D1563681

ATTILA BARTIS

THE END

TRANSLATED FROM THE HUNGARIAN BY
JUDITH SOLLOSY

archipelago books

First Archipelago Books Edition, 2023
The End, A Vége, was first published in 2015 by Magvető (Budapest).

Library of Congress Cataloging-in-Publication data available upon request.
ISBN 978 1 953861 429

Archipelago Books
232 3rd Street #A111
Brooklyn, NY 11215
www.archipelagobooks.org

Distributed by Penguin Random House
www.penguinrandomhouse.com

Cover art: Thomas Wågström.

Portions of Kafka's *The Castle* appear on page 216
in Anthea Bell's translation, Oxford World Classics, 2009.

This work is made possible by the New York State Council on the Arts with the
support of the Office of the Governor and the New York State Legislature.
The publication of this book was generously supported by the Carl Lesnor
Family Foundation, Lannan Foundation, the Nimick Forbesway Foundation,
and the National Endowment for the Arts.

Ez a publikáció nem jöhetett volna létre a Petőfi Literary Fund nagylelkű
támogatása nélkül. Support for the translation & production of this
book was provided by the Petőfi Literary Fund

PRINTED IN CANADA

THE END

Must buy cradle. Gently used will do.
advertisement in a Transylvanian daily

PART ONE

As I headed for the airport early Saturday morning, the fog hadn't lifted yet, and as the cab left the outskirts behind and made for Terminal 2, we saw a black dog lying in the middle of the road—its hind legs still twitching. The speeding car just ahead of us must have run over it. The cab driver slammed on the brakes, pulled over, and got out. He drew a piece of steel cable from inside his jacket, struck the dog twice on the head, grabbed its hind legs, and dragged it to the side of the road. Sorry about that, he said when he got back in the cab. That's all right, I said.

I'm András Szabad, fifty-two years old, a photographer. Fairly well-known. Actually, very well-known. Which is no reason, of course, for a person to go public with the story of his life.

I had to go to Stockholm for a medical examination.

I haven't picked up a camera in two years. Not since Éva died.

But before proceeding any further, I should make something quite clear. I do not believe in God. For a long time I wasn't sure, but now I am. Which, needless to say, is not about God, it's about me. I lack faith. Hope without faith is just balancing the odds, and of course such calculations are always a bit ridiculous. For instance, could the doctor in Pest have mixed up two test results? Yes or no?

At the same time, I should keep in mind that even if I am personally ill-suited to figure out where God came from, a providence of sorts is clearly present in the world, and it is greater than we are. Or maybe He comes from us.

Kornél said I should get my life down on paper, because when you see the big picture, such questions have a way of resolving themselves.

(Budapest, fall, 1960)

Actually, the darkness is all I remember from those days. The gloom. I spent three years in the same gloom that my father and I had encountered three years before, when we got off the train at the Keletin railway station reeking of tar. And it made no difference that the morning brought light, the light just made the profound gloom even more visible. On the other hand, this gloom was altogether different from the gloom of the previous three years, because we knew when that would end. The official paper, signed and stamped, spelled out that it would last only three years. It didn't state, on the other hand, that instead of my father, only his shadow would emerge through the prison gate, or that by the time he came through our front door, the three years of waiting would kill my mother. But we knew it would be three, and no law of nature, no implacable formula of physics exists that is more important than the certainty of these three years. Three years. My mother wouldn't have died for anything in the world during the first or the second year. If it's three, then let it be three. We will wait until my father's shadow comes home.

We looked for a tobacconist where he bought some cigarettes, then we walked to this apartment building, where I still live, mostly. His shoes pinched. They fit just fine to begin with, but his feet swelled up when he packed, and by now he could hardly walk, even with his cane. I told him to give me his suitcase, but he wouldn't, and so we stopped on every corner to rest. He knew the way. He'd been here before, so at least we didn't have to ask anyone for directions.

There were some people out and about and the shops were opening up. The super was just dragging the garbage bins outside. My father had met him before, too. He introduced me, then we headed upstairs.

The key got stuck in the lock, and there was no light in the hall. The rooms were lit by a single bare bulb, twenty-five watts each. But at least they worked. The kitchen had a hundred-watt bulb. My father asked which room I wanted. I looked out the windows. The view was the same from both rooms. I said it's all the same, then chose the second, the one we happened to be in. My father brought my suitcase in from the hall. He stood around for a while, undecided about where to put it, then placed it in the middle of the room. Meanwhile, I kept looking at the house across the way, where an elderly woman was watering her flowers behind a lace nylon curtain.

The apartment wasn't completely bare, though. The previous tenants had left a couple of mattresses behind, and also there was a table and a chair between the two windows in my room, both made of particle board. My father's room had a wardrobe with the door hanging off its hinges. There were also the inevitable tile stoves, one in each room. In the kitchen stood a cheap stove and a red sideboard – also of particle board – and a sink to go with it. That was the first thing I discarded after father died.

I grabbed the chair and placed it next to the suitcase in the middle of the room. I felt better sitting next to this suitcase. The suitcase, at least, was mine. Father asked if he should close the door connecting our adjoining rooms, and I said yes. They're double doors, so I helped him press down the sliding bolt, and from then on, we never opened that door again.

I heard him snap open his suitcase, and then I heard him cry. He stopped after a while and clicked the suitcase shut. After that, I never heard him cry again.

He called through the door that he was going out for some rolls and cold cuts. I said fine. After I heard the front door close, I waited a bit, then decided to go take a leak. A cockroach scurried across the bathroom, so I turned off the light and relieved myself in the kitchen sink. Then I let the water flow until father came back with the rolls, some bologna, and a map of the city.

We ate in my room because it had a table. I sat on my suitcase, and Father sat on a chair. I threw the crumbs and the paper bags into the toilet, then Father spread out the map and showed me where we were.

Remember. It runs parallel to Lenin Boulevard. You get off on November 7th Square, then head towards Heroes Square along People's Republic Avenue. You can take the underground, but it's not far. Or else you head down Mayakovski. Remember. Szív. Szív Street 8. Keep this with you at all times, son. So you won't get lost.

I folded it up neatly and put it away, and from then on, I had it with me for years, and though at first I had no idea which tram would take me to November 7th Square, I barely ever lost my way. It took me a day to realize that I was of the city now, but I hadn't yet set foot outside the apartment. And so I opened the map and checked how I could get down to the Danube. Turn left at the first corner, then right on Lenin Boulevard, then walk until I come to the river. Judging by the map, it was the same distance as the woods from our former home. In short, there was no need to take a tram.

(on the bridge)

The tobacco shop on the corner opposite was still there at the time. Later, we went there to make phone calls, but just then I went to buy a pack of cigarettes. The man asked what brand. I knew only one, the Sellő my father smoked, so I bought a pack of Sellős. It was the cheapest brand and cost just two forints. I forgot the matches though. I found my way to the Danube without difficulty. It was getting dark by then. I went up on the bridge so I could see both banks of the river at the same time. I asked a pedestrian for a light. I'd never smoked before, although I easily could have. I knew I'd feel dizzy, so I held on to the guard rail. The current swirled below me, a tram clattered behind me. The bridge quivered.

A woman came toward me with a child. Then two men, then another woman in a light gray overcoat. From a distance, she looked just like Imolka. The first cigarette made my head reel, but not as much as I'd have liked. When I asked for matches to light the second cigarette, the man gave me the whole box, so I wouldn't have to hit anyone else up. Despite the tram, lots of people crossed the bridge on foot. During this stretch of time back home, I'd have run into at least five people I knew. By the time I'd finished the tenth cigarette, the chill wind had gotten into my bones. I waited, hoping that the woman who looked so much like Imolka would come back the same way, but she didn't. To my right the former Royal Palace, to my left the Parliament, and in the middle, a big barge.

(the warehouseman)

The truck with our furniture was supposed to arrive in three days. I bought a broom and a mop. The super lent me a pail and a ladder. His name was Gyula Korbán, and he lived alone. His service flat was downstairs in the back, next to the shared toilets. He took out the garbage bins, come winter he sprinkled salt on the sidewalk, and he reported on people. This was just about the extent of his duties. It seemed to me that except for my father and myself, everyone in the building was afraid of him. We had no reason to be afraid of him. People much higher up than the super were turning in reports on my father. I cleaned up, not that there was much dirt around. Our transister radio was in the truck, so I couldn't listen to music as I cleaned the place, but I polished the floor with a waxed rag, just as Mother had taught me. When the three days were up, our things had not yet arrived. Father waited an extra day, then decided to make inquiries. There's something amiss with the shipping form, they said over the phone, that's why the truck hadn't come, but it is sure to be here in two days. Another time they said that we gave the wrong address and they sent everything back to Mélyvár. We did not give the wrong address.

Father started work on our third day here. He got a job as a warehouseman in a rubber factory behind a cemetery. At least this didn't make his feet any worse. Ever since he was released from prison, he had trouble walking without a cane, though he used one even before that. He'd been using a cane since he was a child. He managed to get me into a decent high school, though that didn't make much sense, I wouldn't have been admitted to university anyway. Of course, I wouldn't have cut it. That's not where my talents lie. I attended just enough classes so I wouldn't get kicked out. Also, that way, if the police stopped me, I wouldn't be a public hazard, a man shirking his job. Before Adél Selyem came to our school, I had little contact with anyone there.

From time to time, Father looked up one of his old friends from Pest. Some, as soon as they saw him in the door, asked him not to come again, while others did the same only when they found out that he'd just been let out of jail. On the other hand, some of his friends invited us for Sunday lunch. Others gave me clothes, sometimes even books. As a matter of fact, there were a lot more of them. A lot more. And it wasn't their fault that they, too, were swallowed up by this darkness. Those who dared open the door only a crack, without unhinging the chain, were also swallowed up by it.

We were supposed to spend Christmas with friends, but they called it off. They were not afraid and they were not mean-spirited. Their child had to go to the hospital. And so, father and I stayed home. The vendors were already packing up in the nearby market, but he managed to get hold of a Christmas tree. The wooden stand and the ornaments were in the truck, so we stood the tree up in a corner. We had candles, because a couple of weeks previously a fuse blew and we asked the super for some. I lit them, then we stood by the tree and sang "Silent night, holy night, all is calm, all is bright." Then Father went to his room and came back with a Zorki and a roll of Forte film.

Merry Christmas, son.

(the Zorki)

The first shot I took was of the Danube, provided I don't count the ones I had taken of my dead mother. But they never really existed, because the film got jammed up inside the cartridge, and so for hours on end I was taking pictures of nothing. On the second day of Christmas I went back to the bridge, which had become a habit by then. I placed the Zorki on the rail to steady it, because the passing tram made the bridge shake. I'd have liked to take a very different picture, but I had to make do with what I saw, to the right the Palace, to the left Parliament, in the middle an icebreaker.

It had grown dark, and though I thought that exposure with the camera's open diaphragm would take a full minute, I opted for half a minute – the streetlamps and icefloes would give off light. I pressed the shutter, counted to thirty, then released it. Except, I didn't take into account that whatever is in front of my eyes for a second would not be there a second later, that during the thirty seconds the car lights would snake past and the river would sweep the boat and ice floes along with it.

The second picture I took that night was of the naked lightbulb hanging from the ceiling. It got overexposed. The third was of the Christmas tree standing in the corner. Then I put the camera away and didn't pick it up for days. I had no reason to. Then after New Year's Day, a woman moved in, one floor down, across the street. She was around forty. Not pretty, rather nondescript. Every morning she threw the window wide open and put out her pillow and blanket to air. She wore a blue quilted robe and a kerchief. On Sunday mornings she always got up at the same time as the old woman living across from me, so I was able to take some pictures of her airing out her bedclothes, and of the old woman watering her flowers on the floor above. Basically, after the Christmas tree, I only took pictures of them. I also took a picture of the carpet beater down in the yard, just so I'd use up the roll, and then I found a photo lab on the Pest-side of Elizabeth Bridge, where the entrance had been before it got blown up during the war.

I ordered small postcard-size copies of all my shots. The man in the lab, thin, around fifty, surely meant well, and out of sheer goodness of heart, he enlarged only six out of the thirty-six shots. He said the others were all alike. Seeing how I squandered the film, we might as well save on the paper. They all show the same windows. He wonders why. And also, the Danube and the light bulb, what a waste, one was blurred, the other overexposed. I said yes, I see. Which put the wind in his sails, and he said the pine, too, what a waste of film. It's just a pine tree standing in a corner, nothing more. It's a Christmas tree, I said, but he ignored me. As for the carpet beater, it lacks interest. If only someone were beating a rug, let's say, and the photograph projected something dynamic or revealed something about life, that would be different. But as it is, it's just an empty carpet beater in a desolate yard. As for the windows, he can't even begin to guess. What's so special about those windows? Why take thirty pictures of them? I have no idea, I said, paid him, and left.

The man's comment about the carpet beater bothered me most of all, because it was the best. The light bulb wouldn't have turned out any better even if the shot had not been overexposed. There was nothing in that picture except for a light bulb dangling from a gray wire. As for the pine, no one except for me could have seen it for what it was. It remained a pine, it was not transformed into a Christmas tree. That would have taken something extra. On the other hand, three years later, I took a proper picture of it. As for the woman airing her duvet with the old woman watering her flowers above her, it would have worked only if there were no curtain. However, as it was, hardly anything showed except for the old woman's dim shadow. But the carpet beater was just fine, much better than the pine tree. Its presence made the yard look a lot more desolate. The truth is I'd taken that picture just to use up the roll.

(the note)

After three and a half months of waiting, our things finally arrived. We were way past Christmas and New Year's by then. The cartons were soaked, the clothes and bedding were moldy. For the most part, the furniture was intact, only the mirror had cracked, and also, the painting with the full moon had a visible tear the size of your palm. The freight company had sent a bill for the storage. The movers had a signed document saying that my father had asked that our things be delivered only at the end of January. It would have made no sense to lodge a complaint. We paid the fee, and the movers began cursing us for living on the fourth floor. At one point they even dropped the piano. It was then that I began helping them carry the cartons upstairs.

When he saw the truck, Father asked what I'd like for my room, and that's how Mother's things ended up there. There was no room in there for the flower stand, but I got the china cabinet, filled with all the bits and pieces of broken porcelain, mother's desk with the letters Father had written her, the wardrobe with her clothes, her escritoire stripped of its secrets, her cracked mirror, her armchair, and her bed. For lack of space, I pushed the piano up against the door between our rooms. We never opened it again. There was barely any room to move about. I closed the shutters and lay down on the bed. I knew that anyone else but me would suffocate in there, even my father. I was home at last!

My father tried to arrange his room just as it had been at one time. A writing desk, armchair, books. A sofa with a small round table, a reading lamp, a glass of water. Also, a small wardrobe for his shirts and two suits. When they searched the house, they took his typewriter, and the telescope he sold when I was still a child. He used the money to buy an Agfa enlarger. Thanks to some miracle, they did not seize his negatives and photographs, despite the fact that the officer in charge said that there was something fishy about a man taking pictures of the sky. What, he wondered, was behind the clouds. To which Father replied, you're right, Comrade Major, there's something behind the clouds. God. And he took all those pictures hoping that God would show his face, and then he could show it to Comrade Major. At which Comrade Major – right in front of Mother and me – dished out an ungodly backhanded slap. But at least they didn't seize his photographs. They saw that there was nothing on them. Except, after three years in prison, my father would never again be so sure that he'd want to show the face of the Lord to an agent of the Secret Police.

What couldn't be squeezed into either of our rooms we piled up in the hall. From that point on, a veritable Tower of Babel made up of broken side tables, worm-eaten cupboards, and torn armchairs stood between the kitchen and the bathroom. Father said, We'd be better off selling this stuff. I got off the stool I was standing on so he could look straight into my eyes, and said, Never.

That night he knocked on my door and asked if he could come in. I said of course, but on the threshold he stopped short. He'd come to ask me not to hate him, but he was afraid to ask. I couldn't tell him either that I didn't hate him, it's just that there was nothing he could do to help me. Still, it's good knowing that he's in the room next to mine. Finally, he told me that he'd made some potato soup.

I went to the kitchen. He ladled the soup straight out of the pot. The potatoes were whole. He asked if I had enough money. I told him I did. He'd been paid, and put the money in a drawer. I should help myself if I need it. I thanked him for dinner and said it was very good, then I went back to my room. I'd already turned off the light and was about to drop off when I remembered that it was his birthday.

I got up and looked around for something I could give him. I didn't want to give him anything that had belonged to Mother, but I had nothing I could call my own. Then I went through my photographs and found the picture with the carpet beater. On the back I wrote, *To my Father, Budapest*, but then it dawned on me that I couldn't give it to him, because it's just like a prison yard. On the other hand, we'd put the pine tree in the corner, so at least he knew that it was really a Christmas tree. I wrote the same thing on the back of that one. By that time he was fast asleep. He went to work at the crack of dawn and I didn't want to wake him. I put it down on top of his table, and in the dark I added, *Happy Birthday*. In the morning I found a note in front of my door: *Thank you, son.*

(at the factory)

Early one morning, I had to go see Father at the factory. It was still dark, and by the time I reached the railway station it was raining. Dirty gray water trickled between the cobblestones, and over the water trickled the light of the streetlamps. I went looking for the main entrance, and when I found it, I slid open the iron door. In the porter's cubicle a bare twenty-five watt lightbulb dangled from the ceiling, under it sat the porter in his uniform. He was around fifty. Not fat, but with a spongy face, and a thick mustache. The keys, like towns on a map, were hanging on the wall behind him. I stopped by the small window and said I'd come to see my father, András Szabad. He works in the warehouse. The porter didn't even look up as he continued playing with a rat. He'd tied the animal's tail to the phone with a string, and when it tried to chew away the string, he struck the rat's head with a bunch of keys. The blood was smeared all over his desk. I repeated: András Szabad, warehouse. He works here. He's my father. At last he looked up. He had nice, clear eyes. So the lame man's son has come to see him after all, he said, but the rat claimed his attention again, and he had to clobber it again because it was chewing on the string again. Number 7, he mumbled. All the way in the back.

Scattered piles of rubber tires were burning in the yard. An emaciated dog was wandering about in the smoke. It was shedding its hair. As soon as he saw me, he scurried away in the direction of the smokestack. Inside, between the red brick walls, a machine was slowly breathing in and out, as if it were asleep. The windows were still dark. All the way in the back, at the end of the yard, stood the seven warehouses, like adjoining hangars. Inside, under the cold artificial light, the black tires were arranged in orderly columns. By the last door stood a desk with a telephone, exactly like the porter's cubicle. My father sat behind it, above him a twenty-five-watt bulb, next to him his cane. I went over and said he should come, because the bones were done. Mother already had dinner on the table. He said nothing. He just kept staring at some invisible spot. The spot where I was standing. When I woke up I realized that I was the invisible spot.

I heard him sleeping. Breathing in and out like the machines in my dream. I thought he'd be late for work, but then I remembered that it was Sunday. I looked around for a notebook. I tore out my history lesson and began to describe the porter, the dog, and Father. That was my first entry. Then over the next thirty-three years, I filled enough notebooks to fill up an entire wooden chest. For all I know, my dreams may be more reliable than my photographs.

I went to the kitchen to get something to eat. Father kept his photographs in a box in the pantry, on a shelf just above the sugar, salt, and flour. I took it down and looked at them. A couple of pictures of our garden in Mélyvár, a couple of me and Mother. The rest were of clouds. On the flip side in block letters he noted the type of cloud, location, and the time with a pencil. He must have wanted to catalogue them.

How could he possibly think, I wondered, even if for the bit of time it took for him to get that slap in the face, that sooner or later there'd be someone behind those gray clouds? I'd forgot to go shopping, but I found some eggs. While they were cooking, I thought that when it comes right down to it, photography is not worth the trouble. Just as Father couldn't manage to capture God's image behind his clouds, I too would fail to take a picture of that dog wandering about in the smoke-cloud of burning rubber tires. Where God might show his face for a moment, the film tears.

(the FED)

One morning, I ran into Father in the kitchen. I asked if he'd like some fried eggs as well. Ever since his release, instead of pajamas, he wore a robe. It looked a bit like an overcoat. He thanked me. While the eggs cooked, he'd get dressed. He didn't feel comfortable in a robe. He always wore a suit. It was more convenient. Or perhaps it was just force of habit. He used to wear a suit when he taught, and he wore one when he was called up to forced labor. He wore a suit wherever he went. Now it happened to be a rubber factory.

In 1956 he was caught on camera placing soup bowls from the corner diner on the main street of town. It appeared on the front page of a British daily. It's that picture that got him arrested. And also, because the soup bowls were lined up so neatly on the street the Soviet tanks were reluctant to plow through them. In that picture too Father wore a dark suit, his cane dangling from his arm. When he came back fully dressed, I asked him if he would use his camera again.

Certainly not, he replied.

I sat down too, and for a while we chatted pleasantly. He told me that he first owned a Leica, but it got lost while he was in forced labor. He bought the Zorki after the war. Or, to be more precise, originally he had a FED but after learning that the camera was named after Felix Edmundovic Dzherzhinsky, who helped establish the Cheka and the OGPU Soviet state security organizations *and* the ÁVH, the military academy of the Hungarian State Security Authority, he was disgusted and exchanged it for a Zorki.

I asked him if the Leica had been better.

He said he couldn't feel the difference, only saw it. But in time I'd feel it.

What makes you think so, I asked.

You are completely different from me, he said.

I almost let slip that it was true but decided to keep it to myself.

He said that his talent lay in taking pictures of what he saw. Precise, well-structured pictures, without any disturbing elements. That's what he liked about astronomy, too. That you need to see clearly. You need to see the full picture as well as the details, all at the same time. And for that, all you need is an eye for proportion and a good camera.

I'm not so sure, I said.

Well, I am, he said. You take after your mother a lot more than me. If you become a photographer one day, you will want to capture what's not visible.

You can only take pictures of what's visible, I said.

Oh please, son. What can be seen is only a means to an end, just like a camera, he said. But in order to capture the invisible, you need to forget the camera in your hand.

Yes, that would be nice, I said.

Well, the perfect camera can help you with that. It simply becomes part of you. The lens your eye, the film your memory. A mere copy, on the other hand, can never be perfect.

Well the Zorki is perfect, and if it can't become one with me, it's my fault, and not because the picture is just a copy.

I was sorry that I ever brought up the subject. We were only a step away from him offering to help. I knocked my knife off the table as if by accident so I'd have to lean down for it, and then I might as well clear away the dishes. But while I was washing the plates he asked if I'd like him to set up the enlarger in the afternoon. He still has some photo paper and chemicals in one of the boxes, and he'd gladly show me how it works. And so washing the dishes didn't do the trick. I couldn't get his mind off helping me. I appreciate it, I told him, but let's do it some other time. Just as you wish, he said, then he left for the factory, and I went back to my room to read *The Insulted and Humiliated*.

(the cafeteria)

There was a cafeteria on the corner of Mayakovski Street, where I'd go from time to time for a hot meal. It was cheap. You put your bread and cutlery on an aluminum tray. The soup you had to ask for at the counter. They also served cooked vegetables with small slices of meat swimming in fat, noodles with cheese, pork stew, schnitzl, side dishes. . . Then you moved on to the cashier. The cutlery was also made of aluminum, and so were the ladles and the parallel bars along which you had to roll your tray. A hundred years earlier, you could have bought a house from that much aluminum, a big one with a garden, bright sunshine, and carrier pigeons. Then, all of a sudden, there was too much aluminum. Sometimes I had to wait for an empty table, but never for long. People came here only to eat. There was a pitcher of water on each table. A woman carried them from the kitchen, four at a time. She was around fifty. She wore a white apron and calf-length canvas tie-ups, just like the two women behind the counter and the cashier. Her hair was gathered in a bun. She painted her eyelids a thick green and penciled her brows. Her gold rings knocked against the handles of the pitchers.

I went to this cafeteria with Father first. He wanted to cook at home but left the pot on the stove and the chicken wings got burned. We had to keep the windows open for hours. That's when he remembered that he'd seen this cafeteria on the boulevard. I was far from elated, because it took half an hour there and back, plus the time it took to eat. The apartment was a different story. We'd already worked things out, when we'd meet and how much time we'd spend together. But if we go anywhere, my room is not within reach, I can't retreat. Our silence will be uncomfortable, our conversation awkward. But when I saw how desperately he was trying to scrape the four charred chicken wings from the bottom of the pot with a knife, I said, Sure, let's go.

In the end, it turned out just fine. He told me that he might get a job as a school librarian. It would depend on whether he was barred only from teaching, or from working in an educational institution in any capacity. He didn't know yet. My hunch, I told him, was that the only thing he couldn't do was teach, that it made no sense to keep him from working altogether. A school custodian works in a school as well, doesn't he? That's true, he said.

That was when I first saw that woman. I was still on the street, but there were no curtains, so I could see her placing the water pitchers on the tables next to the window. The following day I couldn't get up my nerve, but on the third day, I went back. She came over and replaced the pitcher on my table, even though it was nearly full. She sized me up, but then didn't come near me again.

I wasn't really hungry, but I wanted to see her, with her dark, dyed hair stacked on top of her head, the greasy paint on her eyelids and lips as she carried the pitchers with those eight gold rings on her fingers. She seemed as thoroughly out of place as Father in the rubber factory warehouse. Though actually, that's not true. She walked around the place as if she owned it, along with all the dirty dishes, the people working there, and the hard-up customers they served. In Warehouse 7 my father owned nothing, not even his own shadow as it fell over the rubber tires – provided he had a shadow in there to begin with. As a matter of fact, I couldn't be sure that he was at all visible there. Which is one reason I never went to see him.

It took days before I dared take the camera along, but then I couldn't get myself to remove it from its bag. It then took another three days before I got up the nerve, placed the Zorki on the table next to my plate, and when the woman came through the swinging door carrying those heavy pitchers, I pressed the button. Except, as soon as I pressed it, I realized that half the picture was taken up with the back of the chair across from me, and that hardly anything of the woman would show. She walked along a row of tables, then headed straight for me. I froze. She glared at me as if she'd caught me stealing. Don't try that again, she said, then left me high and dry.

It wasn't even noon, but I didn't get home until evening. I drank some coffee at one of the Calvin Square stands, went to the station, and checked when a train would be leaving for Mélyvár. Then I went to City Park and sat on a bench for a while. Mothers were walking their children, old people were walking their dogs. All was in order. On the corner of Szív Street, I decided, not for the first time that day, that I'd go back and apologize to the woman, but ended up instead giving the cafeteria a wide berth for years to come. Later that night, my stomach was still in knots from the shame of being caught in the act.

Father asked where I'd been. I told him I'd gone for a walk. He asked if I'd taken any pictures, because he saw the camera hanging from my shoulder. I said no, then went to my room. Imolka through a basement window, relegated to the pages of a notebook when I was twelve, or just barely. A cupboard and faucet on the right, a sofa to the left, in the middle Imolka seated at the table, in front of her a plate. On the right a cupboard and faucet, on the left a sofa, in the middle Imolka at the table, darning a sock. And Mother, dead. And also the woman across the way behind the shutters, with her pillow. I knew that if I'd raised the camera to my eye properly, if I'd looked in the view finder, if I hadn't been afraid, she might have not minded at all. And I also knew that knowing this was no help to me, because unless someone poses for me of their own accord, I'd just be sneaking around my whole life.

(the signature)

I soon realized that I was wrong. My father was barred from working in education. They wouldn't hire him to sweep the floors, much less supervise a school library. Not that he knew anything about being a librarian. He knew no more about it than what he'd heard from my mother at the dinner table. On the other hand, he knew even less about working in a warehouse. Where would he have learned? I felt strange that he was looking for a job as a librarian, but I didn't say anything. You can't go around telling your father that he ought to look for a job that was different from the one your mother had at one time.

One night when I got home, the door was locked. I tried to open it, but father had left the key in the lock. I thought I'd knock, but then I thought I should wait a bit. I heard noises inside, as if people were walking about. And moans. For a split second it even occurred to me that he was with a woman. The thought made me happy, though I don't know why. Maybe because in that case, I wouldn't have to share Mother's memory with him. Yes, I think that's what it was, though I have no idea why I should have thought that my memories of Mother had anything to do with him.

Then I heard him talking to someone. He was drunk. For you, you scums? Never. You think you can smear my name? Never. Never, you henchmen, understand? Then I heard a bottle or a tumbler break. Then I heard him reching as he kept saying, never, never, never. Then I heard the water running in the sink. I'd rarely seen my father drunk. A bit tipsy, of course, on holidays when Mother was still alive, but drunk, hardly ever. It didn't take much imagination to figure out why he drank.

I went down to the street, thought I had no idea which way to go. The station was out of the question. Late at night, the police regularly checked your papers. In the end, I went to a café on the corner of Dohány Street. I'd been contemplating the place for weeks through the large panes of glass, but I never went inside. I don't know why. Perhaps because it was usually crowded. But not now. I ordered a coffee and kept my eye on the minute hand of the big clock. I tried to count to myself so that it should jump ahead just as I reached sixty, so that if I take pictures at night, I should be able to gauge the seconds without having to look at my watch. And also, to keep from thinking of Father. I didn't manage the time, not once. Fifty-six was the best I could do.

There was hardly anyone in the café. It was a huge place with gold columns and a fancy restaurant downstairs with frescoes, as if a church had been converted into a catering facility. At the time, I had no idea that this was the New York, one of the best-known cafés in Europe.

It was spring, so only a single coat hung in the cloakroom. The attendant was intent on her crossword puzzle. Further off in a corner, behind two elderly ladies, a young man was sitting with his back partly to me. He was reading. A newspaper stuck out of his jacket pocket. From a distance, he looked like an older version of myself, perhaps by about ten years. Or possibly five. Only the newspaper, that was not me. And when he turned to the waitress to pay, I saw that he was not the least bit like me, though by then it made no difference.

I watched as he handed her a hundred forint bill, pocketed the change, then took it out again and placed some of it on the table. A tip. Then I watched as he asked the cloak-room attendant for his coat and, through the large window pane, I saw him rush off in the direction of the tram. They closed at eleven, so I had to leave as well. I paid with a two hundred forint bill and tried to guess how much the man must have left on the table. In the end, I left it all. The waitress called after me and gave me back a hundred forints. You forgot this, she said. It was an awkward moment, but she was nice. At least, there was nothing humiliating either in her voice or in the look in her eyes. I thanked her, put it away, then headed home.

I knew that the key would still be in the lock and would stay there until morning, but I gave it a try, just in case. In the end I went to the shared toilets in the back of the yard, then up the back stairs leading to the attic, almost to the iron door. I sat down on a step and waited. I was afraid to sleep because I didn't want a neighbor to see me like that, not that anyone was likely to go up to the attic in the middle of the night. Also, I wanted to know when my father would be leaving. I didn't want to bump into him at the door.

Later on, I saw him leave. He was in a hurry and quickened his pace, to the extent that the cane didn't hamper him, of course. Then I went upstairs. The apartment was in order, the pieces of broken glass were in the garbage can, and so was the empty bottle of vodka. I slept a while, then I read. I had taken to reading the books with Mother's bookmarks, from cover to cover. She cut up notebook sheets and she used them as book-marks. Sometimes she'd even write a word or two on them, such as "Alyosha, Alyosha!"

When Father came home from work, I pretended that I had just woken up and was on my way to the bathroom, as if we'd met in the hall in front of the Babel-like pile of useless furniture only by chance. He was flustered, but before he had a chance to say anything, I quickly said that I'd just woke up, I came home at noon. I met a man in a café the previous day, and we spent the night talking. I also said that he can rest assured, I went to him for some matches, and that's why we started talking, because I saw that he was reading the same thing I was. In short, that he's not an informer. How old was he, my father asked. In his last year of college, I told him, which put him at ease, as if a college student couldn't be an informer. Then he headed for his room, but when he reached the door, he turned to me.

I'm sorry. I left the key in the lock, he said.
I know, I said, that's why I went to the café.
And where did you sleep?
Here, on the attic steps.
Don't be mad at me, son.
I'm not mad. But I think you should sign it.
For a while he said nothing.
What?

You know what.

He looked at me as if I weren't even there, like in my dream, when I went to see him at the factory.

Would you sign it, son?

No, I said without hesitation.

So why would you say that?

I was never in prison. But you were. And for what. For nothing. Sign it. Think of your prison years as an advance on your wrongdoing.

I didn't spent time in prison for nothing, son.

That's not what I meant.

A bargain like that is out of the question.

Who would you be hurting?

Myself.

But would you be hurting anyone else? Would you have to put something in your report that would land another person in jail?

Father said nothing.

What are they blackmailing you with?

They said I got hold of this apartment illegally.

But I thought you bought it, didn't you?

No, son. It's a council flat. The money was needed so that they'd assign it to us, and so we could move up to Pest. You can't move from the countryside to this city just like that. It's difficult enough for anyone, especially people like us. It either takes special permission or a great deal of money.

But what can they do?

They can evict us.

I will not move out of this room, ever.

So I take it that you'd sign for the sake of a room after all.

I said nothing. I knew that I would never sign, and I felt like a rat, because I wanted him to sign. It didn't occur to me at the time, but the truth is that it would have felt good, having a reason to hate him.

Another silence ensued, then Father said, forgive me, son. But the answer is no.

But all I've got is this room.
In which case, you won't even have that.

But as things turned out, they did not evict us.

(the roots)

When I try to dig down to the roots, I see that my mother, my father, Hitler, Stalin, and Imolka decided the course of my life. On the other hand, except for Imolka, it's the same with us all. Though come to think of it, we all have our own Imolkas.

When I take stock of my life, I see no reason to launch into some big family history. I haven't got what it takes, nor do I have the means. I can't very well ask Mother and I can't ask Father, and as for my grandparents, I never knew them. Besides, the story of my family is nothing out of the ordinary. One might even say that along with all its uniqueness, it could just as easily serve as the prototype of the history of *the* Hungarian family. Or even the history of a Middle-European, middle class, non-Jewish family. Though come to think of it, they are pretty similar to Jewish family histories. Discounting, of course, what cannot be discounted.

Still, there are stories in my family that I consider important because, like repeating patterns, they too are repeated over and over again. Knit one, purl one. But their importance does not depend so much on repetition as on the clandestine way they have of remaining hidden and unseen, sometimes for decades. It took me all of thirty years to see – and Father never did realize – for instance, that we had lived in an apartment doing our best to keep out of each other's way, just as my father and my grandfather had done at one time, and just as my grandfather did his best to keep out of my great-grandfather's way.

And also, there are stories for which I can find no parallels, but which I like. It's as simple as that. For instance, my maternal grandmother going nuts and sleeping for years at a stretch. Or my paternal great-grandmother going nuts and hauling bits and pieces of the carcasses of dead horses up to the apartment. Though who knows. It may just be a matter of time before we can find the parallels.

(my great-grandfather, András Szabad)

As for my great-grandfather András Szabad's occupation, he owned an entire street in Kolozsvár along with a couple of hundred hectares of pine forest. When my grandfather, András Szabad, finished medical school, my great-grandfather András Szabad, bid farewell to him by advising him to go back to Pest, because here, he said, there's no need for a doctor. Here, the mountains and the forests cure the locals, and if that doesn't do the trick, the person eats coltsfoot or goes to the stable and hangs himself.

My great-grandfather wouldn't have objected to my grandfather studying law, except, within a hundred-kilometer radius from Kolozsár, there was no need for lawyers either. In his eyes, it'd have made no sense. The truth is that in order for my great-grandfather András Szabad to see any sense in any profession my grandfather might have chosen, my grandfather would have had to be born from a different mother. My grandfather knew that, and being a gentleman, he thanked my great-grandfather, András Szabad, for supporting his studies, and moved back from Kolozsvár to his mother in Budapest, where he was born. Then he applied for the position of district physican in Mélyvár and bought the house that had once belonged to the Jerecián family.

To be perfectly fair, I should add that my great-grandfather András Szabad never harbored any great affection for his wife. He never promised her a rose garden, nor did he marry her of his own volition. After the compulsory first night as newlyweds, he had my great-grandmother move to Pest with her impoverished family in tow. On the other hand, he saw to their support, just as he supported their only son, the fruit of their one night together. Then during his secondary school years, he had my grandfather live with him after all, because he was hoping that he'd get to love him. He didn't, but it was through no fault of their own. He had three schools built in three different villages. In Kolozsvár he founded a gymnastics club, he donated to charity, supported the arts, and cast church bells, but the only person he ever loved his whole life was his first cousin.

He fell in love with her when he was still a child. And after his first cousin, Debóra Farkas, died of consumption, my great-grandfather walked home from the Házsongárd cemetery, loaded his dueling pistol, and pulled the trigger. The bullet missed its mark, but my great-grandfather's life had ended just the same. For two years he lay on a couch blind and crippled. His servants bathed him, his peasants fed him, his relations robbed him of his possessions. During the two years he spent wasting away, he saw his son just once. He asked his son what he'd like from him to make up for not having loved him as a father should.

My grandfather András Szabad chose the hunting lodge in the Maros Valley where he'd spent a couple of weeks with his father when he was in secondary school, and where, thanks to the storms at Istenszék and the mushroom pickings that ended in diarrhea, they nearly forgot that they didn't love each other. I would have chosen it myself, son, my great-grandfather said, and by all odds, this was the moment when my grandfather made up his mind that should he have a son of his own, he'd also be called András Szabad. Just a couple of months later, his wish was granted.

Then came 1919 and in Versailles they signed Europe's death warrant, which according to popular lore happen the following way. They spread the map of Greater Hungary out on a table and Romanian, South-Slav, and Czech whores danced on top of it blindfolded until they ended up tracing, with the heels of their shoes, the borders of Lesser Hungary. It may not have happen this way, but considering the end-result, it very well could have happened this way. And who is to say that it had to end this way? The Treaty of Versailles might not have been a death warrant if only they'd have had the drunken whores dance on other maps as well, and not just the map of Greater Hungary. After all, there were a lot of other maps on hand. Germany, for one. Be that as it may, from the moment that the new borders of Hungary were drawn, whereby Kolozsvár and the Maros Valley were suddenly as distant from Hungary as Ulan Bator or Darjeeling, my grandfather, András Szabad, considered the hunting lodge in the Maros Valley as his birthplace where, truth be told, he'd spent just one summer in his whole life.

Later, my father considered it his own birthplace as well, whereas he hadn't spent even a day there. He familiarized himself with his native soil by pouring over maps and revisionist photo albums, and by the time my great-grandfather András Szabad's hunting lodge could have become my native soil as well, the Tigris and the Euphrates became two tributaries of the river Maros, and Istenszéke towered above mounts Ararat and Sinai. Which just goes to show you. Mythology is written the same way as history. And the life of a human being.

Be that as it may, in 1940, when Hungary's borders were redefined once again, this time more realistically, except it was the Nazis who had a sense of reality this time, my grandfather, who was not endowed with an abundant sense of reality himself, boarded a train and bought back the house in the Maros Valley from a wine merchant by the name of Petre Armenis. He could have gotten it back gratis, except he didn't think it right.

Although my grandfather had spent nearly his entire fortune on the house, its purchase carried only symbolic significance, because in exchange for renovating it, he let Petre Armenis continue to live there. This was grandfather's way of offering Armenis protection against the new Hungarian administration of the district when Northern Transylvania reverted to Hungary, and thus Armenis could continue to buy up the wines of the Küküllő region and haul them in large oak barrels to sell to the priests and tavern keepers of the Transylvanian highlands until the Second World War, when along with my grandfather's house, the Romanians repossessed Transylvania. As for Armenis, his oak barrels and truck were soon claimed by the new Communist state.

Come to think of it, of all the András Szabads, I had the best chance of actually being born there. Except, it was 1943, I was born in Mélyvár, and I'd been living in Pest for months, and if I were not to count myself which, of course, is impossible, basically three people decided what my life would be all about. Father, János Kádár, and Gagarin. And also the superintendent – which goes without saying – the guy at the corner grocery store, the ticket inspector on the tram, the waitress in the café, the old woman across the street who watered her flowers every morning, plus all the people who passed me by on the street. Plus Imolka. Which, when all is said and done, just about covers it.

(my grandfather, András Szabad)

Just because we do something wicked now and then doesn't mean that we will remain wicked for the rest of our lives. My grandfather said this to Father when he returned from the front only to find the Jerecián house barren, because the neighbors had made off with its everything in it. Though actually, that's not when he said it. He said it years later. He brought it up with respect to mankind as such, he being the one exception.

He'd bought the house from an Armenian rug merchant who had kept one of his lovers there. I don't know what she was called, so let's call her Terézia. Then when Terézia tired of him, he gathered up the torn pillows, the ripped underwear, and the shoes worn down at the heel from dancing, and went out to the yard, made a bonfire, and by the time the fire turned to ambers, Terézia had to leave with the one suitcase she'd brought with her to town. Go back and feed the chickens, if this place isn't good enough for you, you peasant hireling!

When he poured the petroleum on the bonfire with the props of their lovemaking, my grandfather was still secretly hoping that Terézia would fall to her knees and beg his forgiveness, but he was wrong, because by then Terézia held the feeding of the chickens in higher esteem than having to wait around in silk stockings, and so she threw the matches at Jerecián. Go on, light it, you mountain Jew.

It was mostly this mountain Jew jab that made up Jerecián's mind to light the bonfire, and he did such a thorough job of it that half of the hundred year old walnut tree burned down as well. Mountain Jew. The nerve. She washed her hair in champagne, she treated her hands – used to chicken shit – with the finest of creams, she lived like a veritable film star, and she had the nerve to call me mountain Jew, he raved for the benefit of my grandfather. There's no Jew who'd sell you this house below cost out of sympathy.

Because I'm selling it on emotional grounds. Mountain Jew. The nerve of that filthy whore. And in fact, he really did sell it below cost or, at any rate, for the sum that my grandfather had at his disposal, and he even left him the furnishings.

And so it came to pass that my grandfather András Szabad bought this dump of ill repute from the Armenian, whose floorboards still reeked of perfume when my grandmother died in childbirth, and my grandfather made up his mind that if, being a doctor, he could not save my grandmother, he would never remarry but would bring up my father with his dislocated hip and die on the Russian front.

By all odds, this must have been why he made the lives of the district physicians after him a living hell, because as he examined them, he had the peasants of the nearby villages commit the Hippocratic oath to memory. Take a deep breath, Uncle Ádi, and now repeat after me: the doctor serves life, and not the rich or the poor, so be sure to take these powders every night, and put those thirty eggs back in your pantry, because I'd only break them on my way home. Then he mounted the buggy and headed home to continue my father's education from where the nanny had left off. And so, some people considered him a saint, while others suspected that he was just plain nuts. Really, he was neither.

As for whether my grandfather András Szabad was a saint or not, let me just say that he always insisted that his patients take the sides of bacon back to their pantry, and no one ever saw him drunk. On the other hand, after he died, two-hundred and nine empty pálinka bottles were found in the back of the attic. Each label had a date and the title of a book written on it: June 2-5, 1936, *Père Goriot*; November 9-11, 1938, *The Charterhouse of Parma*; February 3-13, 1940, *The Brothers Karamazov*.

Except for these labels, he left hardly any other documents behind, and, with the exception of a stereoscopic image of my grandmother, he didn't keep family photographs in the house either. The wooden box with the spyglass stood on his desk next to his medical bag, like some sort of physician's instrument, or like a consciousness-altering gadget that, with the help of the two glass positives and the light filtering through my grandmother's eyes, could reach the brain through the neural pathways behind the eyes, and somehow transform one's sense of guilt into a sense of duty.

In short, my grandfather was neither a saint nor was he as mad as a March hare, he was just unhappy, and, like unhappy people in general, he reminded himself of it day after day. Day after day he looked through this spyglass, which provided him direct access to his unhappiness. After all, happiness and our unhappiness seen from a distance are the same thing.

I might even say that only Grandfather's sense of duty kept his depression at bay. He really wasn't a saint because he knew full well that unhappiness wouldn't absolve him from anything. And so, apart from looking into my grandmother's eyes every day and letting pálinka put him to sleep every night so he wouldn't have to remember his dreams, he did everything possible in the interest of his physical, mental, and psychological wellbeing that he needed to perform his duty. For instance, with the same sense of duty that kept him from touching the maid servant before discharging her for the day, he'd buy a bouquet of fresh flowers once a month and head for the brothel on Szemere Street. He made no secret of it and told people where they could reach him in case of an emergency. As for the prostitutes, he thanked them for their help, which in the balance of a man's life is as vital as the help he gives others.

All the same, he made more mistakes than you could shake a stick at. For one thing, he decided that doing without a mother was better than accepting any sort of stepmother, and for another, he believed that books stave off loneliness. He also was convinced that a man with a limp would be condemned to loneliness all his life, and so he made sure that Father would learn to read, write, and count before he was of school age, just as I did, though I couldn't count. On the other hand, I didn't limp.

My grandfather was right when he thought that with a bit of attention, his son wouldn't need a wheelchair, but he was wrong when he thought that a tutor would be better than limping to school. He was right when he thought that nothing provides a sense of freedom as much as the starry sky, but he was wrong when he thought that nothing would make his ten-year-old son as happy as a telescope. He was right when he said that after the war the Russians would drag away the Hungarians, but he was wrong when he said that the Germans would let the Jews go home. All in all, numerically speaking, he was right in about as many things as he was wrong, and so the end result – zero – does not indicate a saint, it indicates a mere mortal.

In short, in the summer of '24 my grandfather András Szabad ordered the latest Zeiss telescope from Pest along with a stand, a compass, and a crateful of books on astronomy, because he calculated that the more his son studied the heavens, the less he'd move about, and the less he moved about, the less the dislocated hip bone would wear away the pelvic bone. But possibly, he was right about this as well. Possibly, it was thanks to the telescope that my father never had to use a wheelchair. Or possibly, thanks to cancer. I don't know.

At the same time, thanks to the self-same telescope, sometimes he wouldn't see his father for days, as if the kept woman, the banished Terézia, had put a curse on the house, keeping the two lonely men out of each other's way for years on end. All the same, grandfather was right about one thing: unhappiness cannot serve as an excuse for not doing the right thing.

(my great-grandmother)

By the time my grandfather came home from the front in 1918, my great-grandmother had lost her mind, and died before long.

By all odds, fear had made her lose her mind. Above all, she was afraid of starvation which, considering that it was wartime, was not unreasonable. And so, whenever she saw her chance, she paid a veritable fortune for a piece of shank, shoulder, or rump of a dead horse. She would take a razor, cut the horse's shank into thin slices, tie it up with string and hang it in the larder to dry. Then she'd hang the dried meat on the valances throughout the apartment. She had read somewhere that that's how it's done. The shreds of horsemeat hung in the Angyal Street apartment much like flypaper hung in the houses of peasants, except that the shreds of horsemeat didn't kill a single fly.

She was also afraid of the dark. This too was a reasonable fear, it's been reasonable since the dawn of history. And so, besides the carcasses of dead horses, she also got hold of a couple oil lamps and a pitcher of petroleum. She didn't trust electricity.

She was afraid of many other things too, from peddlers to the Spanish flu, but basically, the source of her fears was death. Except, while prayer or the compulsive washing of the hands or writing poetry offered some relief to others, it offered none to my great-grandmother, neither the horse meat nor the petroleum, and the fact that since her wedding night her husband had been supporting her from Kolozsvár – five-hundred kilometers away – and she was already a grandmother, didn't help alleviating her fears either. And to make matters worse, her son became a widower, then left my father in her care while he was doing service in various field hospitals. And so, with an unfortunate sweep of the tenderizing mallet, she broke the glass pitcher, and the fifty liters of petroleum flooded the house, which did not catch fire, she made sure of that, but she managed to slip so that she banged her temple against the tile.

At this juncture, the young housemaid Melánia decided that there was nothing more she could do here, it was bad enough standing by as Her Ladyship gradually lost her mind. She soaked up the petroleum, threw out the shreds of horsemeat, shooed the hordes of steel-blue buzzing flies out the window so as not to bring shame to the house when the neighbors found my great-grandmother, then she took my father with her to her father's cobbler's workshop.

In short, when the First World War came to an end, my grandfather András Szabad found his son in a cobbler's workship in Angyalföld, and since he had no other business in this poorman's district of Pest, he grabbed my father and took him back to Mélyvár.

By the time they reached Mélyvár, the neighbors had carried off what was left of Terézia's things, her pouffes, her rugs and mirrors, and the slits in the parquet floor now exuded the stench of mouse rather than the scent of perfume. But this couldn't keep my grandfather from picking up his practice where he'd left off before the war. The Republic of Councils be damned, he hired a maid, had her scrub the place clean, got in a buggy and made the rounds of his former patients, the ones that had survived the consequences of Franz Ferdinand's assassination, that is.

On his way home, my grandfather saw Mrs. Gajdos in the adjacent yard beating a rug taken from the Jerecián house. When Mrs. Gajdos felt his gaze on her, she turned around, pale as can be, and with the hatred that comes from the hell of shame, she screamed, "Stop staring, Doctor! You and your son, you both survived! But where is my son? So stop staring!" At which my grandfather said he was sorry, at which Mrs. Gajdos broke into tears and ran inside the house.

The next morning, when my grandfather found the carpet from the Jerecián house leaning against the stairs, he decided that he would never put anyone in Mrs. Gajdos's situation again. He didn't even want to know who got hold of his stereo-photography set or the bed on which my grandmother died in childbirth.

By the time Béla Kun took off from Budapest's Vérmező and headed for the safe haven of Soviet Russia dangling the gold of the former counts from his plane – this was after the fall of the Hungarian Soviet Republic – despite his best intentions, my grandfather András Szabad had gotten back just about everything that had once been taken from him. A curtain here, a physician's manual there, a silver candelabra lying on the bench under the walnut tree, a small side table by the raspberry bush. Or it might be six Meissen tea cups with saucers, a reading lamp, bed linen, and even my grandmother's likeness in a mahogany box equipped with a loupe. This made him happy.

Sometimes at night he'd hear the gate creak, or someone moving about in the garden. When this happened, he'd turn to the wall. But certainly, even if nothing had been returned to him, he'd still have been convinced that despite all our evil deeds we're not altogether depraved all our lives.

(my father András Szabad)

All considered, my grandfather was very much mistaken in thinking that nothing could make his son as happy as watching, night after night, the distant, unreachable skies through a spyglass. Come to think of it, it was more like this: he merely passed on the magogany box in which he had been keeping his own unhappiness. Or, thinking further about it, I have spent three decades myself looking through the viewfinder of a camera in search of something I will never reach. Yet it was thanks to that Zeiss telescope that Father discovered the exploded star that prompted Anna Hollós to run after him along the university corridor.

Hundreds of amateur astronomers discovered that spot of light on the edge of the universe when Father did, but Mother couldn't have cared less. She wanted to live in this apocalyptic light. And she had every reason to do so. She hadn't yet gotten over her brother's execution, but she was over a marriage that had lasted just a few months, as well as the death of a child. But these last two things, she forgot to tell me about.

Father was able to handle Anna Hollós's beauty far better than the knowledge that other men also found her beautiful. And so, after their first night together, as soon as he was alone, he packed his things. He cleaned up, washed the dishes, stripped the bed of its linen, and wrote two letters. One was addressed to the owner of the rented quarters in which he said how sorry he was for having to leave on such short notice. He attached the month's rent to it. The other was for Anna Hollós. But then he tore it up, because he felt he was being silly. And he was probably right.

As always, my grandfather was glad to have his son back, and in keeping with his character, refrained from asking awkward questions. In the evening, when they sat under the cankered walnut tree, all he asked Father was why he quit university, to which Father said that it was the right thing to do. And my grandfather acquiesced to this answer without qualms. Then once the jug of wine was empty, one of them would return to Balzac, the other to his spyglass, and they made a point of keeping out of each other's way. They lived in peace for weeks until Anna Hollós appeared on the steps of the porch, her hair down, wearing a French dress, and she said to Father, András Szabad, you should be ashamed of yourself, you coward.

When my grandfather returned from his patients and saw that his limping son wouldn't necessarily need to live the rest of his life in solitude, it didn't make him as happy as he'd have liked. To his credit, he gave a polite greeting, but with that he considered their conversation over. He withdrew and for hours busied himself looking into his mahogany box with its loupe.

He didn't make it his business to exchange a few words with Anna Hollós until the next morning. Only after waiting for his son to start packing again, did he emerge from his room with two cups of myrtle wine in his hands and sit down by Mother's side under the cankered walnut tree.

I have no right to question your feelings, and I respect your admirable humility, without which you surely wouldn't have come here. But I'm afraid that you're too beautiful to ultimately make a man like my son happy.

Anna Hollós thought of many things she'd have liked to say, but in the end, all she said was that even so, she'd like to try. She finished her myrtle wine and headed for the bathroom, and by the time my father packed up his notes so he could take the exams he missed and continue with his studies, Anna Hollós had gathered her waist-length hair into a twisted knot that stayed, it seemed, for the rest of her life.

(the countess)

Behind the building, under the stairs leading to the attic, lived a mother and daughter. At least for some time I thought that they were mother and daughter. One of them must have been around eighty, the other around sixty. One wore a gray coat, the other mink. Then, as the weather improved, she switched to a long, tobacco-yellow coat. I hardly ever saw her because the older woman did most of the shopping. I saw her carry a basket when she left home. The younger one never carried a basket, just a string bag now and then, though, come winter, her mink didn't go very well with it. Of course, it may have been some other animal. It couldn't have been Persian lamb. Mother's coat was Persian lamb.

We ran into each other in front of the entrance. She'd come from the farmers' market and her hands were full. I opened the door for her. I asked if I could help carry her bags up. She sized me up. You should have seen the look of disappointment in her eyes. You must never ask a woman a question like that, my dear. In this house you of all people should know that.

When I took the string bag from her, all I knew about her was that when she crosses the inner courtyard, the superintendent Gyula Korbán never misses a chance to comment, Putting on airs, comrade? Putting on airs?

Pardon. May I, I said, and held out my hand for the string bag.
At least, you know how to get yourself out of such an infinitely awkward situation. You may take it, she said, and she handed me the bag as we headed for the back stairs next to the shared toilet.

Mária, dear, we have a guest, this young man. . . . Pardon. As you see, burdened down with so many potatoes, even I am wont to forget my manners. Countess Éva Szendrey, she said, and she offered a hand.

I am pleased to meet you. I am András Szabad, I said, and I was grateful to Mother for having taught me when to shake and when to kiss hands.

I introduced myself to Mária as well, then she took the potatoes meant for their potato soup from me. She wore ash-gray at home, just as she did when, from time to time, I saw her heading for the farmers' market. She flashed a triumphant smile. The kitchen couldn't have been more than six square meters, hardly big enough to contain that triumphant smile.

Did I or did I not say that sooner or later the young man would pay us a visit? Well, did I, or did I not, she asked.

You did, Mária dear, you did, the countess said. But let's not embarrass the young man. I can offer you English tea, my dear, or sour cherry liqueur, she said turning to me. I opted for the tea, because it was clear as day that in this place I couldn't very well light up as I drank the liqueur.

In the living room, which was somewhat larger than the kitchen, books and *Life and Sciences* magazines lay on the small table, and a Lux broadband radio stood next to the armchair. Above it hung a painting by Munkácsy showing peasants bending over their task in an autumn landscape. Above my armchair there hung a painting by Rippl-Rónai, a girl with a parasol in the garden where the white light was reflected by the bark of the birch trees. The same woman was sitting across from me now, except her face was covered with a network of fine wrinkles, gray instead of blond, and with a deep scar on her eyebrow. The china cabinet held French porcelains. One book case contained German books, the other English. The Hungarian books were lined up in four rows under the window, poetry, all of them, and works by Márai. The oil radiator stood under the other window.

Mária served the tea, and the countess proposed that this might be the best occasion to open the cookies from across the ocean – don't you agree, Mária dear? And so we were served the American cookies, too, on a glass plate.

Is that you, I asked with reference to the girl with the parasol. I knew it was her, except I had to say something, seeing how I'd accepted the invitation.

No, my dear, it's not me. But it was. There was no trace of bitterness in her voice, she said it the same way she'd say any bon mot. Still, this painting, which she'd be looking at for another seven years, hung right across from her armchair.

By the time we drank our first cup of tea, I learned that Mária was neither the countess's mother, nor her aunt, but a lady's maid, who after the war was urged politely to go on her way, but she stayed, and now they lived off of the packages from across the ocean, two each month, one for them, and one for the customs officials, and not from their pensions. The scar, missing from the Rippl-Rónai, made its appearance during the political upheaval – at the time of nationalization she behaved badly. But I dare hope it left a trace only on my vanity, she added. Mária would have surely let on had my appearance been marred because of a silly backhanded slap.

In turn, I told them what I could about myself . . . that we moved to town from the provinces, that Mother died, Father was released just recently and is now working in a warehouse, but before that he was a teacher. The countess asked what I did, I told her I'm attending secondary school.

But it's Tuesday, she said.

I know.

I see. . . Surely it would be tactless of me to inquire what you have against public education.

It wouldn't be tactless, except I don't know the answer.

In which case it's something of a mystery. By our next encounter I shall have solved it. I hope you like enigmas.

Only if I must.

Must? Of course not. There is no such thing as must. But believe me, there is nothing more intriguing than knowing why we do something. And now I'll let you go. It is nearly siesta time.

Thank you for the tea.

It was our pleasure. And next time you lock yourself out of the apartment, my dear, there's no need to sit on the attic stairs.

All right, I said, slightly taken aback.

I do realize that an aristocrat should not snoop around, it is not *comme il faut*, but what can I do if the kitchen window looks out onto the shared toilets?

In that case, next time I'll ring your doorbell, I said.

Quite right. Though you may do that anytime.

Thank you.

Mária dear, kindly see the young man to the door.

(Kádár)

One fine day János Kádár happened to say, whoever is not against us is with us. People heaved a sigh of relief. After all, had not Christ said the same thing? Except, from then on, like it or not, whoever did not show the whites of his teeth was with him, whereby, like it or not, with this single sentence, he finished off an entire country.

In short, one fine day we woke up to the fact that even if it came with a price tag, Kádár had pardoned Hungary. It was five years after the revolution, and on the morning of August 26th, everyone had been hanged. And the truth is that even those who benefited from this new Workers' Militia gray lovefest, like Father, had least expected it. Though he was still barred from teaching, after a couple of months he found work in a branch of the district library. It was all the way out in Rákos, but at least he didn't have to spend his days in a warehouse sorting tires, v-belts, and pipes destined for oil rigs.

(the singer)

When I was a child, a beggar used to come to our house. Two or three times a week he would stop at the bottom of the stairs leading to the porch and sing. He sang operas, brandishing his white stick for accompaniment, as if he were conducting. He showed up at lunch time and sang until he got his mug of soup.

Each time he wore the same freshly laundered shirt with the frayed collar and cuffs. He also wore a suit, a pale yellow tie, and a pair of army boots. He didn't stop until the porch door squeaked and Mother or I would take him his cup of soup and a slice of bread. He knew by our gait which one of us was bringing his lunch. May God repay you, madam, may God keep you in good health, young gentleman. Not once did he get it wrong.

He hung his cane on the banister, sat down on the bench under the walnut tree, spread his napkin over his knee, and placed the bread on top of that. That's how he consumed his lunch. Then he brushed off the crumbs, folded the napkin into a triangle, and put it back in his pocket. Then he walked over to the garden tap next to the bench and rinsed the dishes. He always returned the cup and spoon sparkling clean.

Mother would often cook especially for him, because he would eat nothing but soup and bread. Once we tried giving him chicken wings, and once some thin cabbage stew which, with a bit of good will, could be considered a transition between soup and non-soup, but the old man said thank you, but he can't eat anything like that. Which, to put it mildly, Mother could not fathom. Once she even asked what the gentleman has against proper food, and to oblige her, the old man explained that alas, he's got a difficult nature, and the pain of having to give up eating meat yet again tomorrow would far outweigh the pleasure those few bites would give him today, and so mother had to take the chicken wings back and prepare his usual soup from caraway seeds, all the while quietly railing against the eccentric old man. This time I had to deliver the soup, since Mother declared she wouldn't deal with him ever again. God keep you in good health, young gentleman.

I must have sat next to him more than a hundred times while he ate his lunch, yet it never occurred to him to tell me the story of his life. He did not wear dark glasses; the sockets of his eyes were not empty, a gray silky netting had not covered his irises. His gaze was clear, blue as the sky. You knew that he was blind only from the way he looked into the void.

We didn't even know his name. I respectfully called him Uncle. Mother and Father called him Sir. Once Father introduced himself, but that was all. András Szabad, he said, and as for the old man, he just said that the pleasure was all his, he thanked Mr. Szabad for his goodness, then excused himself, saying that he wouldn't want to embarrass anyone by divulging his name.

It was sometime in the summer of '52 that he sang in front of our door for the last time. Then in the early autumn of that year, Spinster Lórántffy began letting on that the Secret Police had taken the singer into the nearby woods, strung him up by the feet, and beat him to death because they were on assassination prevention maneuvers, in case Comrade First Secretary should visit the town.

We knew perfectly well that just like nearly all of Spinster Lórántffy's nightmares about the Secret Police, this too was rubbish. Not that there wasn't plenty of reason for such nightmares. On the contrary. Except even nightmares have their limits, Father said. If it were a parish priest or a comrade gone astray, then yes, it might make sense hanging them by their feet and beating them to death. But if there's not a single, solitary perspective from which a killing like this could be seen as logical, then there's no explanation, save one. Madness. And where there's madness, there's chaos, and there's no chaos here, so calm down, Anna. If it was in fact his boots the mushroom pickers found, and he was in fact beaten to death and found hanging by his feet, then it wasn't the Secret Police, but a madman. Or if it was the Secret Police, then there's something here we don't know. Then the old man was either a member of the Arrow Cross and no better than a Nazi, or a count, or a monk. Or an old-time communist, Father added to put Mother's mind at ease, for as much as he loathed the communists, after the debacle of their reign of terror, he could still not comprehend the logic of the new order, filling everyone indiscriminately with dread.

Even under the Arrow Cross, people knew who should be afraid. The Jews, the communists, the members of the resistance. In short, everyone. But even so, people knew who should be afraid and why. It's one thing if the reason is unacceptible or incomprehensible, and quite another if there is no reason to begin with. A regime as deplorable as the former is simply impossible, Anna. It would fall apart at the seams. It couldn't function, dear, Father said, and so refused to accept that in fact this was the very logic of the regime. And then it came to light that Spinster Lórántffy herself, the former aristocrat, had the rank of major within the Secret Police.

Now that she relented and saw the light, the aristocratic spinster's duties were not limited to arousing fear with her terrifying nightmares. Thanks to her training, she was also tasked with acting as advisor to the team whose job it was to sow the seeds of those nightmares. For instance, it was Spinster Lórántffy who came up with the idea that once a day at dinner time, an automobile should stop for three minutes, no more and no less, in front of the window of the editor-in-chief of the local newspaper, a maneuver that should continue, she advised, until Comrade Blénesi hangs himself. If the State Security comrades do their job properly, this should transpire within seven to eight days, the Spinster Lórántffy predicted, except she overshot the mark by two days, because by then János Blénesi had an inkling about the nature of the new regime.

It was also upon Spinster Lórántffy's advice that they opened up the blind windows of the police basement, so that the screams of those being tortured should be heard on the street during the night, and also, that whenever there was a funeral at the Catholic cemetery, they should hold dog training or target practice on the nearby field. But Comrade Prosecutor, I am just a simple class alien, an old maid who studied psychology in Vienna. Yes, that's true, I offered a few bits of practical advice in the interest of the protection of the state, I admit it. But how can anyone so much as imagine that I had beggars beaten to death? That's nothing but phantasmagoria, Comrade Prosecutor. Phantasmagoria. This is what she said at the trial, when with respect to a couple of cases, new comrades capitalized on the old conception. In the end she confessed to the charges against her and got ten years, and as for her house on Szabadság Street, it was given to an agricultural engineer, a civilian like herself, who had studied in Moscow, and who had the blind windows of the police cellar blocked up once again.

(the *zú*)

It's not true that I don't like enigmas, except it bothers me that I can't solve them, I told the countess the next time I saw her.

That's not fair play, my dear, she said.

What's not, I asked.

I racked my brains for days, wondering what our young friend has against public education, and then you come out with the answer.

Did you find it satisfactory?

I wouldn't call it satisfactory, but it's not bad for a start. One thing is certain. Few things hold a person back as much as the fear of failure. Fortunately, there are many ways of avoiding failure. And one of these is tackling the problem.

I said nothing, so she continued.

But be that as it may, I value the other route much more. That of finding the solution to the problem. What can I say, it is part of my inheritance, even though, undoubtedly, the solutions were at times unfortunate, to say the least.

Aren't unfortunate solutions still solutions?

Certainly. At least, to the extent that an effort has been made, in which case, the main obstacle, the fear of failure, is overcome.

I don't think it's just the fear of failure that's keeping me from attending school.

I quite agree. That's why I said just now that it's not bad for a start. Are you willing to engage in a bit of constructive failure?

Must I?

I told you the other day. There are no musts, my dear.

All right, then. I'm game.

Mária dear, would you bring us the *zú*?

I hadn't seen Mária till then. She'd been sitting by the window out of sight, next to the radiator. She now put down her needle and darning egg, went to the china cabinet, and

50

withdrew a silver box the size and weight of a large brick. It bore a coat of arms on its lid. The countess told me to go ahead and open it. It was just like a jewelry box, lined with black velvet, and amid the black velvet there lay, in a small niche, a dark brown wooden disk.

Well? she asked.

I took it out. It was barely larger than a coin, though a bit thicker. It had some sort of symbol carved on one side composed of seven or eight lines; the etchings were painted white. There was nothing on the reverse side, just the tree's rings, of which there were quite a few. It was hard, heavy, and battered. It had clearly been used a lot, though I'd have been at a loss to say for what. The symbol resembled a double cross, though it could just as easily have been something entirely different. I couldn't even be sure that it was a symbol at all.

Well, my dear, what do you think it is?

I don't know, I said.

Think. You won't know the answer, but I'm sure you will come up with some intriguing ideas.

I turned the side with the symbol every which way.

Is it some kind of seal? Except, they don't make those out of wood, do they?

No, they don't.

Well then, money?

Money? Funny how no one has ever thought of that.

Some sort of money with no value? You know, like a red cent?

Not bad, my dear, but contrary to popular belief, red cents were never in circulation. It must have referred to something.

A figure of speech, like a red herring.

Too bad. If it were a genuine red cent, it would be worth a fortune by now.

To me it is precious. It's been in the family for three hundred years. At one point, my great-grandfather had this silver box made especially for it.

But what is it?

That is precisely what nobody knows. And that is why it's been so carefully guarded. The container was made when my great-grandfather took it to Rome.

Why Rome?

Because in Rome, my dear, they know everything. There are very few places where they know everything.

And what did the pope have to say?

I'm sorry to disappoint you but not even my great-grandfather had access to the pope. One of the subordinates claimed that this was the model for the mark with which the first Christians were branded.

So mystery solved.

But the Christians were not branded, my dear.

Maybe they reconsidered.

As we all know, they came up with countless excellent ideas. . .

How did it end up with your family?

It was a present. Solomon Szendrey went to Constantinople at the head of a delegation of Hungarian noblemen to negotiate with the Sultan, and the Sultan gave it to him. The story is probably not true, not a word of it, because Solomon Szendrey was a great liar. But be that as it may, this whatchamacallit – please forgive me – made it into the family through him.

Except, if that's all you know, then there's no use guessing, because who is to say whether we're right or wrong?

Just a week ago, you'd have been right about that.

Do you mean the mystery was solved?

It simply came to light. This is a peasant, my dear boy.

A peasant? What are you talking about?

This is a Chinese chess piece, my dear. A pawn. She laughed as she showed me the latest issue of her *Life and Science* magazine. This is the Chinese chess piece of the smallest value. The Chinese call it a zú, or foot solider, the English call it a pawn, while we call it a peasant. A peasant in the Szendrey family's treasure box, she laughed. Three centuries of guesswork, and it turns out that the family heirloom is a chess piece, she smiled as she placed the wooden disk back inside the silver box bearing the family's coat of arms.

What's so funny? Aren't you disappointed?

Disappointed? Don't be silly. I haven't had such a good laugh since we were stripped of our wealth and nationalized.

You laughed when you were nationalized?

Of course. What could I do, my dear. A couple of wretched, dispossessed men show up with two State Security people at the helm who had already lined their pockets, and they think that by confiscating the family silver, they're liquidating the aristocracy.

Which they did.

You think so? Mária, my dear, in your opinion what is the aristocracy?

Zú, she said, and laughed.

And the honorable working class?

Zú.

And our young friend here?

Zú, from top to toe.

And unless I am gravely mistaken, I too am a zú, don't you think?

Yes, your ladyship, from top to toe, and what's more, so am I, Mária said.

I believe Mária is right.

In which case everyone is zú, I offered.

Bravo! You're quite right, the countess said. A pawn in an elegant box has kept an otherwise undoubtedly well-educated family of high repute in the dark for centuries with its secret. Though come to think of it, the countess continued after a short pause, hasn't it kept all of us, from the nobility to the Secret Police in the dark? Even you, for that matter, my dear András.

Yes, I see what you mean, I said.

I'm glad you do. Truth will out, she said. Off you go before you start imagining that this old countess is ready to take the place of the Hungarian public school system.

But the two are like night and day.

I will take that as a compliment.

(the summons)

Every time I came or went, I always checked the mailbox downstairs by the front door. Not that it made any sense. Father didn't subscribe to newspapers and he corresponded with only a couple of people. I corresponded with no one. In spite of this, I would slip the key into the lock, turn it, open the creaky door, close it, turn the key back again, and move on. I'd do this six to eight times each day. It really made no sense, if only because the mailman delivered mail just once a day, and Father only got mail once every two or three weeks, and when he did, you could see it through the slot.

When the lock on the mailbox went bust, I still used the key, out of habit I guess, to pry it open. Using my finger would have been easier, I wouldn't have had to search my pocket, except I got used to doing it this way. I could have changed the lock, but what would have been the use? If something came for Father, I put it on the table in his room. I didn't even check the sender. As I said, I wasn't expecting anything from anyone, but at least, this checking of the mailbox made me feel that I was at home. You don't go checking mailboxes in other people's houses, do you?

Once I was leaving the house just as father was coming back. We ran into each other downstairs at the entrance. He was just opening the empty mailbox, and that's when I realized that he checked it every time himself. Though who knows. He may in fact have been expecting something. He asked if I had any money, and I said thank you, I do. He asked if I'd had anything to eat, and I said yes, I'd bought a roll and some salami. Then we parted ways.

The sun shone so brightly outside that after leaving the building's grim, dilapidated entryway it came as a surprise. And when the sun shone in my eyes, I almost turned around to tell him that I'd brought him a roll, too, it was in the cupboard. But then I didn't turn around. I figured he'd find it anyway. But what I really wanted to tell him about is how we both check the mailbox.

When I placed the envelope on Father's table, like I always did, it didn't even occur to me that the letter might have been meant for me. Then he came home, read it, and knocked on the door to my room. His face was ashen and his lips quivered, ever so slightly. You'd think he was about to cry. This came for you, son.

Neither one of us had counted on this letter. Neither one of us had ever counted on all the things that an ordinary family could count on, months or even years in advance. We simply weren't like that. Of course, we were hardly what you'd call an ordinary family. The letter was from conscription headquarters, informing me when and where I needed to show up for mandatory enlistment.

My first I thought was to hang myself. Then I thought that they'd never find me back in the backwoods near Mélyvár. Then I thought of sneaking across the border. I didn't really think about doing any of these things – not in the strict sense of the word, the way you do, for instance, when you decide you'll go and buy three rolls and some salami. Only the pictures rolled past my eyes, like on a movie screen. A man is running through a cornfield, another man cocks his gun, aims, waits, grins, fires. When the images vanished, I saw Father standing in the same place, just like before.

You survived the three years as well, didn't you, I said.

Just the same, you will not be a soldier, son, no matter what, he said.

Thank you, I said, hoping to put him at ease, even though I knew that there was nothing he could do. Even Party secretaries couldn't get their children exempted, let alone a recently paroled warehouse man. Or even a teacher.

(the old woman)

I bought a ticket and boarded the morning express. I spent my time counting the stops to Mélyvár. An old woman sat across from me. Sweat ran down her face, and she kept wiping it. After a while, her hair was wet, too. And then her clothes. She wore a brown sweater with big wooden buttons. When the conductor came in, she started rummaging through her handbag. Her hands, too, were drenched in sweat. The conductor punched her ticket in disgust, and didn't even bother checking mine. On his way out, he closed the compartment door. I asked the woman if there was any way I could help. There's no helping this, she said. All the same, I opened the window, hoping the draft would help her dry off. Then a pigeon flew in as we rounded a bend.

I'd never seen anything like it before. On the other hand, I rarely took the train. When I was around two and Germans soldiers were billeted in our homes, a peacock flew into the room. This I remember. My mother peeled it off me. And now a frightened pigeon was fluttering about in the compartment. It knocked against the old woman's suitcase, the mirror, the sliding door. I tried to steer it toward the window, but that just made it more desperate, so I sat back down in my seat and kept still, hoping it'd calm down. Meanwhile, the old woman kept wiping herself. Then she put down her rag and without so much as a sideways glance, she grabbed the bird, with a sharp snap she broke its neck, and flung it out the window, at which point the old woman's skin started drying up. And I woke up screaming. Luckily, Father had left home by then, taking my conscription orders with him.

(the peacock)

During the last days of the German occupation, Dr. Col. Johann Wolfgang Adler presented Mother with a peacock wrapped in a blanket. It was a farewell gift. His men requisitioned it from the Gypsies living on the outskirts of town, but only after they'd shot each and every one of them to death with the exception of seven young girls, though later, after they'd made good use of them, they shot them in the back of the head as well, then sacrificed two cans of gasoline for the cremation.

The peacock was already deposited on the porch when Mother came home that evening, with only its crowned head and tail feathers poking out from under the army blanket tied around with string. She unwrapped the blanket and flung the bird out into the yard, where it landed among the jeeps, motorcycles, and sidecars, and good riddance to it. She sent Évike from next door home, fed me, put me in bed, then served up the billeted Germans' supper.

After dinner, Dr. Col. Johann Wolfgang Adler entered the room carrying a bottle of wine. He begged to be excused for the inconvenience, and told Mother how sorry he was that the war had to end in this inglorious fashion. And also, we should take things in stride, because new Gypsies would soon come to replace the old.

Are you sure you won't have some wine, dear Anna?

At which Mother let on with a single glance that she remained adamant about not striking up a conversation with Coloner Adler, not even if it was his last night.

A pity, because right now I have urgent need of advice, Coloner Adler said. You understand, having to obey two contradictory sets of commands is confusing for us all. Now, for instance, in accordance with Colonel General Friessner's order of the day, and in accordance with martial law, I should have Blumann and the others summarily shot, because a German soldier is not a criminal, he does not steal, he does not set people on fire, he does not commit murder or rape women. On the other hand, not even a retreating German soldier is immune to the plague of wandering Gypsies. How would you resolve this quandary, Frau Anna?

Whereupon mother cleared the plates off the table.

Never mind, I'll resolve it somehow. Of course, my problem is a mere trifle. Just think of the poor English, who are wondering to this day if it's wise to arm the Negroes with weapons, because what if those Negroes should happen to take aim not at our racial theories, but their own officers?

Whereupon mother took the dirty dishes outside, then came back for the tablecloth.

Please stay. You know perfectly well that we'll be gone by the morning. Think of it this way. By talking to me, you are making a sacrifice for your country. Surely, your country deserves as much, because it's in big trouble. We'll be defeated, but you'll be liberated, and liberators can never be despised wholeheartedly, not even if, like my own soliders, they'll shoot Gypsy girls in the back of the head after they've had their way with them.

Whereupon mother removed the tablecloth, which at least had remained clean, and for years to come, we ate supper with this tablecloth on the table.

Do you know what I think, dear Anna? That as of tomorrow, there will always be people here who will think of our Gypsies as having been defiled and massacred, but will think of their own Gypsies as an excusable excess, a lamentable lapse. And there may even be a grain of truth in in, no more, but that grain will suffice to cause contention, and it's this contention that will bring this country down. On our last night here, let this be my farewell message to you and your country, my dear Anna.

Whereupon my mother didn't leave, though the folded tablecloth was already in her hand. She could have, had she wanted to.

You could have gotten along very well without your Jews, Gypsies, queers, and communists. You could have hated us with all your hearts very well without them. And hatred imparts strength. It imparts a lot more strength than faith, hope, and charity. But the contention and division that will now follow will be the ruin of this country. Mark my words, it will become weak, sad, ridiculous. We are in no position to justify this or that act of ours, because there is no justification for them whatsoever. On the other hand, from now on, we'll come in handy for this rabble, their excuse for everything. This is the only reason why I am sorry that we've lost this war.

At that point, Mother commented that he needn't be sorry for her sake. Or the country's.

Whereupon Colonel Adler thanked Frau Anna for talking to him after all, and poured himself another glass of wine. According to Mother, he was a decidedly handsome man.

Believe me, dear Anna, I have no desire whatsoever to live in your wartime memories as the humane Nazi, through whose example you can teach your sweet little boy that a German is also a human being. I haven't sunk that low. We needn't clink glasses either. But please drink a glass of wine with me. It is no good, drinking alone. . . But if not, then not, the colonel said after a short pause. Though you are wrong.

Whereupon my mother began meticulously folding the tablecloth, making sure the sides were aligned, not that it made sense, because it soon landed in the laundry basket anyway.

You know, I had a teacher in college once, the colonel went on. His name was Professor Klaus Klaus. What a funny name! He held a demonstration. He called up three students and asked them the simple question, who wrote the *Nichomachean Ethics*? He handed each a slip. They had to write down the answer. Needless to say, all three wrote down Aristotle's name without a second thought. And here I must add that there was

59

nothing funny about Professor Klaus Klaus, except for his name. He glanced at the three slips and was satisfied with two of the answers, but he told Helga Müller to come to his office after class because he wanted to talk to her.

As for Helga, she didn't dare ask why, but two minutes later, she started sobbing, at which Professor Klaus said, it's all right if you remember now. Stand up and say the name in front of the class. Who wrote the *Nichomachean Ethics*? Well, miss? Let's hear it. Whereupon Helga screamed, sobbing, I don't know, and forgive me Professor, forgive me, forgive me! So much for the sense of security that comes from knowledge, Professor Klaus said, and then he reassured Helga that she'd given the right answer, but apart from the fact that she will pass with flying colors, she will never benefit from Aristotle's ethics, or anyone else's ethics, for that matter in the days to come.

The truth, dear Anna, is that I wasn't afraid of Professor Klaus, and so I couldn't understand Helga. Let's put it this way. Knowledge *has* given me security, and as we imagine, freedom hinges on a sense of security, and as for freedom that makes you quiver with fear, who wants that?

I wasn't afraid of Klaus, I wasn't afraid to call my PhD thesis "The Ethics of Freedom." I wouldn't have been afraid to desert either. Except I didn't consider it the right thing to do. In short, I am not here out of fear. Which doesn't mean that I'm not afraid of anything, because, for instance, I'm afraid of death. I'm merely saying that I'm not a victim of my system. And at the risk of disillusioning you, dear Anna, my conscience is clear. Way back, near Warsaw, I let a couple of truckloads of Jews run, I have not executed anyone with my own two hands, and so on and so forth. Yet at the same time, I don't think I have done anything good either. I merely avoided committing evil. By the way, I don't hold a clear conscience in high regard. The greatest baseness has been committed in its name.

In short, if I were to take my own life, the colonel went on, I would not do so out of fear, or because of a guilty conscience. And certainly not because I couldn't decide if it is hypocritical of the English, not arming their Blacks at this particular point in time, of all times. Because, you see, I have a strong suspicion that it is hypocritical. In short, I wouldn't be doing it out of ethical considerations, nor because I've lost hope. I am pretty sure that after a year or two as a prisoner of war, I'd be invited to teach ethics at one of the top universities. If I were to take my own life, I would do it solely because... This wine is terrible. You were quite right not to have accepted it. And now, dear Anna, may I ask you to open a window for a second?

Of course, my mother said, and while she was occupied with opening the window, without fear, and with a clear conscience, Dr. Col. Johann Wolfgang Adler shot himself through the mouth.

The orderly was the first to come running, and he asked mother to stop this inarticulate screaming and help gather up Colonel Adler. And needless to say, he would bear witness to what happened, so needless to say, no harm would come to Frau Anna. For the moment, however, he begs Frau Anna to collect herself. After all, there's a war going on. And then, after mother had more or less composed herself and helped convey the colonel's body to Father's room, who was in a forced labor camp at the time, the peacock came flying through the window. It strutted around the big table with Dr. Col. Johann Wolfgang Adler's wine glass on top of it, it perched itself on the blood-spattered armchair for a while, and then it alighted on the china cabinet, and from there it flew in the direction of the voice calling to him. It then strutted along the hallway, came to my room, and landed atop the tile stove, where it shifted about for a while, like someone who can't quite decide what to do next, even though I was screaming at the top of my lungs by then. But at last, it flew across the room, its rainbow-colored tail trailing behind.

This bright, technicolor comet is my first memory.

After that, a heavy blanket of warmth buried me and the house fell silent. It was a silence more profound, even, than the silence that followed the sound of the gun. It was this silence that made Mother rush into the room and shriek, Murderers! and tore the Gypsies' bird off me before it could peck out my eyes and before I could find my peace, too, once and for all.

(Dr. Zenta)

A couple of days after my summons, Father brought home a stranger: Dr. Zenta, a neurologist. He wore a gray suit, and his hair was also gray, though he was more or less the same age as Father. He had the head of a vulture, or God knows what. He bore a slight resemblance to my mother's brother, Ivan, who was shot by the Arrow Cross. This was the first visitor we had since we moved into this apartment.

Father asked that I come to his room, but there were only two chairs, so I brought a stool in from the kitchen. Dr. Zenta said that like in the country in general, there had been a thaw in the military as well. My father asked what that meant. Dr. Zenta explained that they still don't like malingerers, but of late those with suicidal tendencies have been exempted from military service. The high death rate among the conscripts was hurting the army's image, and they would like to improve it. And also, that it was lucky, me reaching military age just now, because you never know, perhaps a year or two from now the hardliners might be back.

I asked if I should hang myself. He said definitely not, because that's what malingerers usually do. They hang themselves, jump off bridges, take an overdose of sleeping pills, and then they live to regret it, just like the seminarians. In the worst case scenario, they might even end up under lock and key for years. Anyone who really wants to die dies. Technically speaking, it is much easier to kill yourself than somebody else. Still, there must be exceptions, I said. Someone may want to die in earnest, but botches it up. That's true, he said.

At this point I thought that Dr. Johann Wolfgang Adler botched it as well, and that he was counting on Mother catching his reflection in the window, turning around in the nick of time, and forgiving him.

So then, what's it to be, Father asked rather impatiently, then fell silent, probably realizing that his question made it sound as if he were clamoring for my suicide.

We'll find a way, Dr. Zenta said. Have the boy come see me tomorrow at four for further guidance. Then he glanced at his gold Schaffhausen and left.

I took the stool and the glasses back to the kitchen. First the lightbulb burned out, then one of the glasses broke. I lit a candle and swept it up. The shops were closed, but then it occurred to me that I could bring the light bulb from my reading lamp.

Father was sitting on the bed as if it were a bunk bed, his cane resting by his side. I asked him who our visitor was. For a while he was silent, then he just said that he'd known Mother in the old days.

I went to my room and opened the drawer of the china cabinet that held a box of family photographs that didn't make it into our albums. If I see something in a photograph, I remember it for life. I even remembered that the watch said five minutes past four. I found the picture at the bottom of the box, mother as a young girl in some park or at the edge of the woods, looking up at the sun. Her hair is swept by the wind. With her right hand she is holding the hand of a man. His Schaffhausen says five after four, and there the picture ends.

(in the hospital)

At four p.m. the following day I showed up at János Hospital. The doorman was a gnome. He said Dr. Zenta won't see just anybody. I said he's expecting me, but he clearly did not believe it. After a while, he decided that he's taking less of a risk if he calls upstairs just the same. Excuse me, Comrade Chief Physician, it's Sanyi, yes, Comrade Chief Physician, the doorman, there's a young man here to see you, Comrade Chief Physician, yes, I understand, Comrade Chief Physician.

He looked hydrocephalic, and when he got up off his chair, he was even shorter than when he was seated. Rushing up ahead of me all the way from his doorman's cubicle to the chief physician's room, he opened all the doors for me, then hurried back with the same officious gait.

Dr. Zenta was a lot more cordial than he'd been at our place the night before, but he didn't so much as hint at where he knew my father from, so I didn't ask. He asked if I'd like some cognac, and I said no, just some water. On the other hand, I accepted the American cigarette. He explained in great detail what I must do, what I must say; he even acquainted me with the manner of speech of the recruiting officers.

He said that he thinks everything will go smoothly, at most they'll order an examination, though not necessarily, but even if so, I had nothing to worry about, the diagnosis he's giving me will do the trick better than any physical handicap. I understand, I said, and I recalled the way Father had been sitting on the bed, with the cane leaning next to him. Also, I thought how they'd have never exempted this man with his vulture face, and probably he wouldn't have even tried to avoid the draft. But then, I thought that it was all bullshit. Not only did Mother's younger brother try to be a soldier, he was shot in the back of the head for it, whereas he looked like a vulture, too. On the other hand, he got a Jewish woman pregnant at the worst possible time.

Dr. Zenta took a sealed envelope from his briefcase. He'd written what's inside the night before, he said, then he warned me that I should not hand it over until they ask for it. And also, do I realize that he could be sentenced to five years in prison because of it. Along with me. I know, I said. Then he asked me to refrain from opening it, its contents have nothing to do with me, but it bodes no good to anyone if they see the name on the slip such as this. I said that naturally, I would not open it. Still, I should know something about what's in it, in case they ask. He assured me that they wouldn't ask me about the diagnosis, he's sure of that. But for my information, incipient schizophrenia. The point is that they should exempt me, but not order compulsory psychiatric treatment. But otherwise, the illness is ideally suited for the purpose. There is nothing wrong with me at the moment, I am a useful member of society, and will continue to be a useful member of society for a good while to come, but there's no knowing what I might do under pressure. I asked what that meant. As far as they're concerned, it meant that there's no knowing when I might empty the barrel of my gun into the drill sergeant. But I would never riddle the sergeant with bullets, I said. Of course not. After all, there's nothing wrong with me.

I asked if others are also let off the hook after submitting such a diagnosis. He looked me steadily in the eye for some time, and his gaze did not waver even as he lit a cigarette. If it bears my signature, he said from behind a haze of cigarette smoke, then probably yes, and then he stubbed out what was left of his cigarette with such force, it broke in two.

He got up, fished a key out of his pocket, opened the medicine cabinet and took out a vial. He wrapped it in cotton and slipped it inside an empty pill box. He said I should drink it before I leave for the recruitment office. It's a simple sedative, I'll feel a bit woozy, nothing more. But it will help reduce the tension, so I won't forget how I must deport myself. Also, it will alter my appearance, because I'd look too handsome and healthy otherwise. Just like my mother, he no doubt thought.

He still had something to attend to, he said, but if I waited, he'd take me to Pest by car. I told him thank you, but just now I'd rather walk. We then shook hands. I was very grateful for that slip of paper. I had my doubts when he handed me the sealed envelope, but when he broke the half-smoked cigarette in two, I knew I'd be exempted.

It took more than thirty years to find out who Dr. Zenta was. I learned that at the time of my discharge he was no longer a neurologist but a high-ranking officer with State Security. *Emotive influence exercises an especially significant role with regard to agents active in the art world, especially with regard to women, with whom emotive influence comprises a natural and incidental element of emotive and logical involvement.* This is the sort of instruction material he wrote.

(the circle)

On my way back from the recruitment office I took the tram, and at one of the stops I saw a woman leaning against the sign post. She was licking half a lemon. She didn't budge until everyone got off, as if she weren't waiting for this particular tram. None-theless, the conductor did not slam the door in her face, even though with women approaching forty, they generally do.

Everyone saw, not just me. The whole tram with its wooden benches, including matrons and expectant mothers saw. She licked the lemon a couple more times, then took a piece of cellophane, wrapped it up, and put it in her handbag. She gave the impression that along with her keys, makeup, and personal documents, she always had half a lemon with her to lick as she listened to the male passengers gulp over the clatter of the tram's wheels.

From the moment she got on, I watched her only through the reflection in the window. I tried to make myself think that she was the lover of a State Police agent or a Party secretary. But it didn't help much. It seems that political, religious and moral affinities do little to alter our innate inclinations. In any case, it's pretty embarrassing when half the passengers on a tram know when your salivary glands spring into action.

Even though I was the only one on the tram who didn't stare at her outright, she decided to sit down across from me even though there were plenty of empty seats. I didn't get it. Why me? There really were at least twenty passengers staring at her – not indirectly but obviously – the way most people do.

On the other hand, I had played the half-wit barely an hour before so well that I contin-ued in my role. I could have easily snapped out of it, I could have easily looked anyone in the eye, but it just wasn't happening. Even though it was clear as day when she got on the tram that she wouldn't be getting off alone.

With some women, it's obvious at first glance. To be exact, every woman has a moment like this at least once in her life, when, if she has a mind to, she could lure Christ down from his cross. She may be granted this power just once in her life, and she may not even take advantage of it, because her conscience or her upbringing won't allow it. But even if only for a single moment, her power over the universe is real.

I had no idea what I'd say to her if it came to that. I couldn't very well say to a woman that in line with Dr. Zenta's instructions, barely an hour ago I played the fool at Conscription Headquarters. You hand them this envelope, and no matter what they ask, aside from your name, you say, I don't know. You don't play the fool, but calmly, soberly, and without batting an eye, you say, I don't know. After that you can say whatever you want, it won't matter. Do you like cabbage soup? I don't know. Maybe. Would you pick up arms in defense of the Hungarian People's Republic? I don't know. No. Was your father a dirty traitor to his country? I don't know. Yes. Have you ever attempted suicide? I don't know. Not really. And meanwhile, you don't bat an eye, understand? Don't forget that part, because it's more important than anything. If they call your mother a whore or say they're going to enlist you, you don't bat an eye. You just give them a blank stare. Just make sure you take that medicine before you leave. And keep in mind, I'm a friend of your father's, and don't try to deny it, because they know. And the only reason you looked me up was to ask for some sleeping pills, because you haven't been able to sleep for months. That's when I examined you.

I can't very well say to a woman that I'm on my way home from the recruitment office with an E Category army certificate in my pocket. I can't very well say to her that it's no use licking that lemon, I won't be going home with her, because Father is waiting for me, desperately wondering if I'd been conscripted or not.

Come to think of it, Dr. Zenta was right. Once you've said I don't know, there isn't much left to say, either to the draft board, or to a woman, a complete stranger sitting across from you on the tram. Then after three stops, she leaned toward me.

You must have driven lots of women to distraction by not looking at them. Am I right?

I don't know, I said. I wanted her to stop talking to me. Her voice was spent.

It's sexy when a man doesn't know something. Usually, they like to know everything.

I don't know, I said. Possibly.

It's a fact. Take my word for it. . . Do you believe me?

I don't know. Yes, I said.

In that case, close your eyes, she said, and I did so. She stroked my eyelid with her finger.

What color are mine?

I don't know. Blue?

What kind of blue?

I don't know. Ice-blue. With a brownish speck in the left eye.

Okay, time to open yours. It's rather exciting to find a man who knows nothing at all. We're getting off here.

I got off with her at the Hotel Astoria, even though I was supposed to stay on until Deák Square.

Wait for me here. It won't take more than ten minutes. I just have to pick up my working papers.

I nodded and began following her to the hotel entrance.

Wait here, she said. Right here.

She drew her lipstick out of her handbag, got down in front of me, and drew a circle on the asphalt of the station platform. She clearly wasn't concerned with the passersby, who hurried past in consternation.

Wait right here, and don't try getting away, because that would make me very sad. You may not know much, but by now I'm sure you know that.

As for me, I stayed inside that circle drawn on the asphalt as helpless as a kitten in a tree, all the while I was thinking I would never, ever have such power over anyone as she had over me. As I was waiting, I tried to figure out what I'd say to her, because once she was back, I'd have to say something.

Obviously, I couldn't tell her the truth, that I just wanted to look at her, to have her sit on the kitchen stool and just look at her through the Zorki's viewfinder in the weak light coming through the air shaft until she looks as immortal as Mother when she died, and then press the shutter release. And then ask her to leave. Or not even ask, because she'll know.

Which of course I can't say to her. There's no woman alive who wouldn't think that I'm just some pathetic Oedipal weirdo, looking for his mother in her. Who would believe that for me, my mother is not a woman? I can't tell anyone that you're wrong, my dear, it's not my mother I see in you, nor any tangible. What I see in you is eternity. I don't want you to cook, do the wash, clean the house, I just want you to die for me in front of my eyes, again and again, night after night.

After I'd taken the hundredth or the thousandth picture of her sitting on the kitchen stool, I felt as if I'd been waiting within that red circle for an hour or two, but no, that's impossible. She was just going to pick up some papers.

Then as night fell, I realized that I hadn't been waiting for an hour or two, but nearly half the day, that she must have given me one last look from an upstairs window and decided that I really don't know anything, that I don't know anything so thoroughly that even the know-it-alls, are better than me, and then snuck out a back door. Every hotel has a back door for the staff. And when they turned on the street lamps, I was left with nothing except the urge to hate her. At least, to hate her. But she was right. Even is she played this dirty game with someone every single day, this time around, she was right. How else could I have followed Dr. Zenta's instructions to the letter. Still, it would take that extra stop to Deák Square to free me from that goddamn red circle.

Then I went home and told Father that he could stop worrying.

(the mannequin)

That night I sat down at the piano and opened the keylid, but it was late to play, so I lowered it back down again. Besides, I hadn't played the piano in this apartment. Ever. Next door, my father was talking in his sleep. Two-thousand six-hundred, he said from time to time, the round number he'd been assigned in jail.

I thought next day I'd go to the tram stop and take a picture of the red circle. It's bound to be there. Things like that don't disappear from the pavement overnight. And then I thought, what's the use? It would make more sense to ask my father if I talk in my sleep too, if I ever say zero.

Actually, I was sorry I hadn't been enlisted. At least, something would have happened to me. Or I don't know. Be that as it may, it took that red circle to make me realize that I can see all of life, I can see anything, even things that others need pointed out to them, and all this because of the view finder of an old, battered camera. Yet I also realized that's as close as I'd ever get to what I see.

There was a ladies' tailor down on the corner of Rottenbiller and Lövölde streets. Rosenberg & Son, except the Son had passed away. The previous winter I inherited a coat from someone, but its sleeves barely reached my wrists, it needed new cuffs, so I decided to take it to the shop. But when I went past the shop the morning after my visit to the enlistment office, I saw that Rosenberg was clearing shop. Some of the furniture was already outside, and he was busy stuffing rolls of fabric in boxes. He'd placed a chair and a mannequin on the street to reserve a spot for the movers. I waited for him to come outside with one of the boxes and inquired if the mannequin was for sale.

He asked what I needed it for. The question surprised me. I wasn't counting on having to justify my need for a slightly battered shop window dummy that a ladies' tailor had used for decades to display his best suits for the benefit of the passers-by. Then, for lack of a better idea, I said I needed a roommate.

Annushka, you got yourself a husband, the old man said and grinned.

No she hasn't, I said, my color rising, she's just going to stand in a corner and keep an eye on me.

Same difference.

I wouldn't say so. Hope you don't mind if I give her another name.

For fifty forints, you can give her any name you like.

I had only twenty forints on me, and Rosenberg said that he wasn't the one who wanted to sell in the first place. Which, after all, was true. I might have said that I didn't leave home wanting to buy a window dummy either, but relented and thanked him for his time. That "you got yourself a husband" and his wide grin were pretty shabby business. I was already at the intersection when he called after me. All right, give me the twenty and be done with it.

Annushka was just a torso, a wooden frame propped her up from the hip, and she didn't have arms. Judging by her painted hairdo and puckered lips, she must have been made before the war. I picked her up. She was as light as a feather. On the way home, it started to rain. I covered her with my jacket so she wouldn't get wet. People had sought shelter in doorways, they were all occupied with keeping dry, so at least they didn't stare at me carrying that dummy tucked under my arm. I decided not to name her anything at all.

I tried to figure out what I'd say to Father. Telling him that I wanted to take pictures of her seemed the obvious thing to do. I can practice positioning the lights on her. Or I could say that I found her on the street and brought her home to prevent her getting soaked. But then I realized that there's no need to worry, Father would never ask.

(the piano)

In the summer of '52, we received a message from the colonel in the Interior Ministry. Mother cleared out half the living room the same day. Part of the living room furniture ended up in the attic, the china cabinet was moved behind the dining table, the flower stand was relegated to the porch. Then we cleaned house, just like before Christmas and Easter. Practically no one skips these holiday cleanings, not even in wartime, so that the Lord can come into a clean household, or if a person should die, they should leave a clean household behind.

There were few things I enjoyed as much as these pre-holiday cleanings that stretched into the night, Mother in a worn evening gown waxing the floor, and me waiting until she reached the window, then skating after her with rags fastened to my feet. But I enjoyed the last stage of cleaning most, when she also fastened rags to her feet and we skated around to music from the radio until the floor was as shiny as a mirror and one of us fell headlong on the parquet. We invariably stopped after the first fall. It was the sign that we've done a good job.

On major washdays the sign was that the soapy water would boil over in the huge laundry pot. Then, using long wooden spoons, we transferred the steaming rags to the big tub. We could barely see each other in the hot mist that filled the kitchen. After a while, we ran the clothes under the garden tap, then hung them up on the steel wire stretched out between the walnut tree and the woodshed. Father mounted a winch on the side of the shed. If the wire sagged under the weight of all that laundry, the winch could be used to tighten it. It was like a tuning key.

Mother and I joined forces to wring out the sheets and the duvet covers. We held the two ends of the rag-serpents in a tight grip. We always turned it to the right, though from where I was standing across from her, she seemed to be twisting it to the left, something that for years I couldn't understand. I couldn't decide which was real. Just take my word for it, son, Father would say, all it takes is looking at things from more than one perspective. If we stand facing each other in reverse, we'll see each other in reverse.

Next, we'd shake out the wrinkled sheets. Our reward was the cool mist, and sometimes the rainbow of our own making in the middle of the garden when the mist scattered the sunshine into its component parts. We also shook the towels dry, or nearly so. As opposed to the right-left quandary of wringing out the laundry, it took me next to no time to grasp the rainbow. After all, what could be more natural than that, just like the beveled edge of the large mirror or Father's reading glasses on the window sill, a drop of water should also scatter the light.

When Mother hung up the wash, I would hand her the clothespins from an old tin of Franck's Chicory Coffee Substitute that grandfather András Szabad's servants had passed down to us. In the winter months we didn't really need the clothespins, because in no time at all the bedsheets froze stiff as armor. During these months we washed the laundry in the bathroom, threw on warm clothes, then ran outside to hang up the wash. Meanwhile, Mother made hot tea. In winter, we always started hanging up the wash at the woodshed and progressed toward the walnut, so that before we froze to death, we would be close to the house and the steaming hot tea. Strange how neither mother nor I could figure out how the wash could dry in such bitter cold, so we resigned ourselves to the phenomenon without trying to fathom the mystery. Once she said, ask your father, son, I don't know, and I don't care. The only thing I care about right now is the tea. And I confessed that I was more interested in the tea myself.

I have no way of knowing what it was like for her to be my mother. All I know is what it was like for me to be me, and this is what it was like.

From time to time, a bed sheet that was now coming apart would remind her of a family story. For instance, that my grandfather was not just an architect, he was also a first-rate mushroom gatherer. He had his own mushroom knife and a mushroom outfit and a mushroom backpack, and he could tell a death cap from a button mushroom from a distance of thirteen feet. But once he unquestionably made a mistake with regard to some coral mushrooms, and on his wife's birthday, of all times. My grandmother was first to her feet. She made it to the bathroom and quickly locked the door, leaving her thirteen friends and relatives to soil themselves out in the hall amid a general burst of laughter.

I loved these stories, because they seemed so true to life. They seemed so true to life that I didn't realize until twenty years later that I had never actually met either my grandfather or my grandmother. This happened in my rented room in Budapest, when I pinned my eyes on the cracks in the ceiling as I related these stories to Éva. The realization came as quite a shock.

But Mother never told me stories about her brother, Iván Hollós. She talked about him just once in her life. This was just days before Father's release. It was evening and we were sitting on the two stools in the kitchen, just like we'd been doing every night for the past three years. Then she got to her feet, went outside, and came back with Iván Hollós's notebook. From now on, I place this in your care, son.

I wanted to ask her why, but she began talking about Iván, and I didn't want to interrupt, and she didn't stop talking until dawn. Even her last cigarette was gone by then, the one she hid on top of the cupboard. She spoke like an automaton. Then she got dressed, because she had to be at the dressmaker's for the early morning shift. She kissed me on the forehead, and I was left to fend for myself with page after page of godawful poetry, an unfinished essay about the inevitability of existence, and Iván Hollós's weighty presence.

Then I pulled myself together and did the dishes. After that, I looked over my homework. I still had an hour before I had to leave, but I was afraid I'd fall asleep. Ever since they threw Father in prison and made a seamstress of my librarian mother, I couldn't afford to be late for school, even if I ran a fever. But I'm getting ahead of myself.

In the summer of fifty-two, the colonel sent word about the piano. We didn't know his name and we made no effort to find out, because Antal Szakonyi, an old friend of Iván's who got in touch with the colonel, had asked us not to. In short, we cleared out half the furniture from the living room, which now looked like the salon of a stranded cruise ship that had run aground and in which the tables and cabinets had slid one on top of the other.

A couple of days later, the colonel sent word that he hadn't forgotten his promise, just that something had come up. Then he sent word again that it'd be in the early fall. It was now late November, and we'd practically gotten used to living in what felt like a stranded boat, when early one morning a military truck pulled up in front of the gate, its sides covered in green canvas.

Six soldiers jumped out and opened the gate as if they owned the place. The vehicle backed into the yard and stopped near the porch steps, and by the time we threw on some clothes and Mother opened the door, the soldiers had already rolled up the canvas, and there it sat on that early November morning, like a giant coffin, a piano – and a Bösendorfer at that.

Getting it down proved quite a challenge. The six privates fixed the heavy strap in place, and as if it were really just an oversized coffin, maneuvered the piano off the vehicle. Father showed them the way, but Mother remained standing on the porch with a coat thrown over her nightgown, smoking and staring into space.

I couldn't really help the soldiers, so I went and stood by Mother's side, and that's when I saw that she wasn't staring into space. If you stare into space, you don't see anything, and your tears don't come flowing in streams down your cheeks.

I asked her why she was crying, but she didn't hear, or else didn't have a ready answer. She didn't even ask me to leave her alone, and so we remained standing beside each other like that even after the soldiers had hauled the piano inside. When one of them came back out for the legs, only then did Mother open her mouth: Let's go, son, and she make them some coffee. By the time we finished, the Bösendorfer was standing to the right of the window, and its black heft had restored the equilibrium of the long-askew room.

The soldiers gathered up the straps, gulped down their coffee as if it were pálinka, Father told the driver to convey his regards to the Comrade Colonel, and they were off.

Father leaned against the door frame. He was alone, because Mother was gazing at the garden or perhaps something else through the curtain. And I was between the two of them.

Mrs. János Veres from next door broke our solitude. She rapped softly on the door, came in as if on tip-toes, and asked in a whisper: Are you really being deported? We had an answer ready. No, dear Emma, we're not being deported. On the contrary. In honor of my brother's heroic death, Comrade Minister has decided that the Party would gift us Iván Hollós's piano. Of which only the Party, the Comrade Minister, and the gifting was not true, but the piano, at least, was, there it stood for all to see, just like the army truck that had backed into our yard earlier that day. Upon which, Mrs. János Veres, née Emma Kozma, left satisfied and obviously relieved, and decided that she wouldn't be mentioning the incident in her report that day, because it would be a bit like denouncing the Comrade Minister, not to mention the Party.

Mother hesitated for a bit, then stepped over to the piano, raised the lid, and ran her fingers over the keys. Barbarians, she said, then lowered the black lid in place.

(Gagarin)

In the spring of '61, Gagarin was sent into space. I thought it was great. The countess objected that Gagarin was just over a meter and a half in height and spent less than two hours up there. But all things considered, the news made her happy as well. After all, Gagarin showed us a way out, she reflected, though she predicted that those hundred-and-eight minutes would spell the end of Yuri Alekseyevich's marriage and he'd find solace in alcohol, because though he may have been promoted to the rank of major while he was up in the sky, he is now surely the loneliest man on earth. And as we know, women will not tolerate a man who feels lonely by their side.

Needless to say, the countess had been right. A while back I read that before the Russians attempted a manned space mission, they sent thirty-six dogs into the starry skies. The Americans had sent apes. Then the animal tamers from the circus convinced Comrade Chairman Khruschev that a man resembled a dog more than an ape. And how right they were. When push came to shove, Khruschev knew whose opinion mattered most. In short, when the dogs came back alive three times, and the spacesuit-clad test dummies returned unscathed, Gagarin was given the all clear. But regardless of his impeccable training, those hundred-and-eight minutes in space did the trick, so that even years later he said, I still don't know for sure who I am, the first man in space, or the last dog. If you ask me, he knew. One generally knows such things.

(the pantry)

One evening someone got stabbed in our building. Not counting the countess, there were seven families living in the back; what I mean is six, plus the super. Of the six families three were Gypsies, one a family of musicians, plus two regular Gypsy families, who didn't flush the toilet and would occasionally howl. The Gypsy musicians wouldn't talk to the others. They wouldn't even deign to howl with them. The man played in a restaurant. He took a cab there and back every night, and when he got out of the cab in front of the house, he was drenched in sweat and his bow-tie was loose. He always paid with a hundred-forint bill and told the driver to keep the change. Their son must have been a year or two younger than me. He also played the violin and wore a bow-tie. I'd occasionally see him with a violin case, though I never heard him practice. The wife didn't work. On the other hand, she made sure that their apartment should be spick and span. She wouldn't talk to any of the tenants except the countess, and went about in fur coats she'd bought from her. They divided up the kitchen and installed a water closet at their own expense, so they wouldn't have to use the shared toilet. When the new toilet was installed, the "regular" Gypsies spilled a pail of urine on her. The superintendent took matters in hand and the police showed up, gave the tenants a warning, and all was quiet for a time.

Then one night I heard a woman scream like a stuck pig, and soon after, I heard sirens shriek as two Moskvitch cars came from two directions on the one-way street, followed soon after by an ambulance. Three blue lights were flashing in front of the entrance. I watched from the window. First the musician's wife was carried out on a stretcher. She was still alive, though they'd stabbed her in the chest. Behind her came her son flanked by two officers, handcuffed. Before they hustled him into the police car, he managed to spit on his mother on the stretcher. Nobody ever learned what happened, except for the fact that the boy stopped practicing, put down his violin, grabbed a knife, and stabbed his mother.

I couldn't figure this out. How could he have been practicing, when I never heard him play? Then it turned out that soon after they moved in, the tenants complained because of the noise, and they soundproofed the pantry. They didn't want to be targeted. They nailed heavy duvets to the walls of the two-square-meter chamber, including the ceiling, and the boy had to practice in that hole six to eight hours every day. And I thought, if only my mother had padded the walls of our own pantry with duvets instead of Persian rugs, the neighbors wouldn't have heard Klára Meyer's birth pangs, and the Arrow Cross men wouldn't have shot my uncle in the back of the head along with his Jewish lover and their two-day old baby boy.

And I also thought that the only reason I could possibly have for killing Mother is that she died. And then it occurred to me that I'd never be able to take a proper picture of that boy, because there's no way that the picture could reveal that he's playing a violin locked in a two-meter square pantry stuffed with duvets, especially one with a fourth wall. Photos of prison cells have at most three walls.

Early in the morning, after Father had left, I took the stool into the pantry and shut myself inside. At first I sort of liked it. That is until my thoughts started leaping in all directions one after another, indiscriminately, until they were gone. They just stopped, my mother, the garden, Imola, the rubber factory, the stabbed Gypsy woman, the Danube, the man from the café, my father's drunkenness. Nothing. Only the pawn that the Chinese call a foot soldier and we call a peasant remained. And it was no use, me knowing that it's just a foot soldier from Chinese chess, for hours on end I couldn't take my mind off it, as if a tunnel inside my head had caved in, holding one single thought captive. I thought I'd go nuts. When I emerged from the pantry, I thought it was late afternoon but hadn't been inside for more than thirty minutes.

(the execution)

It was around that time that I got into the habit of playing the piano, though that's not quite true, because I can't really play the piano. I just strike certain keys, then repeat it, and that's about it. This approximates music not so much because of the order of the successive notes, but rather, because of the repetition and the rhythm. But it certainly helps to keep my mind off of things. On the other hand, just because there's silence in your head doesn't mean your heart has stopped beating. The sound and the silence are a bit like light and shade. A photograph doesn't necessarily have to depict an execution to make your chest tighten. Black, white, black, white, pigeon, black, white. Basically, that's all it takes. Once, when I took a picture of Éva, I showed her this André Kertész photograph taken of a New York building and a flying pigeon. May you be as lonely, I said. All right, she said.

That Gypsy boy playing his violin in the pantry reminds me that Iván Hollós played the piano more or less like I did, meaning not at all. Still, he sat in front of the family's Bösendorfer every morning, struck a few keys, took a sip of his coffee, exhaled the cigarette smoke, then struck the same keys again. Generally, he stopped when he finished his second cigarette, though a few times he didn't. Maybe four. By the time he finished his coffee, he'd find something. A couple of chords, that's all. Or else, he simply forgot that he couldn't even read music.

Though come to think of it, at such times, my brother may have gone a little crazy. Or God knows what happened to him, son. He'd sit at that piano for hours, while I stood in the door, listening to him. I didn't dare move, though I'd have liked to see his face. On the other hand, perhaps it's for the best that I didn't. Those bad chords and misguided notes made me feel as if they'd dragged me through a bunch of basements and tunnels, right into the belly of the earth, into the fire from which everything originates. But except for our mother and me, no one ever heard him. Except for maybe the neighbors.

Actually, my best friend Klári heard him once. And then my brother disappeared, and the Bösendorfer disappeared as well. Though from time to time, Iván would come back for a decent meal and a change of clothes. Then one time he came with a van and six movers, for the piano. He said to our mother that the neighbors had complained, so he's taking it, a friend had offered him an apartment. That's when I took the train to Pest.

A friend? What friend? A you-don't-know-them friend? You're taking our piano to a you-don't-know-them?

Yes.

Is that where you sleep and get up in the morning? Is that where nobody complains? And you come home from there once a week for clean clothes?

Yes.

Well, don't you think I have a right to know what's happening with you? Where you live? And what you're up to?

And then he hugged me so tight, I couldn't breathe, then he kissed me on the forehead and said that as a matter of fact, I'm the only person who has a right. Then he left without another word.

And as for me, I didn't understand, and though I wrote Klári repeatedly, telling her that I'm in Pest, she didn't answer my telegrams either. So the following morning I went to see them in Buda, and I could already hear our piano from out in the middle of the street. And I was so enraged, I felt so betrayed, deceived, cheated, that I knocked Klári out of the way, barged into their room, and was about to slap my brother across the face. But all I could do was cry and I ask, why are you two doing this to me? Whereupon Klári and my brother threw their arms around me and said, because I wouldn't have approved. And I had no clue what they were talking about.

What do you mean, I wouldn't have approved?

You wouldn't have approved because Klári is a Jew.

Is that why? Is that why you've been hiding from me? Is that why I'd have disapproved? She's my friend. I've known since elementary school what she is. Why would I have disapproved? Why?

Because we're leaving. Klári's father has already arranged for the papers.

And then my mother calmed down. She was as calm as a statue of the Virgin Mary. And then she glanced at the mirror, and saw no one there.

You're not going anywhere, she said.

She was just as composed when she went to see Chief Counsellor Abonyi at the ministry. The guards couldn't believe their eyes when His Grace came to greet her in person. I wouldn't like anything to happen to my brother and Klára Meyer. You owe it to our mother, she said. And as for Abonyi, on account of some old, obscure debt, it was actually the least he could do. All right, Anna, he said. I understand.

And so neither Iván Hollós nor Klára Meyer went anywhere at all.

His Grace, however, enjoyed the protection of the National Guard only as long as Vice Admiral Miklós Horthy was at the helm, and by then it was too late to leave. Then Mother put me in the care of our neighbor Kati once more, went up to Pest again, emptied the pantry of its preserves and canned food, lined the walls with the family's Persian rugs, and oversaw the birth. Afterwards, Iván and my grandmother moved the heavy sideboard in front of the pantry door. Except, Klára Meyer wouldn't do what she was told. She might have been a Jew, but when she went into labor, she screamed just like any other woman bringing another human being into the world, and the Persian rugs nailed to the pantry wall were no help. Even the expensive silk rugs of the Hollós family weren't enough to convince the neighbors that they hadn't heard anything.

And so, barely two days after Mother had returned to Mélyvár, the Arrow Cross soldiers pushed aside the sideboard and did their duty. In a sense, they were charitable. They were satisfied with just three crimson holes in the rugs, and basically, they didn't give a shit about my screaming grandmother. One of the men held her down and stuffed his leather glove into her mouth, but that was all. Their major concern was that Iván Hollós should see everything down to the last detail, and that the bullet should penetrate the two hemispheres of his brain only after the helplessness had driven him out of his mind.

A sight for sore eyes, I must say. We understand. It stood up. But do you really have to knock up every Jew-whore you meet? What would become of our people if everyone behaved like you? Is that a nice thing to do? Well? Is it? You see how hardy they are? How they hang on? She's got a bullet through the head, but she's still holding on to her bastard. I said they're hardy, didn't I? This is how they suck the nation's sacred blood dry. With this hardiness. Wouldn't it have been wiser to have given her a good fucking and called it a day? Just look at the little bastard, it's in his blood. He'd suck a corpse's tits dry, too, if he could. You see? You see why you mustn't – not with these people? Do you see or don't you? Oh, I think you're beginning to see. Dip your wick, and good riddance. I'm not saying it's no good. I've fucked my share of Jew-whores myself. We all fucked them, boys, haven't we? But where did you leave your good Magyar sense when you knocked up the likes of her? Replacing those fine preserves with Persian rugs? But at least now you see what they're like, or don't you? If there's no milk, he'll suck his mother's blood dry. The little leech, look at him writhing. Shoot, soldier. I said *shoot*. Like this. See? No more writhing. And you, there, stop your twitching. You'll never become a good Magyar if you carry on like this. That's for sure. You think we need sick livestock in times like these? These are difficult times for the Fatherland, Iván Hollós, and you, writhing like a sick sheep because of a Persian rug with a few holes in it instead of stepping up and doing your part? Do you think you're of any use to your country? No, you are not, take my word for it. Now shoot. Did you hear me, soldier, I said shoot. Well, Your Ladyship, we're done here. You can put the preserves back on the shelves now.

Éva asked me once how I knew these things, when I wasn't even there. And I told here that the apostles were all sleeping, too, when Jesus went to the Garden of Gethsemane, yet there is little about which we can be more certain than his words: the spirit is willing but the flesh is weak.

(the café)

One night the young man I'd seen before was again sitting in the café. He was with a girl, and they were arguing. Actually, from what I could make out, the girl was giving him an ultimatum of some sort. As for him, he was trying to explain to her that there was no choosing between the two things, because there was no real connection between them, and so it's not an either-or situation, to which the girl said that she's the connection. Or was. Then she got up and left. She was very beautiful.

The young man continued to sit there with his coffee and glass of soda water until closing time. Once he took a slip of paper from his pocket and wrote something down, and once he went out to the cloak room to make a phone call, but that's about it.

The following day, as I passed by, I saw him sitting at the same table, so I went inside and ordered a coffee, even though I had other plans.

Two days later I saw him with the girl again, who again ran off. Then the fourth day I saw him sitting alone again. He didn't show up for two days, then I saw him with the girl again. Then he was alone again for nearly a week. But still, there was no one to introduce us to each other.

(Adél Selyem)

About six weeks before our high school graduation, our literature teacher, József Kállay, died. Some said it was an accident, others said it was of his own free will because his daughter got pregnant and he couldn't bear the shame. Be that as it may, before it pulled into Keleti Station, the Debrecen Express scattered Kállay's remains along with a batch of corrected papers from 4B into the wind, and then our Hungarian classes were suspended for a couple of days.

Then a woman called Adél Selyem, who'd just received her diploma and who, unlike the other teachers, left her teacher's robe unbuttoned, came to fill in for him. She wore a white blouse and a black suit, her skin, too, was white, her bag black, her nails white, her hair black, just like a black and white photograph that someone had just started to touch up. Except for her red lips, there wasn't a hint of color on her. Even her eyes were slate-gray.

And she was no taller and weighed no more than Gagarin when he hovered in space for a hundred and eight minutes.

During her first class she said that she'd like to review what we'd learned about the poet Endre Ady. Then she asked us to take out our notebooks and write down what we consider most important about ourselves. I wrote that my name is András Szabad and I can stay in a pantry that's just a meter-and-a-half square for thirty minutes of my own free will.

The next morning I showed up at eight, but I must have gotten the schedule mixed up, because there was no Hungarian class. I sat through history and biology, then during the main recess, headed home. I always tried to get away from the street where the school was as quickly as possible. It wasn't out of fear but shame. I felt ashamed that

I couldn't care less about being punished. There were no stakes attached. So what if I get kicked out? At most, I'd have to look for work a couple of months earlier to avoid being considered an anti-social work dodger, which actually does have repercussions.

Just as I reached the corner, I heard a woman's footsteps coming up behind me. I slowed down so she wouldn't have to run. She stopped, but then resumed her steps, quickening her pace. I knew it was her. There was no one else who'd run after me like that.

And how long could you hold out in a twenty-square-meter cell? she asked after we'd taken a couple of steps in silence.

Probably the same, provided I were alone, I said.

Why did you try it?

Because I wanted to find out what it was like for my father in prison, I said for want of anything better. I couldn't very well say that it was because the Gypsy boy next door stabbed his mother, though I suppose I could, except she wouldn't understand.

You'll never find out, not in a pantry.

Yes, now I know.

And why can't you stay put in a classroom for a couple of hours a day? There you're not alone.

I stopped. The sun shone through the locust tree, and the shade of the leaves danced on her face. Her lips were slightly parted. After that *you're not alone* she forgot to close them.

I'll stay put, I said. If that's what you want.

Yes, that's what I want.

Why?

For one thing, because you'll get kicked out otherwise.

Yes, I know.

Don't you care?

Now I do.

Thank you.

Thank you, too.

You do know that I could get kicked out myself because of this conversation?

You know perfectly well that I do. You wouldn't have come after me otherwise.

It's just that I saw you from the entrance, and figured. . . I have to go back. I have class.

Go right ahead, I said.

What about you? You just said you could put up with it.

I'll show up tomorrow, but I want to be alone now.

Fine.

Also, I don't want to discuss anything with you in front of thirty complete strangers. Not even about Ady.

I need to call on you at least once. If I can take it, so can you.

That's true. Except, I'm not sure it'd be true the other way around.

Are you so sure?

Yes. And now go, Adél Selyem, or you'll be late for class.

(Ferenc Vándor)

At night, after Father had fallen asleep, I tried to image the unimaginable, to the right, the locust tree, to the left the Soviet embassy, and in between, the parted lips of a black-and-white woman. But I couldn't do it. Imolka was the only person I saw before the mind's eye.

All the same, I showed up the next morning, as promised. Hungarian was the last class. She spoke about Ady, but apart from the fact that she never once glanced at the back window where I sat, I remember nothing. At the end of class, one of the boys near me who was going to study liberal arts and who surely must have become a teacher of the humanities, commented that this was great, this is what a Hungarian class should be like, and that Kállay should have flung himself in front of the train long before this.

I went to school the following day as well, even though there was no Hungarian class. After school I saw her get in a car. She wasn't driving. I went in the following day too. When class ended, she said that it wasn't compulsory, but if anyone was interested in manuscripts and other relics, she'd gladly take them to the Literary Museum on Sunday. I, for one, was interested.

Saturday night, I hardly slept at all. Father had left the radio on, the broadcast ended, but the crackle of the airwaves continued, as if the sounds were coming from outer space, whereas it was just the transmission tower broadcasting nothingness. Then at dawn I had a dream – it was more like a waking-dream. Ferenc Vándor was kneeling in my place, slumped over like a sack. I said, don't kill them. He just looked at me and said, three is invisible, one is visible, and then the water came pouring out of his mouth. It was horrible. It wasn't horrible because I knew he'd hang himself, but because I knew he was wrong, that it's always the one that is invisible, and that I always see. That's what

I woke to, that and the radio, which started up again, and then to Father who turned off the radio, shaved, and got dressed. His cane tapped the length of the hall, then the key in the lock.

(Imolka)

Actually, Imolka's full name was Mrs. Ferenc Vándor, née Imola Kocsis, and she was the only woman in town who was terrified that her husband might eventually come back from the POW camp. Because you have no idea what Feri is like. And as a matter of fact, people didn't, though they knew that Feri had busted the church door in Nyárfalva in the middle of the night and rang the bell and roused the town just because of Imolka, because she wouldn't do it before the wedding, which just fired up Feri's jealousy all the more, and at the wedding he managed to smack the vicar, Imolka said, and also, that he can grab a bull-calf by the horn with one hand tied behind his back, and the war, too, came to such a miserable end because somebody had made a mistake, and Feri was called up too late. And so, Imolka was the only woman whom the neighbors comforted by assuring her that it's not that easy finding your way back from Siberia, most of them don't even survive the camps, they're worse than the war. Actually, when they said that it was absurd, Feri coming back, acting the way he does, they were comforting themselves more than Imolka.

Imolka was all of twenty-four, and in her haste, she invariably neglected to do up the top and bottom buttons of her dress, and she made sure that this state of undress should seem like simple negligence, nothing more. She'd often call attention to the fact herself, oh, dear, how careless of me, and she would first lean over to do up the last button, all the while making sure that her hair shouldn't cover her unbuttoned top. Then she would stretch to her full height so that all eyes could see how uncomfortable and sweaty she was, but decorum dictated that she button her dress all the way. And she could button up with such lack of guile that even the abandoned, forsaken war widows forgave her. You'd think that Imola's sorrowful blue eyes would make them break out in a sweat themselves, but they all mothered her instead, because it's high time, they said, that you should put that Feri Vándor out of your mind, you can get a divorce in two minutes flat, dear, just don't turn sour, like a pickle, on account of a good-for-nothing like him, and now let's just do up those buttons, and they buttoned her up nice and tight around the bosom, while all the while she kept saying, oh dear, oh dear, how careless of me, how careless.

The men, though, were on to her, her shenanigans were so far afield that from that distance they could safely jest and say things like, for two gilded roses like that, I'd gladly trek home from Kamchatka, just don't tell my wife. At which Imolka berated herself yet again for her carelessness, buttoned up, and told the honored agronomist that it's probably because she doesn't have a proper mirror. And the very next day, the agronomist's wife brought her a proper mirror herself, whereas she knew perfectly well that the mirror had nothing to do with it, and Imolka was profuse with her gratitude, and in her embarrassment she even spilled the tea. Imola came by an iron the same way, as well as a vase and rollers for her hair and an umbrella, they were all carried to her house by the wives, who were grateful that she didn't settle exclusively on their own husbands, and played no favorites.

I, for one, saw her button up when I was just twelve years old. She even let me carry her string bag. Just look how careless I am, would you take this for a second? And I stood there looking at her as she held the bag out to me. Well, aren't you going to take it? And when I took it from her, she bent down to do up the last two buttons, but she noticed how dusty her shoes were and asked if she could borrow my handkerchief. Then she dusted off her sandals the way Mother would the porcelains with her feather duster, then took the string bag from me and said, thank you, András. I didn't realize that she was talking to me for a moment because no one had ever called me András before. Of course they had no reason to, because I was still Andriska, through and through.

Then in the evening, when mother was gathering up the day's laundry, she asked what happened to my handkerchief, and I told her that Sanyi Asbóth had a bloody nose so I gave it to him, and since you can't get blood stains out anyway I just told him to keep it. At some point I realized that I sounded like a robot. Mother just looked at me for a while, and then all she said was it's all right, son, you did the right thing, giving it to him. Only then did it dawn on me that the Asbóths had been taken to an internment camp the week before. I was overwhelmed by a hatred I had never known before. I would have liked to send Imolka to an internment camp, along with her revealing dress and dusty sandals, for her never to return, whereas at the time I had no way of knowing that just thirty seconds' worth of fidgeting with buttons in the dusty summer sun can change a person's life as drastically as Stalin or Hitler. Or almost as drastically. All I knew was that because of something that could not be put into words, I was lying to Mother for the first time in my life. Because of a partly unbuttoned woman, a complete stranger, I was forced to do something I didn't want to do.

Then all of a sudden Ferenc Vándor showed up, but actually no, not all of a sudden, but with the first transport the Soviet bureaucracy dispatched by mistake. They wouldn't make that mistake again. People were confused, because you couldn't have imagined a quieter, more peaceful man than Ferenc Vándor. Yes, I was a prisoner of war in the Soviet Union, but we were treated well, so you can rest assured, Aunt Magda, because sooner or later, the rest of the men will come home too, or if not, it won't be because of the way they're treated, because, take my word for it, they treated us like human beings, not the way we treated others, and believe me when I say, Aunt Magda, your husband will benefit from the time he spent there. No, we didn't meet, it's a big country, Aunt Magda, you can't meet everybody, but all I can say is, your husband is in a good place. And then Imolka's tears began to flow and she said, come, Feri, let's go home, and they thanked Aunt Magda for dinner and they went home, and Feri Vándor didn't so much as consider slapping the vicar again, and at four a.m. on the dot every morning, he'd present himself to the officer on duty at the police station: see, I'm here, I haven't skipped town, and by four-thirty he'd be at the construction site next to the Kiserdő woods to start work – he'd climb up into the sky in the crane's cabin, from where he would watch the town until nightfall.

Then on Sunday, the wife of another POW invited them to dinner, yes, they're being treated well, so rest assured, Aunt Emma, the other men will come home too sooner or later, or if not, it certainly won't be because of the way they're treated, and Imolka took his arm again, and they went home, except after the tenth dinner invitation her tears didn't flow anymore, she just stared into space like her husband, who, back in Nyárfalva, could grab a bull-calf by the horn with one hand tied behind his back.

And so it transpired that hardly a month or two had passed, and Imolka forgot to leave her dress unbuttoned, and day by day, she became more real, for nothing can bring a person down to earth quicker than unhappiness. She soon became so real that the men stopped making jokes about her and meanwhile the women came to realize that she had always been a whore.

Of the men, the veterinarian, Comrade Party Secretary Dr. Dorvai, was the first to detect her newfound realism, for he knew very well what it meant when from one day to the next, a woman buttons up, and also, and that when this happens, any talk of full-moon breasts and wasp-waists was ill-advised. At such times, it's the soul that needs comforting, Comrade Assistant, and you'll see, that dress will come right off. Take my word for it, old man, it will come right off. No joking around and no cheering up, that's the golden rule. Sympathize, sympathize, until she forces her filthy slit at you. But even then, you play hard to get, like a Catholic priest. You get my drift, Comrade Assistant? And now, Comrade Assistant, hand me that puppy.

He knocked on their door on Sunday. He waited till Sunday, because he knew that Ferenc Vándor would be at home, and he didn't want any misunderstanding, on the contrary, he barely glanced at Imolka as he discussed the matter with Comrade Vándor. It was only when the conversation turned to a dog's loyalty and the close spiritual bond between man and beast that he glanced at Imolka who said she had no interest in keeping a dog in their tiny basement apartment, but how could she say no to a dog's loyalty, and then, before her husband could say no, Comrade Dorvai hastened to mention the two kilos of chicken backs that, and this goes without saying, he'd supply every week, because chicken backs are pretty hard to come by unless you're a Party functionary, and then Ferenc Vándor glanced at Imolka, and he said, alright.

And so the following afternoon, Comrade Dorvai barely stopped by with the chicken backs, but declined both the Russian tea and the chicory coffee, because I'm swamped with Party work, before long I'll have to choose between my family and the Party, I swear. Believe me, Comrade Vándor, he said turning to Imolka, there's nothing worse than being forced to choose between one's family and the Party. But never mind, that's the cross I have to bear. Not all women are as considerate as you. So it's Buksi, is it? What a nice name, Buksi. And now, if you'll excuse me, I must be off.

Then on Thursday, he couldn't even stay as long as before, because he needed to attend a meeting to address the complicated international situation. However, just before he left, he added with a modest blush, that there were two chicken legs among the backs. On Monday he accepted the chicory coffee, unbuttoned his top button, and put the only surviving puppy of a litter of nine on his lap, Buksi, good, bite, that's it, just like that, what a smart dog, and he said he was grateful that he had a place to rest and some human contact, if only for a moment. Also, your Feri seems like a very decent working man, he deserved to be brought home with the first transport, but what I can't seem to understand, Comrade Vándor, is why you seem so down in the dumps. After all, neither the international situation nor matters of animal welfare are weighing on your shoulders, but forgive me, who am I to meddle.

And then on Thursday, something inadvertently slipped out of Imolka's lips, she didn't mean to say it, especially not to this man, namely, that Feri hasn't been his old self since he entered the camp, he's like a stranger, but she bit her tongue right away, and she was grateful to Comrade Dorvai for having brushed the subject away with a come now, being a POW takes its toll on everybody. As they parted, he placed a hand on Imolka's shoulder and gave her a look that said you're not just a sensitive woman, Imolka, but a wise woman, too, so get this nonsense out of your head. Whereupon Imolka nodded, all right, József, and once he was gone, she could still feel the weight of this man's hand on her shoulder, and only then did she realize with a start that she'd called Comrade Dorvai József, and she decided to tell Feri that very same day that they should return the dog. He was the one who wanted it, so it was his responsibility to come up with some excuse, but they must give it back, and that man must not visit them again.

On Monday, after school, I went to the Balogs' garden and climbed into the woodshed behind Kossuth Street 17, because the shed was nearly joined to the back wall of the house. There was barely half a meter between the plank fence and Imolka's basement window. They didn't have curtains. After all, except for the rain, the cats, and me, no one ever went there. I pried loose one of the planks so I'd have an unobstructed view of the sideboard, the water faucet, the sofa, and the table. Only the bit right under the window was hidden from view. In short, I climbed in there every day with my handkerchief soiled with Imolka's sweat and the dust of her sandals. The Balogs thought that I came this way to take a shortcut, in at Red October 35 and out to Kossuth Street 17 through the woodshed, except I wasn't taking a shortcut, I was taking the first photographs of my life.

A photograph won't be any good, son, unless you think it through first. By the time you press the shutter release, you have to know exactly what'll be on it. You have to see it so clearly that you should be able to describe it beforehand. In the middle a walnut tree, to the left the fence, to the right rabbit cages, though of course, that's not enough for a good picture. You need to know why the walnut tree is in the middle, what you mean to convey by it. But this *what you mean to convey by it* got me confused, because I had no intention of conveying anything. Nothing could have been further from my mind. I just wanted to take pictures, pure and simple, and so I decided to forget the whole thing.

But then in May of '56, when I found that slit on the side of the woodshed from where I could see Imolka's basement window, I suddenly knew what should be in my pictures, even though I'd seen nothing of interest for weeks. Basically, when she's alone, she's not very interesting. Mostly, she just eats, reads, brushes her teeth, or just sits and rests. But day after day, I waited for the right moment and meanwhile made a note of what I saw, to the right the sideboard, the water faucet, to the left the sofa, and Imolka in the middle darning socks at the table, to the right the sideboard, the water faucet, to the left the sofa, in the middle Imola at the table, looking straight at me, but not seeing me. I kept these descriptions, or nascent photographs, if you will, committed to sheets of graph paper in a notebook that I kept in our garden in a Franck coffee tin hidden under the straw in the empty rabbit hutch. In a sense, this was my first photo album.

Then one day Buksi was tied to the sofa leg with some sort of leather strap, and Imolka was lying face down on the table among the tea cups, saucers, and chicken backs. Her toes just barely touched the ground. Her dress wasn't even unbuttoned, it was just folded above her hips. Dorvai gripped her wrists behind her with one hand and squeezed the back of her neck with the other. He held her as if he meant to kill her, while Imola screamed, oh my god, oh I can't take it anymore, take me! I didn't want it to end. I didn't know what would come next, just that they're about to destroy Imolka. Annihilate her. But the more she screamed, the more certain I was that she wanted it. She wants to be destroyed, annihilated. Then Dorvai pressed her against the side of the table with such force, Imolka practically split in two. Take that, you mutt, take that, you bitch. And then suddenly it was over, and the three of us lapsed into an eternity of silence. Dorvai slumped over her, and I slumped down to the ground. Imolka had long since cleared the table, changed her clothes, and aired the place out before I felt the splinters clawed under my fingernails and recovered my senses.

Then once when I saw from our window that the veterinarian had arrived, I rushed to the woodshed and found Ferenc Vándor kneeling in my place, much like a half-filled sack a bit slumped over in the middle. I stopped in my tracks. He sounded surprisingly calm. Is this your place, kid, he asked, and I nodded that it was. Then he said I should go home, and I nodded again, except I couldn't move. He then got up, grabbed my shoulder, and dispatched me into the bright afternoon sunshine. He wasn't rough, but rather, as if he were helping an errant butterfly back outside. Okay. Off you go now. And then I said, please don't kill her. He smiled. Relax, kid, I'm not going to kill anybody. He even smiled. After he shut the door, I went home and watched from the window to see if the veterinarian would make it out. True to his word, Ferenc Vándor did not kill them.

Then the following day, when work began at the construction site, the foreman shouted, fuckinghell, will you look at that! And up high, at the end of the crane's arm, like some gigantic gallows, there hung Ferenc Vándor, who once roused the whole village in the middle of the night when he rang the church bell and slapped the vicar across the face and grabbed a bull-calf by the horn with one hand tied behind his back, until they shipped him off to the Soviet Union, that is. Later that same day, Imolka took a piece of cardboard and wrote I WAS BAD on it, and with a length of rope hung it around her neck. Then with another length of rope she hanged herself.

Then, sometime that fall, after the revolution was over and Father was back from Pest and we had finished dinner, Mother hastened out to the kitchen, though at such times we were in the habit of staying at the table together. Father fidgeted with his fork for a while before he spoke. I'm sorry, son, this is awkward for both of us, but they're going to search the house in a couple of days, and not just my room. You understand? Possibly even the garden. So if you have anything to burn, today would be the day to do it. And I said I understood and stood up to get some matches from the kitchen. I was already at the door when Father called after me. It's a shame, son, because I like your pictures very much. But these people would never believe that the sideboard is really a sideboard and the sofa is really a sofa. And then I went out to the garden and made a little bonfire from the straw in the rabbit hutch, and without even going through them, I burned all my pictures. For the first time in my life I felt no shame, nor joy, nor fear, nor pain, and this feeling of emptiness was so overwhelming, that I was suddenly convinced that this emptiness was me. Then, when the straw was gone, I poured a can of water over it from the garden tap and covered what was left with dead leaves from the walnut tree, so the people who searched the house wouldn't have anything to ask us about. Then I went up to my room with this feeling of emptiness still inside me.

(the non-obligatory)

When the authorities insist that something is not obligatory, it is still generally ill-advised not to do it, because all the non-obligatory things that you fail to do lie dormant in the subconscious of the authorities – the May Day parades you missed, the class outings and the union meetings you skipped, and when you're finally at the point where you're hoping that they'll call you to account at last, kick you out, lock you up, humiliate you, ruin your life, because it's best to get it over with, only at that point do you see the recognition flickering in their eyes that ah, of course, you were the one.

The authorities can also ruin you at any time for doing something that they had made obligatory just the other day, and then, with impeccable logic they will then explain why they had no other choice the other day, and why they have no other choice today. But they will never hold you openly accountable for what was not mandatory, not even in the execution chamber. After all, they're a self-respecting lot. Just like you and me. And by the time you're eighteen, you know this.

If someone encounters the authorities every day for years on end, waking up with them in the morning and going to sleep with them at night, going on class excursions with them, cheating them, escaping them, getting fake medical exemptions for them, then the authorities have reason to believe that a person who has reached his eighteenth birthday is ready. Knows his place. You can trust him with assignments more complex than his algebra homework, without it presenting the authorities with any sort of risk.

By now you know without having to be told that if the authorities have a soft spot for the poet Endre Ady, it would be unwise to risk missing a non-obligatory Ady outing just before graduation. And so, almost the entire class showed up at the Literary Museum to take a look at Ady's manuscripts. I tried to time it so I wouldn't be there too early.

(in church)

An American magazine had a picture of a woman standing on a balcony. She was photographed from the back and not much of her showed, just her back and her hips, down to where her dress had been torn. She's leaning on the tin balustrade, looking at someone. She's obviously looking at someone just leaving rather than at someone she's expecting. Her dress is like a ruptured embryonic sack. It is also clear that if the person she's expecting were to take this picture of her, she'd plunge to her death from the balcony.

This was the only picture in the magazine in which the woman's face was not visible. That's why I bought it at the flea market. It was the only picture where you could see Imolka, even if, instead of a table, she was leaning over a balustrade, and instead of the basement door about to close, she's looking at the deserted street.

On Sunday morning I opened the magazine, found the picture, and kept looking at it until I could see Adél Selyem in it.

It could have happened just as easily that Kállay didn't die, or that Adél Selyem hadn't come to take his place. Or that she came, but during her first class with us, she hadn't dropped those two sentences written on a sheet of paper that I'd handed her, or that when I leaned down for it, she hadn't pressed her knees together like a frightened animal. On the other hand, I realize that whichever eventuality might have played itself out, it might have changed the course of my life, but not the essence.

The truth is that I knew perfectly well what I was writing on that sheet of paper. I knew it as surely as I knew whose steps I heard hurrying after me as I walked toward People's Republic Avenue. I didn't wish it, I didn't want it, I knew it. I knew it with the same certainty with which Mother knew that God existed, even if she didn't know it because of a slate-gray stare when the Lord came in to substitute for a man who'd committed suicide.

When I ripped that sheet of paper out of my notebook, I didn't think of Adél Selyem as a high school Hungarian teacher – I would have had to have thought of myself as a high-school student for that. And by the time I finished those two sentences, there was no trace either of fear, hopelessness, or shame left in me, nothing of what I'd felt in the wretched circle that Mrs. Ferenc Vándor, née Imola Kocsis, and her veterinarian, Comrade Dorvai, had drawn around me.

It was also clear that this fearlessness did not originate with me. I hadn't changed. It was something Adél Selyem carried inside her. I likewise knew that it had nothing to do with love. As I said, my mother did not fear God, and I realized that I wasn't afraid of Adél Selyem.

I got in the tub and let the lukewarm water run over me. I sat there till nearly eleven. Sometimes I'd fill my mouth with water, then slowly empty it, much like the way Ferenc Vándor's soul came trickling into my dream. Then I got dressed, but it was still too early. On my way to the museum, I went inside the Franciscan church. They were holding Mass. Since I moved to Pest, I had never been to church. The last time I went to church was with Mother in Mélyvár.

The front pew was occupied by a couple of elderly worshipers. Behind them came the yawning emptiness of thirty empty pews, like some stranded galley long since deserted by the able-bodied passengers who could swim to shore. I sat down in the back row near one of the side chapels with the small marble slabs. The graveyard of grief.

WITH THANKS TO THE IMMACULATE ONE, THE JONAS FAMILY IS GRATEFUL FOR THE INTERVENTION OF THE VIRGIN MOTHER, IN THE NAME OF LITTLE GYURI'S ORPHANED PARENTS

It occurred to me that the same stonemasons who carve all these *we give thanks* and *in gratitudes* also carve *born, died, lived* nine or sixty-nine years on tombstones.

An elderly, slightly hunched Franciscan friar was speaking. He said that we all forget about the procession of the Holy Ghost, whereas the approaching Pentecost is at least as important as Easter and Christmas. He spoke from the heart. He felt genuinely sorry for the Holy Ghost.

Then at Thykingdomcome, the swinging door creaked, and the man in his mid-twenties whom I'd seen in the café a number of times entered. He sat down by the side chapel opposite me. It was only at peacebewithyou that he started to look around for people whose hand he'd have to shake, or to make sure that no one was near him, and so he wouldn't be offending anyone if he remained seated.

I stood up. I don't know how it happened, because I couldn't have done it either on a bus, or in a café, or at a social gathering. I've never been good with introductions. Luckily, I rarely have to introduce myself anymore, and even then, it's mostly a formality, in which case, no one pays attention to names.

I stood up as if I'd come to the Franciscan church for this purpose alone. There was no trace of the usual anxiety my name gives me, that when I say, I am András Szabad, Szabad as in *free*, someone may counter with, You've *got* to be kidding! I caught up with him at the little newspaper counter.

András Szabad, I said as we shook hands.

Peace be with you, he said.

Kornél Erdős, he added with a touch of unease. Then, with an ungainly sweep of an arm, he indicated, even more embarrassed than before, that this was a church, where it wasn't allowed, but that it wouldn't be long before we'd meet up again at the coffee shop.

(in the museum)

By the time we reached Kosztolányi's hat, half the class had disappeared, and soon the rest dispersed, saying they had homework to do. I wandered from room to room, and at Babits's shrapnel-scarred typewriter I stopped and waited for Adél Selyem.

She pretended to be surprised that I showed up, I didn't think this sort of thing would interest you.
    Of course it does, I live in a museum myself.
    What sort of museum?
    Let's make a game of it. Take a guess.
    Fine. I like games.
    I thought so.
    Oh? So then, how many guesses?
    Just one.
    I'm not sure I'll manage it.
    I think you will.
    Are you sure?
    Yes, I'm sure.
    Completely?
    Completely.
    That's no good, that scares me.
    It's okay.
    It's okay? Which would you prefer, that I guess or that I should be scared?
    Not the latter, certainly. But that doesn't depend on me.
    In short, you want nothing to do with my fear, even if you're the cause of it?
    I have nothing to do with your fear of failure. You had it in you before you read your first Ady poem. It doesn't seem to bother you that I'm your teacher.
    If I didn't go back to school, you wouldn't be my teacher.

I wouldn't like that.

All right, then I'll go back. I couldn't care less.

You do know, don't you, that there's something scary about you, András Szabad.

If there is, it scares me as much as it scares you, Adél Selyem.

She cast an uneasy glance at her watch.

I must leave soon, she said. Do you have anything planned?

No.

Then let's see one more room.

Yes, let's. Just as long as you don't have to leave that other room right away.

I'll have to call someone. I saw a telephone in the cloak room.

Are you going to call the man whose car you got into the day before yesterday?

For the first time she looked me straight in the eye before she spoke.

Yes, she said after a while. My father.

I see.

He's busy. But on Sunday afternoons, we have tea together.

I do the same thing with a countess.

Well, the tea may be the same, but my father is a far cry from a count.

Which means what?

Let's change the subject.

As you wish.

Will you tell me what's in your museum?

You told me you'd guess.

Why don't you guide me through it?

A bed.

Is that the most important object?

Not at all. Except, I thought I'd start in a clockwise direction.

Ok then. . .

There seems to be a lot that makes you uneasy.

What makes you say that?

Never mind. There's also a cracked mirror.

What happened?

Somebody looked into it.

Who?

My mother. She looked into it after she died. No mirror can survive that.

I'm sorry.

So am I. Then there's a china cabinet, a small escritoire, a window, a desk, then another window.

Are the windows part of the museum?

Yes.

That's good.

Yes. Especially at dawn.

Anything else?

A piano.

Do you play?

No. But sometimes I give it a try. And behind the piano there's a closed door.

And behind the closed door?

My father.

I'm sorry. At least as sorry as I am about the cracked mirror.

So am I. And so is he.

Which one of you closed that door?

We both did. Along with a prison guard. And a grave digger.

I see.

Yes, I know you do. I wouldn't have mentioned it otherwise.

And do you have visitors to your museum?

If I did, we'd be going to literary museums together.

Is that because you won't let anyone in?

No. For instance, a dressmaker's mannequin is a permanent visitor.

That's not very encouraging. And, alas, I'm not a mannequin.

I wouldn't feel bad about that if I were you. Nor would I protest right away.

All women would protest.

If you ask me, we protest when something hits us where it hurts.

Well, that would hurt anyone.

Not me.

That's because you're a man.

Five minutes ago I was still a high school student. What should it be?

It's no use talking to you.

I didn't ask anything impossible, just that you make up your mind about who you're talking to, instead of your father, on this non-mandatory Sunday-afternoon museum excursion. You invited the entire senior class after spotting me from the school gate during break and chasing after me.

That's not true! I did no such thing.

Then she grew quiet. She stood before me, looking into my eyes, motionless, like someone who had lost consciousness, as though she were under a spell.

Never mind. But let's please not go back to addressing each other so formally.

You're horrible. Like a lead bell, whose heavy clapper clangs into a person and crushes them.

We were only talking about a piece of papier maché light as a feather.

But you were talking about it as if it were me.

I wasn't.

Yes, and that's how you look at me, that's how you demand to know whose car I get into, and even how you put that slip of paper into my hand about your twenty-square-foot cell.

Is that so?

Yes, that's so. As if I were a papier maché doll, with whom you can do whatever you want.

Your words, not mine.

Is that so? What, may I ask, are you thinking?

That you're afraid. And I'm sure there's a reason. But I'm also sure that it's not me. And that for the first time in my life I'm not afraid, and I don't know why. And that I never want to be afraid, ever again. Also, I feel tired. I'm not good at charming women. Let's go have a drink somewhere.

You know I can't do that.

Fine. Just let's get out of here.

I have to call my father first.

Fine. Call him.

It really was my father.

I know. And there really hasn't been anyone in my room aside from my mannequin, and I don't want the two of you to meet.

(at the new housing estate)

Adél Selyem lived in a new housing estate near the Árpád Bridge. It was a tiny sixth-floor apartment with its windows looking out onto the sky. We took a cab. She was right. Being seen together in public wouldn't have been wise. Her room was just as black-and-white as she was, with the exception of a scrap of red rag hanging from a nail above her bed. If her room were a face, this rag would be the lips.

You realize they'd burn me at the stake for this, she said, and sat down on a chair.
I think I should leave, I said, and sat down on the bed.
Stay.
What's that rag?
Nothing. Just a rag.
I see that. It's pretty red.
Yes, it is. What is your mannequin doing at home now?
She's sitting on the piano bench.
I thought you were the one who played the piano.
We take turns.
I really don't know why I got so worked up before. It was silly of me. After all, I have no idea what it's like to be a mannequin.
Nothing could be simpler. For forty or fifty years, you stand in a dressmaker's shop window wearing the dressmaker's best two-piece suit. Except, unlike you, he grows old and decides to close his shop and puts you out on the sidewalk, and then someone comes along who's never had a mannequin in his room before, and he looks at you and sees that you've painted your lips red, and he makes an offer. The old dressmaker would like to get fifty forints for you, but in the end, he settles for twenty, and after all those years, all he can do is laugh and say, Annushka, you found yourself a husband.
Is that really what he said?
Yes.

And what did you do?

I handed him the twenty forints. Then it started to rain and I threw my jacket over her and took her home.

Did Annushka thank you?

Let's not call her Annushka, but she's been grateful.

How does she express her gratitude?

With silence.

And her red lips.

Yes, red-lipped silence.

Is she still wearing the suit?

No. That wasn't part of the deal. She's also missing her arms and legs.

So she's just a torso?

Let's just say she's half-length.

I have a bottle of wine. Will you open it?

Only if we stop talking about mannequins.

She's your mannequin. I don't see why it should bother you.

Because it reminds me that when it comes to knowing what to say to a woman over a glass of wine I'm at a loss.

I don't have the sense that you are.

Well, it's the truth.

There are some women for whom it doesn't matter what you say. And there those to whom you don't need to say a thing.

I'd prefer the second. And what does a woman who doesn't expect you to say anything do?

With her, you don't need to ask such questions. She just knows.

I'll bring in the wine.

I heard the sound of glasses knocking against each other in the tiny kitchen, then I heard water running from the bathroom tap, then the swish of a piece of clothing. I looked at the books on the shelf, her desk with two stacks of papers, the corrected quizzes and the ones she hadn't gotten to yet. The French existentialists. Sleeping pills on her nightstand.

She'd changed clothes. She came in barefoot, wearing a white summer dress. Her lips were freshly rouged. She brought the wine and two glasses. She sat down on the bed next to me and placed the glasses on the floor. I opened the wine, poured, then we drank without clinking glasses, as if it were water.

It's gone, I said.
What?
The fearlessness.
So let's bring it back, she said, stood up and closed the curtains.
You're the one who's afraid of being seen, not me, I said. Besides, with a seventh-floor window, there's not much to worry about.
And what is it that you're worried about?
I have no idea.
I know you've never been with a woman, and yet I now feel better with you than with anyone else.
It's not what you know that scares me, but what you don't know. What neither of us knows.
It which case, it's no use me trying to guess.
No use at all.
In which case, pour some more wine.
Take my word for it, it'd be better if I left now, I said, and stood up.
But not for me, she said, and reached for my pants.

Needless to say, over the course of eighteen years I'd imagined this movement a thousand times, and I knew, too, that it wouldn't turn out like I'd imagined. But no, I now realized with a jolt – it was exactly as I'd imagined. But beyond this sense of exactly-as-ness, I felt nothing. Nothing at all. I wasn't scared. Instead, I felt a bitter resentment turning to stone inside me, the realization, somewhere in the pit of my stomach, that it could be anything, anything at all, including the first time a woman touched me, that it would be exactly as I'd imagined it through my eighteen years. And that this is hell, that no one can give me anything, nothing whose primordial imprint had not existed in me before, and that I wasn't even ten when they returned that goddamn piano and I stood on the porch, watching my mother cry, and I already knew what it would be like when she died; and the time they came to search the house, they hadn't yet slapped my father across the face, yet already I saw him as the ghost of his former self; and Dorvai hadn't taken that stupid puppy to Imolka yet, and Ferenc Vándor hadn't found my spot in the woodshed yet, but I could already feel in my groin the archetypal imprint of what was soon to transpire.

I leaned over to kiss her, but she turned her head away.

Please don't. Just this one thing. No.

I think it'd be better if I left now.

No it wouldn't. It wouldn't be better for me, and it wouldn't be better for you. Trust me. And she began undoing my belt, and I unbuttoned the top of her summer dress.

Are you saying it'd be better for me if I never kissed anybody, is that it?

Yes, that's it. Don't even think about it.

Nobody, or just you?

Nobody. But definitely not me, she said as she grabbed my dick. Her nipples were rock-hard, and rough. You'll need to come quickly now. But trust me, you'll like it.

Why?

Because you can't come inside me. Also, I'll want you to get it up again and keep it up for a long time afterwards.

I said nothing. She looked at me. Her lips were like a red ring. Then she started working her way up my dick, further and further up, until, after a while, I couldn't look anymore, and I turned to that goddamned red rag on the wall, and by the time I realized what that rag was for, she had me inside her, up to her throat. Then she suddenly grabbed me by the hips, forcing me further inside, then began swallowing me as I leaned over her like I'd done before on top of that woodpile, except this time, instead of splinters under my nails, it was flesh.

You see? I told you you'd like it, she said when I came to. I tried kissing her again, but she quickly refilled my glass and gave it to me.

Yes, you did, I said, overwhelmed by a feeling of emptiness the like of which I'd never known before. It was nothing like the emptiness I'd felt when I burned the pictures I'd taken of Imolka. To the right, sleeping pills, to the left quizzes on French existentialism, and in the middle, a red rag.

You're not drinking?

No. I want to feel your taste in my mouth. I like it.

I felt that if I didn't get to my feet that instant and flee that apartment right away, I'd go crazy, that I must run down seven flights of stairs and be done with this new housing estate, toward the Danube, back to Mélyvár, into 25 Red October Street, across the woodshed, and back to 17 Kossuth Street.

She took the glass from my hand and leaned her head on my shoulder. It was as light as a feather. Her white summer dress still hung loosely around her breasts. She was really quite beautiful.

From now on, you must never forget how handsome you are. Handsome. Every part of you, she said, as she placed her hand on my groin once again.

My first thought was that apparently, there are men who, when they make love for the first time, like being told how handsome they are, but then I stopped thinking, because I saw her lean over me again and take my dick in her mouth again, until I was ready to come again. Then she grabbed my hand and put it between her thighs so I could feel her desire.

She had nothing on under that summer dress.

Grab me.

I let go.

Grab hard. It won't hurt.

I know.

Please. As hard as you can.

Give me another glass of wine first.

She reached for the bottle on the floor, ready to pour, but I took it from her and drank straight out of the bottle, and that's all there was inside me, that half bottle of wine, and nothing else. Not even the air I was breathing.

I then stood up, lit a cigarette, went to the door, and looked back at the two of us, me grabbing her hips and pulling her to me, watching how she knelt in front of me, her dress pulled up to her waist, how she succumbed to my weight. I watched her shriek, no, that's not allowed, then she saw her reaching into the air screaming, I can't take it, stuff it in my mouth! But I don't understand, or I don't want to understand. She manages to reach the rag and pull it off the nail and stuff it in her mouth to keep her from screaming, just like a small child who, waking from a nightmare, stuffs its diaper into its mouth.

When she came to, she broke into silent tears, so I sat back down again.
  What's the matter?
  Nothing. It's just that you can't imagine how good it is with you.
  That's for you to know, not me.
  You didn't come inside me, did you?
  No, of course not.
  She reached for me, but I stopped her hand in midair.
  Don't you want it?
  I do, I said, but I need to go now.
  You said you had nothing to do.
  That was at noon. It will be evening soon.
  What's going to happen with us?
  I don't know. Nothing.
  I can't go and teach that class. Not after what happened.
  Sure you can. I'm not showing up anymore.
  I can't ask you to do that.
  It's not up to you.
  You need to graduate.
  You know better than I do how close I am to flunking out.
  We shouldn't have met.
  That's true. We shouldn't have met, and God shouldn't have created the universe. Still, admit it. We're grateful that he did.
  Will I see you again?
  Yes, of course. But now I need to get going. Someone is waiting for me.
  Who?
  You don't know him. A friend.

(the sleeping pill)

It was clear I wouldn't go to school anymore. Though I did go back one more time to take care of some paperwork, and to be able to say that my decision had nothing to do with Adél Selyem.

It was also clear that I'd never see Adél Selyem again. It didn't turn out that way, but that evening I had every reason to think so.

When I got home, Father was in the kitchen, spreading butter on a piece of bread for his dinner. As we greeted one another, he was about to put the bread on a plate and take it to his room. He'd been eating in his room for some time by then, especially if I was home, so he wouldn't be in the way. I mostly ate in my room as well, for the same reason. I didn't want to disturb him with my presence.

I haven't eaten yet either, I told him, and put some stuff I found in the pantry on the table – liver paté, tomato paste. He still wouldn't sit down, so I said that I needed his help. I pulled a chair out for myself but waited for him to sit down first.

   What happened? he asked. Nothing, I said, but in the fall, I'll be needing a job. Or even earlier. He said that even if I don't go to university, he thinks I should try one of the vocational schools. Things were loosening up, I might get admitted to one of the less competitive faculties. I told him, It will take more than things loosening up, because I won't be granted a high school diploma. He said that as things now stand, they're sure to give me one. And I said, it's not up to them. I've quit school. That's why I need a job.

He kept his eye on my slice of bread with the liver paté and tomato paste, and said nothing. He drummed on the side of his plate with two fingers, but that didn't break the silence either. All the diplomas and doctorates he'd ever envisioned for me now amounted to nothing more than this half-stale slice of bread.

It's still not too late to think it over, son, he said.

There's nothing to think over, I said. I'm in no position to do so, I added, as if this helped clarify things.

Do you have any idea what you'd like to do?

For the moment, I just need a job. Any job. I'll look through the classified ads, but maybe one of your friends could come to the rescue.

As you wish, son.

He stood up and headed for his room. At the door he turned back and said that Vermesi is sure to help, that he'd call him tomorrow. I thanked him. Then I heard the door to his room close. His buttered bread was still on the table. He'd only taken a bite. I thought I'd take it in to him. Then I thought that I'd tell him that maybe a year from now I'd go to night school and get a diploma. And then I thought that before he goes to bed, I'd ask him to take the Agfa out of its box along with the chemicals and trays, and teach me how to enlarge photographs.

When I went to my room and saw the mannequin on the piano bench, it reminded me that I hadn't thought of Adél Selyem since I got off the tram. And then I thought that it wasn't her fault, it was mine, that when something happens to you for the first time in your life, you shouldn't observe it from three meters away, because then it doesn't really happen to you. And you shouldn't know what it'll be like years in advance, and you shouldn't wax nostalgic about it afterwards. And suddenly I felt a frantic desire that surpassed even what I felt when Adél Selyem screamed that it wasn't allowed and stuffed that goddamn red rag in her mouth.

I picked up the mannequin and took it out to the hall, and getting up on the stool, I managed to stuff it on top of the Tower of Babel. Although the reading lamp was still burning in father's room, I tried not to make any noise. And then I picked up the Zorki.

I walked to Óbuda. It was night by the time I got there. I took a picture of the new housing project where Adél Selyem lived, and then I ran out of film. On the third and fourth floors the lights were still on. The front door opened and a man walk out. I hurried away. I looked up again from the far side of the street. It was dark on the sixth floor. She must've taken a sleeping pill.

On my way home, I sat down on a pier by the Danube and fell asleep. When I woke up, I felt numb all over. Dawn was breaking. I checked the time. Public transit was up and running. I liked this city at dawn – the way they swept the sidewalk, the way the street lights went off, one by one, the way delivery men dropped off milk and bread in front of the shops. A city shouldn't be blamed for the fact that a person can't live in it. There must be people who can't live in Mélyvár, people for whom twilight begins as soon as Kossuth Lajos Street is swept up and the bread crates and milk boxes are dropped off in front of Szorovka's shop.

(the enlarger)

I met Father at the door downstairs. He asked where I'd been and I said I took some night photos. Then he told me he'd call Vermesi about a job. I thanked him and said, any job will do. I was about to say goodbye, but as if somehow apologizing for our living in the same apartment like strangers, I asked if I could unpack the enlarger. Would he mind?

Would you mind?
Of course not, he said. I'll come back up with you and show you how it works,
There's no need. Besides, you have to go to work. You can show me in the evening, or whenever. For now I'll just unpack it, to see what it looks like.

I already regretted bringing it up, because he darted back upstairs with me as if I'd given him a new lease on life. They'd have had to wipe the three years of jail from his memory for that. Or maybe if the Lord would raise Mother from the dead, bathe her, and seat her on the bench under the walnut tree in the garden of our home in Mélyvár to smoke a cigarette after having cleaned the house. It would have also helped if his son hadn't just returned home from a housing estate with a poorly exposed negative of a prefab building where, after having swallowed a sleeping pill, a woman was sleeping under a chewed-up piece of red rag hanging from a nail over the bed. By all odds, the same things would have given meaning to my own life. Though come to think of it, the sheer inevitablity of nonexistence also gives life a meaning of sorts. Except, you can't keep that in view day in and day out.

His cane knocked against the steps. The rubber tip had worn away. We we moved in a year before, he didn't have to hold on to the balustrade yet. We should have looked for something on the ground floor, I thought.
The box was in the pantry, up on the top shelf. I took it down along with the trays

and chemicals. With the exception of the drier, I found everything you need – tongs, thermometer, timer. I placed the red lamp on the spice rack, because it was near the socket. I placed everything else on the table under it. We mixed the developer and fixer in a tray and then he prepared the papers whose expiration date had passed. They're fine to experiment with, he told me. Then I helped screw the stay plate to the baseboard, and the head to the stay plate.

I asked if he'd get in trouble if he showed up late for work. He said no. He's on good terms with the doorman, he can arrange it. I brought a reel of developed film and he showed me how to wind it on the spool and place it in the tank. Then he explained how film is developed. He said it's got to be pitch dark because unlike paper, which is orthochromatic, film is panchromatic and sensitive to red light. He said not to stick my hand in the chemical mixture but to use a clip, otherwise it could damage the skin, and that exposure must be precise. You must attend to every second, son, he said, the developer must always be twenty degrees, and you must never wipe film clean with your finger, son, but blow on it or use a brush. Aside from the washing, the fixing is what matters most.

Then I turned off the light, closed the door, and there we stood, the two of us, in the red light. I blew the dust off the film, he placed a piece of paper on the baseboard and set the enlarger to the correct height. He showed me how to position the film. He didn't keep it rolled up, he cut the negatives into squares. Using a roll is not ideal, he explained, there's nothing more practical than a strip of six. If it's in a roll, you can't make contact copies. Also, he kept only the best negatives, he said. That's why he cut the strips into squares.

Then I handed him the roll of film for him to feed it, and he turned on the projector in the Agfa. And then, as if it were God's own curse, Mother appeared on the paper. She was sitting under the walnut tree in black and white, smoking a cigarette after she'd done the laundry.

Father and I stood there like two murderers, whereas neither of us could be called that. Forgive me, son, he said. He turned off the lamp and walked out. I heard him close the door to his room, leaving me alone, with no idea how to proceed. I took the paper and immersed it in the developer. It turned black. It must have been exposed to the light when Father walked out.

I knocked on his door. He was sitting on the bed. I said he should go to work, it's not that late. I thanked him for showing me the magnifier, and said I could handle the rest. When I looked out the window, I saw him enter the tobacconist to make a phone call. He stood around on the corner for a while and then headed in the opposite direction.

I retrieved the film from the Zorki, fed it into the tank and developed it, then used a paper clip to hang it on the kitchen lamp to dry. It looked just like fly paper.

The last frame was barely visible. Two sheets got ruined, but the third turned out just fine. At the same time, I knew without the shadow of a doubt that I would never use clips or a timer, and that I'd count the seconds as if I were underwater, and that I must feel the paper with my finger. Until the image appears, it's as slippery as if it were covered with seaweed. Nothing approximates death as closely as photography.

(Kornél)

I reached the café at around ten. There was no electricity. Kornél was sitting with his back to me, watching the street through the curtain. The light from the approaching cars filtered through to his white shirt in circles and lit up strands of his uncombed hair. Two elderly women were sitting at the other table, waiting for the bill. The cloakroom woman told me they weren't serving customers. That's all right.

I don't remember our first conversation. According to him, the Church never came up. According to me, he excused himself for his Godbewithyou. According to me, I spoke mostly about Mélyvár. According to him, I told him about one of my dreams. According to him, it happened years later, according to me, it was back then that he said how it would have been better had his father also ended up in jail after '56 because then at least he'd know why his life went off track. According to me, I never said that he didn't know what he was talking about, and anyway, even if an outside source can be found, one's life is no less of a fiasco.

According to him, I let on that I'm a photographer to be reckoned with, someone you can love or you can hate, but sooner or later everyone will have to decide which, whereas I had made my first enlargement only that day. According to me, I merely asked about the notebook that he quickly closed and hid in his briefcase. I didn't even bring up photography, I remember that clearly, because of the passionate way he articulated how much he disliked psychologists, directors, actors, and photographers.

According to him, he might have said something like that, though he doesn't really dislike them, he envies them. Also, he's afraid of them, because the world lays claim to them more than to a great Hungarian novelist. According to me, when I said he didn't know what he was talking about, it was in response to that, rather than what he'd said about his father not having gone to jail.

According to him, I spoke about Adél Selyem as if she were the love of my life. That's out of the question, according to me, there was no love in my life. According to him, I spoke about other women the same way. According to me, if I spoke about other women that way, I'd made a mistake.

According to him, when I told him about Mother that time in the café, I broke a glass. According to me, I was reaching for it when the lights suddenly came back on. Also, I'm absolutely certain I never said that the whore is not the woman who does it for money, but the one who dies, but I could never have said anything that ridiculous, not even at dawn after a night of drinking.

According to him, after the café closed, we went to a wine bar. According to me, I picked up a bottle of wine from home and we went down to the Danube. According to him, we never picked up cigarette butts at a bus stop as day was breaking. According to me, the thirty-three-year-old cigarette butt I keep in my drawer is from that bus stop.

And he definitely did not recite Lőrinc Szabó's *For Nothing, Entirely*, because he would never recite that poem out loud. Ever. Even to himself, it would be in silence, so he wouldn't have to hear it. Let's face it, at one time or another, everyone ends up reciting it to himself. Besides, he is absolutely certain that I was the one to blurt it out: *"It's horrible, I know, but it is so; / If you love me, you cease to be, / or nearly so. . . . / I'll soar above the law, / so I can love you; / Like a lamp now extinguished, / don't live if I don't say so. . . ."*

According to him, I'd made up my mind about everything even back then, and even back then, he was the freer of the two of us. According to me, he'd made up his mind about everything years before we met, and neither of us had ever been free.

According to him, what matters is what becomes of someone in thirty years' time. According to me, back then is what matters, that the present contains the past. According to him, after leaving the Danube, we walked up to Castle Hill. According to me, we stole some bread from the front of a shop and ate it in a park.

For him, university started at eight. For me, that's when the liquor shops opened. According to him, the second bottle was also wine. According to me, it was vodka. Afterwards we went to the university, just so in the dining hall he could show me a letter he'd written to the woman I hadn't seen him with for weeks.

According to him, he was no longer in love at the time. According to me, that was the last time he was in love. To him, ruining one woman's life is a mistake, but ruining the lives of two is a sin. To me, ruining anyone's life is a sin, even our own. According to him, we didn't go to their house in Budafok that day. Not yet. According to me, the third bottle was wine again, and his mother had to put us to bed.

I don't remember that first day. When I woke up, I found three cats sitting on the bed. When I threw up in the bathroom, I tried to make as little noise as possible, then I shook him awake and asked him where we were.

Has my father seen us, he asked, but before I could answer him, he dropped off to sleep again. The makeshift stairs that his father had temporarily thrown together years before creaked under my feet. And the garden gate let out a creak too. It was pitch dark, and I wandered around for a while before I found the bus stop. For the first time in my life, I had a hangover. And for the first time since my arrival in the late-night gloom of Keleti Station, I was actually looking forward to the next day.

(the printer)

Father found me part-time work as an assistant gatherer at a printer's. It was mostly night work. They all thought I gathered up typefaces, and after a while I stopped trying to explain what a gatherer actually does. There's a long track that's more or less waist-high. It's shaped like an upside-down wedge. The sheets hang from it, folded in half. The sheets of a daily, let's say. The first batch consists of the first and the last page. The second batch consists of the second and the next-to-the-last page, and so on, hanging in long rows along the track, and I walk along it and gather up the sheets one by one, until the newspaper is complete. And that's about it. What can I say? It didn't require a high school diploma.

I was the only male among the gatherers. There weren't many of us. We helped the machines. The gathering machine's capacity was much more limited than what could be produced. One of the women was on maternity leave. I was hired to take her place.

There were two tracks resting on two bucks. The two tracks were needed so you didn't have to make the return trip empty-handed. The flooring of the workshop was made of beams much like the sleepers and they were also treated with tar, which made the room smell like a train station. I wasn't always able to separate the two smells. The station smell made me think of Kállay, and Kállay made me think of Adél Selyem. I tried to pretend that she was walking in front of me in her bare feet gathering the sheets, wearing a white summer dress, her two finger tips covered by rubber glove ends. The Political Committee has taken a firm stand today. Must buy cradle. Gently used will do.

All the women wore the same calf-length canvas lace-ups with cut-out heels that waitresses and saleswomen wore back then. I can't remember if there were seven or eight of us, just that we were always one short, because as soon as one of us came back from the smoking area, another would take her place. If someone didn't want to light up, they'd let the next in line go outside. But this hardly ever happened. Since the shop was filled with combustible materials, it was off limits for smoking.

Some of the women would smoke two cigarettes, or they'd go to the bathroom, or take a quick bite or two of their sandwich, but nobody minded. There was no time to talk. There was no one to talk to anyway. The window of the staircase where the women took short breaks gave out on a firewall, on which weeds had sprouted up through the cracks. No one talked very much inside either. There was the machine noise to contend with, and we saw only each other's backs as they swiftly approached and passed us. From time to time, the gatherers would exchange a word or two, but any exchange was drowned out by the noise of the workshop.

In between batches the shiny pair of tracks could be seen, hovering waist-length above the legs, like the ghost of a railroad track leading nowhere. Then the men showed up. They loaded the new batches on the tracks, cracked a couple of dirty jokes, the women laughed, then we got back in line. I barely existed for them. As for me, if any one of them were to come towards me on the street, I'd recognize her quicker than any of my former schoolmates.

I had this job until Father died.

(the automobile)

Early one morning when I came back from the printer's, I saw a police car parked in front of the house. It wasn't the usual blue and white, but the kind that's given away only by its license plate. My heart skipped a beat, and I froze at a distance from the building. I was sure that they'd come for my father. I couldn't begin to imagine why, but I was sure that the car was for him.

I couldn't decide whether to go in or wait on the street. As if it made the slightest difference. Then I realized that I couldn't just keep staring at a police car out on the street. I looked around. The tobacconist hadn't opened yet, so I couldn't go in there.

I didn't want to hide. On the contrary. I wanted to be present at the most opportune moment. Let them know that I see them. That I see them getting in the car with my father. Go up to them and say, the Kereszt family is expecting you for lunch. Don't forget. As if it made the slightest difference. But I wanted them to know that they have me to reckon with, and the Kereszt family, and the whole world. They have to consider that my father had finished his prison term, and nothing had happened since, nothing that would warrant their coming for him in their car painted in civilian colors so early in the morning.

As I said, the tobacconist hadn't opened yet, and I couldn't stay on the street, so I decided to go upstairs. Worse comes to worst, we'll bump into each other on the stairs. From what I could tell, only one person was sitting inside – in the back seat – smoking. When I passed he turned his head in my direction, almost imperceptibly.

Since there was no driver, I concluded that it wasn't a high ranking officer who'd come, because they always have a driver. Besides, it was pretty late, and they know that my father goes to work. They must have counted on not finding him at home. In official cases, State Security men usually show up in pairs, which meant that there were two of them upstairs. I was sure of it as I pressed down the handle of the downstairs door.

I knew that they'd have my father sit in the back, and also, that in case of possible resistance, there's always someone waiting there. Waiting for him. Opening the door, and if need be, pulling him inside, or restraining him. So if there's someone's sitting in the back, it means that they're going to take someone away, though in my father's case, they hardly have to anticipate serious resistance. On the other hand, they must adhere to safety precautions, even while leading away a man with a cane. As I closed the downstairs door, I turned around to catch one last glimpse of the automobile. The man in the back seat still did not look my way. If someone opens the front door of a house, especially if it's a house where they have come in an official capacity, it's only natural to look. Perhaps they wish to give the impression that they're not interested, or that they don't see, but they've still assessed the goings on. That slight movement of his head in my direction was enough for him to know who I was. They would surely recognize the son of the man they'd come for, even if they had only seen his back.

I stopped by the mailbox and fumbled with the key in the lock, hoping that I wouldn't bump into them on the landing, where they'd rush past me, but downstairs where I was standing. That way I could be present when they shoved my father into the car. If I turned around after them on the stairs, or followed them, it would seem like aggression on my part, and that wouldn't be advisable. In short, my first appearance mustn't appear aggressive, it wouldn't be good for Father, they'd just take it out on him. Right now, my job is to somehow warn them with my presence, to let them know that they can't be aggressive, they can't do whatever they want, at which point I stopped fumbling with the mailbox key. They still hadn't closed the door upstairs.

I was just headed upstairs when I saw two men in civilian clothes come out the countess's door. By all odds, I should have felt immensely relieved, but I felt dizzy and disconcerted as I watched them take their courteous leave of the countess. The countess closed the door and the two men headed down the backstairs. Then I thought how my father is almost never home when I get back from the printer's, and also, that they know this better than I do. I didn't have a ghost of a chance of knowing what might happen, either to my father, or myself. There I stood on the landing, crying like an idiot, and all I could think of was that they're stronger than I am, that if two men in civilian clothes should come ringing our doorbell, I'd be utterly helpless.

After they'd left, I pulled myself together and went to see the countess.

What happened? I asked.
What do you mean, what happened?
Why did those two men harass you?
I wouldn't call it harassment. They paid me a visit, we had tea, and they left. It's a far cry from harassment, my dear. A far cry. If you get this worked up because they stop by for a chat, what will you do if they should decide to pay you a visit?
That's different, I said.
No, it isn't. It's the same thing. This is how things stand, and from now on, it's only going to be more so. And then it will pass. Rest assured, they meant no harm. We had a little tête-à-tête about my family. It's a rather big family, and we're scattered all over the world. It must have escaped your attention, my dear, but they put up a wire fence around West Berlin in the course of a single night, and there are Szendreys living there as well. That's what we talked about. But these cars are not those cars, they're not black, just gray.
Yes, I know.
Okay, then. Mária, dear, will you prepare a light breakfast tea for our friend?
As you wish, your ladyship.

(a game of chess)

Come to think of it, why don't you go home?

I go home every day.

That's not what I mean. I mean Mélyvár. Even if just for one afternoon.

I can't.

Why not?

Because I can't. I have nowhere to go. It's that simple.

As long as there's a train to Mélyvár out of Keleti Station, you have a place to go.

I don't understand you. You can't abide the thought that you don't wake up in the heart of town because your parents never made it past the outskirts.

That's not true. I don't mind.

That's not how I see it.

And I don't understand why. Whenever I ask about you, you change the subject right away and start talking about me. As for wanting to live where you live, it doesn't follow that I hate the very idea of Budafok, and it most certainly doesn't follow that I blame my parents for it. You want to know what I think?

If you're going to say again that I had made up my mind about everything beforehand, don't bother.

But that's exactly how I see it.

It's your move.

And not only did you make up your mind beforehand, but. . .

One. I did not make up my mind about anything beforehand. Two. . .

Three, four, five, six. Seven: Thou shall not kill.

Check.

Yes, I see. And I wish you'd believe me when I say that I didn't make up my mind about anything beforehand, and I do not punish anyone, and when it happens, I'm fully aware of it. For instance, I know when I punish my father. And I know when I punish you.

And yourself.

Yes, I know that too. And I make sure not to do it.

I suggest you resign. I'm taking your rook.

I've already made my move. I resign. Or you know what? From this point, let's consider it a new game. You won the first.

I didn't. You made a mistake, like I did with the pawn.

Except, whether someone makes a mistake with the pawn in the opening or a rook in the endgame makes a hell of a difference.

From the point of view of the mistake, it makes no difference.

Except, it's never only the simple fact that matters, but the consequences as well. I doubt that you'd care about the simple fact of a gun going off if someone's head were not in the way.

Except, no one's pulled the triger of a gun now, right? It's a game, right? We're paying chess because both of us like to play chess. This difference you're talking about, I don't see it, because you can overlook a pawn, or a rook, for that matter, without someone dying as a result. Without a sin being committed. But as far as you're concerned, one goddamn mistake matters as much as someone being shot in the head.

One. It is not the same. Two. I had to beg you to put back that pawn.

And so I did. But I didn't say, let's forget it and start a new game.

It wouldn't make much sense at the third move. Besides, I put back my rook, didn't I? And let's not consider it a new game. Check.

Yes. It seems so.

Indeed. And I'd be grateful if you'd let up with this you made your mind up about everything in advance business.

You play better when you're uptight.

If it were that simple, I'd have beaten you at least once.

This time you just might.

Yes, I just might.

Go home. At least for All Saints' Day.

Don't count on it. Especially on All Saints' Day.

I'll take your rook.

And I'll take your knight.

Take the bishop instead.

Why?

Because that'd make it a stalemate. You can't checkmate with a knight.

I didn't know that.

I still think you should go home.

(Mélyvár)

When Father got a decent job, I spread the map out on the table to look for Rákos. I took a pencil and checked off the streets where I'd been so far. Others do the same with maps of the world. The military barracks was the furthest I'd been. And also, Budafok. I'd also been to János Hospital, Margaret Bridge, Keleti Station, City Park, Moszkva Square, the Castle, the Astoria, Kálvin Square and Rákóczi Road, and needless to say, People's Republic Avenue, and the Boulevard. I remembered some of Father's friends who'd invited us for dinner, but I couldn't remember where they lived, so I couldn't check them off. Two of them lived somewhere in Buda, and one in Angyalföld. They drove us there. My winter coat is from them. But that's about all. The streets in Mélyvár, on the other hand, I knew like the back of my hand. Of course, Mélyvár is not a big city. At best it's run of the mill. Its railroad station and churches are run of the mill, even its hills. Its zoo and its barracks. And so is its river.

One castle, one textile factory, one waterworks, one academy, one library, one Heroes' Square, one mill, one foundry, one slaughterhouse, one museum, one market, one barracks, one lime-burner, one dairy, one police station, one tram, one pool, in the winter one ice skating rink, one daily paper, one junkyard, one theater, one crematorium, one Party Headquarters, and one former Jew. Also two Calvinists, two post and telegraph offices, two movie houses, two buses, two gas stations, two high schools, two hospitals, two housing estates, two vineyards, two hotels, two savings banks, two former aristocrats. Three Catholics, three doctors' offices, three cafés, three nurseries, three circles of friends, three tomato farms, three cemeteries, three former houses of ill repute, and three direct flights to Pest.

(my father's lover)

No doubt about it. Our lives would have taken a different turn had I not taken that map and marked the places I wanted to see, had I not decided to walk down the major streets to see how I could live here. But that's not true. There's no denying cause and effect, but no single effect is due to a single cause.

I started with the district and the two adjacent ones. I used a map. I mapped out where I'd go before leaving home each day. I wanted no street uncovered. I took the Zorki, but rarely used it. I felt a strong, inexplicable aversion to devoting my life to taking pictures of flaking walls, scaffolded houses, and dim doorways. Once I took a picture of a child on a scooter. He was facing the sunlight, it had just rained, and the wet cobble stone reflected his image. That picture I liked. I had a scooter myself when I was a boy. Because of his leg, my father couldn't ride a bike and so he couldn't teach me. Of course, we didn't have a bicycle to begin with. But later, I learned all the same.

One day I decided to walk all the way to Thököly Road. It was fall and getting dark, and I was cold. There was a wine bar on the corner of Thököly and Hungária roads and I decided to go inside. I saw Father sitting facing the door. The woman with him must have been his age, more or less, and he was holding her hand. I didn't know what to do. He stood up. The woman was clearly embarrassed. She was beautiful. Just like my mother. I'm sorry, I said, and left. I knew that something that should never have happened had just happened. I was at the corner when he caught up with me.

I don't want you to misunderstand the situation, son, because it can easily be misunderstood.

And I said that he could rest assured, I didn't misunderstand, and he should go back in, his friend must feel very uncomfortable now, at least as uncomfortable as he and I feel.

And then something happened that had never happened before. My father began shouting at the top of his lungs that he's not feeling awkward, and he has no intention of doing so, because except for my mother, he never had anything to do with anyone else and never will, ever. He's not an animal, he doesn't need another woman, he has a wife, so I better not defile my mother's memory by accusing him. Come to think of it, what am I doing there anyway? Why am I spying on him like an informer, a squealer? I have no idea who that woman is and why he's with her in there, and why he's holding her hand. She's his cousin, his cousin once removed, and they haven't seen each other since they were young, and she lost her husband, and now she's a widow, and not some whore, so I better not accuse him of anything with his own cousin. He knows perfectly well what I think about him, he's known for months, the way I smear all the filth of my own imagination on him, but he's clean, and that's a fact, he has no secrets. He's never taken pictures of whores who sell themselves from the window opposite, and he doesn't hide dirty magazines in his drawer, and if I go on like this, he'll soon be ashamed of his own son, who is so perverse, he lives with mannequins.

I said that I don't live with mannequins, and I didn't hide the American magazine, I just keep it in a drawer, and I'd be keeping it there even if I knew that he went about searching my room. Then he grabbed me by the arm and screamed in my face that he never searched my room, ever, he just needed my birth certificate, so I better not dare question his decency again.

All right, father, I said.
I repeat. Don't you dare! Understand? It's because of my decency that I've gone through hell!
I know.
So don't you accuse me of anything! And don't spy on me. I don't have a lover!
Fine. I believe you. But you might as well have someone. There's nothing indecent about it. You can't cheat the dead, and my mother is dead. She's dead because of your decency, among other things.

He let go of my arm and stood under the lamplight as if it were the gallows.

A bus pulled in. I got on and began crying like a baby. He didn't come home for three or four days.

But I have to stop now because of the ant.

(the ant)

I was sitting in the garden watching an ant. It crawled away, then came back, then crawled away again. It moved back and forth along a stretch of about a meter and a half. From time to time it stopped, took a few steps to the right, then a few to the left, but then returned to his original path. Actually, it was an invisible path. There was nothing to mark it. At least, nothing that would warrant us calling the edge of a meter and a half stretch of concrete garden road a path. When I sat down on the ground at the base of the wall of the house, the ant was already there. At first I thought it had lost its way. Except, someone who has lost his way won't be taking the same couple of hundred steps there and back. Someone who has lost his way will keep at it until he finds the road to take. Or until he gets off course even more. Or he'll stop and make a fire, shout, wave, give out signals and pray in desperation, hoping he'll be found. But with regard to this path, the steps the ant sometimes took to the right and to the left made no sense either. There was nothing there. No proper road, no food, no other ants. Which is probably why it kept returning to its original path.

Now and then it would stop and with its two forelegs fix something on itself. Just like a fly. Except, unlike a fly, an ant can turn around as if it had a spine. Or like a dog when it bites its tail. And this fixing something, this self-cleansing was no more logical than the moving there and back. There was no visible dirt sticking to it. Nothing that it was doing for minutes on end made sense, nothing at all.

If it would eat, or at least look for food. If it would talk to another ant. If it would propagate the species, or build a castle. Or it if would just leave. After all, he's got no business here. Things like this would make sense. But this, this back and forth, as if it were in a cell – even though it was at liberty to climb off the garden ledge and head for the grass – was puzzling. Also, it can't see, though it must sense some light stimulation. But seeing things the way I see them, the thorn bush across the way, behind it the garage that's been put to use as a junkyard, the unfinished statue of Christ in the garage window, a bit further off the pear tree and the rotting plank fence with the cat sitting in front of it, all this it can't see. It has no brain. It has no memories. If I were to put it down a meter and a half further off, it'd walk back and forth the same way.

I know why I'm sitting on the ground against the wall of the house. It's because I'm waiting, something that, here and now, gives meaning to my life. Of course, I could just as well be sitting here not knowing why I am doing it, but even so the things that surround me, what I think about them and what I feel about this green garage thrown together from coarse strips of cheap wood, with God only knows how much stuff inside and an unfinished Christ in the window, these might still give some sort of meaning to my life.

But even if me being here had no meaning, neither visible, nor invisible, if I were blind, if I couldn't see that dusty garage window, if I were not aware that someone was squatting over me, watching me, and that judging by his yard stick I barely exist, if he were to ponder that my life is subject to a single movement on his part, a whim. . . .

You're so skinny again, boy.

How are you, Aunt Emma. I'm not skinny. It's constitutional.

Constitutional, constitutional, come in and eat, and like some sort of bait that will make me mend my ways, she swings the string bag with a loaf of fresh bread in front of me.

Thank you. We'll be in soon. I'm waiting for Kornél. He's gone swimming.

That'll be a long wait. An hour, if not more.

I know, Aunt Emma.

If you know, just imagine how well I know. Just don't go out drinking this time before you have something to eat.

We're not going out drinking, Aunt Emma.

No? Watch what you say, boy, because I know everything, she said and laughed as she wagged a finger at me.

A person who knows everything need not weigh things. He knows everything as one. For him cause and effect are not separate things. There's nothing godlike in my freedom to weigh whether this ant should live or die. In fact, this freedom may well be the most human of all things. The entity in whom all things are as one, me, the garage, the unfinished Christ, this ant, doesn't think. He can't make a decision of any kind.

Seen from the vantage point of an omniscient being, there is no mercy. It wouldn't be logical. My sin would have to fall outside of him. From his vantage point, I may not even exist. I am not separate from the whole. Only man can say, your kingdom come. Only man can say, peace be with you. Only man can say, to hang by the neck. Only man can say, at least, give it a try.

Seen from the perspective of an omnipotent being, it wasn't much, but seen from my own perspective, it was at least more than nothing. Which is more or less as far as I got in that garden at the age of eighteen as I watched the ant that finally caught a scent and left. Provided it could smell at all. Still, it must be open to some little stimulation. Something drives him on. And as I sat across from the garage window with the unfinished Christ that Kornél's father had carved twenty-six years before, thinking, again and again, that he'd botched it up, simply because it wasn't perfect.

(the mirror)

I have no idea who that woman was. I never saw her again and neither did Father, I think. I'm not even sure that he spent those couple of days at her place, whereas it'd have been better for both of us had he done so. It's better for us to live with the living rather than the dead.

On the other hand, I don't know what it takes to survive the dead and retain one's sanity and the soundness of one's soul. Some people manage, others don't. It probably depends a lot more on the dead person than on the living. It may well be that I was not the only person who couldn't get himself to throw his mother's clothes into the garbage. Probably nobody in the world could have done it. And it may well be that while some people don't know how to live, others don't know how to die. This may well be the only way in which Éva resembled my mother.

When Father came home, I didn't leave my room for a day and a half. He knew I was home, but he didn't knock on my door either. After a day and a half I couldn't keep it back anymore and I peed into the majolica vase. I tried aiming for the inside wall so as not to make any noise, but he must have heard, because a couple of minutes later the key turned in the lock, and he left. It was only for the time I needed to go to the bathroom and wash up and for him to do some shopping. Then when he came back, he closed the door to his room loud enough so I'd know it was all right to go to the kitchen, that we wouldn't run into each other. The door between our rooms had been closed since we moved in, while the door to my room had been closed since Mother's furniture had arrived. His door now closed once and for all. A week passed.

Then we realized that this was no way to live. One morning we bumped into each other in the hall, and then we did the worst possible thing, we acted as if we'd met the night before, as if nothing had happened. He asked if I had enough money, I told him I did, he said he'd just been paid, if I needed money, I should take it from the drawer, and I thanked him. The only thing that changed was his closed door. It was a tactful gesture. He kept it closed because of me, so we shouldn't be forced to look at each other when I go back to my room from the kitchen. Two days later, when I needed money, it was in the drawer along with a pack of cigarettes. They had filters, so I wouldn't have to smoke the same stinging Selló cigarettes that scratched his throat. This daily allowance of cigarettes could just as easily have been kept in the kitchen, but this way I had to go to his room every day to get it.

Then one morning when I went to the bathroom, I found him standing in front of the mirror, his mouth wide open like a child's at the doctor's. He was looking at his tongue. I asked what happened. I've got a lump on my tongue, he said. It hurts. I feel it every time I swallow. There was an unfamiliar fear in his eyes the likes of which I'd never seen before, not even when, years ago, they took him away. I said I'd have a look, then told him it's just a tiny white aphthae. I had it myself, you can pick it up in any of the cheap cafaterias. I hope you're right, son, he said. Don't worry, I'm right, I said, there's no reason for you to imagine the worst because of some aphthae. And in two days, it was gone, except from that point on, I often found him standing in front of the mirror, examining his tongue or oral cavity, the entrance to his tainted soul, for thirty minutes at a stretch. A year later he was diagnosed with cancer.

(the space research)

I tried to be at home as little as possible. Except apart from Kornél and the countess, I had nowhere else to go. When Mária was ill, I went to the farmers market to do their shopping, and the countess gave me some books. We read the issues of *Life and Science* together. She was especially interested in the latest findings in space research. She thought it was ungodly. I asked why not biology, and she said, oh, my dear, nothing amuses God more than his two creations, the priests and the biologists. She was also interested in the Nazca plateau and the Easter Island statues and Mohenjo-daro, because she considered the clumsy efforts to at solve their mystery the last bastions of mythical thinking.

It wasn't just the fact that two-thousand years before Rome, Mohenjo-doro already had flush toilets and running water that intrigued her, anyone with a bit of self-respect can do that, dear, she explained, but that they haven't found a single temple in the entire town, not even a cemetery. Nor weapons. Sometimes I tend to think it wasn't inhabited by humans. Or else, it was a matriarchy, she added with a chuckle. The second option is more plausible, I said. Atlantis, on the other hand, did not interest her. It doesn't matter if it existed or not, she said. Take the Lost Paradise, for instance. It's not the Lost Paradise that's intriguing, but why we lost it. We don't believe in a god, dear. We believe in half a god. All we have is the Good Lord, and even he scares us half to death. It's all right if he's partly anthropomorphic. Why not. And just imagine what a great big shadow this mighty big Good Lord casts in the bright sunlight at noon. A shame you're short on languages and diligence. If you could read German, I'd lend you a book about Job. It's a book to be reckoned with. Those who believe in a half-god break into a cold sweat over it.

I assume you did, too, I said.
You're right, my dear. But the fact that I break into a cold sweat over it doesn't mean

the other person can't be profoundly in the right. If you manage to learn this golden rule, your life will be a lot more difficult, but you will also be able to part with it more easily, I should think.

I thought we need a good half-god in order to let go of life more easily.

No, my dear. For that you need a clear conscience. And the more unimpeachable truths a person amasses, the more dirt will adhere to his conscience. Unimpeachable truth is the quagmire of the soul, my dear.

She considered space research ungodly, because with its help, man is looking for a way out of earthly existence. This, she added, obviously involves him going and continuing his shenanigans someplace where, if he were naked, he'd freeze to death before he could suffocate. If that's the case, I asked, why does she find space research so intriguing? Because, my dear, when it comes right down to it, I'm as curious as the next man.

(the Book of Job)

Once during biology class Áros Szűcs asked if God didn't create man, and he didn't create animals and plants, not even mushrooms, then what did he create? At this Comrade Teacher Kozma's face turned ashen, though behind that ashen countenance something of the real Kozma was nevertheless visible, the man who'd have liked to see the world as one, in its entirely, to understand it in its entirety. But such an eventuality was not granted to him, just as it had not been granted to anyone during the past couple of millennia. He had only some vague ideas, but these ideas were quite vague. His logic was far from faultless, and so were his convictions, not to mention his knowledge. Only his goodwill was without blemish.

God did not create anything, he said, though you could feel that he's not saying God's name with a small g. Not a capital G either, but certainly with a medium-sized g. Or a capital G, except with a dot over it that weighed a ton, to crush it.

But Comrade Teacher, he had to create something to kick-start evolution, so the animals could evolve in line with Comrade Darwin's guidelines, Szűcs said.

You are mistaken, son. In order to create, you first have to exist, and god does not exist. If he existed, then naturally, he'd have created everything. But he doesn't.

But how do we know, Comrade Teacher? Szűcs persisted.

We know because Marx, Engels, Lenin, and above all, Comrade Stalin realized it and they told us. Comrade Stalin studied to be a priest, but then he saw the light. Had he not seen it, he wouldn't have turned into Comrade Stalin.

Comrade Stalin may have been mistaken, Szűcs said.

He was not mistaken. None of them were mistaken, ever. What they say is sacred, and don't you forget it, son.

But the Pope is never mistaken either, and he's sacred, too.

Except the Pope is just one man, but Comrade Stalin and the others are four.

The fascists also outnumbered the Jews, but they weren't in the right, Szűcs said. At this point Comrade Teacher Kozma snuck a desperate look at his watch, but there were still ten minutes left till the end of class.

What is your father? he asked, hoping to lend new momentum to his dialectic.

An engine fitter, Szűcs announced with a triumphant ring to his voice.

And then I knew that it was him. Starting with fifth grade, there's an informer in every class. When school began Father had warned me to be cautious.

That's just it, son. If Comrade Stalin were mistaken, then for example, your father wouldn't be a machine fitter now, because in that case, he wouldn't have free will. God does not create machine fitters, because when they invented him, there weren't any machine fitters. That's the point. Your father wanted to be a machine fitter of his own free will, and that's what he became.

My father was originally a journalist, Szűcs said.

And then the chalk snapped in two between Kozma's fingers.

He must have written something where he had made an error of judgment but admitted his mistake, and in order not to make any more mistakes, he decided to become a machine fitter. Which just proves that God does not exist, because if he existed, mistakes would not be possible.

I see, Szűcs said.

Very good. As for the Bible, it was written by men with the best intentions, but without any basis in fact. Remember that, son. Only man is capable of creation. He crosses a horse with a donkey and creates a mule. A hybrid. An animal that hadn't existed before. Had God created everything, we wouldn't have mules, would we?

That's true, Szűcs said. Except, mules can't propagate the species.

They will. For the moment, they may not, but they will!

Comrade Teacher, is man also a hybrid?

Some are and some aren't. A mestizo, for instance, is a hybrid, but the whites are not.

Not even the Magyars?

Now that, son, is a very good question. When it comes down to it, the Magyar is also a hybrid. Many kinds of people mixed in the Carpathian Basin, because they had to mix, because it's very difficult, finding your way out of it. And eventually they became the Magyars.

In which case I'm not a Magyar, and Comrade Teacher is not a Magyar, but we're hybrids, Szűcs said. At which several boys in the class guffawed, but just now, Kozma was in no position to worry about the troublemakers.

That's right, son. We all have all kinds of blood flowing in our veins. Cumanian, Turkish, Armenian, and also Jewish and German and Russian. All kinds. The Magyar is a combination of these. Though actually, there's no such thing as a Magyar. Magyars as such don't exist. And that goes for God as well.

Did Comrade Stalin say that?

No, he wasn't concerned separately with the Magyars. He's occupied with more important things. Though on the basis of his guidelines, and with the application of a little logic, it's possible to come to the right conclusion, Kozma said. Then he snuck a look at his Pobeda once again, but there were still two minutes remaining.

In which case a Cumenian or a Turk or a Jew is not a hybrid, but a Magyar is.

I didn't say that, Kozma cried, at the end of his tether. He's no more hybrid than a Jew, and don't twist my words. I only said that there's no such thing as pure blood, because we're all mixed. But they're still people for all that.

Okay, all right, I understand, Comrade Teacher, and thank you for your guidance, Szűcs said with a grin, at which point the bell sounded at long last.

As for me, all I could think about on the way home was that my maternal grandfather was Polish, which makes me a hybrid, too, but that's all right, because there's no such thing as a Magyar.

But then, after dinner, when I helped Mother with the dishes, I told her that I wasn't a hybrid.

What do you mean, son? she asked, stunned.

I'm Magyar, and I believe in God.

144

Of course you are, dear.

I'm Magyar, even if Grandfather was Polish.

What do you think? What makes you Magyar?

I'm Magyar because I was born Magyar.

In which case, was a Janissary Hungarian or Turkish?

I said nothing.

If you ask me, you're Magyar because we brought you up as a Magyar. And as for your grandfather, he was Magyar because he wanted to be. You might decide one day that you're Polish, and then you'll be part Polish and part Magyar because you won't be able to forget that you're Magyar. At most, you won't bring up your children as Magyars.

But I can't decide that I'm Black.

No, because black is not the opposite of Magyar, it's the opposite of white. White is a race. You have to be born white, but you have to learn to be Magyar. Come to think of it, a black man can also decide that he's Magyar. Of course, that's not an easy decision to make. Also, people wouldn't believe he had really turned into a Magyar, which would take the wind out of his sails.

But I can't decide that I'm neither?

No, son, you can't. You'd have to have lived alone in a cave at the end of the world from the time you were born.

What about a Jew?

What about a Jew?

Is a Jew Magyar or Black?

That's an ify question. You can't become a Jew just by learning the Torah.

But you have to learn it even if you're born a Jew.

In which case I can't be a Jew, but a Jew can be a Magyar.

Something like that. Except, all he has to do is learn it, but you'd have to be born into it.

I'm not sure that's fair.

I'm sure that it's not. It's every bit as unfair as the fact that a bird can fly, but you can't. Injustice exists only if someone has a choice. Understand, son?

And God. Does God exist or not?

He does, dear. Except, that's an even more difficult situation than the Jews. In that cave you would definitely not be a Magyar or a Jew or a Pole. On the other hand, you'd probably believe in a god of some sort. We all do, even if we all believe in a slightly different god, even though we insist that we believe in the same god.

Communists don't believe in God.

Are you sure? If you ask me, Stalin is every bit as much a god to them as a pharaoh or a Chinese emperor was in the past. A primitive god. At one time even animals were gods.

Stalin is not God. He's filth, but God is good.

Mother laughed.

As you say. Filth. But that's not why he's not God. God isn't always good either. I prefer to say that he's all-powerful. He's basically good, though he can also be bad.

He can't be bad. Satan is bad, I said.

Yes, he can. It wasn't Satan who put poor Job through all that torture, but the Almighty, even though he knew perfectly well that Job was not guilty. And when he showed mercy at long last, his sole goodness consisted in sparing him more of his cruelty. And let's admit it, that's insufficent in itself to be called goodness, Mother said. But just then Father appeared in the door, so she couldn't finish what else she wanted to tell me about Job and the Almighty.

Father wasn't crying, but his eyes were misted over.

It's over, he said. London has just announced that Stalin died yesterday.

And then Mother clipped me in an embrace and started sobbing, it's over, dear.

You see? I was wrong, and you were right. He's not God after all.

(the darkroom)

From the time the kitchen was turned into the darkroom, there weren't many doors left in the apartment that could've been closed. Mostly, we met in front of the bathroom in the morning, when he went to look at his throat in the mirror. It was horrible. Once I told him that maybe he should go and get examined, that might put his mind at ease. He must have doctor friends he trusts. Yes, you're right, son, he said, but then I remembered that he knew just two doctors, one was his father, in whose hands his own mother died, the other was Dr. Zenta, whose hand with the golden Schaffhausen is holding my mother's hand in a torn photograph.

Then a year later, when there was something to take a biopsy of, after a routine surgery, they called me into the physician's room. I had no idea what these holier than thou doctors meant by the words they used, and when the doctor told me confidentially that the diagnosis was positive, I was as happy as a child. After all, in a sense, that's exactly what I was. And then he said that I misunderstood, and I told him that now I understood, and then he said that the patient must not get wind of the diagnosis.

Then why did you tell me?

Because we'll need the cooperation of the next of kin, and you're his next of kin.

No, I'm not next of kin.

What do you mean?

I'm his son, not his next of kin.

That amounts to the same thing.

I've never hit anyone in my life, but you better watch what you say. I'm his son. Get it?

He sees that I'm in a state of shock, which is only natural, but it will pass, and then I'll be able to cooperate.

What do you expect? You want me to lie to my father and pretend that he's fine, when he knows perfectly well that he isn't?

He can't be sure.

My grandfather was a physician.

Still, he can't be sure, and it's been proven that it's better for the patient if he doesn't know.

Who proved it? Tell me. Who?

He expected more of me, he said. He thought that I'd act like a grownup, but it seems he was mistaken.

Fine. So I'm a grownup. What do you want me to do?

First and foremost, make sure that your father's peace of mind is not disturbed.

Don't you think it's too late for that? He'd have needed his peace of mind to keep him from contracting cancer.

This is not a psychosomatic illness. No one contracts cancer from nerves.

Why don't you try it, I said, and left the office, careful not to slam the door, because Father was waiting outside in the corridor with its flaky walls.

From the time I set up the enlarger, I spent a third of my life in red light. Especially my days. I spent my nights at the printer's, because at the crack of dawn the papers had to be ready to ship to the distributor. Then, while it was still dark, the paper boys spread them around town like a disease. By the time I got home and fell asleep, they had infected the town a second time.

As I hurried along the track, I'd sometimes catch a glimpse of a sentence or two. It made no difference whether it was a lead article or a classified ad, I invariably felt a perplexing sense of shame. Political Committee to Take a Stand Today. Must buy cradle. Gently used will do.

Of course, it would be nice to know whether what I felt was actually shame or bewilderment. Shame doesn't adhere to bewilderment, only afterwards, like an explanation gone awry. Did I in fact feel it shameful for the Political Committee to take a stand on anything, for it to exist in the first place, or did I take the Political Committee for granted and it was only their "taking a stand" that turned my stomach?

The latter alternative seemed more likely. What we thought about God in '61 can be retrieved with a lot more clarity that what we thought about the Political Committee that same year.

But that's not what I meant to say. I meant that when I was spending my afternoons in red light, I didn't touch the Zorki for months. I was too busy enlarging the old negatives, although there weren't many of them. I enlarged some of them ten times, others as many as a hundred. Some I didn't even have a chance to see because the man in the lab said they were flawed, or of no interest.

Only now did I realize that I hadn't seen the negatives my father had enlarged on soft, shiny sheets of paper. Not yet. My negatives are stiff, that's why I need soft paper, he explained. I had no idea what stiff negatives meant. On the other hand, these postcard-size pieces of paper told me where I'd been. To the right a cupboard and a faucet, to the left a sofa, in the middle Imolka peeling onions.

For instance, I hadn't seen the picture I took of the waitress in the cafeteria before. I didn't go back to because I felt ashamed. He was right not to have enlarged it. It was a terrible picture. Two-thirds were taken up with an out-of-focus table top, the rest, on the left, with the back of a chair. And somewhere in the distance, the waitress was just coming through the swinging door. Only half of her shows, from the waist up. In her hand, the water pitchers. I pinned it to the wall and studied it, and was at a loss. I was at a loss to understand what made it so mysterious. What made it better than all the other pictures I'd taken. The paper gradually dried and rolled up. I soaked it and pinned it up again. It took two days for me to realize that the woman's eyes were closed, that that's all it takes, a pair of eyes in the distance, barely visible, shut for a split second; in short, it all depends on whether I will ever see the whole picture as one. To do that you must first see everything separately, down to the tiniest detail. To understand that you can neither catch that moment too early nor too late, you must see which direction the dust swirls as a gust of wind sweeps it along the street. You must see it as a unified entity a split second before its light reaches the brain. It makes no difference whether I happen upon that moment or create it myself, whether I set up the lights myself and tell her to close her eyes. If I don't want blind chance to be the author of my pictures, I must see the whole thing the way no one has seen it before. And I felt as helpless as a man whose mouth is gagged with a rag and whose hands are tied behind his back.

(the gatherers)

One night the door of the basement corridor was locked, so I had to go by the type-setters. That's when I saw that there was a lab. Until then, I didn't know that they took pictures in a printing house. The red light was on over the door, which meant no entry. I decided to come back after work, but the light was on again, and the next day, and the day after that.

I read up on it. I wanted to find out how they divided up the screen plates and what kinds of cameras they used. If the photographer would let me, I could enlarge one of the negatives and see what the eyes of a man walking along the street looked like.

There was a woman with the gatherers, fiftyish. We usually worked one behind the other. Sometimes she was up front, sometimes I was. Our timing was just about the same. She had trained me when I first started. She gave me a piece of rubber for my fingers. You wouldn't believe how difficult it is to separate one sheet from another without rubber on your fingers, but they make your hands sweat. So the women cut off the tips of their rubber gloves and pull them over their fingers. This way, only the tips of their thumbs and index fingers got sweaty.

The woman who trained me was called Gizella Vámosi. Her daughter was my age and her husband was a machinist at one of the factories in Csepel. That's all I knew about her. And also, that they owned the complete works of Mikszáth and Jókai. All she knew about me was that I'd moved to Pest from the countryside, my mother died, my father was a librarian, and that I was planning to finish high school at night. It was hearing about Father being a librarian that prompted her to tell me about the Mikszáths and Jókais, and it was Mother's death that prompted her to bring me a sandwich now and then. I asked her if she knew the photographer, and she told me that it would be pretty hard getting transferred to the lab without a skilled worker's diploma. I was just curious,

I told her. Her husband liked to take pictures as well, he has a Smena. When my shift was over, during her cigarette break, she took me down to Karcsi.

Karcsi was around thirty-five and had curly blond hair. An unbuttoned shirt revealed his hairy chest, and he wore a wide belt. After we made our introductions, he asked me how he could help me. I said that I was just curious to see how photographs are made in a printing press. He invited me in. He showed me the equipment park, then the adjacent lab. He explained how the plates were made. Then he said that it was impossible to make it with the girls with such large equipment. That would require a Rolleiflex instead of a camera that covers your face, because women don't go for that. It puts them on their guard. Eleven out of ten women spread their legs like dogs. For virgins and married women, you don't even have to put film in the camera. He placed a hand on my shoulder.

I was disgusted and I never went back there again.

(All Saints Day)

On All Saints Day I went out to the Kerepesi Cemetery. I found a candle in the pantry to take along. It was dark and damp when I got there, with thousands of flickering lights, and a crowd. Which is the last thing I wanted. The relatives of the dead came carrying chrysanthemums. Some only visited the graves of relatives, others also paid their respects to the great men of the nation. I stopped by Ady's grave. I had every reason to do so. Then I spotted Adél Selyem and left. She was with a big, bearded man, an intellectual by his looks. She reached up to his chest, if that. I imagined the man tearing the red rag from its nail even without having to be asked, and stuffing it in her mouth. She'd found a partner, I thought. And also, that by tomorrow, or by this time next year, she'd be desperately looking for someone else.

Fortunately, she didn't see me. I scurried away before she'd have to pretend not to see me. I left the main path, and then the crowd started thinning out. I think I got lost, because I found myself among the children's graves close to the rubber factory. I was shivering with cold, I'd have liked to flee, but that damn candle was still in my pocket. Then at a spot from where nothing of All Souls was visible anymore, I set it on top of a piece of stone and lit it. A feeling of despair swept over me. I can cry my heart out over a police car, but not over a candle, I thought, not even when a bit of rain puts it out.

It took thirty years for me to realize that when we moved to Pest, the rubber factory where Father had been a warehouseman was situated on the other side of that fence. It also took thirty years for me to learn that one of the gravestones among the weeds of the corner of the cemetery that I continued to visit for some time on All Souls Day bore the name of my half-sister, Johanna Zenta.

(bitterness)

A person who can't be happy is a person whose pain I can't believe. It wasn't one of the András Szabads but my mother who said this. She said it the first Christmas when they locked up Father. The two of us were left in that immense goddamn house and Christmas was upon us, and I watched Mother in the living room carve the stump of a pine tree with a small ax until it fit into the stand, then decorate the tree with glass balls and the walnuts she'd painted with silver furnace paint. I would watch her carefully sweep up after one of the balls broke. She then set the table and put on her black silk dress, lit the candles, and ladled the soup into our bowls. Only then did I remember that I didn't have a present to give her. Nothing. Nothing at all. I'd forgotten all about it, and I was suddenly overwhelmed with shame. My shame turned to anger in seconds, and instead of taing a sip of the soup, I said, we're not having Christmas this year.

> What do you mean?
> I mean that you shouldn't be happy now. And neither should I.
> Are you sure?
> I'm sure. Nothing could make me happy now.
> She said nothing.

We shall see, she said after a while, and turned off the lights, so she could light the candles on the tree. Outside, the wind howled through the branches of the walnut tree like a tortured animal. And when all the candles were burning as bright as the fires of Hell, and only "Silent Night" stood between me and my shame, I broke into tears. Please, please forgive me, I didn't mean to forget. And then Mother put her arms around me and said, thank you, son.

I didn't understand. I could understand her forgiving me, but her thanking me was beyond the bounds of reason. And then she said that her child being able to say what he really feels is the best present for her. Even his shame. This is more important to her than anything I could have given her. Everyone forgets things. For instance, for the last three years, she has forgotten her brother's birthday, and believe me, she explained, the fact that he's dead doesn't make it any easier, it makes it worse, because you can always ask the living to forgive you, while asking the dead is a lot more difficult. But instead of the anger or hatred provoked by my feeling shame I'll be able to ask for her forgiveness, or anyone else's for that matter, if she's been a good mother to me. She was sure that I'd have many more occasions to feel ashamed, because one can't live a life without it. But if I should ever catch myself lying or finding excuses or throwing aside my dinner or hating the person I've offended, she'd be the one to blame. Now that my father couldn't be with us, she needed to know that she's been a good mother.

Tomorrow, I'll give you a present, I said.

I'd like that very much. But I couldn't possibly give her a better present than what I just gave her, even if I didn't mean to.

Then we lit the firecrackers and sang "Silent Night."

Then she handed me a small package. When my fingers touched the tissue paper, I already knew that she'd given me something that could never be mine, Father's pocket knife with the ebony handle, a present from my mother, but also from my father.

The best present for me is that you forgave me, I said.

Nevertheless, you should enjoy the pocket knife, I know how much you wanted it, she said.

The worst thing that can happen to someone is to be incapable of distinguishing happiness from sadness. As far as Mother was concerned, this was the saddest Christmas, even more bitter, perhaps, than the winter of forty-four, when Father was called up for forced labor. But she didn't want that to eclipse everything else. Had Christ just threatened or chastised, had he just suffered, had he been incapable of appreciating the Last Supper, his words wouldn't be worth a single forint.

A bitter man will sow the seeds of hatred in the world, because he sees nothing but the cause of his own bitterness in it. A bitter man is invariably unfair, because fairness is contained only in a broader context. Invariably, a bitter man makes those he should be grateful to feel ashamed of themselves. He will find allies in those who indiscriminately accept his right to anger. And in the end, he always turns his back on his allies, just as he turns his back on those who won't be his allies because they care for him.

You should be wary of those who refuse a present, Mother told me, saying they don't deserve it, or else they accept it as if they were doing you a favor. In that case, you become their ally or servant, only to wake one morning to the realization that they've plucked your soul clean, leaving you to fend for yourself.

A bitter man is a solitary man. When he admires a mountain or the sea, he is admiring the setting of his solitude. He always stands alone in this setting. For a bitter man, even the loves of his life, his wife, his parents, or his children are nothing more than part of this setting. They're shadows and monsters with whom he wrestles alone, and who attack him with the same rage that he feels himself. For a bitter man, all his hurts, ire, and thirst for revenge are justified, and his being called to account for the pain he's caused is, he believes, unjust. He doesn't turn away from people, it's just that there's no place in his truth for anyone else.

Also, Mother warned, sometimes it takes very little to feel bitter. Some people do not turn bitter even from war, while for others it suffices that they feel ashamed, perhaps even once. We have no way of knowing how much it takes to make an individual bitter. However, one thing is certain, the Lord does not help the embittered individual. In the eyes of an individual who can't find solace in another individual, God himself will be no more than part of the setting of his bitterness. So I should allow myself to be happy with this pocket knife, it will take nothing away from the pain I feel because my father is behind bars. There's no need for me to feel either shame or guilt because of it, otherwise I will never be able to see things for what they are, or as part of a whole. I will be blind. My soul will lack eyes.

In short, this is more or less what my mother taught me. Then in a little less than two years she decided to die before she could grow bitter and blind herself. She was as terrified of bitterness as Father was of cancer years later. She didn't realize that fear is the root of bitterness, and so she didn't take into account that there is nothing more frightening than finding your mother dead.

(the poem)

One day my father knocked on my door. He was holding a newspaper. We never went to each other's room with a newspaper. I knew it must be something important.

His name is Erdős, isn't it?

Who, I asked, nonplussed because I didn't understand the question. I'd have never found a connection between Kádár, the Political Committee, and Kornél.

Your friend Kornél.

Yes.

That's good. Very good. He is at least as good a poet as the poets of the *Nyugat*.

He's not a poet, I said. He's been mucking about with a family novel for years, but he doesn't write poetry. I would know about it.

My mistake. There must be two.

Can I see?

He handed me the paper and left, leaving me with three poems, and it took just one line for me to know that my father had been right. And also, that the bitterness stuck in my throat would suffocate me.

What's this, I asked, and put the paper down in front of Kornél.

He said nothing.

Just don't try sending me back to Mélyvár, ever again.

I don't understand what's eating you.

I realize that. And you probably never will.

All right, enough. If something is bothering you, please tell me.

You know what you are? A colossal, cowardly hypocrite. A pretend good person with pretend honesty and pretend modesty.

Stop it!

And I'll have no more of your lies, the only person I thought was close to me.

What lies? Tell me. What?

Don't pretend you don't know. At least, not that.

Oh, I see. You're upset because three of my poems got published in the paper.

No, Kornél. You're way off track. And you know it.

If this gets you so worked up, I'm sorry, and I apologize. But I am not a hypocrite and I wouldn't lie to you. Take that back. It just never occurred to me that they might interest you. My poems.

It didn't occur to you.

No.

It didn't occur to you that I, of all people, might be interested.

No. Or anyone else, for that matter.

Is that so? For your information, this paper has a circulation of a hundred-thousand.

Yes, I know, and I sent them in because that's what one does. If a person writes a poem, sooner or later, he'll send them to a newspaper, and sooner or later, the newspaper will either publish it, or reject it. And if it gets in the paper, a person is either capable of feeling happy as a consequence, or not. And if he is capable, he will enjoy a good night. And if he's not, he'll have a miserable life.

They're damned good. All three of them.

Thank you.

Don't mention it. They're better than good. Just don't pretend you don't know. At least, not with me.

Why do you find it so incredible that someone may not know?

Some people may not. But you do.

That's an unfounded accusation.

It's not an accusation, just fact.

I can't begin to imagine where you get your facts from.

They come from the fact that you're a coward. You're as much of a coward as I am.

I'm not a coward. Besides, what does this have to do with cowardice?

You would never send in a poem unless you were absolutely sure that it wouldn't be rejected.

There's no poem that might not be rejected.

But a poem like *Early Morning Drunkenness*? Come on, it's too good.

Which doesn't mean it can't be rejected. By the way, I'd never think of you as a coward.

Well then, it's time you started.

I won't. Nor will anyone else.

I don't care about anyone else, but you're free to think so.

You see? I'd never be able to say such a thing. That I don't care about the opinions of others.

You know perfectly well what I mean.

I do. But still. The way you say it. Putting it out there like a rock.

Here you go again.

I said rock, not two stone tablets.

Because a rock is bigger.

Are you sure that your photos are good?

On the contrary. I'm sure they're not.

Well, I happen to like them.

How many of them have you seen?

I don't know. Three, possibly. The one with the bridge that's hanging over your bed, the waitress, and one other.

Why didn't you see more?

Because you didn't show me more.

And why didn't I?

I have no idea.

Well I'll tell you. Because of the *and-one-other*.

Don't twist my words. I'd never say I liked them if I didn't. And you know that. You know it perfectly well.

I'm not twisting anything. It's my *and-one-other*, not yours. That's why it'd have been enough for you to see just two, and why I've never shown them to anyone else. Not one. It's because you'd never send a bad poem to a paper, because it's all you have, your poems, and if they sent it back, you'd be left with nothing. It's this fucking fear that fires ambition.

I'm not ambitious.

Sure you are. Except, you feel even more ashamed of it than I do.

The carpet rack. The carpet rack in your old backyard. The picture you didn't give to your father because it looked like a prison yard. That was the third.

(the dream)

Around that time, I had a dream. I rarely have erotic dreams; as for black-and-white dreams, I've only had four, and the kind that showed me what was to happen years later, that happened only once. I was sitting on a bench in a park. It was night. I went there, hoping to take a picture of Gagarin, because my father said he walks around there every night. Not far from me, a couple was making love leaning against a wall. A lamp with a tin shade was hanging above them. From time to time, the wind shook it. The man stood with his back to me. He didn't know I was there. But the woman kept looking at me over the man's shoulder. She was saying something, but though her lips were moving, no sound came out. She kept repeating two words, over and over again. She wanted me to read her lips. But I couldn't. That's what woke me, that I didn't know what she was trying to tell me. I felt no physical desire, neither in my dream, nor when I woke up, but every movement of the woman's lips stayed with me. In the morning, I stood before the mirror and repeated the movement of her lips until I understood what those two words were.

Years later, that's how I met Éva, except she didn't say anything. She just looked.

(the Kádár villa)

That winter I found out where Kádár lived. I don't mean the address, just the general area. The husband of one of the women at the printer's was a plumber, and she told Gizella Vámos that her husband had fooled around with a faucet at the Kádár villa the day before. He was at it for hours. Gizella Vámos didn't want to believe it, but eventually she did. Apparently Kádár wasn't home, but his wife was very nice, she even made a sandwich for Gizella's husband. They're not at all like we think. Until then, it hadn't even occurred to me that Kádár lived anywhere at all.

I took the bus to Pasarét and wandered around for half an hour. I was sure I'd find the villa and catch a glimpse of the kitchen or bathroom window, or see the wind tear at the trees in the garden, or see that the street is every bit as slushy as Szív Street, and then it might seem more real. This was one of the idées fixes throughout most of my life, that whatever is real, whatever is tangible is easier to understand, and what we understand, we can tolerate better. Manage it. Keep it in hand. Or avoid it.

Come to think of it, my life and Éva's life were spent under this misconception. It ruined our lives. It was the things she didn't talk about. For her, the idea of acknowledging the truth was intolerable, while for me lying was intolerable, and these two views were at loggerheads. I was right in thinking that lying condemns a person to solitude, and I was also right in thinking that sooner or later, reality will inevitably triumph over lies. Except I didn't count on one thing – that reality was more terrible for her than her lies were for me.

In short, I went to Pasarét just to make sure that the wind tore at the trees in Kádár's garden just as it tore at the trees in his neighbor's garden. Other Party functionaries had villas in the neighborhood, too, and cars with tinted windows stood in front of their villas, too. I didn't see anything. The sky was blue, and János Kádár's villa was comfortably perched on the hillside, just like all the other villas. Actually, this was the hardest to bear – that in one of these streets there lived the man who realized that it's not fear that keeps the world subservient, but grayness. That's a lot more reliable.

(the Leica)

One day when I went home, I found three Gypsies in the apartment, a fat one and two scrawny ones. They wore hats and corduroy pants. They were busy disassembling the Tower of Babel. Hawkers. Father sold them Mother's useless antique furniture. I thought I would go out of my mind.

Father was leaning against the door, looking on. When I went to my room, the big guy tried to follow me. I said he'd have to kill me first, and closed the door. But one quick look inside my room sufficed, and he made an offer to His Excellency, as he put it. The offer amounted to the price of half a house. I heard Father say that they weren't for sale because they were being used, at which the Gypsy upped his offer.

I went outside and as quietly as I could manage, considering that I was trembling with rage, I said that as long as I'm around, and I don't just mean in this house but on this earth, the Gypsy better not make any more offers for my mother's furniture. Okay, alright, he was just trying to help. Just carting this junk away, and he'd have to cut his losses. In which case, don't bother, I said. It's too late, he said, business is business. We agreed, didn't we, Your Excellency. Whereupon Father said, yes, we agreed. But nothing else is for sale. I took a look at the ramshackle armchairs, side tables, and chandeliers. The mannequin was lying in front of the bathroom door. I'm sorry, but she's also staying, I said, and picked it up. Then I stopped in front of Father for a second, but then decided to keep my mouth shut and went to my room.

One of the scrawny Gypsies protested. In that case, it would be a hundred forints less. We agreed, Your Excellency, to buy everything in bulk. The big guy told him to shut up and just keep packing. Father, who felt that he owed them an explanation, said that the mannequin was his son's, he should have said so right at the beginning. The Gypsy gave no reply, but my father couldn't bear the silence and added that his son was an art photographer and needed the mannequin to adjust the lights.

I watched them load the stuff into their truck, and then settle in beside the disassembled Tower of Babel. A Magyar was at the wheel. Generally, Gypsies can't drive, so they hire someone. This is especially true of the hatted Gábor Gypsies of Transylvania, who don't go in for construction work. I grabbed the Zorki and snapped a shot just as they threw the canvas over the junk. Then they drove off.

I stopped in the middle of the room. The mannequin was lying on the bed, where I'd tossed it. I heard my father sweeping the hallway. I knew that if I were to go out now, we wouldn't speak to each other for weeks, or even months. But I went anyway. He was leaning on the broom as if it were his cane.

You might have said something, I said.

We'd have to talk more often for that, son.

I doubt that we ever will.

I'm sorry, but we needed the money.

Well, I didn't.

You live here, too, don't you?

I do. That's why you should have said something before you sold my mother's things.

These are not your mother's things, but my father's things. Everything, with the exception of the piano, and I don't need my son's permission to sell the things I grew up with.

Well, you should, because I grew up with them, too.

They were falling apart. Just taking up space.

Well, now there's plenty of space. I hope you're pleased.

Goddamn it, I told you, we needed the money. Is that so difficult to understand?

No. Not at all. Just don't speak to me this way, ever again, whether you're drinking with your cousin or selling what's left of Mother.

As he stood there, the broom or cane or whatever it was shook in his hand. The veins above his frayed collar, throbbed on the sides of his neck. His lips tightened, as if he were about to shout at me, but he didn't.

And another thing, I said. I am not an art photographer. I'm not going to be an art photographer in this fucking lifetime. Not now, not later. You may have been, but not me. I could puke when I hear that word, I said, lowering my voice. I'm not an art photographer, I said again, then retreated to my room.

On Sunday morning, I headed for the flea market but couldn't find any of our things. I didn't bump into Father either, not in the kitchen, nor the bathroom, nor the hall. This went on for nearly a month. One time he was just leaving the apartment as I was coming up the stairs, so I quickly turned around and headed back out of the house. He probably saw me, but at least this way I didn't have to humiliate him by not saying hello.

Then one morning when I came home from the printer's, I found a horrendously expensive Leica M3 on my desk with a note propped up against it. It said: This is what the money was for. Happy birthday, son.

(the first picture of my father)

I left the apartment, careful not to leave any telltale sign that I'd been there. This this-is-what-the-money-was-for hurt more that all the damn junk he sold, because I knew perfectly well that he was lying. I went looking for Kornél at the café, then at the university dining hall. Then I took the tram out to Budafok. The emptiness of my narrow life dragged me down and I fell asleep. When we reached the last stop and the conductor woke me, at first I thought I was on a train speeding over a vast empty expanse of plain, but God had left the window open and the wind came rushing in and the light streamed in through the window.

I walked back one stop. Kornél's father was fixing the garden gate. He didn't seem happy to see me, but I knew that his grumpiness wasn't aimed toward me but rather toward the gate, his ill health and, basically, his whole life. Go on in, he said, Kornél is upstairs. He then added that Kornél must be very busy if he can't find the time to fix a hinge. I asked if I could help. He said that he was nearly done. And I said that Kornél must've thought that it could wait. Nothing can wait, he told me, because life is happening right now, it's sweeping you along with it right now, otherwise it'll leave you behind. It's the one thing he wanted to teach his son. Nothing else, just this one thing. And I said that he did teach him, I'm sure. And he said, the two of you see eye to eye, boy.

I went upstairs and told Kornél what I could. He said he didn't know, and happy birthday.

> But what makes you so sure he's lying?
> I'm sure because I know how much a Leica costs.
> Still, he managed to buy it somehow.
> But how? That, I will never know.
> Are you sure you need to?
> If your father showed up with a car, you'd want to know how he got it.

He might have sold other stuff, not just the rickety old furniture.

That would have been a very stupid move on his part.

I think what got your gander up is that note, that he felt he needed to explain. But the point is, he thought it was important. Like calling you an art photographer.

That word makes me puke.

But not him. Now that you've quit school, he needs something to hold on to.

Well, I need to hold on to something, too, but not that.

If you ask me, you need a good camera. You also need to start talking to each other instead of hiding from each other like two lost souls. You need that, too.

But I don't need lies.

A person doesn't always lie out of bad faith.

Sure. He can lie because he's a coward.

Didn't you say once that you're a coward, too?

That has nothing to do with this.

Are you sure? Because it seems to me that you're being a coward right now.

What do you mean?

You're afraid to be happy with a camera that any other person would love to have. And that's because you're a coward. You're afraid to knock on his door and thank him.

You know what? Why don't you go help your father fix the garden gate?

What has that got to do with anything?

Simple. Your father is just fixing the garden gate downstairs. Go down, he'll hold it steady while you drive in a screw. Or whatever.

Will you please not badger me. I told him I'd fix it. I told him at lunch that it's loose and I'd fix it in the afternoon.

So why didn't you?

Because he wouldn't let me. He said it's gotta be fixed now or never. Though come to think of it, he may have thought that I'm just a good for nothing who can't even be trusted to drive in a screw, when the whole house is falling apart.

It's not falling apart.

Sure it is. Because his son is a clumsy good for nothing who can't even mix cement or fix a leaky roof.

I'm sure you're as good at it as he is.

And I won't even finish college, or be the next man on the moon!

If you ask me, you'll manage both.

The point isn't what you think will happen.

And for me the question isn't why you think my father is a coward.

No more of a coward than you.

I'm sleeping over.

No you're not. Go home, thank him for the present, then go take some pictures. Or take a picture of him.

I'll go home tomorrow.

No. Go now.

I bought a roll on Kálvin Square, then sat down in the museum garden for a while. Evening came at last, and I headed home. I saw him through the curtain of his door, reading by the small table. He didn't turn around. I went to my room. I sat down and studied the camera. It was just like the Zorki. Though actually, not at all.

I had a leftover roll of film. I loaded it into the camera. When I got up, the parquet floor creaked. I stopped. I thought I'd have to stand there till the end of time, like that dog in the pitch-dark skies locked inside an iron box. Then I went out to the hall. He was still sitting there. I tried to gauge the light through the curtain, then I set the focus. To the left, a flower stand, to the right, the small table with a glass of milk and a slice of bread. In between, Father, reading. Except he wasn't turning the pages. Then I pressed the shutter release button. The Leica was equipped with a quiet shutter release so it couldn't be heard through a closed glass door.

(the bicycle)

Mother said that because of the upheaval caused by the war, they forgot to baptize me. At the time, I believed her. But in retrospect it seems to me that when they executed her brother, she got disgusted with God. She found her way back to him, but by then nobody thought of my baptism.

She thought of it when they arrested Father, though actually, it was a couple of months later. She'd been fired from the municipal library and was working as a seamstress. She sewed on buttons. One fillér per button. She had to sew on a hundred buttons to make a forint. Our bread cost us two hundred buttons. She said not to worry, she'd get the hang of it, and by the second week, she satisfied the norm. Then, when Father's sentence was legally binding, they called her to personnel. We have good news, Comrade Szabad, the head of personnel announced with a grin, and Mother was promptly transferred to the company's new department to sew uniforms for the Workers' Militia. The militia had just been set up, hundreds of uniforms were needed, and the norms could not be met. She'd work for ten or twelve hours at a stretch sewing the gray uniforms with gray thread. She hated the Militia. Which is why they made the transfer. If she produced a reject, they took it out of her wages. Half a loaf of bread cost one forint.

I had an easier time of it. I just had to go to school. I couldn't be late, I couldn't be truant, I couldn't be given a mark of distinction or excellence, but by then, it made no difference. And needless to say, I couldn't attend the high school where Father had previously taught, just a vocational school. I studied to be a fitter and fashioned hammers from small steel rods. The shop overseer handed out the four-by-four-by-fourteen centimeter rods, we drew the pattern, placed the rod in a vice, and grated it until we reached the designated line and the hammer was ready. Then the sharp edges had to be filed down. The seniors drilled the eyes for the handles. Meanwhile, in another shop, the girls varnished the beechwood handles and affixed the hammer heads.

I liked making hammers. The shop was located in back of the phys ed yard, and in the afternoon the sun shone through the screen grate over the window and fell on the first work station, where I was. One work station was fitted with three clamps, and there was room for thirty-nine of us in the room. The grinders and the cutters were in the back. The sunlight didn't reach that far, so they had to work by lamplight. My left foot in front, my right hand gripping the file handle, my left palm placed on the end, and me leaning over it. My whole upper body pressed forward, and then pulled back the same way. Meanwhile, I didn't look out the window. As a matter of fact, that's what counted, that I didn't look out the window but concentrated on the iron shavings accumulating on the oil-stained workstation under the clamp, and the sunlight on them. If I take my eyes off them and break the rhythm, the black iron shavings begin to blind me, and not with yellow light like the lamps, but with white light. It's crucial to keep my eyes away from the window and keep my breathing steady. Leaning forward I exhale, leaning back, I inhale. If I managed to do this, then after a couple of minutes, I'd no longer hear the horrible bray of the thirty-nine files and I'd forget about the smell of the iron shavings and the used-up oil. The space and people around me ceased to exist. It's not that I was alone, it's that I didn't exist. It's not that I didn't exist, it's that I was the iron shavings.

A couple of years ago, while I was staying in the guest lodgings of a monastery in Kyoto, I realized that for three years, while my father was in prison, I was what you might call a meditating ironworker-monk. Or at least, this was true while I forged hammers. And now that my father is gone and so is Éva, and my camera is not within reach either—though I may stare at the cracks in the wall for hours on end—I can no longer turn into iron shavings. The precondition for a man to stop existing is that he exist first.

During one of our training sessions, I had to make a hammer. The shop overseer wore the same blue coat that we wore. He must have been around fifty. He had a paunch. Because of this paunch, we called him Pretzel. He told us every single time that these hammers would end up in shops and people would work with them, and we mustn't forget that they're meant for the home. If any of us filed past the line, we'd get slapped. He knew that my father was in prison, so he always gave me a lighter slap. His real name was József Berecz.

The vocational school was located on the outskirts of town, past the station. You could take a shortcut in the direction of Ace Worker Road and cross the tracks. If I hurried, the trip from home took forty-five minutes. We didn't have a bicycle. Father couldn't ride one because of his dislocated hip. When I was a child, the bread man we called St. Anthony taught me to ride one, but I haven't ridden a bicycle much since then.

A lot of the students had bicycles, Csepels or Ukraines. Once during break, between classes and shop, I borrowed someone's bike. There was a space in the cement wall of the phys ed yard in the back, and you could slip through it and head for the Backwater. Break lasted fifteen minutes. I had gone as far as the greenhouse, but couldn't make myself stop. I kept wheeling that damned bike on and on under the willows. My chest, I felt, was about to explode. The sun beat down on me and the wind found its way under my shirt. I was happy. I'd never felt as free.

When I reached the cement wall and pushed the bicycle through the opening, I found József Berecz standing there. The others were back in the shop. I held my head so that when he slapped me, his hand would land on the back of my head.

Don't try that again, he said.

All right, I said.

What were you thinking, you of all people? You want to get me fired?

No.

Fine. Go on in. But if you don't finish your hammer, I'm going to beat the daylight out of you.

I will, I said.

You're lucky to have a father like that, kid. You don't know how lucky you are.

(the assistant)

When my father and I first arrived at Keleti Station, the bridge at the far end of the avenue reaching from the station to the Danube led nowhere. For a long time, it was the longest suspension bridge in the world. The Germans blew it up, but the pylon on the Pest side of the river remained. At dawn, when the Buda side was obscured by fog, it looked like the gates of Hell. They'd left it there for that reason. It rose above the towers of the nearby church. The trams turned around under it. Sometimes I'd go and look at it.

Then they dismantled it and built a new bridge. It took three years, maybe four. I don't remember. But it didn't make me happy. If I stood facing this gate to nowhere, in one of the side streets to the left stood the photographer's studio where I used to take my film to be developed. I'd found the place by chance. Now and then, the man and I had some pretty awkward conversations, but at least he wasn't nasty. Going to the printer's night after night was pretty awful, so I thought I'd shoot a roll of film and take it there to be developed, and if he remembered me, and if we had another chat, perhaps I'd ask him if he could use an assistant.

The man wasn't there, just his assistant. He must've been my age or at most a year or two older. Since I was there, I decided I might as well remove the roll from the camera and give it to him. He put it in a drawer, wrote out the receipt, and told me three days. I stood around for a while, pondering if I should ask him how a person becomes an assistant. He raised his eyebrows and gave me an inquisitive glance. I left.

Three days later, when I came back to pick up the film, I found him there again. He gave me the negatives, looked me over, then offered the comment that if I own a Leica,

I might want to learn the proper technique, because my pictures are appreciably under-exposed. My stomach heaved, but then I said nothing, except that I'd try.

You can study up on it. There's plenty of literature on measuring light, he went on. And also, perspective and framing.

What is your problem, exactly, I asked.

He had no idea what I was talking about. Why do you think I have a problem? I was only suggesting that if someone feels the overpowering urge to hang an expensive camera around his neck, he might as well learn to take decent pictures.

You're right. I'll do that, I said, and walked out.

Hours later, I was still shaking all over. It was the first time someone had taken an instant disliking to me at first sight, and I was surprised that such a thing was possible, and that this phenomenon would probably accompany me all my life. I'd hoped to sleep an hour before work, but I couldn't close my eyes. I thought I'd go back the following day and tell him that my pictures are not appreciably underexposed, they're one f-stop underexposed, sometimes one-and-a-half. And then I thought that it didn't matter. The worst thing I could do was to go back there. Even if I took a perfectly exposed roll of film there, I could do nothing to undo those raised eyebrows and that contemptuous tone of voice.

I reflected that there's nothing to protect you when, with the pretended calm of intense hatred, someone says, I don't know what you're talking about, as if no one knows better than he.

I got out of bed and opened an American magazine, thumbed through it, then put it back in the drawer, thinking that it's at such times that men slap their wives. Or their children. In the bathroom, Father turned on the faucet. I could hear the water hit the bathtub. I knew that while he waited for the tub to fill, he'd be examining his oral cavity. I thought how he'd never slapped me in my life. I went to the bathroom. He was standing in front of the mirror. I told him that he should go see a doctor the next day. He gave me a blank look. For a second, he didn't know what I was talking about. Then he understood and said, fine. And I said he was right, there's no comparing this camera with the Zorki. And he said that he just wanted to make sure that the quality of my pictures should depend on me and not my camera. I asked if I should go with him to the clinic. He smiled and said, there's no need, son.

(Johanna)

I finally had a girlfriend. Johanna Vészi. We met at the bus stop. It started to rain and she held her umbrella over my head. I thanked her. She asked where I was going. I said that I was just out for a walk. Which would have been true if I didn't have the Leica in my pocket. Except that's nobody's business but mine. She said she was going to Liberation Square to meet her girlfriend in a café. She said I could go with her if I liked. It's raining too hard for a walk. I said I didn't want to be in the way. She said I wouldn't be in the way. She just had to give her friend a book. Besides, she didn't want me to get soaked to the skin.

She wore a gray three-quarter-length coat and a pair of thick tights. White. Her hair reached down to her shoulder. Her face was narrow, her features regular, undistinctive. At least, that's what it looked like in the light of the street lamps that had just been turned on. Only her eyes betrayed something demonic, though what we often mistake for demonic is merely that moment in the struggle between yearning and taboo when yearning gains the upper hand.

Her girlfriend was already at the café. Johanna introduced us, then asked her friend to accompany her to the restroom. Her name was Enikő. She had on the same white tights as Johanna. Their coats were also similar. None of us took off our coats, just unbuttoned them. Because of the thick cigarette smoke, the woman behind the counter turned on the fan. Even their gestures were similar. They moved to the dictate of some inner voice. They didn't move at the same time, but they moved the same way. Only their faces bore no resemblance. Johanna's friend had a beautiful, if stern, face. Cold. I knew why she'd been called away to the bathroom. When they came back, Enikő asked if Johanna had brought her the book. Then she quickly finished her soft drink and apologized for having to rush off, she had a ticket to the Pushkin movie theater.

When we were alone, I said that there was no need for her to send her friend away. She drummed her fingers nervously on her bottle of soda, then said that she hadn't sent her away. Then she started to talk about Enikő, that she's her best friend and they'd known each other since they were kids. They attended the same secondary school.

Which one?

She drummed her fingers again and said, the Catholic Girls School.

I didn't know there was one.

It's the best high school around. Not easy, but they teach you everything.

For instance?

Everything.

The rain stopped, the Leica was in my coat pocket, and I'd have liked to leave, but felt that I couldn't. I thought that pretty soon she'd ask where I went to school and then she'd be disappointed and then I could leave at last. Or maybe I'd just tell her that I have a girlfriend.

Isn't Enikő beautiful, she asked.

I didn't notice, I lied. For a second it occurred to me that I should say that as far as I'm concerned, she's more beautiful than her friend, but couldn't get myself to do it.

Well, I should take it from her. Enikő is one of the most beautiful women in the city.

She's cold, I said, and that, at least, was true. And then something happened that made the chair sway under me and blur my vision of the interior.

You're mistaken about her, she said. Enikő is the one who taught me all about kissing.

There sat across from me a girl in a gray coat and thick white tights who had attended a Catholic school, and who'd been taught everything. It hadn't been twenty minutes since she held her umbrella over my head. Except for my name, she knew nothing about me, not even that I was hiding a camera in my coat pocket. I took a sip, then drummed my fingers on the bottle. I had no idea what to do next.

She didn't mean to embarrass me, she said. And that I mustn't think anything bad, this happened years ago, they were still children, practically. And that she told me only so I'd see that when I think that someone is cold as ice, it's nothing but appearance.

She hadn't embarrassed me, I said. It's just that if she were to tell this to someone after they'd kissed a hundred times, I'd understand, but I was a complete stranger, she didn't know anything about me.

You're wrong again. I know everything about you. Everything that matters.

Are you sure?

Yes, I'm sure. From the moment I saw you pull your coat tighter around you in the rain. I'm sure because you're exactly like my brother.

I said nothing. Then, that I couldn't be exactly.

No. You are exactly like him. Even your first names are the same.

And did you tell your brother as well that your girlfriend taught you all about kissing?

She said nothing. Then she said, no. Her brother had defected six years ago.

Not six years ago, but in '56, I thought.

Where to, I asked.

She didn't know. He'd severed all ties with the family. Once they heard that he was in New York, but she's sure he's not in New York. Her brother had gone much further than that.

Where to?

Papua New-Guinea. Or Cape Town. The further the better.

From here even Vienna seems far, I said, and it's less than three-hundred kilometers.

Vienna may be far from Budapest, but not far enough from their family, she said, then fell silent again. Then after a short pause she added, my father is an animal.

I didn't know what to say. Then I said the rain had stopped. If she felt like it, we could go for a walk. We walked towards Kálvin Square. When we reached the Literary Museum. Adél Selyem came to mind, and her father. I should take a picture of Johanna Vészi here, in her gray coat and white tights, I thought, and reached for the Leica in my pocket, but couldn't bring myself to take it out. I didn't want this woman, who thinks she knows everything about me, to know anything at all about me. If she were to ask me something, that'd be different. Then I'd tell her.

Why is he an animal?

I thought you'd never ask.

It'd be pretty hard not to ask.

And even harder to answer. But he's an animal, take my word for it. My brother was right to leave at eighteen. I'd like to leave.

Where to?

Anywhere. The moon. The stars. But please don't ask about my father. I can't talk about him now. Why don't you take my hand instead, she said, then took mine in hers.

We'd gone past the dark Museum Garden and she was still talking about her brother András, and there was nothing demonic about her anymore. At the front door of a house on Szentkirályi Street she said, this is where I live. I thanked her for the umbrella. She asked if she would see me again. I said that it depended on her. And she said no, not on her, and pulled me inside the front door.

She clung to me so tight, she sucked the air out of my lungs. She groped down to my throat with her tongue and pressed my hand to her groin. I could feel the heavy tights getting wet, then I felt her grabbing my member through the fabric of my pants. More, more, more, she panted with every movement until her body went into a spasm and my pants were soaked through as well. It was terrible. The way I grabbed her flesh, the way I tore her cotton tights off her, the way the world turned dark and collapsed over me, that was the worst of all.

She panted heavily as she leaned against the peeling plaster. I gathered her coat around her.

Well, did Enikő teach me how to kiss?

She did, I said.

Will you come by again tomorrow?

I will.

You do realize that you can't sleep with me.

I know, I said.

My family is like that. A girl, if she's Catholic, either flees to the end of the universe or remains a virgin until she marches down the aisle.

At the printer's that night, I made mistake after mistake gathering the sheets. You'd think it was hardly possible. I gathered some sheets double, and skipped others entirely. During the first cigarette break I felt sick and went to throw up, but couldn't. Gizella Vámos told me to go home.

The next day we met in the same café on Liberation Square. Going to see Adél Selyem in the new housing estate would have made more sense. She wore white tights, just like the day before. We had a soft drink, and she talked to me about how much she hates her mother.

I asked her why.

Because she's a coward who puts up with everything. She even put up with her father chasing István from their home. Also, at night he drinks himself stiff with cheap Lánchíd cognac.

I asked who István was.

Her brother. She told me so yesterday.

I thought he was András.

Both. István András.

I'm just András, I said.

The light was on in Father's room. Until we were inside, it hadn't even occurred to me that he'd be home and that I must say something. It hadn't occurred to me either that except for himself and Kornél, no one had ever been to my room. I told Johanna to wait in the kitchen.

I knocked on Father's door and said I'd brought someone with me.

He asked if he should go. I said no. And he shouldn't be mad at me, I'll try to arrange it better next time. He said I needn't bother, he doesn't mind, he's glad that I'm not alone. I thought how I wouldn't mind if he weren't alone either, but there's no way I'd tell him that for as long as I live. Never. He asked if I wanted to introduce them to each other and I said next time.

I found Johanna sitting in the kitchen just as I'd left her. When we went to my room, she sat on the bed. She didn't even look around. I asked if she'd like to meet my father. She said she wouldn't like to meet either my father or my mother. I said fine. And I couldn't meet anyone in her family either, ever. Enikő is the only one who knows about me.

And then I heard my father's cane knock-knock along the hall after all, and the front door closing, too. I asked Johanna if she'd like a glass of wine. She said yes. My glass was on the side table, and I went and got her one from the kitchen. I asked if she'd like me to turn off the light. She said no, because she'd like to see me.

After a while, we settled into a routine, and she came to see me twice a week. We didn't even meet anywhere else. Her glass was on the side table. I poured, she got undressed and stretched out on the bed. My father locked the door and left. We kissed, then she had me sit on her belly so she could watch the spunk cover her from her breasts to her belly button. Meanwhile, with her other hand she pleasured her clitoris. We climaxed together. Her body arched like a bridge, then collapsed into itself. She screamed like someone falling from a great height. For a brief second or two, her face was beautiful, as if she weren't the same woman who'd come to my room just a little while before and who'd be leaving soon. These seconds made it worth my while to wait for our Tuesdays and Fridays, to wait for her to speak up at last and ask where she was and who I am. Or let her not ask, just say something other than that she longs to be among the stars and hates her father and her mother, her schoolmates, and the Catholics. Then she smeared me all over her. Her breasts and belly were shiny with slime, then she watched, like in biology class when they study cell division through a microscope, the sperm crack as it dried. She never said, but I think that she didn't take a bath at my place so she could take the ungodliness under her blouse home to her father and mother. She usually stayed an hour.

Kornél asked why I do it. I said I didn't know. Whereas I knew. He said that she's a confused girl. She may not even have a brother. She can't love me, and why not admit it, I don't love her either. And I'll hate myself more and more every time we meet. And I said I know.

She always gave two short rings, so that my father knew not to answer the bell. Then once, when I heard the two rings, I put my camera on the side table. I hadn't planned it, and I wasn't thinking of what I was doing. This was the only time she asked me something. She asked why it was there. I said that I'd like to take a picture of her face while we made love. She said fine.

Had I expected anything at all, this is not what I'd expected. Not by a longshot. Had I thought it through, I'd have probably put the Leica away as I'd done for the past three months. I expected to see the same face as I'd been seeing before. She threw off her clothes and wrapped herself around me. What's keeping me from taking those pictures? she asked.

I sat up and picked up the camera. And then she went wild. More. Look, she said, and pushed me off of her. Look at me, all of me. I want it, she said, and grabbed herself between the thighs. As she lost all restraint, she kept repeating, look at me, look at me. She probably didn't even notice that I'd turned on the reading lamp as well, and that I kept pressing the shutter, that I even changed rolls, or that I was concentrating only on her face. That I kept looking into her misty eyes through the view finder, waiting for her to perish.

When she recovered, she asked if I'd like it, too. I said not now. She got dressed and left. For the first time I opened the window and watched her walk away. I cried. Then I went to the kitchen, mixed the chemicals together and developed the rolls of film. I hung them in the window so they'd dry faster. Each of the pictures was blurred and underexposed. I chose three and without making contacts I enlarged them on hard paper, then fixed them to the drawing board with tape. The next day Kornél came to see me. He said he didn't know that it was possible to take a picture of the moment when the soul leaves a person. I said, thank you.

They were really good pictures.

Then on Friday, when I was waiting for the bell to ring twice, someone came banging on the door. Fortunately, my father had already left. I asked who it was. A woman said I should open the door. It was Enikő. Johanna Vészi was standing on the landing further down without moving. Enikő pushed me aside and came in.

Just what do you think you're doing? If you think you're going to ruin my friend's life with your perversion you'd better think again.

I said I don't have any perversions and I'm not ruining anybody's life.

You bet you're not, she said and demanded that I hand over the photographs. We went to my room and I took them off the drawing board.

You're sick, she said. A perverse animal.

I tore them to shreds and handed them to her. You better leave now, I said. She slammed the door and I never saw her and Johanna Vészi again.

Fifteen years later, when Éva defected, she stole the negatives, among other things. For weeks I didn't realize that they were gone. When they invited me to America on the occasion of the first exhibition of my life, I saw Johanna Vészi again hanging on the wall of the gallery, framed and with a price affixed. I told them to remove the pictures, but Éva said that I couldn't do that here.

(the isle of the dead)

Checkmate, I said.

And so it is.

Indeed it is.

You bet it is.

Just don't congratulate me. It would sound high-minded, coming from you.

I wasn't going to. Still, let's order some chocolate mousse cake. We deserve a treat.

Chocolate mousse case is expensive, I said.

But this is a special occasion, he said and waved to Évike, and Évike waved back as if to say hold on a minute.

I folded up the board and we packed away the chess pieces. Kornél drew a notch on the inner side of the board.

This was game number what? I asked.

Eighty-six, he said. I hadn't expected you to beat me before we hit a hundred, but eventually I knew you'd beat me with one hand tied behind your back.

What makes you so sure about such things?

I'm not sure about such things, but I was sure about this particular thing. And I was sure because, unlike you, I grew up with chess puzzles, and so, unlike you, I know not only that I'm no good at chess, I also know how bad I am. But as you see, I was wrong again, and I can admit it. So please. . . .

Two chocolate mousse cakes, Évike, I said.

Is it a holiday of some sort?

Yes. Also, please bring us two kitchen knives.

Are you out of your mind? Really?

I glanced at Kornél. He laughed, then told Évike that two desert forks would suffice.

You're nuts, the both of you, Évike said. Then we watched her walk away to place our order.

I don't think she ever walked away without us looking after her. She was blond, around thirty, and she tied her apron tight around the waist, and wore her hair gathered in a ponytail. I thought she must be the daughter of a Russian liberator. Kornél calculated that in that case she'd have to be younger than eighteen. He always paid more attention to such details than I did. Évike was just as beautiful when she came toward us, except we didn't dare look at her the same way. I venture to say that we were both a little in love with Évike, except we didn't believe that this is all there was to love.

She placed the two chocolate mousse cakes and the two glasses of soda on the table in front of us, then, making a show of it, the two desert forks. These are instruments of murder as well, she said, except it's a more painful way to go.

We shall use them strictly according to regulation, I ventured.

You're a lot less likely to believe that than your friend, she said.

You see, Kornél said.

You know what I see? I see that with that innocent look of yours you lead everyone down the garden path. Unless I'm somehow mistaken, you were the one who was all over the place when Évike came over.

And unless I'm somehow mistaken, you were the one asking for the knives.

After we wolfed down our chocolate mousse cakes, I pulled out a postcard from my pocket.

Look what I found, I said.

One side bore a reproduction of Bocklin's *The Isle of the Dead*, the other an address and *Where are you?*

What's this, he asked.

Adél Selyem, I said.

I don't recommend you go.

Of course I'm not going.

You'd be wiser asking Évike to marry you. Buy a Moskvich, and take loads of pictures of her until she gets old and fat. But you're through with Adél Selyem, right?

I just said I wouldn't go over there.

Wait until someone send you *Pilgrimage to the Isle of Cythera* rather than *The Isle of the Dead*.

I just said I'm not going.

Fine. I heard you. Except, I know you're going.

What do you think I am? A psychological cripple?

Of course not. Just the opposite. You may not be one, but you sure as hell know what it's like. You attract people with mental problems like spoiled meat attracts flies.

Or they attract me, I said.

No. It was Évike who pulled you in. As for the psychological cripples, you're simply curious. You want to reassure yourself that you're not like them.

Okay. I'm not going.

(the cabbage)

Mother and I were in the kitchen, having dinner. The blinds in Father's room were down. We didn't use the living room much. At first Mother would set the table there now and then, but soon we found ourselves mostly in the kitchen. She was tired, and it was more comfortable in the kitchen. Thanks to a friend of hers, she got hold of the newspaper that ran that picture of Father. She knew some English and tried to read the article, and what she didn't know I looked up in the dictionary. There was nothing of real interest in the piece. They praised the revolution, that's all.

She couldn't figure out how they managed to identify Father. After all, his face wasn't showing. He's just leaning over. Two of his colleagues are clearly visible in the background, but all that you see of Father is that a man is leaning down in the middle of the Grand Boulevard, placing a plate on the road. At first, I couldn't figure out how either. Then I noticed that his cane was hanging from his arm.

She was proud of Father, not that she had a choice. When half the teaching staff headed for Budapest in an old, discarded bus and stopped in front of our house and Father grabbed his coat, that's when I first heard Mother shout. She held onto the coat and screamed into Father's face that he was lame, he didn't have to do this. And Father said, oh yes, I do, we all have to. I was standing in the hall with them. Not only was this the first time I heard Mother shout like that, it was also the first time I heard my mother use the word 'lame.'

After the bus left, Mother sat down in the kitchen and started crying. Actually, she wasn't crying, but her tears began to flow and she smoked one cigarette after another. She smoked three or four cigarettes before she realized that I was there. She said, forgive me, son, I didn't mean to say that about your father. And I said there was nothing to forgive, because she was right to say what she did. No, she said.

There were three men at the trial, Father, Zakariás, and Kövesdi. The accused. Father said, excuse me, I'd like to point out that as we know, they weren't mines, just soup plates from the takeout place around the corner. Is that so, the public prosecutor said. Am I right in thinking that you wanted to make fun of the Soviet Army? This is how eighteen months turned into three years. Of the fourteen teachers who were on that bus, nine got off. Tordai, who drove it, got six years, the others eighteen months or three years. After two and a half years, Zakariás died in prison. They notified his family only when his sentence was up.

We were just trying to make sense of the article in the American paper when Aunt Erzsike Kormos came over. She lived two houses down and was tiny. You'd think she had stopped growing when she was twelve, though later she gradually turned gray and accumulated deep wrinkles. She permed her hair with rubber-padded tin springs, which added five centimeters to her height, and another half a centimeter was added thanks to the thick rubber soles the shoemaker glued to her sandals.

They had made stuffed cabbage, and she'd brought some over for us. Two servings for me, two for my mother. After Father was locked up, once or twice a week she'd knock on our door and bring us cake, or something else. We were pleased, and we were not. Had she asked fewer questions, we'd have been more pleased, I think. She didn't scare us, just her questions. For instance, are they going to relocate us? No. Thank God they didn't think of it, and let's hope they won't, she said.

She was worried about what would become of Father's leg in prison if he couldn't use his cane, and what would become of me if I didn't go to college? And what would happen to Mother, if they threw her out of the clothing factory, what would happen to us once Father was released, and what happens if Kádár turns out worse than Rákosi? She wasn't an informer, she was sincerely in search of answers, just like us. It's just that those two portions of stuffed cabbage couldn't compensate for the anxiety her questions stirred in us.

But there was something even worse than her questions – the circumstance that she knew someone who knew someone who knew someone who knew one of the prison guards, who was a good person. Erzsike, dear, I'm not sending any letters. I can't take a chance. What if that prison guard isn't such a good person after all? Then my husband will get into even deeper trouble. And I was thinking that this was a little like when our blind beggar wouldn't eat the chicken wings, but I kept my mouth shut.

When the porch door opened, Mother quickly slipped the newspaper under the pillow on the stool. The dictionary was still on top of the table. Aunt Erzsike placed the small pot with the four cabbage rolls on the table, then asked what the book was. Mother's lips began to tremble, because she'd have to tell a lie, which she hated as much as the jackets of the Workers' Militia. Before she could speak, I quickly said that it's an English dictionary, Aunt Erzsike, and I'm learning words from it in the evening. Good for you, she said, you should never stop learning. Then she took a deep breath and said that she sent word to Father through the prison guard just the same. She didn't do it in writing, just verbally to avoid any problems, but she sent word that we're all right, and Father sent word that he was all right, too, that he misses us and sends his love. That's all she wanted to say.

Mother's eyes filled with tears, then after a while I said, thank you very much, Aunt Erzsike. Thank you very much for the good news. And for the cabbage. I'll return the pot tomorrow. Then I saw her out and locked the garden gate.

I'm going to kill that old woman. May God forgive me, but I'm going to kill her. I'm going to strangle her with my bare hands, Mother said.
Maybe he really did send a message, I said.
How could he, son? Through whom?
She meant no harm, I said.
No harm, showing up with her cabbage and spewing a bunch of nonsense?
We haven't tasted it yet, I said. It may be worth it. And then Mother finally laughed and we spooned the cabbage out of the pot and decided that we wouldn't do away with Aunt Erzsike after all, and when she said that this cabbage is even worth an actual letter from Father, we screamed with laughter so hard, the cabbage spilled out of our mouths.

(the exhibition)

I went to an exhibition. I read about it in one of the papers at the printer's. A celebration of the past. Then the following day I learned that for them, the past began with the first of May fifty-seven years before.

It was pouring, but I had an umbrella with me and I was there by six. The place was packed. I was afraid they might not let me in because I didn't have an invitation, but nobody bothered with me. At the opening, some president or other held forth about the responsibility of the photographer and the role of photography in shaping society. He heaped praise on the Hungarian art photographers for their strenuous efforts in recording the strenuous exertions of the workers, the peasants, and the intellectuals, along with the Hungarian countryside and other industrial complexes. He compared Hungarian photography to capitalist photography and concluded that the scales are tipped in favor of socialist photography, because unlike capitalist photography, socialist photography is not decadent. He then greeted the photographers who were present. Some people sniggered at the mention of the Hungarian countryside and other "industrial complexes," but they were clearly satisfied with the rest of the speech, especially the part when the president tipped the scales in favor of Hungarian photography. I had no problem with *the landscape and other industrial complexes*. A mistake like that is unfortunate, but just about anyone can slip up that way, especially in front of a hundred people. On the other hand, the repeated mention of art photographers got my goat. To my mind, it was not quite so clear cut that every good photograph is, at the same time, art, though admittedly, I'd have been hard put to say what it took for photography to turn into art.

I tried to guess who in the crowd might be photographers. When people started circulating, they congratulated a lot of them. One related the circumstances of how the photo was taken, how he was lowered into a pit, another talked about what the old woman peeling onions told him, and another said how friendly the famous pianist turned out to be. Here and there I stopped and listened. Some of them were likeable, others less so. I tried to imagine us having a conversation. I failed, even in the case of those who seemed likeable. I thought that if I knew just one of them, I wouldn't feel like such an alien among all those photographers. But I was wrong, because this sense of isolation wasn't alleviated even later on, when I was the one being congratulated in a variety of foreign languages.

I looked at the photographs. On the whole, they were good. Almost every one of them contained something of interest, a quality that was wholly missing from my own. One of them I couldn't even figure out. It showed a mailman riding his bike along the street of one of the new housing estates. I studied it for quite a while, trying to figure out what made it so odd. Then I realized that what the photograph showed we never could have seen from street level. The walls of the prefab buildings were perfectly vertical. The parallel lines did not tend toward each other. I decided that I'd check up on the technique in one of the books at home, but then forgot all about it.

There were pictures of circus acrobats, horse herds, smelters, children and old women, high-voltage wires, and ballerinas. There were subjects that I'd photographed myself, except mine were terrible. For instance, there was a beautiful picture of a woman watering her flowers behind a lace curtain.

All in all, the president was right in his opening remarks. The photographs showed Hungarian reality as it was. Together like this, the many flickering side-lights and shadows, children, horses, peasants, old women, blinding show drifts and falling leaves, lamp lights in the dark, all that is life incarnate, formed into a gray morass, as if the Danube had emptied its waters into the sea, leaving only its muddy bed with its occasional flickering puddles behind.

I tried to imagine my photos of Johanna Vécsi on the wall, but failed. They didn't fit in.

As I studied one of the pictures, a woman came over to me and said, isn't the wrinkled face of this old woman beautiful? I said it was. She must have been around fifty, she had bleached hair, and she stood so close to me, I could smell her face powder. She was about to say something else about the beauty of old age, but a man took her arm. Come, Ági dear, let's go.

And then I found myself standing in front of a picture. On the left Gagarin was sitting with János Kádár's wife. Behind them Gypsy musicians with champagne glasses, looking at the dancers and smiling. The caption under the picture said, Yuri Gagarin's wife dancing with Comrade Selyem. Among the dancers in the back I spotted Adél Selyem. I thought I'd suffocate.

(the long sleep)

My maternal grandmother was the other crazy person in the family. In honor of the millennium of the founding of the Hungarian State, my grandfather, the architect Oszkár Kiepski, changed his name to the Hungarian-sounding Hollós, because he felt that the Poles were every bit as duty-bound to be patriotic Hungarians as the Jews and the Armenians. Then in a side street one day, the Hungarian people, led by People's Commissar Béla Kun, accidentally trampled him underfoot. He had just enough strength to drag himself home, but by the time the family physician arrived, he'd expired. And so, not long after my paternal great-grandmother, my maternal grandmother Júlia Hollós also went out of her mind, except she didn't hoard either horse meat or petroleum. She just fell asleep and entered another world.

She slept through the Hungarian Soviet Republic, the entry of the Romanian Army, the Trianon Peace Treaty, the White Terror, and the Vienna Accord. She was still sleeping when Miklós Horthy attempted to break with the Axis powers. In her dreamworld she idolized her husband, while in real life, her children idolized her. In the space of just one year, Father introduced himself to her three times, the last time as her son-in-law. But Júlia Hollós did all this with such somnolent charm, that no one thought ill of her. What worried her the most throughout the war was that they were ruining poor Oszkár's beautiful buildings. Even the birth of her grandson in the pantry didn't stir her from her slumber. She woke up on the second of February, 1945, when the soldiers pushed the sideboard aside and shot her son in the head. She managed to stay awake the entire afternoon. Then in the evening, she died from shock.

I know of no other crazy people in the family, though there, in front of the photo of Comrade Selyem dancing with Valentina Gagarin, I thought that I'd lose it myself. On the way home it was still pouring, and the raindrops were knocking against the black canvas of my umbrella. My brain picked up the rhythm – on the left Mrs. János Kádár, on the right Comrade Selyem, in the middle Gagarin. On the left Mrs. János Kádár, on the right Adél Selyem, in the middle Comrade Selyem. On the left Mrs. János Kádár, on the right Adél Selyem, in the middle me. On the left sleeping pills, on the right the existentialists, in the middle a red flag.

(in the library)

The next morning, I asked Father whether he'd mind if I went to see him in Rákos around noon. I said that I wanted to see the pictures in the papers. He was surprised, but pleased. The last time I sat in the reading room of a library was when Mother was still a librarian. Of course I don't mind, son, he said.

The trip to Rákos took over an hour and a half. I looked at the ongoing construction. Housing estate, no man's land, housing estate. Further off, some sort of garden city. I walked at least ten minutes from the stop. There'd been a broken watermain some-where, a long plank led from the elementary school to the road. As the children walked over it, they kept shoving each other, and some of them ended up ankle deep in water. They loved it.

Apart from Father, two college professors, a mining engineer, and Sára Rónai also worked at the library. Sára was the only bona fide librarian. One of the professors and the mining engineer had been in jail, the other professor had merely been fired. After their release, if they had a bit of luck plus a diploma, plus connections, people could find employment in such remote libraries instead of having to work in factory warehouses.

When I opened the door, I couldn't see Father anywhere. The man behind the counter said that I should check the reading room. He was just arranging some books. When he saw me, he was embarrassed. He probably hadn't thought about how it would feel to see each other there. Nor had I, for that matter.

Before he introduced me to the others he asked me to go with him through the emergency exit to the yard in the back to have a cigarette, where he told me who was who. The professor that was seated was probably an informer. Be careful with him. The mining engineer is okay. The other professor, who was behind the counter, was a professor of philosophy, he's not all there, poor man, you couldn't talk to him about anything besides picking mushrooms. They'd executed three of his students. I asked how someone who'd been in prison could become an informer. He said, it's easy. They're probably the easiest to rope in, son.

There was no ashtray, so we stamped out the butts on the narrow cement walk, then we flicked them into the grass with the toes of our shoes. Then before he opened the door he added that I'd also be meeting the head librarian, who is a very decent person. He had her to thank for his work in the library. Once inside, he introduced me to the philosophy professor and the mining engineer. The chief librarian and the informer were at lunch.

I asked Father for the issues of various dailies stretching back several years and sat down with them in the reading room. I wanted to find out about Comrade Selyem. For some reason, I thought that the papers would tell me. Although a part of me knew full well that they wouldn't, I felt that I'd been cheated, defiled, raped. I felt like taking the first bus to Óbuda, and then I'd lash out at her, tear her apart, and it's no use her begging and screaming, I wouldn't let her reach that fucking rag.

There I sat in the reading room of a library in the middle of nowhere, and just as scientists look at cell division through a microscope, that's how my crystal-clear mind observed my anger, bitterness, revulsion and rage turn into sexual desire.

I asked Father where the bathroom was. He told me. When I entered, I didn't turn on the light. Then I went back to my place. Across from me, an elderly man was reading Thomas Mann.

I found nothing about Comrade Selyem, not even a hint that he existed, and after a while, I gave up. Or rather, I lost interest. I didn't want to have to go to the bathroom of a library like that ever again. I started reading the news, both old and new. A sightseeing airplane crashed in Lumumba Street. The Citadella has been renovated. They've started reconstruction on Elizabeth Bridge. They'd installed a television in the Corvin Department Store. And for security reasons, they've secured passage from East to West

Berlin. When I got to the point where they'd executed Eichmann in Israel and scattered his ashes into the sea, I suddenly realized that it wasn't Comrade Selyem who didn't exist. I didn't exist. When Father and I got off the train and were met by the lurking darkness of Keleti Station, I fell asleep for years, just like my maternal grandmother had done many years before me.

(the baptism)

So then, as I said, one night it occured to my mother that during the upheaval caused by the war, she forgot to baptise me. She asked me what I thought. I said it made no difference. I saw that this hurt her feelings, so I said that to my mind it made no difference, because I had taken it for granted that I'd been baptized, so I felt baptized, so whether they baptize me now or not, I'd be the same person I've been all along. The only way I wouldn't be the same person is if I'd been a communist. But I wasn't. At which she laughed and said that I was right, at least, insofar as I take communists as my point of reference, but if it's Christianity, then at most, I'm a sympathizer.

I said I didn't mind. But what if she remembered wrong? Maybe I was baptized. Living, as we were, in the middle of the war had caused her to forget my baptism. Wasn't that more likely than that she had forgotten to baptize me altogether?

She pondered this for a while then said that she wouldn't have forgotten, it's out of the question. It's like forgetting your wedding.

You can forget anything.

No, son, there are things you never forget. You may survive it or forgive it, you might regret it or make amends, you might even deny it, but you never forget it.

I think you're wrong. I think it's possible to forget.

That takes a sick person, son, a person suffering from the saddest of all illnesses, the fear of reality.

Basically, I have to accept what you remember on faith.

You're being impertinent, she said.

No, I'm not. But the fact is, I'm at the mercy of your memory because, let's admit it, there's no way I could remember my own baptism.

At which point she sighed. Poor child. Would you like another slice of Hitler bacon as compensation?

Yes. Aunt Erzsike brought us the Hitler bacon. Their garden was full of plums, which they made the Hitler bacon out of.

When she put it in front of me, she said that I deserved it only in part, because it's not quite as I said, my being at her mercy, because people remember a lot more than they think. There are even prenatal memories.

She saw that this got me thinking, so she gave me five minutes to figure out what prenatal means. She said she'd fire up the furnace in the meanwhile, so we'd have hot water to take a bath, but first she took a spoon, grinned, and scooped out the corner of the jam.

I heard her splitting the logs on the tile floor of the bathroom to heat up the furnace. Luckily, right before they took Father away, the wind uprooted the pear tree in the back, and we chopped it up and gathered up the dried branches, so there was plenty of kindling.

Have you figured it out? she asked when she came back.

Yes, I said. But I don't have any memories like that. The first thing I can remember is the peacock.

A gleam came to her eyes. She said, see, with this peacock, she was no longer out on a limb, and I wasn't at her mercy, because if I remember the peacock, I could just as easily remember my baptism. Provided that it ever took place. Except, it didn't. At which point, I pulled the plate closer to me and covered it with my hand, before she could take another chunk out of the jam.

Fine, I said. Let's get it over with. But the risk is yours.

What risk?

If you ask me, being christened twice is a mortal sin. If you can't get married twice, you can't get baptised twice.

She's going to check, but she's sure that being baptised twice or any number of times is not a mortal sin.

Eventually we agreed that she'd go talk to the priest the next day.

Father András was around eighty, and he was in charge of the small Franciscan church up in the vineyard. Actually, he was the only Franciscan. In 1950 the big yellow building of the order had been nationalized, and they moved in the employees of the waterworks. Only Father András's cell remained. It wasn't much good as an apartment, because it opened up to the sacristy. The church was a way off, but from time to time we walked up there, mostly at Christmas and on Good Friday.

Once, Comrade Varga told my father that it's ill-advised for members of the teaching staff to go to the church on the main square, whereupon Father said, no problem, Comrade, though the other day the Lord said that it's also ill-advised to be a Party Secretary. Whereupon, red as a lobster, Varga yelled, you're going to burn your fingers one of these days, András. You have no idea how I keep covering for you, the chances I take, solely out of respect for your district physician father. Who, let us not forget, saved your life, Father said. That's right, Comrade Varga countered, except, you're abusing your position. Are you bent on ruining me? Whereupon Father said, fine, from now on I won't be going to the parish church on the main square. That's when we first went up the hill to the Franciscans for midnight mass.

Father András was unrelenting. He chastised the faithful every chance he got. It wasn't much fun, I can tell you that. When we slipped into our winter coats before setting out, mother always said, come, son, let's go for our slaps in the face. Then on our way home, we counted the number of slaps. At times Father tried to make excuses for the old man, saying that basically, he's right. But he was alone with his reasoning. I don't want anyone scaring me with the fires of Gehenna on Christmas Eve, Mother said, and especially not because the church is empty. Idiots that we are, we go, and right away, a slap to the right, and a slap to the left, while those that have enough brains to stay home get off scot free. Father had to concede that what Mother said was justified.

On the other hand, we were secretly grateful to Varga because, for one thing, the masses held by the preacher on the main square were so boring that Christ himself fell asleep on his cross, and for another, our only real objection to Father András's fiery sermons was that we got our share of the fire. Also, we enjoyed our walk up to the vineyard, especially in winter, when the main square was one big salted pond of slush, while the snow up on the hill was pristine.

True to her promise, the very next day, Mother went to see the priest, but when she came back, she was fuming mad. She said that she refused to speak to that senile old man ever again. Instead of welcoming her, he berated her as if she were a naughty child. A good thing he didn't strike her palm with a switch, like in school, because I hadn't been baptized.

I asked her what's next, and she said, nothing. They had agreed on Sunday morning. Let's go, get it over with.

I asked what I'd have to do, and she said, you'd have to be about eighteen months old. She was awfully mad at the old Franciscan.

On Saturday night she washed my white shirt, but it didn't dry in time. She tried ironing it, but the iron was too hot and the collar turned yellow. I wanted to say that we could go some other time, but I saw that she was looking into space. Had she been mad, really mad, that'd have been a lot better. But as things now stood, she just lit a cigarette, took a couple of drags, then put it out, then she took a big breath and went to Father's room. It was dark inside, except for a bit of pale light that filtered in through the slits in the blind. I heard the light being switched on, then the creaking of the wardrobe as she opened it, then the hangers being pushed aside on the copper bar. Then I heard her stop as she considered. This is his gray suit. And the black. And here are the shirts. And his winter coat.

Put this on, son, she said, and handed me a white shirt.
It's too big for me.
Slip into it. Let's see.
I slipped into it, and she helped button it at the neck.
A perfect fit, she said.
It was lovely weather, a lovely summer morning in spring. The locust trees lining the road leading to the Franciscans were almost in bloom.

I liked this church. It was as deserted as a hangar. Centuries before the Calvinists had whitewashed the whole thing, and it subsequently stayed that way. Only the altar piece and the Stations of the Cross were put back, and a statue of St. Francis talking to the birds.

I stopped by the altar, while Mother went to the sacristy. I heard the priest grumble that it was against the rules.

My husband is in jail. I'm not going to ask anyone to come and be a godparent, Mother said.

Up above, the sun shone right through God's eye.

There we stood side by side, me in Father's shirt, Mother in a white dress. I bent my head, and in the name of the Father, the Son, and the Holy Ghost the old man sprinkled water on me. I thought how I'd forgotten to clean my shoes. Then my eyes rested on Mother's legs as she stood by me on the dark stone slabs of the church in her snow-white sandals.

When we came out of the Lord's hangar, I could tell that she was relieved and happy. We then went to the café near the church, at the top of the path.

Down below, on the corner of the main square, a man was heading toward us. When he passed, he said, why aren't you in jail, fascist whore?

I didn't understand what he was talking about. And as soon as I did, I wanted to go after him and kill him.

Mother grabbed my hand. Don't you dare, son.

(Mária's death)

Mária died. She fell asleep. The countess waited until seven a.m., then sat on the side of her bed and said, Mária, please. Get up. It's time you got up. Pull yourself together this instant, you hear? Then she came over and asked me to go down to the tobacconist and call an ambulance. She stood in the door with a coat flung over her nightgown. She had never been to my place before. I took her inside. She followed me like a child. She stopped in the middle of the room, looking for a place to sit. She then sat down on the piano bench. I said I'd be back soon and she should wait for me.

The man on duty asked in what capacity I was calling.
     We're neighbors, I said.
     Doesn't the ailing person have relatives?
     She's not ailing, she's dead.
     That's not for you to decide. Why doesn't a relative call?
     Because she's in a state of shock, I said.
     Is that so? And how would you know, if I may ask.
     I know, because she's in my room, playing the piano, asshole! That's how. I can hear the Bösendorfer even from down here at the tobacconist.
     Will you send an ambulance for the body already?

I also heard her on the staircase as I came back. It may have been Chopin. I can't remember. When I entered, she stopped.
     Forgive me. I didn't even ask if it's all right.
     Of course it's all right, I said.
     Bring me a spoon of sugar, dear. And a glass of water.
     I did. She scooped out some sugar from the paper bag and gulped it down, then drank the water, and then her tears began to flow.

I am so ashamed of myself, she said. I am so ashamed, and the tears began to flow from the corners of her eyes down the furrows of her wrinkled face onto the collar of her winter coat.

Why are you ashamed, Éva?

Because I am afraid, she said, and her body convulsed with sobs. Because I wanted to be the first to die. I thought that I deserved as much.

I walked up to her and put an arm around her shoulder.

Good God, I am so scared. It's so unfair. The Lord is right, not leaving such decisions to us.

When she stopped crying, I saw her home. Mária was still lying in the same position, as if she'd just fallen asleep, her hands clasped over the forget-me-not duvet cover. She looked beautiful in death, her face smooth. Poor darling, the countess said as she ran her fingers over Mária's forehead.

And I thought that the man on duty may have been right, that it's not something we – a doctor, or anyone else, for that matter – can determine, and that perhaps there's something we don't know, and those people are right who say that Mária is looking down on us now from somewhere the height of the curtain rod, and then from above the soaked-through girlders, and then from above the roof tiles, and then from a place that only God knows. The greater the distance, the sharper her vision. After all, it's always easier to set one's focus on the infinite. Once she sees everything as one, and I do mean everything, she will pity us, because we don't know what she knows; she will pity us, and her heart will bleed for us, because one way or another, she has died, and it's high time we accept the fact, and if not here, then there, in that blinding light, she has ceased being Mária, and the I that we become in God's heart will no longer recognize the I that we had once been down below, because that other I has never burned the scrambled eggs, never kissed, and never tried bribing gravediggers. There is probably no better place than God's heart, if only God's heart did not come with such a horrendous price tag, if only it were not so terrible letting go of the fleeting years of autumn grime and springtime sparkle in which, after all, I am I.

Then the ambulance came and they took María away. When the man filled out the form, he asked the countess what her relationship was to the deceased. We were standing in the kitchen. The countess pinned her eye on the aluminum tea kettle sitting on the corner of the kitchen stove and said nothing.

I wish I knew, she finally said.

I'm sorry, but you must know. I need to write something here. Relative, co-tenant, or whatever.

I am her sister, she said.

See? Now that's something I can write down. Sister. In which case, please accept my condolances.

For a second I thought she'd fling the tea kettle at the poor man.

Thank you. Thank you very much, she said.

And then, at long last, they left.

You go, too, my dear. You probably haven't slept yet.

Should I bring something from the store?

No. There are some leftovers. She cooked for two days. She knew I wouldn't throw anything out.

Fine. I'll come over in the afternoon.

Come over whenever it suits you, my dear. I am fine now. I've accepted it. It is difficult only until we accept the new reality.

Is it really easier afterwards?

Of course it is. Face it. Accept it. Take it in. Usually, this is the most difficult thing, because at times we find reality inconceivable. But thank God, I am pretty good at it.

Not me.

I know, dear.

At home I closed the shutters and went to bed and dreamed that a screech owl was flying around my room.

(the accident)

Once, when I was headed for Margaret Bridge along the boulevard, the glass front of the Western Railway Station was shattered into smithereens. A train that was backing up crashed through the guard rail and the glass front of the station and plowed its way onto the Boulevard, not coming to rest until it had nearly hit the tram tracks. No one died, but at that moment, there was no way I could be sure of that. When I got closer, it turned out that the train was empty, the loudspeaker warned people of the runaway train in time, and an old woman, the one person who'd been injured, was being taken care of. They were waiting for the ambulance.

I had my camera with me, though there was nothing exceptional about that, I nearly always had it with me, just like my father his cane, something that became part of him, and of which he always felt a bit ashamed. And at moments when he felt most ashamed of it, he had a way of showing off with it, to make him feel secure. Cane, glasses, artificial heart valve, camera. It all depends on your illness.

So there stood the empty railway carriage clear across the Grand Boulevard. The people had already scattered. In fact, they got used to it in no time at all. The newspaper vendor on the corner was doing a lively business again. With the derailed carriage behind them, people were waiting for the tram. I looked through the viewfinder. I focused on the man on the sidewalk who was leaning against the first wagon, reading a newspaper. But I couldn't get myself to press the release shutter. I knew that if I were to bring the photo to a newspaper, I might not have to work nights at the printer's. Still, I couldn't do it. It might even be exhibited, I knew that, too. But I had no personal relationship to that runaway carriage. I'd just happened to be there, that's all. It just burst into my life. That's when I realized that since Johanna Vészi, I hadn't pressed the shutter release button once.

(the castle)

Not much else happened before Father got cancer.

Though actually, maybe something did.

One day when I got home, Antal Lovas, Kőszegi and Pál Demjén were sitting in Father's room. Father's former cellmates. Lovas had saved Father's life. After contracting an infection, he vomited and had the runs for days. They told the guard to call a doctor. The guard said he had a better idea, and kicked Father in the stomach. Shit that out, he said. Lovas then had someone steal coffee grounds from the kitchen's garbage disposal, and also potatoes burnt to a cinder, and my father was able to keep the water inside him.

Kőszegi was locked up first under Horthy as a communist. He was still just a child. Then he was a POW in Siberia, then under Rákosi he was locked up as an anti-communist. Then in '56 he was in charge of obtaining petroleum for Molotov cocktails. Then thanks to some stroke of luck, he barely escaped a death sentence. His partner, who could have testified against him, died of a heart attack at the hearing. So he, too, was given just three years for carting the wounded.

Demjén had been an actor. He hadn't really done anything, he'd just been in the wrong place at the wrong time, and seeing how he was there and a true character actor through and through, he proceeded to recite the National Song, *Shall we be slaves or men set free, now is the time, so answer me!* According to my father, he tried to sleep through his eighteen months in prison, which he more or less managed to do. He was among the first to be released, and before long, he set out to write his memoirs. Not on paper, which would have been risky, but in his head. Actually, he wrote, memorized, burned what he'd written, wrote, memorized, burned what he'd written and collected the ashes in a Zsolnay vase. Even the Almighty couldn't tear '56 from his grip. Often, there's no greater boon for a dilettante than a failed revolution.

Just as I was taking my coat off in the hall, I heard Father say, Pali, I can't do it.

Someone's moving around in the apartment, Kőszegi said.

It's just my son getting home.

Lovas was sitting across Father in the easy chair, the other two were sitting on the bed. I'd met them before separately. There were glasses, two bottles of wine, and some cookies on the small table. That's when I realized that it was October 23rd. I couldn't decide if I should go in to say hello, or whether it might be better not to interrupt. I had no objection to Demjén, except that he was ridiculous and I felt awful in his company, partly because I didn't want to think of anyone as ridiculous. I'd been at their place once not long after we came to Budapest. He showed us the Zsolnay vase with its revolutionary ashes. He'd secured the top with cellophane, as if it contained jam. He didn't want dust to mix with the ashes. He recited some passages from his memoirs. I could tell that Father felt as uncomfortable as I did. It's going to be exciting, Pali, you must finish it, everything surrounding '56 in important, and thank you for the dinner, Klára, dear, it was nice, having some proper food for a change. But now we must be off.

On the way home I asked if he meant it, does he really think that everything is important, even Demjén's cellophane-covered ash jam.

We stopped and he lit a cigarette.

As a matter of fact, yes. I meant it.

I'd pick and choose myself, I said.

That's why it's important, son, so you'll have something to choose from in the future. How we remember something is secondary. What counts is that we should remember at all. Worse comes to worst, we'll lunge at each other's throats over the how. But what we don't remember doesn't exist.

Well, I don't know, I said, perhaps it's better if we don't come to blows over our memories.

That's the logic of the hangman's assistant, Kádár, Father said. Forgetting, and hanging those who stand in the way of remembering.

I said nothing. I knew that he was wrong. That there are other options, and the fact that

I don't know what they are doesn't mean they don't exist. They must exist. It was late, and it seemed a lifetime that we waited for the tram. Then it pulled in and we fished change out of our pockets and said nothing more all the way home.

It was really because of Kőszegi that I decided not to go into Father's room. He was intelligent, sober, guarded, and ruthless – the only true revolutionary among us, the type who, if he won, would plough up the cemeteries before sowing the seeds of a new country.

When we first arrived, we went to see him, too. He lived alone. He didn't want to jeopardize the safety of a woman or a child. He lived somewhere in Buda in a converted laundry room. The place was clean and orderly. He was a good cook, he laid a white cloth on the table, and a red vase held fresh-cut flowers. He was nearly manic about making sure that there'd be no hint of the mildewed dejection that all too often settles into the homes of bachelors and widowers. I was sure that he'd never burn chicken wings so badly that he'd have to air out the place for hours afterwards. I was sure that he set the table for himself even when he didn't have company, and that he would never eat bologna from soaked-through wax paper. And I saw the awe on Father's face, that because of the fresh-cut flowers, the cigarette hanging nonchalantly from the corner of his lips, and the collected works of Lenin and Stalin that took up half a wall, he believed, pardoned, and allowed this man to do whatever he wanted. I saw his mute nodding of the head when Kőszegi quoted from that shit the way the parish priest says Luke nine-eleven. You need to know the enemy, he said. I saw Father reflecting on a cliché he'd heard a thousand times before. I saw how pleased he was when Kőszegi spoke with me as if I'd also spent three years in jail, that because of his own years there and Mother's death, he considered me a human being.

I began to hate him when he said to Father that there are no unnecessary victims, no unnecessary sacrifices. The more of us they put behind bars, the better it will be for us in the long run. But in your case, you could have stayed home with a clear conscience. With your cane, nobody expected you to take part in the street fights. Nothing and no one, except for your own vanity.

I felt like toppling the table over on him, along with its white tablecloth. I glanced at Father, waiting for him to say something to this jackass.

And then Father gazed into the empty space past the fresh-cut flowers and said, yes, János, I know. You're right.

On the way home, I told Father I didn't want to see that man ever again. He said he understood, but that doesn't change the fact that Kőszegi was right, and it didn't change the fact that his words wouldn't alter anything at all. Whether his decision had been right or wrong when he got up on that bus, his future had been decided, and Kőszegi, with his hell-bent truth, is as much a part of it as Demjén with his dilettante memoirs. Each of the men who got on that bus wanted to head in a different direction.

Someone's moving around in the apartment, Kőszegi said.
It's just my son getting home.
Why can't you do it? Are you afraid? Demjén asked.
Yes, I'm afraid, but not of what you think.

I went to my room and softly closed the door. I knew that Mother had been right when she'd said, you're wrong, son, it was not in vain. If we can live like human beings in this country someday, we'll have your father and the others to thank for it. I knew without the shadow of a doubt that this was the truth, except it suffocated me every bit as much as Kőszegi's irrefutable truth that Father should have stayed home.

What are you afraid of? Demjén asked.
That those among us who will die before this communist insanity is over will be the lucky ones.
András, I can't believe my ears.
When the time comes, remember what I said. Those of you who will live to see the end of communism will all become unhinged. And if I live to see it, I will too.

I got in bed and decided to finally finish *The Castle*.

Still, would you mind expanding on your pronouncement, Lovas said.

Fine. When do you think this thing will end?

In less than ten years, I should think. The economy won't hold out much longer. It's impossible.

It doesn't seem impossible at all in my view. In my view, it seems better and better, thank you.

How am I not telling the truth?

You are not just a landlady, as you make out.

Well, you're very sharp, I'm sure.

The U.S. will not stand for this much longer, Demjén said.

What? Unless my memory is deceiving me, they let the Ruskies march right in, didn't they?

They were in a bind. Don't forget the Suez crisis, Demjén said.

Don't be silly, Pali. Are you serious?

I see only that you appear to be a landlady to me, but you wear dresses that don't suit a landlady.

It was an unfortunate coincidence. The whole world was indignant because of what happened to us.

At most half the world. Also, who do you mean by us?

You, for instance.

That's what I thought. Me and you, and Anti and János. It didn't take six years, and we can all be named, it wouldn't take more than ten minutes.

You're just like a child who knows some silly joke and can't be brought to keep it quiet. So out with it. What's so special about those dresses?

You'll be angry if I tell you.

No, I shall laugh, because it will be just childish nonsense.

The U.S. will bring the Ruskies to their knees economically. That's what the Cold War is about, András. Economics. No one's going to use the bomb, Lovas said.

That's what I'm talking about, Father said. So grab a piece of graph paper and figure out how long, in spite of the U.S.'s mighty efforts, we'll be able to afford our Sunday stews, and you'll see that nothing will change here within our lifetime.

So now we have it. They are old-fashioned, over-trimmed, and what else was it? And how do you think you know all that?

I can see it. One doesn't need any training to know such a thing.

It doesn't take the U.S., or the Cold War, for that matter, for every dictatorship to implode from within, Kőszegi said.

No, János, I'm afraid you're mistaken, Father said. Not every dictatorship, but every regime, and that includes Athenian democracy.

You can see it, just like that. You know at once what fashion demands. You're going to be invaluable to me, because I do have a weakness for beautiful dresses.

See? That's why we need this organization, Demjén said. Because of what you're saying. Because something has to speed up the implosion.

We already have an organization. It's called the Workers' Militia. Did you have something similar in mind, Father asked.

I don't appreciate your cynicism!

Have it your way. Just don't offer me honey-coated shit for dinner.

Honey-coated shit? What exactly are you accusing me of? Is it what I think it is?

No such luck, Palika, I'm not accusing you of that. You are not an informer, because you're too dense. Feeble minded. How should I put it? Dumb.

You were a supercilious know-it-all even in jail. Except, in there, we had to forgive you!

I'm sorry, Palika, but it's the truth.

Don't Palika me!

I heard Father's door slam, and then the front door.

I admit that this organization is not perfect, András, but it's not all that bad either. What, exactly, is your problem with Pali? Lovas asked.

You want me to tell you? Do you really want me to tell you?

Actually, I'm more interested in why we will all become unhinged, should we outlive Kádár. Demjén is stupid, I admit, but you neglected to tell us why, Kőszegi said.

If you must know, János, it's because thirty years from now, we will still be expecting the same thing we did six years ago, and we'll spit at our grandchildren, who will be wanting something entirely different, and they will spit back at us, and then we will become unhinged.

I'm aiming only to dress well, and you are either a fool or a child or a very bad, dangerous man. So get out of here, hurry up, get out!

We're the ones bringing up our grandchildren, Kőszegi said.

I might, but not you, Father said.

From all that I can tell, even your son doesn't care that it's October the twenty-third.

Okay, enough is enough, Lovas cut in. The two of you don't have to survive Kádár to become unhinged.

You're right, Toni. Let's go.

I'm sorry if I hurt your feelings. I'll apologize to Pali as well, but really, this is what I think, Father said.

I know. No harm done. But let's go, Kőszegi said.

God speed, Lovas said.

K. was out in the hall as the landlady called after him: "I'm having a new dress delivered tomorrow. Perhaps I'll let you go and fetch it."

I waited for him to gather up the glasses, open the window and let in some fresh air, or else grab his coat and leave, go after them, drink himself sodden, to do something, anything but stay in his chair where they'd walked out on him. If only I could have forced myself to go to him and say, Father, you're right.

(Mária's funeral)

The countess decided to put Mária to rest in the Szendrey family crypt. Her Swiss relative was offended and stopped sending care packages. Her Berlin relative came for the funeral. Walter Ulbricht did West Berliners a favor by putting up the wall. It does a person a world of good if he is not simply free, but is confronted by the fact day-in-and-day-out and isn't given a chance to forget that freedom is not to be taken for granted

I accompanied her to the cemetery. It was drizzling, I held the umbrella for her and she took my arm. We looked around for the gravediggers. The office said that they'd be somewhere by the race track if we wanted to talk to them. Two children had climbed on top of one of the graves, intently watching the horses over the wall.

The main path had been swept clean, but on the side paths, we were up to our ankles in leaves. A wet cobweb stuck to her knee, she brushed it off, but then it stuck to her hand. Would you let go of my arm, dear? Of course, I said, and then it ended up stuck to my own hand. I wiped it onto a tree trunk.

This thing they call nature is not quite as enticing from up close as it is from the top of a hill, she said.

I don't mind it, I said.

Not only do I mind it, my dear, I adore it. Not such a long time ago, when I was an adolescent, this was how I rebelled against my mother.

Your family didn't think much of cobwebs?

My mother considered any contact with nature the perversion of the privileged. Though let it be said in her defense that she considered any such activities, from collecting butterflies to discovering primitive tribes, a manifestation of the bad conscience of the aristocracy. She claimed that the butterflies didn't like being collected, and the primitive tribes didn't want to be discovered.

I can see her point. Still, why did you rebel against her?

Because I sided with my father, who waved the flag of discovery.

It's no picnic living in such a divided family.

You're being ironic, dear, but you're right, it's not, especially if you go for walks in the woods with your father so as not to disturb your mother while she is entertaining her boyfriend.

Did you know about it?

Certainly. A child is neither stupid nor blind. On the other hand, it takes quite some time before a child realizes that her father isn't a saint, and her mother isn't a filthy whore – oh, do excuse my language.

It's okay. But why did your father decide that he'd go on those walks in the woods?

Because his stand was that my mother wasn't a. . . you-know-what, she was just unhappy, and he was powerless to change that.

Which is when people get divorced, I said.

Or play cards, or commit suicide, or have a lover, or collect moss. He opted for the latter. With my help, he discovered two previously unknown types of moss. He was in love with lichens and moss.

And when did you realize that your father wasn't a saint and your mother. . . ?

Later than I should have, my dear. Unfortunately, only when I realized that I wasn't like my mother.

What made you think you were?

When you see that the men think you're even more beautiful than your beautiful mother, and you happen to catch your mother kissing someone, you can't help but draw certain conclusions.

You mean about yourself?

Who else? Our mother can't be worse than we are. This truth is independent of class, my dear. If our mother has a lover, and we realize that certain young men get us all fired up, can we draw any other conclusion than that we're no better than the Whore of Babylon?

I guess not.

You see? We feel contempt for our mother, because we saw what we saw, but we can easily feel a deeper contempt for ourselves, and with that, the problem is solved. And if at the same time we consider our father a saint, because he'd rather collect moss than slap our mother and her boyfriend, the die is cast, and we are determined never to ruin a man's life. We'd rather collect moss ourselves each time we feel the Whore of Babylon stir within.

Is that why you never got married?

That's why, my dear.

And what happened afterwards?

What do you mean what happened afterwards? We've just been to the family crypt. My mother and father are lying next to each other, enjoying their eternal rest, while I've ruined the lives of four men, utterly and irrevocably, except, not because I kept a lover, but because I was afraid to love them.

We fell silent. It was lunchtime. The four gravediggers were having their bread and bacon under the shelter of a crypt's molding.

So be careful, my dear, lest you'll be the next, she said.

I'm willing to take the chance. It'd be worth it.

That's very flattering of you, except, you're mistaken. It would not be worth it. If you'll take the advice of an old woman who speaks from experience, steer clear of a woman who won't give herself to you stock, lock, and barrel. It doesn't matter why she's not capable of doing so. But if that's the case, turn on your heels and run for your life.

I'll do as you say.

I should hope so. But if the poor thing gives herself to you stock, lock, and barrel, then kindly value her. And now let's go because I must talk business with those gentlemen over there.

The shortest man with the mouse eyes was the head gravedigger. At least, he was the one who got to his feet when they saw us approach. Before shaking hands, he wiped his on his pants. The countess explained that she was there about opening the Szendrey crypt for Sunday.

It ain't easy opening that crypt, little lady.

What exactly does it ain't easy mean?

Well, little lady, it ain't easy means that it's a whole lot of work, provided you don't want the marble broken, little lady, and my guess is that you wouldn't want that.

You guess correctly. So let us draw the conclusion.

Draw the what?

Discuss the price.

Yes, yes, the price. 'Cause there's the official price, and then there's the actual price.

Meanwhile, this desecration of the dead was making me feel sick to my stomach.

May I ask what the official price has to do with the actual price, I asked.

This gentleman and I will determine that. You just hold the umbrella, my dear, the countess said, and squeezed my arm just like my mother had done once when I said too much.

Dear sir, don't even mention the official price to me, I hate anything official. Just quote me the actual price.

Now we're talking, little lady. I see we understand each other.

Why on earth not? So then, how much will it cost not to have that marble chipped?

Well, seeing how there's quite a bit more labor with it than with a new grave, which is officially four hundred. . .

Oh, dear, dear, didn't I just say that I didn't want to hear about anything official?

Four hundred, he finally said, which is just a hundred per head for us, ain't that so, boys.

Great. In which case, let it be a bottle of whisky per head, plus a package of American cigarettes per head.

That's a deal, little lady.

How did you manage that, I asked once we were back on the main path.

Manage what?

This thing with the whisky and cigarettes.

Where have you been all this time, my dear? Haven't you ever been to the doctor, or the police?

Sure, but I would never know how to do this.

In which case, you really must learn how. The priest, for instance. I'm going to offer him two boxes of Dutch coco. Priests love coco.

Sunday morning she asked that I stay by her side, if possible, because she might want to hold on to my arm. I told her it was only natural. We took a cab. It took us up to the mortuary. I couldn't believe my eyes. There were already about fifty mourners standing by the building, mostly elderly people. I recognized one or two faces from the movies or the papers. But most of them were strangers to me. By the time the priest recited the prayer, there must have been about a hundred of us. No one gave a speech. At a regular funeral, those in the back chat, those up front cry. But here, except for offering their condolences to the countess, no one said a word. We walked from the mortuary to the crypt as if we were at a silent demonstration.

This hurt me. I'd never seen any of these people visit Mária or the countess, and not one of them ever took the string shopping bag out of Mária's hand, or the countess's, and that covered in black from top to toe, with a single white flower in their hands, they were thinking only of their own, long gone Márias. Perhaps I was being unfair, that by all odds, no one takes their string bags from them either, nor do they expect it, and that this silence is meant not only for their own long-lost Márias, or at least, I hoped so, because right now, everything should be about the Mária who had spent fifty of her eighty-two years in the service of the Szendrey family.

To the right the countess, to the left the lady's maid, in the middle a Chinese chess figure.

Come, my dear, take me home, so I can have a good cry at last.

(the rope)

It was snowing heavily. I stood by the window, watching the street down below turn from gray to black and white. The wind blew some snowflakes into the room. From time to time, a car passed by. The tire tracks disappeared like vapor trails. To the left, at a distance, someone was approaching from the direction of People's Republic Avenue. He was reeling slightly, though possibly, he'd skidded along the icy sidewalk. Occasionally he stopped. He held a briefcase over his head against the snow. He'd almost reached the tobacconist when I realized that it was Kornél. I thought he must be drunk. Despite his winter coat and the battered pigskin briefcase that once belonged to his father, because of his bent back and his reeling, he hardly resembled himself.

I opened the door and watched as he brushed the snow off of himself. He wasn't drunk, he was exhausted. Or beaten half to death. Or who knows.
 What happened?
 Nothing.
 Well that's good. There's hardly anything better than that.
 Ask me in already, and make some coffee.
 Fine. Come on in, I'll make some coffee.

We went to the kitchen, he sat down, and I put the water up to boil. The rubber ring had burned out in the coffee maker months before, and I forgot to buy a new one, and when I remembered, it was not to be had anywhere.
 So then, I said.
 Don't rush me.
 Fine.
 I sat down as well as we waited for the water to boil. Then I poured the coffee into the pot and stirred it, so it wouldn't boil over.
 You're going to be offended, he said.

Probably. You're always right about such things.

He took a folder from his briefcase and laid it on the table.

Here, he said.

What it is, I asked.

The volume.

At long last!

I wish I could feel as happy as you.

That's your problem. But don't try to ruin my happiness. Besides, why would I be offended?

Because I didn't show it to you before.

Before what?

Before I turned it in for publication.

You come here with the book you've turned in, and you think I'm going to be offended? I'm sorry, but you're an idiot. And, as you say, offensive.

This is not the volume I handed in, it's the volume I took back.

You mean they gave it back?

They didn't give it back. I took it back.

All right. Let's have some coffee, because this is too much for me.

It's too much for me, too.

Will you kindly tell me why in God's name you took it back?

I took it back because yesterday Tőfalvi asked me to go have a beer with him.

Who is Tőfalvi?

The guy who flunked me in linguistics last year.

What did he want?

Actually, it wasn't beer. He invited me for dinner in Mátyás Pince.

Dinner with Gypsy music?

More or less.

Can I guess?

Go right ahead.

For the appetizer, he said he was sorry for not realizing earlier that he'd making a fool of himself by having you repeat the year.

It was more elaborate than that, but basically, yes.

And what was the main course?

The manuscript.

What do you mean the manuscript? What does he have to do with the manuscript?

The publisher sent it to him for his opinion. From time to time, he gives his opinion. In other words, he censors manuscripts.

This Tófalvi is such an important person?

Exactly.

I thought it takes months for a manuscript to make it to an editor's desk.

I handed it in back in August.

Fuck you.

I told you you'd take offense.

I'm not taking offense. Just go on.

Yes, you are. And I'm sure you're right. But I didn't want to show it to you until it got accepted.

Go on.

So they sent it to Tófalvi.

And?

He talked for an hour about how, instead of the folksy nonsense and the social realist nonsense, this is the sort of poetry Hungarian literature needs today.

Is that what he said? Social realist nonsense?

And surrealist nonsense. And Christian nonsense.

Basically all of Hungarian poetry is shit, but you will pull it out of the quagmire? That's a pretty impressive offer, coming from a censor.

Exactly.

The front door opened, Father entered and shook the snow off his legs. I'd have been happier had he taken his time in this snow. I didn't like Kornél talking to my father any more than Kornél liked me talking to his. We are never able to hear what our own father is trying to say, while it is perfectly clear to someone else. Also irritating is that others are deaf to what we've been hearing loud and clear for years. But possibly, what is even more irritating is that our voice is distorted next to our father's, and our own speech takes on false overtones. Of course, there are occasional exceptions. And, fortunately, this was one of them. But almost every exchange carries with it an uncertainty: is the soloist playing badly or is it artistic intention, and so, we feel ill at ease not only for the soloist but for the composer as well, and for ourselves.

Father asked if we'd mind if he had coffee with us. I said of course not. He poured himself a cup of coffee, then went to stand by the door. Kornél stood up to give him his chair. I felt ashamed that I hadn't realized that there were just two chairs in the kitchen, apologized, and brought in the piano bench. Then Kornél explained to him that we were just talking about the professor who'd flunked him, but had invited him to dinner the night before.

It happens, Father said.

After he made you repeat the year, you became his favorite, I said.

More or less. My book is going to be published next year.

You're kidding. It takes five years even for one of our court poets to get published, I said.

I'm not kidding.

So what's the problem? Father asked.

The problem, Kornél said, is that it's not going to be published.

Why not? What was for dessert? I asked.

For a while, Kornél said nothing, then he said, that.

I knew what the 'that' was, but I simply couldn't believe it.

What do you mean *that*? I asked.

I just told you. *That.*

How was it served up?

Actually, it wasn't.

I don't understand.

There's nothing not to understand. Tőfalvi is no fool. Obviously, he wasn't about to hand me a piece of paper in Mátyás Pince with State Security letterhead for me to sign.

But how do you know what he was after? Father asked.

I know because he said he's eager to get information about people my age, because the rift that divides us is no good for anyone.

And what are you supposed to do about it?

Meet with them regularly to talk. He also said that I should start a paper at the university. I'd be the editor-in-chief and he'd oversee what I was editing.

Is that all he wanted?

No. I mean, yes. He told me they'll be appointing five poets to go to London in January, and he'd make sure that I'd be the sixth.

And report on the other five? I asked.

He didn't say, but it was obvious. I've never even asked for a passport.

Are you sure he wanted to rope you in? my father asked.

I'm sure.

I'm not so sure myself, Father said.

Well, I am.

It happens that someone sees the light and realizes what an idiot he's been and tries to make amends, I said.

Yes, it happens. Except they're generally not former members of the Secret Police, Kornél said.

Was Tófalvi with the Secret Police? How do you know, I asked.

It's common knowledge, he said.

I thought he was an editor, my father said.

So then, you went and asked them to return your manuscript, I prompted.

Yes. I told them that I had been over-precipitous and the manuscript is not ready for publication. I'm working on some more poems that I want to include. I said whatever came to mind.

And what did they say?

They said that there's still plenty of time to make changes before the manuscript goes to press.

So you didn't ask to withdraw the proposal, you just asked for it back so you could make some changes, my father said.

No. I insisted that they return it.

I assume Tófalvi won't like that, I said.

He already knows. I ran into him at the publishing house.

What did you say to him?

The same thing. Also, that after yesterday's conversation, I realized the responsibility and needed to consider a bunch of things.

And what did he say?

He said he was sorry, because he'd been expecting the opposite. Then he issued a veiled threat. He said he hoped that I realized he was not just a simple college professor.

He veiled his threat so well that I, for one, don't even see the threat at all, I said.

Well, that's what it was. He clearly meant that he's not one to be messed with.

I think my son is right, Father said. He could just as easily have meant that he's more than a simple college professor and knows talent when he sees it. At which, we fell silent.

What will you do if he asks you to have beer with him again tomorrow, I asked after a while.

He won't. It's over and done with, Kornél said.

It's never over and done with, Father said. Either you misconstrued his meaning, or if not, then he will try again.

I'm not misconstruing anything, and they're not going to try again.

What makes you so sure?

They're no fools. If I ask them to give back a book they've already accepted for publication, they know that it's no use trying again.

They can try another way. I don't mean to belittle what you've done, Kornél, but asking them to return a manuscript is not such a big deal, Father said. Not even if it's your first book.

He took a few more sips from his empty coffee cup.

I realize that, Kornél said. But they have no more cards to deal. I'm almost ashamed, but I've never done anything they can hold on to. I'm not gay, I don't steal, I can't tell good political jokes, and I've never owned a single counterfeit dollar.

I don't think they will try anything, Father said. But it won't be because you asked for your book back but because they weren't trying anything this time either.

Yes, they were.

Believe me, they never try to rope someone in without the person knowing about it.

They tell you straight out what they want from you, as well as what they will give you in return. That goes without saying. It's a contract. You sell your soul, and they buy it.

That's just what happened, Kornél said. They told me what they'd give me in return.

Without them laying out what they want? That's highly unlikely, Father said. If they need you, they need you lock, stock, and barrel. And for that, you need to know that you've sold yourself. Not guess it, not think it, but know it. This knowledge makes you theirs.

There followed another stretch of silence, then Father spoke again.

My advice to you is, don't be so afraid of them, because then they will find you without fail and rope you in, he explained. Then he got up and left.

What should I do now?

I don't know.

I can't return the manuscript.

Not for the time being. But at least it's ready.

Good lord, why am I such a coward?

If only I could be as cowardly as you.

What filth. May they rot, all of them. May they rot.

By now, the corners of his lips were trembling.

I need to go out, I said. I'd never seen him cry and didn't want to. I went to the bathroom and turned on the faucet so I wouldn't hear.

(St. Anthony)

I must have been around five when St. Anthony took Father for a ride on his bike. His real name was Anthony Keresztes. We called him St. Anthony because in '47, when even the gophers in the wheat fields were dying of thirst due to the draught, he brought us bread.

Don't bother waiting, Miss Doctor, 'cause there's nothing for me to bring. Get your hands on some bran. If it's good enough for the pigs, it's good enough for us, he warned every Sunday, but then he'd show up with some bread all the same, wearing a white shirt, a felt coat, and a hat, despite the sweltering heat. He brought the bread on his bike. It was in a canvas backpack.

In those days peasants more intelligent than he were paid with the family jewels for a morsel or two. The price of art was never as high as it was back then. Art insured your survival. "But my dear sir, this is no fairground bauble, it's an authentic Mednyánszky." "In that case, bon appetit, your ladyship."

Before the war, my grandfather cured the Keresztes boy of diphtheria or some similar disease without charge, and we never forget, dear Miss Doctor, because the Lord punishes forgetting more severely than fornication. And so, out of gratitude for Grandfather, we had our daily bread, even during the famine of '47. And also out of respect for my grandfather, he insisted on calling Mother Miss Doctor, and me Young Gentleman Doctor, and my father Mr. Doctor.

Sometimes he'd hoist me up on his battered Turul bike and take me for a ride around the yard. He came for the last time in '52, just before I could reach the pedals. He didn't bring bread. I'm a coward, Mr. Doctor, he told Father. I wouldn't be afraid to hang myself, except the Lord would forgive me even less for that than for forgetting.

I signed and joined the farmers' coop, so there's no more bread baking, not in the world we live in. May God spare you, Mr. Doctor.

I must have been around five when after a ride, I challenged Father saying that I bet he couldn't ride a bike. At which he said, of course I can, son, I can ride it as well as you. And he got on the rack in the back and St. Anthony took him for a turn as well.

I even remember the shadow of the walnut tree on the wall of the house, the sun beating down on us, the screeching break, and the felt coat I grabbed hold of. It smelled of dogs. I think it must've been sweat that produced that pungent smell. Mother, who was watching from the steps of the porch, laughed, and I got even bolder and said that she should also take a spin. She protested, it's not a good idea, I'm not dressed for it, but Father and I grabbed hold of her and dragged her down and she also got up on the rack and did a round with St. Anthony, to the rabbit hatch and back.

And once each of us took a ride, St. Anthony told us it was time he showed us what a real bikeride was, and he put my arms around his neck, ordered my father to get on the rack, and had my mother sit on the crossbar in front of him. If only someone could take a picture of us now, Mr. Doctor, sir, he said.

That may well have been the moment I decided to become a photographer. It could be that simple, that there's a moment when the promise of eternity takes root in us. We all possess the yearning, but few of us receive the promise.

Of course, this also depends on receiving that promise at the right time. And it seems to me that a five-year-old child wrapped around St. Anthony's neck on a sunny day on a Turul bike with his mother and his father is a good recipe for such a promise. Compared to such a moment, it makes no difference what he may later think about the relationship between a photograph and eternity, because it has been decided.

Of course, there's no way I can be sure that this was the moment. I'm just saying that there are moments that decide your fate even if it's obvious that another moment would have steered your life in the same direction. The magazine of a gun may hold six bullets, but the point is that it makes no difference whether it's the first or the sixth that hits the target. All that matters is that it has. For all I know, without that moment I might have never taken a picture of Imolka. To the right a sideboard, to the left God knows, in the middle incontrovertible transience. Possibly, it was just a single suggestion that decided everything, when St. Anthony said, if only someone could take a picture of us, Doctor, sir.

(the last picture of my father)

When Father and I left the hospital, I hailed a cab. On the way home I spotted a photographer's studio from the window: József Reisz, Passport & ID Photographs. It was in a side street. I tried to commit the place to memory. I'd go back later.

Do you remember St. Anthony? Father asked.

Of course, I said.

But you were so young.

I have no idea what made Father think of him, and he made no further mention of him on our way home.

When we got home, I didn't know what to do, join him in his room, or let him be. He asked me to join him. He couldn't drink because of his surgery, but he poured me a glass of wine. I was afraid he'd ask what the doctor had said to me, because I knew that if he asked, I'd tell him. But all I could really think of at that moment was that I had to look for a new job, because I wouldn't be able to support myself from what I was making at the printer's, and I'd want to make changes to the kitchen as well. The red sideboard would be the first thing to go. I could probably find work with Reisz or some other photographer who specialized in ID photography. Meanwhile I decided that if he asked, I'd say that the doctor didn't know either, it was up in the air.

I'd like to ask a favor of you, son.

Yes, I said, and took a sip of the wine. It was like vinegar. But at least, now I knew he wouldn't ask, that I wouldn't be the one to tell him, that he'd just ask me to take him to Mélyvár. It was high time to return home, Kornél had said so repeatedly. I hadn't been to Mother's grave since the funeral.

It's not easy asking something like this, and I feel ashamed, he said.

So then don't ask, I thought. If Mother didn't say where we should dig her grave, neither should you. I wouldn't ask such a thing of anyone either. Though come to think of it, there won't be anyone to ask. I certainly won't be asking you, that's for sure. I'll need a proper stand for the enlarger where the sideboard is now. Making enlargements on the kitchen table is pretty awkward.

Not that there's anything to be ashamed of, Father went on, but I realize that it means different things for you than it does for me. Like photography, though not only photography.

That's all right, I said. We both knew that I'd take him home to lie next to Mother without him having to ask. On the other hand, what could I do with his pictures? I'm not going to take his collection of clouds and finish it for him, or publish it, or exhibit it. He's still alive, thank God, so let that be his worry. I've never taken a single photograph of clouds, nor will I take one, ever. Clouds don't interest me.

I'd like you to take a picture of me, son.
Okay, I said.
Just so there'll be at least one picture of me that. . . .
Sure thing.
No rush. Whenever you feel like it.
How about right now? But let's go to my room.
Should I change my clothes?
Don't bother.
He followed me like a child.
Sit here on the bed.
It's been a long time since I last sat on this bed. What should I do with my hands?
I don't know. Nothing. Just don't move your head while I adjust the light.
You need a proper lamp, like the ones in studios.
Someday. But for now, this will do.
And a stand.
Yes, I'll need a stand, too. Lean your head down further.
And where should I look, son?
Into my eyes.

(Sára Rónai)

I had to take some medical records out to Rákos, and also, there were some books to return. I stuffed them in my briefcase, then I rubbed my shoes with floor wax to protect against the slush outside. I'd learned this from Mother.

Three-quarter fur-trimmed coats came into fashion that winter, and from the Danube to the Grand Boulevard, all the women wore them. By the time I got to Keleti Station, there were fewer of them, and in Kőbánya, there were hardly any to be seen. I had to transfer twice before I reached Rákos, and on the third tram I boarded, only one woman wore a coat like that. She sat with her back to me. Her hair was gathered up in a bun. We got off at the same stop.

She was the exact opposite of the woman who had licked a lemon on the tram on my way back from the recruitment office, though I'd be hard put to say what this opposite entailed. She did nothing out of the ordinary; she sat, stood up, got off, walked along the sidewalk. I didn't get to see her face. She walked ahead of me, which made me feel odd, as if I were following her. I quickened my pace and got ahead of her. Then I leaned down, as if to tie my shoes, and let her pass me. I'd be hard put to say why. I didn't see her face, and from the back she looked like any other women in her mid-forties, a slender woman wearing a fashionable coat with fur trim. While I fumbled with my shoelaces, the bottom of my briefcase got soaked.

When we reached the library, she went inside.

I stopped to smoke a cigarette. I tried not to make plans, the good side of which is that at least you can zero in on the things you're not planning. You're not going to get in line behind her at the loan desk, you won't look for a book on the same shelf, and when you sit down in the reading room, you won't sit down across from her. I discarded my cigarette and watched the butt die in the wet snow with a hiss. When I entered, I found her standing behind the loan desk.

Except for the two of us there was no one around, so I had to go up to her right away. Luckily, I'd learned when I was a child that all librarians are middle-aged, sad, and beautiful. I'm András Szabad and I'm looking for Sára Rónai, I said. I'm Sára Rónai, she said, and held out a hand. Then she asked about Father.

I wasn't expecting this. It was as unexpected as the fact that this woman got off the tram at the same stop, or that she was headed for the same place, or that I was in fact going to the library to see her.
He's fine. He has cancer, I said.
I realized that I was still holding her hand, so I let go, hoping she wouldn't notice my embarrassment.
I know. Coffee?
Yes, thank you, I said. Then I placed the books and the envelope on the counter.

She went to the office, poured some coffee from a thermos, then placed her coat over her shoulder. She brought out the coffee in two mugs. We went out to the small yard through the emergency exit, where Father and I once had coffee.
Do you smoke?
Yes.
She smoked only menthol cigarettes, she said. And I said I'd give it a try, I'd never smoked a menthol cigarette before. She offered me one, and we fumbled around for a while with the mugs, the cigarettes, and the matches. Finally we put the mugs on the ground, and I offered her a light. The bottoms of the mugs got dirty from the slush and I wiped them off with my handkerchief. She leaned against the door, and the latch bolt clicked shut.

We just locked ourselves out, I said. We'll have to knock.
We can knock till hell freezes over, she said. The door's padded. Then she took a sip of her coffee, took a drag on her cigarette, and kept the smoke in for some time. When

she exhaled, she added that there's no need to worry, we wouldn't be stuck outside. We could go around through the glass door opposite.

Did my father tell you? I asked.
Sure. Who else?
I don't understand why doctors think it's better to lie.
For a while she said nothing.
Why? Would you have told him? she said at last.
I don't know.
Some people would rather be lied to.
I took a drag of my cigarette and held the smoke inside for a while. The mentholated cigarette felt like a chilly wind whistling in my lungs.
Possibly, I said.
I watched as she wrapped her hands around the warm coffee mug and pressed it to her belly. The yard was barely bigger than my room. It was surrounded by four tall, gray walls. The wall opposite had a narrow glass door and a couple of staircase windows. I wondered why they had the emergency exit open onto the yard. But you could see the sky.

I asked if I could have another cigarette. The wind was up again, and while I lit my cigarette, she held her hand up to shield mine, so the match shouldn't go out. I watched her slender fingers, then her eyes. Her eyes were as pure as the sky. They lacked pity, just as they lacked the wish to comfort me. In fact, I discovered no wish in them at all. There was no reason for me to take my eyes from hers.

What did the doctor tell you? she asked.
They're going to try radiation, but he doesn't expect miracles.
She also lit a cigarette, and this time, I shielded her hand from the wind. I don't know what made her hand so warm, the coffee, or something else.

That's three months, six on the outside, I said.
Don't jump the gun, she said.

I'm not. But that's how it is.

You never know.

I'm a lousy Catholic, so I know.

I'm not a Catholic at all, but there's no knowing. You're just making things worse for yourself, and you're not helping him.

It helps me if I know.

I don't think so. None of us are immune to hope.

I've had an aversion to hope my entire life.

Then what would help you?

If he dropped dead by morning. If he died at last. If he rotted already, along with my mother. Along with his jail time. And his cellmates. Take a picture of me, son. Fine. Go on, keep looking at yourself, you shit. I hope you croak before I take a picture of you tomorrow, too, you shit. And the day after. And also, once you've lost all your hair, I thought. I sunk my nails into my palm to keep me from crying. I learned this from my mother, too, just like rubbing floor wax on my shoes.

I'm really interested in what would help you, she repeated.

I don't know.

Why are you so averse to hope, she asked.

Because it requires something I lack, I said.

For instance?

For instance, strength.

I doubt that you're weak. It's more like you're ashamed of your strength.

I said nothing.

Only a person who mistakes his strength for callousness would be ashamed of it.

Fine. In that case, I won't be ashamed of it. Except, I really don't have any strength. Not for the time being.

You will. Take my word for it. Your father has it, and you will have it, too, she said, and her hand reached for mine, then stopped midway.

Your father is one of the finest people I have ever met, she finally said, but she still had to finish that curtailed motion of her hand, so she took the cigarette butt from me and leaned down to put it in the tin can by the door.

Meanwhile, I thought that Mother was the exact opposite of the woman licking the lemon, and then I thought that this woman must be my father's lover, that she's the one I'd seen in the wine bar at one time, and then that that's ridiculous, because in that case Father wouldn't have let me come to this library, not even once.

I believe you, I said when she straightened up. Except that won't cure his cancer.
I know, she said, and her eyes misted over with tears.
I have to go now, I said, which was a lie.

The door opposite led to the street through a stairwell. On the landing inside she stopped, took my wrist, and pressed it to her belly the same way she'd pressed the coffee mug to her belly in the yard.
You must know that there's room for you here as well as your father.
Some little light filtered in through the wire-mesh glass, as if we were in a hospital.
I know, I said, and took the hand wrapped tightly around my wrist.
You're welcome here any time.
Thank you, I said.
No need, she said.

Outside, behind the blurred glass we saw a man. He'd stopped, looking for his keys. Sára Rónai let go of my hand and opened the door for him.

Because of some mishap, the ride home took about two hours. In the meantime, I didn't think of anything. I didn't think of her leaning over, nor the awkwardly located emergency exit, nor of Father watching us through the glass door. My mind hadn't been so clear since I filed those hammers.

I never went there again. And I didn't tell Kornél.

(scrambled eggs)

Instead of three months, or six, it turned out to be a year. Or nearly. It passed like all the others. After his surgery, my father continued to visit the library for a while, and I worked. Once a week, sometimes twice, I visited the countess. One morning, I found her in a huff.

Just look what I've done, she said, pointing at the pan.

What's that, I asked, though I had a fairly good idea what it was.

Scrambled eggs, she said.

I'll help you, I said.

Don't help me. Teach me.

We were standing in the kitchen. I felt strange. I'd never taught anyone anything before. Once I explained to Kornél how a Leica works, but it'd have been teaching only if he were really interested.

Fine, I said. Step number one: let's get rid of this ugly mess.

I didn't ask for your opinion, my dear. I asked you to teach me.

Teaching and giving one's opinion go hand in hand, I'm afraid. If I remember well, it was you who had berated me once for keeping myself clear of public education.

She said nothing. I scraped the oily, burnt mess out of the pan and threw it in the garbage. Then I washed up.

Do you have a shallow pan for crepes? I asked.

Let's concentrate on the scrambled eggs, she said.

That's what we're doing. But you cook scrambled eggs in a crepe pan.

As far as I can remember, Mária made it in this.

I think you remember wrong.

I see.

And now, let's break an egg.

You know, my dear, that's where my problem begins. The truth is that I loathe egg whites. I have no problem with the yolks, but the whites need to be boiled or cooked.

That's what we're doing. As for loathing, it's not the privilege of the aristocracy. That's why we'll try to break the egg so the whites won't mix with the yolk, if possible. Hand me a big, sharp knife.

Mária broke the egg open on the side of a plate.

But she didn't loathe egg whites.

I don't know, my dear. We never talked about it. The knives are in that drawer over there.

I showed her how to hold the egg, how to knock it against the side of the bowl with a decisive motion of the hand so that the shell cracks about halfway, and how to separate the shell without coming in contact with the whites. She cracked the second egg open herself. It went very well. She was so excited, and was about to pour the oil into the shallow pan. I said no. It's all right when making eggs over-easy, but never when making scrambled eggs. When making scrambled eggs, you add the oil to the egg, but never black pepper, because pepper sticks to the pan.

From time to time she objected, that wasn't how Mária did it, but I told her that now I was the one teaching her. We ate the eggs in the living room.

We should have made three eggs. One egg isn't enough for you.

It wouldn't be, except I don't eat this early.

You should. It is time you learned to act like a grownup.

I'm trying. I'm already pretty good at calling an ambulance for a corpse.

There is no excuse for your cynicism, my dear. And pain is no excuse.

I know. My mother said the same thing.

In that case, you now have it from two reliable sources.

Are you sure my sources are not mistaken?

In this case? Absolutely.

I wonder if cynicism, instead of being a feeling in itself, doesn't come from a lack of feeling.

See? I hadn't thought of that before. It seems that in old age I'm not just learning to make scrambled eggs. I'm also learning that there's one person in the world after all who has no feelings. I have it from his own lips. Let's have some orange liqueur to celebrate, she said.

I said nothing.

Do you remember the zú? she asked as she took the two liqueur glasses out of the china cabinet.

Sure, I said.

If I remember correctly, your most intriguing guess was that it was money of some sort, she continued, a Fiat, and took out the silver box.

Of course that won't change the fact that it's a Chinese pawn, I said.

See? We agree on that. For instance, calling something a people's democracy won't make it either the people's, nor will it make it a democracy. And I feel the same way about the individual who says he lacks feelings.

You're right, I said.

Of course I'm right, my dear. Which is why I think that this zú will be in much better hands with you from now on than with me.

But it's a family heirloom, I said.

I know. And fortunately, it's a populous family. Anyway, if in the future you should meet someone who really has no feelings, then give this zú to him.

Fine. I'll keep it with me at all times.

Don't, because you'll lose it. This piece is hundreds of years old, even if it's just a Chinese peasant, or pawn.

I won't lose it.

Okay. Coming from you, I believe it.

I won't lose it. I promise.

Though later, on our last night together, I very nearly gave it to Éva.

(the list)

It didn't take three months, and it didn't take six months, it took a year. Until late spring, you couldn't tell by looking at him that Father was going to die. But then he started acting crazy. First Kőszegi showed up and sat there every night for weeks. The radio was on full blast to interfere with the wire-tapping, in case the room was bugged. If course, by then it probably was. I have no idea what they were doing in there. Then Lovas also showed up, and then the crazy professor of philosophy from the library. Then some men recently released from jail. They came with Kőszegi. I never saw Demjén, though that didn't surprise me. Sometimes five or six of them sat crowded together on Father's bed. They looked at him as if he were some sort of deity. Kőszegi was the most submissive of them, and also the most subservient, as if he'd drawn the necessary conclusions from the collected works of Stalin. I think he was behind it all. They always came up separately, and left separately. Father kept the shutters closed, probably because of the old woman across the way.

Sometimes one of them would show up with a small portable typewriter and leave it there for a couple of days, and then Father would stay home and type. At first he didn't know how to type properly and pressed the keys with two fingers, but eventually he got the hang of it, and after a couple of weeks, he was faster than an office clerk. Then he burned his notes in the kitchen sink, like Demjén did with his memoirs. He hardly talked to me. Or possibly, the opportunity was not forthcoming. Or I sabotaged our talks. I don't know. Once I went to the kitchen when he was airing out the place and asked why there were ashes in the sink. He said they were just some slips of paper he didn't need anymore. The garbage can was good enough for such things before, I thought, but I didn't see any sense in questioning him. So one day I went to his room after he'd left. I asked him when he'd be back, and he said not before noon, he had a lot of things to take care of. Fine, I said, I'll get us some cold cuts and bread by the time you get back.

I found nothing on his desk, and nothing in his drawer. I felt ashamed of myself, but I had to know what was going on with him. And with me, too. I stopped in the middle of the room and looked around. Had he moved some of the furniture, I'd have heard, and the chandelier, no, he couldn't even reach it. There was no room under the rug, and the parquet floor was intact. He wouldn't put anything on the bookshelf because he knew that along with the storage bed, that would be the first place they'd look. There was no room between the paintings and the wall either, he'd have had to carve out some of the wall. It must be in the tile stove. Once when I was little I stole an eraser and hid it in the tile stove. Except, I couldn't sleep at night, so I opened the window and threw it out into the lilac bush.

I went to the tile stove. It was there. A paper box, it just fit inside the flue. It held membrane-thin carbon papers folded in half lengthwise. Kőszegi must have taken the originals with him. They contained the names, addresses, and professions of several hundred people who were either put in jail or left in '56. The pages also contained the setup of their network.

I didn't know what to do. If there was even one informer among the men visiting my father, he was just waiting for him to finish up his typing, so he could have the complete list. I put the box back in the stove, but then took it out again. I placed it on his table, went back to my room, and waited. There was a small crack in the veneer of my desk, and I couldn't take my eyes off it. My body was disconnected from the world as if I were floating in outer space like some botched up Gagarin who'd lost his moorings. Only my eyes kept me grounded, the fact that I didn't take them off this narrow, blackened crack. I didn't know that fear could be like this. I began to fear in earnest, and when I heard the key turn in the lock, my stomach tightened and my palms were suddenly drenched in sweat.

I heard him open the door to his room. He didn't go in, he took everything in from the threshold. Then I heard the boom of his cane as it broke in two on the footboard of the bed, a piece of it flying through the air and landing on the floor. Then I heard my father yell, come here, son! I got up and went out to the hall. My fear was gone. Yes, father, I said.

We stood in the hall facing each other. His face was ashen. I'd seen that look only once before in my life, when he was with that woman in the basement wine bar. But this time there was no trace of desperation, just pure anger. His lips trembled as I waited for him to yell at me again, but he said nothing for a while. If it took me ten minutes to find it, I said, they'd find it in three. Hide it in the enlarger, I said, then retreated to my room.

A couple of minutes later, Father left. He took the papers with him, but first he threw the empty box down in front of my door. Forgetting all about his cancer, I grabbed the Leica, pocketed two extra rolls of film, and went to Óbuda, but Adél Selyem no longer lived there.

(the network)

The day before she died, Mother forgot to wash the dishes. Come to think of it, this was the only act of rebellion in her life. Who we fall in love with is never a matter of decision. But who we love throughout a lifetime is always a matter of decision. And she had decided, and stood by her decision. Even during the last moments of her life, she simply forgot to wash the dishes.

Before Mária died, she cooked for the next two days, whereas surely, she had at least as much reason to rebel as Mother. It seems that death does not dispose all of us to act the same way. Some clean up after themselves, others don't. Then there are those who would like to, but are incapable of doing so.

Father, for instance, put his things in order, except everything he touched got tainted with cancer. His strength turned into defiance, his steadfastness turned into fanaticism, his clarity of vision into something irresponsible, as if the cobalt rays allowed all the things that till then had a secure place in his soul to become unhinged and proliferate.

When he slammed the front door behind him, I thought I wouldn't be seeing him for weeks. But by the time I got back from Óbuda, he was sitting by my desk in my room, looking through some folder, and the radio was on full blast.

I think we need to talk, son.

Sure, I said, and sat down on the bed.

First of all, thank you for warning me. It was probably not a good idea on my part to put that list there, though I wouldn't have kept it there in the long run, that goes without saying.

This in the long run irritated me, as did his quiet way of saying it. And I didn't like sitting next to him on the bed as Lovas and the others did.

Then that's settled, I said.

Actually, to tell the truth, it pains me a bit, that my son is distancing himself from all the things for which others spent time in jail.

I'm not distancing myself, I said.

Well, you certainly haven't shown much interest.

True. I haven't shown much interest, I said.

And you know, son, it's not just offensive, it's embarrassing.

What's embarrassing?

What's embarrassing? When your former cellmate asks you, is it true that your son doesn't give a shit about you, that can be embarrassing.

It took all my willpower not to shout above the radio.

What gives your former cellmates that idea, I asked, keeping my voice in check.

What gives them that idea? The way you pass through this apartment like a ghost without even bothering to greet the people in your home.

I don't remember ever neglecting to say hello to anyone I met.

And I don't remember you ever coming in to see us, son.

That's true. And I don't remember the two of us ever having a talk like we are now.

Maybe that's the problem, son.

You know, I did want to go into your room once, when you sent that buffoon away, along with his cronies. I wanted to tell you that you were right.

That buffoon, as you call him, spent eighteen months in jail. And the fact that I was right regarding what needs to be done doesn't change that fact. It wasn't the sort of organization we need.

If not that, then what?

One that's viable. One that machine guns can't wipe out.

All organizations can be wiped out, and they will be.

You're wrong, son, as in so many other things, you're wrong. They can't do away with a worldwide network.

You organized a worldwide network?

Not I, but we. The men you consider buffoons.

Demjén is the only buffoon. Kőszegi is a public menace. He should be on your list.

So you consider your father a public menace as well.

244

I'm talking about the list.

I drew up that list, son. It contains the names of the men in our network who will counterbalance what the others are doing.

I see.

You should learn from others rather than calling them names.

I knew that the others were the Jews, but we can't say so because of Mother. It's like a swearword or the name of some disease. One doesn't say cancer either. Except, these unsaid words turn my stomach.

I assume that by the others you mean the Jews.

If that's what I meant, I'd have said so. I'm sorry that my son, of all people, should think that. And by the way, Kőszegi is Jewish.

I didn't doubt that for a moment, I said.

You see, son? It's a cynical comment like that that's anti-Semitic, we need to learn something from others. I'm not talking about Jews and I'm not talking about Freemasons, but something that encompasses the whole world, something not restricted to one place or one person. Something whose head can't be chopped off.

Well, I think that if something has several heads, they will shoot several heads from the back, should the need arise.

You can't shoot half the world in the back of the head, son.

But my objection is that five-hundred men are not half the world. And that my father's life, a man suffering from cancer, is not too high a price to pay, as far as Kőszegi is concerned.

Kőszegi's got nothing to do with this.

But the fact that my father, who could tell with such certainty whether my friend was recruited or not, is now hiding a list of names in the tile stove, well, I've got plenty to do with that!

Shut up, son! Shut up, you hear?

You know who would hide something in a stove? A nitwit, that's who! I hid your colored eraser there when I was six, the one I stole from your desk, because, although I looked at it at least a dozen times, you didn't ask if I wanted it.

Why didn't you ask? I don't remember ever denying you anything.

A kid who reads Petőfi at the age of six doesn't need colored erasers, Father.
If you weren't my son, I'd throw you out of this room right now.
Except, as luck would have it, it's my room.

(the swimming pool)

I'm dreaming about Mother. She's divorced Father and she's living in Pest with an actor. I haven't seen her in three years, and this is my first visit. She's been waiting and is very happy that I've come. She's smiling. The actor isn't home. Mother is wearing a sky-blue robe. She leads me to the bathroom along a long, dark corridor. The sink is filled with water and there's a watermelon bobbing in it. It's being cooled down. A knife with a black handle is resting on the rim. My mother hands it to me to cut it in half, but the melon is still warm. I say, let's wait until it cools down. And she says, but I want it now. I split it in two. My mother's heart is inside. She disappears, and her heart remains beating in my hand.

I wake up relaxed. I know it's not true.

I found Kornél at it already, writing something in his notebook. The sun was shining. His response to my dream was that I didn't kill my mother and I'm not going to kill my father either.

I know, but that's not what my dream was about. It was actually a very good dream.

That's not what a good dream is like.

I got dressed and we went downstairs to the kitchen. His mother insisted that we eat something before drinking our coffee, so we ate our buttered bread first. An alarm clock was ticking on top of the cupboard, and next to it stood a bottle of curdled milk. The milk's asleep, I said and laughed. His mouth full, Kornél stared at me. He didn't get the joke. I pointed to the clock and then to the milk, thinking he'd get it, but he still didn't, or else didn't want to.

What's so funny? he asked.

Nothing, I said.

The coffee was ready. He poured us some and was about to go back to his room.

It's beautiful outside.

He made a face, but then we took our mugs and went to sit in the garden in back of the house.

Still, I'm sorry the actor wasn't home. I'd have liked to know what he's like, I said.

And I'd like to know the last time you took a picture.

What's the matter with you this morning, I asked.

Well, since you brought it up, you've been acting pretty strange these days.

You think it's strange for me to laugh at the milk sleeping next to the alarm clock?

You have a home.

Am I in the way?

You're not in the way. I wasn't thinking that you're in the way. I'm thinking that you have a home, and a father, who is ill. You have a camera, and you have. . .

Okay, I'm listening, I said, And I have a what?

You have a life. And it's not normal when you don't go home for days. And it's not normal, when you consider a nightmare a good dream.

I'm sorry, but I don't follow. I think I know best what kind of dream it was. Also, you know what's not normal? When I say that we should go and enjoy the sun and you make a face, that's not normal.

I wasn't making a face because of the sun.

And I didn't ask to sleep here because I can't stand my own home, but because I like sitting out here in the garden for a bit to enjoy the sun. I love the sun, Kornél. Possibly, I might not take a decent picture in my entire life. Possibly, I'll never meet a woman more normal than Adél Selyem in my entire life. Possibly, I'm even more of a coward than you and may not even dare to ask for my own photos back, should they want to exhibit them. And it is an unavoidable fact that my father will drop dead like a dog, howling in pain. And I'll be standing there, listening, unable to help. But despite all of this, I won't hang myself. I love the sun. It may be something to be ashamed of, but that's how it is. I love this damned light!

It's nothing to be ashamed of. So let's sit here for a while.

I love it, understand? Do you understand?

Yes, I understand. Just calm down.

Fine. But don't tell me if my dream is good or not. And don't fucking tell me to go home.

I'm not fucking telling you any such thing.

He took the empty mug from me, went inside, and brought out two more mugs of coffee.

Have you ever been to the Lukács? he asked when he came back.

What's that?

It's a pool. Across from Margaret Island, near the abutment of the bridge.

Yes, I know which one you mean. But I've never been. The last time I was at a pool, I was still a child.

In that case, come. Let's go to the Lukács.

Ok, sure. But lend me a pair of swimming trunks.

I can give you my father's

Is it expensive?

I don't remember. It's been some time since I went there myself.

How come?

I don't know. Maybe because everybody goes there.

What do you mean, everybody?

Actors, whores, politicians.

You left out poets.

And poets.

It must be a big pool then.

It was past noon by the time we got there. The sun came shining through the branches of the plane trees. The row of cabins was just like the one at the May Day pool in Mélyvár. We changed. His father's bathing trunks were a bit loose, but I pulled them as tight as I could. There weren't many people around.

On the sundeck upstairs, a middle-age woman was sitting on a blanket. Two-piece bathing suits were coming into fashion, and she had one on. It was white, and contrasted with her dark skin. She'd wrapped a towel around her head like a turban, and that too was white. She glanced at us and sized us up.

She was eating watermelon.

Let's get out of here, I said to Kornél.

Yes, let's, he said.

(the stroking)

Stroking my camera with my fingers, I said, calm down, Leica. Some objects make you feel safe not because of their benefit or their value, but because of some human trait they possess. A Leica, for example, is reliable. You can depend on it. It won't let you down. It may go to the devil someday, but it doesn't hint at it for weeks or months beforehand. It doesn't keep you in fear. In fact, it has saved lives. We know of cases when the camera stopped a bullet.

When I got home from the Lukács, I took Father's broken cane and went with it to the shoemaker on Lövölde Square. The man told me he couldn't fix it, that I should take it to a joiner. I said that I didn't know of any in the neighborhood. In the end he glued it together and wound it around a couple of times with the thread shoemakers use to sew leather. He wouldn't take any money, though. He didn't know how long it would last. I thanked him and went home. I found father in the apartment.

I'd have appreciated it if he'd been pleased that I had his cane fixed, though when you're just back from radiotherapy, it's pretty hard to appreciate anything. Be that as it may, he did say, thank you, son. He was sitting at his table with a notebook. I asked him what he was writing. Nothing, he said. Then he added that he was making a list of his chores. He didn't ask me to leave, but I felt it'd be better if I didn't disturb him.

About half an hour later he knocked. I told him to come in, but he stopped in the doorway. He said he shouldn't have reacted with such vehemence before and he was very sorry, and that he appreciated the fact that I had his cane fixed. Then after a while he added that alas, he couldn't walk with a cane held together with thread. It wasn't safe. But it doesn't matter. It's the gesture that counts.

Never in my life have I heard my father say that he appreciated me, or that it's the gesture that counts. I looked at the cross on his neck drawn with an ink pencil. He forgot to wash it off after his treatment. I said that I should have thought of that.

How are you feeling?

Fine, thank you.

When he left, I thought that it was all right. If death had nestled inside me, I'd have probably taken it out on others a lot more. When I heard the cane break on the footboard of the bed once again, I got up and went over to the small table, and that's when I stroked the Leica. The gesture calmed me down.

Then I looked for an empty notebook in the drawer. Since high school it was full of empty notebooks. At most, they contained writing on the first couple of pages. I found one with a white spiral binding, it made it easier to tear out the sheets. I wrote on the cover:" a good day," and began revising the pictures I'd taken of Imolka at one time. To the right a cupboard and a faucet, to the left a sofa, in the middle by the table, a woman with a plate in front of her. To the right a cupboard and a faucet, to the left a sofa, in the middle by the table, a woman darning a sock. To the right a cupboard and a faucet, to the left a sofa, in the middle by the table, a woman eating watermelon. To the right a cupboard and a faucet, to the left a sofa, in the middle by the table, a woman, behind her Dorvai.

(Dalma Keresztes)

The following day I went to the Corvin and bought a pair of bathing trunks, and by noon I was at the Lukács. The woman was sitting in the same place, reading a book. When I spread my towel on the ground, she looked me over again, then greeted me with a nod. I reciprocated.

Where is your friend? she asked.

You'll have to make do with me today, I said.

Well, well, she said, then got to her feet and went into the pool. She was cold as ice, but from the moment she recognized me, there was no trace of the fear of failure left in me.

I didn't notice her hair. That night at the printer's, I imagined that it was black. And so it was, though I wasn't interested in her hair or her two-piece bathing suit. The only thing that interested me was her eating watermelon; instead of using a penknife, she used three fingers to tear the flesh from the rind. I glanced at the book. Balzac. That's good. We can always talk about that if need be.

When she came out of the water, she started talking with an elderly man. They were both wearing swimming caps, and so was everyone else in the pool. If she asks why I'm not swimming, I'd tell her that I've come to sunbathe, I decided. But she didn't ask. She moved the book and her woven pool bag aside and lay down to dry, with her feet facing me. She raised her hips for a second, her belly tightened, and with two fingers she fixed her bikini bottom in place, then she flung her arms to the side, as if she were on a cross. Her nipples stood up from the cold water. I tried to fix my gaze on her belly instead as it slowly rose, then sank with the drops of water collected in her navel. I saw that she was trying to breathe slowly, but to no avail. The rhythm was broken now and then, and her abdomen would tighten. To the right the branches of the plane trees, to the left a row of cabins and the men's pool, in the middle a woman about the same age as my mother, trying to hide her fear behind a phlegmatic façade.

She turned around and began reading, but she didn't turn the page for minutes on end, just like my father when he bought the Leica. I decided that she must be divorced, and her children have probably moved away. Be that as it may, there's nothing to prevent her from spending her mornings at the Lukács. She comes alone and goes home alone. And she looks at herself in the mirror alone when she puts on her bikini.

She got up and gathered her things. Since she returned from the pool, she hadn't looked at me once. Standing with her back to me, she spread her legs a bit as she leaned over for her white blanket. She folded it neatly, laid it across one arm, then turned to me.
Well, I made do with you. Your company was not what I'd call entertaining.
Well, goodbye, she said, leaning over once again to pick up her pool bag.
The pleasure was all mine, I said. I'm András Szabad. Szabad, as in free.
That, at least, is a promising start. Have you given me a name as well?
Not yet.
A shame. That would have added to the intrigue.
How about Olga, I said.
Oh, that sends shivers down my spine.
I'm sorry.
I bet you are. Next time, try harder.
I'm sorry. It's the best I can do. And now I'm off to the Corvin to buy a pair of bathing trunks, I offered.
She looked at me but said nothing. Then after a while she said, in that case, there's nothing to keep you here, is there?
No, nothing.
She took her sunglasses out of her bag and put them on to shield her eyes.
I have a car. I'll take you home.
Thank you, I said.
Dalma Keresztes, she said, but didn't offer her hand. Then she added, born Johannis.

I see.

I should hope so.

Are you sure it's a good idea to offer me a ride?

We're not at the point yet where you should be asking questions. Wait for me at the entrance.

She had rented a cabin, while I'd paid for a simple locker. I waited more than half an hour for her to change. I was thinking about how my father had lost five kilos in a single week. Also, by all odds, he'd probably never been to the Lukács in his life, and at this point he never would. Thermal baths can't counteract the loss of five kilos a week. Nothing can. Neither radiation therapy, nor hope, not even a clandestine network. I can't understand for the life of me why people cling to hope like that. Whoever invented it should rot in hell. My father never thought of organizing a clandestine network when he still had something to lose, did he? If I had nothing to lose, I wouldn't be standing here either, waiting like a gentleman, I guess. If nothing else, me waiting around like this is a sure sign that I have something to lose. Or the fact that I'm not grabbing her by her wet bikini bottom and I'm not shoving her inside her cabin like some Dorvai. You're lucky, Dalma Keresztes. My grandfather used to visit the brothel with a bouquet of flowers. I've been taught to have feelings. I even have a Chinese pawn to prove it. So kindly appreciate it. Of course, if a person has a fist-size tumor where his heart should be, that's another matter. He can break his cane in half even on your back, if he wants. As for me, kindly take me home, born Johannis, because you're not going to cheat on anyone with me. You can bet your bottom dollar. And also, kindly forget that fake nonchalant tone. I don't need the affectation of a frustrated, lonely woman.

Where to? she asked.

As she approached from the opposite direction, I hardly recognized her.

Home, I said.

You expect me to read your mind?

You know what? If you don't discard that shield of nonchalance, I'd rather walk.

I couldn't see her eyes, but the corner of her lip trembled. She wore a sleeveless summer dress, though it was more like an evening gown. It was black and nearly reached to the ground. She had pearls around her neck. She took off her sunglasses and took out her car keys.

Come on, get in.

She drove a red Fiat.

I live on Szív Street, I said.

Neither of us spoke until we reached the Pest side of Margaret Bridge. As we crossed it, I looked at the Danube through the car window.

This was the first bridge I crossed, I said.

Where were you born, she asked.

Mélyvár.

It's a nice place.

You've been there?

Several times. I visited the library.

What do you do?

Mostly, I'm a historian. And you?

Mostly, I'm a photographer.

I fell silent. I've never said this to anyone that way except Kornél. On the other hand, there was no one to say it to. It doesn't matter, I reflected.

That's good. Just photographer would have scared me a bit, she said.

What were you researching in Mélyvár?

That's where they burned the last witches.

I didn't know that. In Hungary or the world?

In Europe.

So the burning of witches is your main subject of research?

It's just a fork in the road. My main subject is book burning. Is Szív a one-way street?

I don't know. I don't have a car.

She said nothing for a while.

And what do you take pictures of?

Not you. Your husband wouldn't approve.

I wouldn't be so sure. Besides, I'm officially divorced.

What do you mean officially?

I mean that my husband defected, and to keep my job I had to ask for a divorce.

In '56?

Do I look that old?

You know perfectly well what you look like, otherwise you wouldn't be wearing a bikini.

A woman can never be sure.

Even if she's told?

Perhaps. For a minute or two.

Well, perhaps, for a day, at least, you should know. . . .

Know what?

It wouldn't be proper for me to tell you in detail what I imagined all last night about your lips, your hands, and the watermelon.

Have you stopped imagining?

On the contrary. I'm imagining it more and more.

A good thing you can't take photographs of what you imagine.

Well, I'm trying. It's the door to the right.

If you mean what you just said, will you show me your pictures sometime?

I can't ask you in, I'm afraid.

Don't tell me you're married?

No, I'm not married, but my father has cancer.

I really hope she doesn't say she's sorry, I thought.

She produced a slip of paper and jotted down her phone number.

I know some doctors. Perhaps they can help, she said.

Thank you. I'll call you. Even if they can't help.

He left the country two years ago. You can call any time you like, she said.

I closed the front door to the house and waited for her to start the car and drive off. Father was lying down with a wet cloth on his forehead. I sat down on the side of his bed and asked how he was. He said he was fine, except he had a headache. I asked if I should bring some pain reliever from the pharmacy. He said he'd taken one already, it's probably because of the heat and it would soon be gone.

I don't know what happened to me. The whole thing, what I did with the cane.

It's all right, it happens.

Where have you been?

I met someone and we talked. At the Lukács.

What's the Lukács like?

It's very nice.

(the witch burning)

The last witch of Europe was an orphaned halfwit by the name of Márta Koszorús. The records tell us that she spoke with the birds, remained a virgin after intercourse, and she cast a spell on dogs. Only on male dogs. When she passed by a fence, the male dogs worked themselves into such a frenzy that they would try to relieve themselves between the slits in the boards or would rub themselves against the trunk of a tree.

According to the testimony provided by the graveyard custodian, she spoke the language of birds, and he even saw the thrushes, crows, and starlings of the graveyard follow Márta Koszorús to her mother's grave, and when she asked them, they tore out the weeds.

Her power over dogs wasn't that extraordinary, and as for the birds, saints could do the same thing, Márta went on. But her postcoital virginity stood to prove her converse with the devil. No matter how many men had her, even if five or six fornicated with her in a row, she remained a virgin. Each time she would bleed profusely. And so there was no doubt that she was the elect through whom Satan meant to send his bastard into the world, just as the Lord had given his Son to the world through the Virgin Mary.

Needless to say, no resident of Mélyvár wanted the town to become notorious because of the Antichrist. And so, five years after the House of Habsburg saw the light and prohibited witch trials, they nevertheless prepared a stake for Márta Koszorús in the castle yard. They didn't even choke her.

What do you mean? Did they usually choke them first?

Of course. The executioners usually pitied the victim and choked her. They investigated her case thoroughly, and let it be said to the court's credit, they examined her in a hospital. But though Márta Koszorús tugged at her four tight ropes and talked to the pigeons flying around the hospital ward, and no matter how loud the hospital's dogs howled downstairs, she was found to be a virgin at three of the trials. And so the Anti-christ didn't turn out to be Hungarian after all, and he certainly wasn't from Mélyvár, which is a good thing, we've got to admit.

But he could have been, I said.

(the good picture)

When he came up a couple of days later, I told Kornél I was in love.

Who's the lucky girl?

That woman.

What woman?

The one from the Lukács, who was eating watermelon.

He got up and looked out the window as if I weren't even there.

Don't do it, he said.

Don't do what?

You know perfectly well. You have a nightmare, and then you go back to that woman on purpose?

That's not why I went back. It has nothing to do with my dreams. You eat watermelon, and I eat watermelon. It's summer. I can't hate everyone who eats watermelon just because I had a bad dream.

But it doesn't follow that you should fall in love with her.

I went back because I had to go back.

That's logical. It's so fucking logical, it couldn't be more logical, could it?

Possibly. But that doesn't change the facts.

How many times have you met?

Twice. Or three times, if we count the first. What's this? An interrogation?

So is it twice or three times?

Once with you and once at the pool, when I went back.

Which makes two.

Plus two more times at her place.

That woman could be your mother.

Nobody's my mother, understand?

That's not what I meant. Sorry.

She's not even forty-five, I bet. She's divorced. Her husband went to Switzerland.

So you slept with her.

So it is an interrogation after all.

Did you or did you not sleep with her?

So now I'm an oedipal madman just because I had a dream about my mother? Is that what you're thinking?

I'm thinking that you're bent on ruining your life.

Has it ever occurred to you that you could be asking me about her? Who she is, what she is, and how it is between us?

That's what I asked you just now.

No. You asked if I slept with her, as if that were the only way to have a relationship.

Not the only way. But sleeping with someone is certainly a sure way. At least, that's what I think.

You know what? Why don't you go imagine a bunch of other things to go with it.

For instance? That if she doesn't stuff a piece of rag in her mouth, she might out-scream three Adél Selyems? Because as I remember her, there's not much more that comes to mind.

What exactly is your problem? That I'm in love and you're not?

You're a shit. A great big shit.

Call it what you will.

You know what I call it? Ruining your life.

Ruining my life? That's a good one, I'll remember that. But the fact that I haven't been with anyone since Johanna Vészi, that's what I call ruining my life, because that was a long time ago.

Well, I haven't been with anyone since Judit, and that too was a long time ago.

Good for you. You seem to take it in stride.

You have no way of knowing.

Perhaps.

Why don't you look for a normal woman, one you can live with?

Fine, I said. Then I got to my feet, went to the kitchen, and brought back the two photographs that were drying on the drawing board.

Here. Here's a normal woman. The only one I can live with.

He looked at the pictures, while he drummed on the table with two fingers.

Yes. They're good. In fact, they're very good.

I think so, too. So stop badgering me.

(the two hemispheres)

I liked that apartment. The terrace had a view of Vérmező Park. The books were in one room, the bed in the other, like the two hemispheres of the brain, and the door between them could not be closed. When Father died, I arranged the apartment the same way, though at the time I wasn't thinking of Naphegy.

Generally, I'd bring over the wine and she cooked. Until the autumn rains, we ate out on the terrace. She usually wore a robe. Sometimes she picked me up in her car, at other times I walked up the hill.

Her doctor friends were mostly psychiatrists and psychologists. They couldn't have helped my father, though the first time I went to her place, she actually did take out their name cards. There was some old music playing on the record player, so she turned down the volume. Her nail polish was still out on the table. The books and the pillows were stacked up in piles. On three sides of the room, the shelves reached up to the ceiling. A linden stood in front of the window. A black Continental typewriter, white sheets, and some used-up carbon paper lay on the desk.

The chaos was horrific. It was as hard to breathe as if you were up in the Andes; you had to watch your step because of all the ashtrays, bracelets, underwear, and glasses scattered about. There was nothing in the other room, just a rug and a chandelier. And under the chandelier, her bed. The apartment resembled the two hemispheres of the brain.

A nice apartment, I said.
I know. My husband furnished it.
I thought it was you.
It was furnished to my taste.
And why did he leave?

Because he couldn't find a twenty-year-old for himself in Pest whose two hemi-spheres he could have furnished the same way.

What does he do?

I just told you. He's a whoremonger. And also a genius, alas. Other than that, he's a psychiatrist.

You hate him?

You have to ask?

In that case, what do you mean that you're divorced only officially.

I mean that when my daughter turns thirty, I will probably follow him to Switzerland.

Are you sure that's what you want?

You're young and you're talking nonsense, she said. Right now, I'm hungry.

The terrace opened from the kitchen. She made some sandwiches, and we ate them outside. We watched the dusk settle in the lap of the valley. She told me the story of the last witch in Europe. Today I know that she'd made it up. Though she had been to Mélyvár and they'd burned a couple of witches there, the innocent halfwit that the Antichrist had chosen did not live in Mélyvár, but in a two-room, eighty square meter bourgeois apartment up on Naphegy. She sympathized with the poor girl, and had every reason to sympathize with her. It took me months to realize that she'd do anything to keep that sympathy alive.

I hadn't thought about it before, but it's obviously true.

What is?

That being strangled is better than being burned at the stake.

Much better because, for instance, if the brain doesn't get enough oxygen, that enhances the sensation of orgasm.

I watched her beads stuck between her breasts in the sleeveless dress she wore.

See? I didn't know that.

Well now you do. You just have to do it the right way. Okay, I'll bring us some wine.

When she rose from the wicker armchair, her breasts nearly brushed against my face. She stopped in the terrace door for a second, then without turning around, she said, you can come after me, if you want.

I caught up with her among her books. After we made love, she asked if she'd see me again. I said, of course. Does that mean I'd want her as much as I did today, she asked, and I said that as long as she made me want her like she did today, she wouldn't need to ask. Her body smelled of ambergris.

Did you mean it when you said you don't have anyone, she asked.

Actually, I do. My Leica.

I assume you won't leave your Leica for my sake.

That's out of the question.

If your Leica is curious to see what I'm like, you can bring it along.

You'll be consumed with jealousy.

You bet. But that'll make you and your Leica want me all the more, she said. And I'd like that very much.

When I got dressed, she asked me not to go to the Lukács.

Why not?

Because I chat with lots of people there, they know me.

And what's wrong with that?

Look in the mirror. You're barely past twenty and I'll soon be fifty.

You're lying.

She kissed me. Her lips still smelled of the ocean. I love you, she said. I said nothing.

She and Kornél met three or four times, but I didn't mind. The first time I felt a bit apprehensive, but she said she didn't want to live her life locked up in a bedroom. Why, then, are you telling me not to go to the Lukács, I thought. After all, my place was off limits. She'd been there just once for a short time, when Father wasn't there. I didn't want them to meet. I told her it was because of his cancer, but the truth was, I didn't want Father to know that I'm with a woman closer to his age than mine. All the same, once they bumped into each other at the door. Father was polite and invited her in. She gave me a quick, furtive glance, then just as politely said thank you, next time without fail, but I need to be off now. I asked Father for there not to be a next time, and he agreed, and never brought it up again.

We first met Kornél at the café. Dalma wore a knitted sweater but didn't wear her brace-lets or her beads. Évike looked her up and down and decided that she didn't pose a risk, and when she put our coffees down on the table in front of us, she gave her a friendly smile. After a couple minutes of awkward silence, Dalma Keresztes began talking about book burnings, and we ended up staying until closing time. She didn't just talk about the books burned for political or religious reasons, she also talked about love letters that ended up in the fire, and the manuscripts that authors committed to the flames themselves. Kornél asked if it's considered book burning when someone writes in the sand. It certainly is, she said, and headed to the powder room upstairs.

I was a real jerk the other day, Kornél said.

Yes, you were. Just make sure you don't hit on Dalma.

You're an idiot, he said.

We drove him back to Budafok, and when Dalma said goodbye, she added that she didn't want to make him feel uncomfortable, that's why she hadn't mentioned it before, but she loves his poems.

Once the three of us went to the movies, and once we went for a walk up on János Hill. Then once they met without me. That made me feel a bit anxious.

Just don't tell me you're jealous, or I blow my top.

I'm not jealous. But don't conspire behind my back.

Someone worrying about you is not what I'd call a conspiracy.

If someone suddenly wants to take you to Mélyvár after talking over a glass of wine, I call that a conspiracy.

And I call it love.

Is that so?

We were talking about you. I'm as easily blinded by a bathing suit as the next man. Also, there's your at times scary obsessiveness. But for your information, she loves you.

For your information, Dalma and I converse in a different way.

Meaning?

Meaning that the details are none of your business.

People always talk differently in bed.

Did you know that she went to see my father?

Without telling you?
Without telling me.
And what did your father say?
Nothing whatsoever.
Then how do you know?
I could smell her perfume in my father's room, even the next day.
That doesn't seem plausible.
That smell is more familiar to me than the palm of your hand is to you.
Still, that woman loves you.
No, Kornél. She loves a raped orphaned girl, to the exclusion of everyone else.

(the right)

I'd like to see the photos.

Fine.

I'd enlarged nine pictures by then. I made forty by fifty centimeter enlargements. I put them in a big folder and took them to her place up on the hill. I laid them out on the floor by the window. I thought she'd ask what became of the other negatives, but she didn't, thank God. So I didn't have to explain that camerawork isn't even halfway between reality and a finished photo. After Johanna Vészi, I'd decided that apart from myself and blind fate that no one would ever have a say in what remains and what will not. If someone asks me to put down the camera at any time, I will, with no hard feelings. But once a person has agreed, I won't lock my pictures up in a drawer, or destroy them because of some nervous whim or onrush of vanity.

I told Dalma Keresztes that the very first time. I told her that I'd take pictures of her only if she agreed to it, but then they would remain my pictures. And if not, that would be my decision. It's up to me. It's my right. I know, she said. I told her that wasn't good enough for me. It's not enough that she knew then, because nothing would change my conviction. Not even if she left me, reported me to the police, or killed me. And she said, I know. Isn't that enough for you?

The one where only her face showed she placed on her pillow. It was as if she were lying there across from the huge windows, half dead, looking out into empty space. She then pulled the blanket up to her eyes.

Leave her with me, she said.

I make just one enlargement of each.

Please.

Fine. I'll make another enlargement for you. But I'm taking this one back with me.

You do know that you can do with me anything you like, she said.

I can't do anything I like with anyone, I said.

With me you can. Anything.

She let down the wooden blinds, and the afternoon shed its thin rays of light on the bed between the slits.

I wish you'd believe me when I say. Anything.

It's your choice, not mine.

(determination)

Then one day I found a studio light in her room.

Where did you get it? I asked.

Never mind. You said you needed one.

That's not what I said.

Well, that was my understanding. Aren't you going to try it?

I looked at her lips. Her lipstick was ever so slightly smeared because she'd been drinking. She got up and handed me the camera.

Where should I look?

In my eyes.

You mean the camera? But that's a machine.

For me, it's my eyes.

Then fuck me like a machine.

Shut up.

Let's go.

I said, shut up.

Then one day as I glanced out the window of the café, I saw her standing on the corner opposite. Kornél said that she probably has business there. But by the time I went outside, she'd gotten in her car and had driven off. In the evening, she wore a dress I'd never seen before. It was red and fell just above the knee.

Pretend that I'm another woman, she said.

It wasn't another woman, I said. It was Kornél. Except, from where you were standing, the curtain stood in the way.

I don't know what you're talking about.

I was standing in the space between the rooms, wishing there were a door to close. She went inside and lay on the bed, positioning herself so I'd see she wasn't wearing panties. She grabbed the bottle of vodka and took a swig.

I was playing chess with Kornél. We hadn't played chess in six months, I said.

I know, she said.

Okay, put down that bottle.

I like vodka.

If I'm not drinking, you have no reason to drink either.

I want you to get me drunk.

What do you mean get you drunk?

I mean, force the bottle in my mouth and make me drink.

I would never want to get anyone that drunk, ever.

Of course you would.

Put it down. Please.

I told you. With me, anything. Not what you dare, but what you really want.

In that case, get out of your clothes.

Only when you say what you're thinking.

That's what I'm thinking.

That's not true.

It is.

You're such a coward.

I grabbed her chin, and the vodka dripped down her breasts. She laughed.

You like that? You're enjoying yourself?

Yes.

Well then, let's get started. Get out of that dress, you slut.

(the telephone)

I'd have had no way of knowing what's what, had she not locked me in that last night. I'd have no way of knowing the extent to which the outer limits of carnal desire can be stretched without it crushing the soul. I think that few things weigh as heavily on the soul as when reality catches up with the imagination. Of course, it could weigh just as heavily on the soul if it doesn't catch up with it at all. Be that as it may, fewer people have gone crazy from being poor than from getting rich. And is the desire for wealth stronger than the mating instinct? I have no way of knowing how closely our reality might have approximated our imagination. If anything was left to desire. It took only a second, and I was left with nothing.

I need to go, I said.
I'll take you home.
Fine. Let's go.
I said I'd take you home. You'll be back in twenty minutes, which leaves nineteen for me.
Five, I said.
Fine. Put your hands behind you.
Not now. I really must go.
Put your hands behind you.
I did as she ordered. I felt the belt of her robe tighten and cut into my wrists.

But that's not how it was.
First we had a fight. I told her that I couldn't breathe. I told her it wasn't a nurse I needed.
What do you mean?
You know perfectly well what I mean. You have no business across from the café of

all places, or on the corner of Szív and People's Republic Avenue. You have no business seeing my father in secret.

That's ridiculous, I've never been to see your father.

And if you do, you shouldn't lie about it.

Why would I go see him? What would I want with your father?

I don't know. Why don't you tell me?

In any case, I doubt that your father would have told me. You're making it up. Your father isn't the sort of person who—

She fell silent.

And when did you learn that he's not the sort of person who?

I never went to see him.

Anyone with half a brain wouldn't do this. You know perfectly well that I know.

Are you calling me a liar?

Just don't lie. It's that simple.

Why shouldn't I get to know your father?

Because I asked you not to. That's why.

You didn't ask, you demanded, because you're ashamed of me. You're ashamed because I could be your mother.

I watched her standing by the window in her open robe, the cigarette shaking between her trembling fingers. What was left of the afternoon filtered through the branches of the linden tree, strands of her hair fell over her shoulder. Never, for a single moment, did I ever think of her as an older woman, not even now. No one would think of her as old for many more years, except for herself.

Please don't do that again. No one can replace my mother, I said quietly. You might be ashamed of me at the Lukács, but I'm not ashamed of you in front of my father. I just don't want him to think that his son is ruining his life. That's all. I don't want him to die despairing.

Ruining his life? Because his son is with an old woman?

Please stop with this old woman business.

For your information, he's happy that someone is interested in his son's needs.

In that case, next time, ask me! Maybe that's why I can't breathe.

You can have anything you want and do anything you feel like doing, and you can't breathe? Who are you trying to kid?

I never asked for that anything. What are you? A kept woman afraid of being fired? You think men want you only as long as they can twist your arms when they fuck you? For God's sake, where's your dignity?

She stubbed out her cigarette, went to the mirror, and rouged her lips.

I need to go, I said.
I'll take you home.
Fine. Let's go.
I just said I'd take you. You'll be back in twenty minutes, which leaves nineteen for me.
Five, I said.
Fine. Put your hands behind you.
Not now. I really must go.
Fine.
I got up.
You want dignity? she said. Sit down and put your hands behind you.
I did so. I felt the belt of her robe tightening around my wrists.
Let's not, I said.
This time around, you're the kept woman. So shut up. For five minutes you can take it.

She blindfolded me.
Not my eyes, I said. Take it off.
I don't understand you. You could have said before. I told you. You can ask me anything.
I won't ask now either, and I'm not going to.
Only four left, she said, and started unbuckling my belt.
I said, take it off.
We could bring up a whore sometime if you'd like.

You're out of your mind. Take it off, I said.

Shut up. A servant obeys and keeps quiet.

I need to go.

I told you. Shut up.

She tried to stuff a piece of rag in my mouth.

I pushed her away with my knee.

You're an animal, she said, and left me. I could hear her crying in the other room.

I didn't kick you, I just shoved you! And I asked you to take it off. You know perfectly well that I have to go. I have to be there when the doctor comes.

I heard her throw her coat on over her robe, slip on her shoes, then slam the door. I thought I'd go mad.

It may have been thirty minutes, or it may have been one. It makes no difference. I don't know. Then she came back and took that shit off my wrists. I left her without a word.

By the time I got to the house it was dark outside and I could hear my father screaming with pain from downstairs. I took four steps at a time as I rushed upstairs. The doctor was there already, but the simple pain killer had no effect. While he went to call an ambulance, I wiped the vomit off the floor.

I went along, and they gave him morphine. Luckily, it helped. The nurse let me sit by his bed until the early hours of the morning, when I had to go to work at the printer's. I told the others that I wouldn't be coming to work anymore. They were understanding and said I should stay home until Father was better, they'd arrange it with personnel. I said thank you, even though it was obvious that Father wouldn't get better, and that I wouldn't be coming back, ever again.

Then I went to the tobacconist and called Dalma Keresztes. She asked what I wanted, it was early. I said I know, but I had to take Father to the hospital last night. She said that she just wanted it to be good for me, and out of gratitude, I kicked her like a dog, and I said that I didn't kick her, nor do I go around kicking dogs, and she said that I blame her when I should be apologizing for treating her like trash, and I said that I have never treated her that way, and she said, interesting, considering that except for me and her husband, no one has ever called her a whore. I'm sorry. No, she's sorry, she said, she's sorry for me. Profoundly sorry. But she won't stand for the way I treat her and rape her and blame her for everything, just like her husband. And she would not stand for me blaming her, as if it were her fault that cancer is what it is. I wasn't blaming her, I said, except I didn't want to see her ever again. She said something else, but luckily, the line went dead. I didn't call her back. I didn't see her for seven years. But Kornél said I shouldn't tear up the pictures.

(the wedding ring)

In the morning, Father felt fine, except his testicles had swollen the size of my fist. His kidneys aren't functioning, the doctor said. But he ate, and the nurses were satisfied. In the bed next to his, a man was reading the paper. From time to time, he whistled. Somebody asked him not to whistle. It's all the same to me, he said.

Son.
Yes, I said.
Please call Kőszegi.
Alright, I said.
And Sára Rónai at the library.
Sure. No problem.
Tell her they shouldn't come visit me.
They don't even know you're here.
Then call and tell them. But I don't want anybody visiting me here.
Fine. I'll tell them.
They should come once I feel better and I'm home again.
Fine, I said.
Go on, call them. You must have tokens in your pocket.
I do, I said.

They were pushing a stretcher along the narrow corridor. The relatives of the sick man were sitting by the wall, having a snack. The man on the stretcher tried to rise on his elbows, but the nurse told him to keep still or the tube in his stomach would be dislodged. I looked out the window. It faced the firewall opposite. The sky couldn't be seen even from the fourth floor.

Although there were only a couple of people waiting for the elevator, I decided to take the stairs. On the third-floor landing, I stopped for a cigarette. I was afraid of reaching the ground floor, of going outside. I felt that the only valid reality was here, between these walls, while everything on the outside, the apartment building of which only the firewall was visible from the hospital window, the sidewalk smeared with dog shit along with the moving traffic, the bicycle chained to a lamp post, its wheels gone, stolen, the young mother, drunk, with the child she kept slapping, the woman who had stared at me on the tram, the mailman and the obese flower vendor, the railway station, the pedestrian crossing, the buffet, the notions shop, from that moment on, none of it was real, from that moment on, all of it might as well have stopped existing.

A patient stopped next to me and asked for a light.

A relative? he asked.

No. Just an acquaintance.

People from Pest are lucky. They get visitors. I get visitors only on Tuesday. I'm from Biatorbágy.

I'm sorry, I have to go, I said, though usually, I would add some other lie to the apology. Then taking two steps at a time, I fled that morgue, out the gate, to be among the drunken mothers, petty hustlers and bicycle thieves, back to the only valid reality.

Barely an hour had passed, and Kőszegi was at the hospital. Father was still sleeping. We were standing in the hall, and he patted me on the shoulder.

You should be proud of your father, kid, because what he did he didn't do for his own sake. He was a brave man.

He's still alive, I said.

He turned red, the artery on his neck throbbed with agitation.

Of course he's alive. Men like him don't die. Ever.

He's going to die in a day or two. Just like you, and all the rest. And Kádár. And me.

Still, we'll have to see eye to eye, little Szabad.

In that case, do something about it.

You're arrogant, kid.

Call me kid once more, and I'm gonna fucking throw you out the window, you shit.

279

He grabbed the back of a white chair. He was trembling from head to foot. Me, I felt calmer than I'd ever felt in my life. To the right Kőszegi, to the left, the ward. I looked. My father was awake now, watching us from the bed. He was at a distance by the window, so I knew he couldn't have heard us. He seemed pleased that we were talking.

Ten minutes, I said.

Is that an order, kid?

What did you say to my father once? That he should have stayed put in '56? Ten minutes, while I go downstairs for some coffee. But he's not going to spend his last day with you, understand?

There was a cake shop across the way. The relatives brought cake and cold drinks for the patients from here, provided they were allowed to eat it. From time to time, a patient also showed up, with a robe thrown over his pajamas. The place had three-legged chairs with red seats and was spruced up with plastic flowers and aluminum ashtrays. I sat down at a table from where I saw Sára Rónai arrive, distraught, then run up the stairs leading to the hospital entrance. I was hungry and ate a cream puff. It was delicious. She and Kőszegi left the hospital about half an hour later. Rónai was crying. Kőszegi had his arm around her. I waited for them to round the corner, paid for the two coffees and the cream puff, and went back to Father.

They're good people, son. They're going to be a great help to you.

Yes, I know.

And that nice woman. What's her name? Dalma?

Yes, Dalma.

She also loves you very much, son. It's just that we've always found it difficult to talk about such things, you and me.

Look what I bought for you, I said.

What's that?

A landmine, I said, and placed an ashtray on the nightstand by his bed.

He laughed.

The nurse told me I had to go home for the night. I couldn't stay, I should get some rest.

I want to stay by his side, I said.

You'll have plenty of time for that, young man. Take my word for it.

Everything will be just fine. You should go on home now and get some rest.

I stopped in his room and looked at the glass of curdled milk on the table. A half-eaten apple lay on a plate. It had turned brown. Medicine. And next to the bed, his new cane. The one he smashed on top of the garderobe. On the floor, books and a newspaper with a picture of a Hungarian working woman fervently embracing Kádár on one of his factory visits. Father had accidentally put his foot on it when I tied his shoes. It was wrinkled. I'm going to save it, I thought. But the curdled milk needs to go.

I knew that he would never return to the apartment, that none of this was his anymore. I'm at liberty to open all the drawers, I can even look inside the tile stove, and I can open the door to our adjoining rooms. The apple is going into the garbage, the curdled milk into the kitchen sink. But I'm keeping Kádár. You can fly all you want, Gagarin, but you will never be as lonely as in your Father's room, on Earth. The apple into the garbage, the curdled milk into the kitchen sink. Day was breaking, but I still couldn't cry. Then I saw his wedding ring by the table lamp. He'd pulled it off.

(the last day)

I fell asleep on the floor and it was past ten by the time I woke up. At first I didn't know where I was. I'd never slept in my father's room before. Then I realized that I had no time to lose. It was snowing heavily and the trolley did not come, so I set off on foot. Fortunately, the hospital was not far. By the time I got there, the doctors were making their morning rounds. A nurse said, half an hour. Or three-quarters. I hadn't seen this nurse before. I asked how my father was doing. András Szabad, room seven. She said he's probably fine. What do you mean *probably*, I asked. If he weren't, she'd know, she said.

Luckily, the tram was running by then, and the snow had let up somewhat, so I went to the café. Évike gave me some paper, and I left a message for Kornél saying I was fine. By the time the doctors had made their rounds, I was back. Father was glad to see me. He was able to get out of bed, so we went out to the landing. A doctor who passed us warned him that smoking was unhealthy. He laughed. You should tell my son that. As of tomorrow, I won't be smoking anymore.

I asked if I could bring him anything. He said he didn't need anything, but he'd like to see the future. I said there's no need for that, everything would be just fine. It's not his own future he'd like to see, he'd like to see mine. I told him not to worry. I'm not worried, he said, but it's not good that neither Mother nor he would know what's become of me. I don't know that myself, I said. He looked down at the floor. In that case, give me another cigarette, son.

Do you know what I'm most proud of in all my life?
You have lots of things to be proud of, I said.
I'm most proud of the fact that I gave you your first camera, and that I was the one to teach you what the aperture and the shutter speed are.

You have lots of other things to be proud of, I said.

Also, I taught you to see the big picture. That you need to see what's to the right, what's to the left, and what's in the middle before you press the shutter. And that often that is more important than the shutter speed.

Yes, I said.

Believe me, son. This is what I'm most proud of. Not that I think there's such a thing as superfluous knowledge. I don't think that that plate was empty. It wasn't empty at all, son.

I don't think it was empty either, I said.

By the way, you know what Kőszegi said to me the other day? That I shouldn't take his idiotic comment to heart, when he said that I should have stayed put. I don't even remember, but he said that you do.

I seem to remember something he said when we were at their place, I said. But what counts is that he remembers.

Never mind, son. As I said, that plate was not empty. Except back then, they could laugh right in our face. If there had been a network that could have helped, one with leverage abroad, one whose reach extended to the American government, then things would be different now. Then this country would be like Switzerland.

Yes, that would have been good, I said.

He laughed.

What is it? I asked.

It's already almost like Switzerland, he said.

How so? I said.

Had they gone at it with a Ruski fly swatter, he said with a laugh, Switzerland would be as flat as Hungary.

To the right a window and the firewall, to the left the banister.

I think you're definitely better. We could go to a pub, I said.

Tomorrow, son. We'll go tomorrow.

He grew tired and I saw him back to the ward. The nurse said I should go and let him sleep till the afternoon.

I have no intention of sleeping, Klára.

I'm the one giving the orders here, Professor.

So it's Professor, I thought.

Father glanced at me.

Klárika said that only serious people could court her.

And not someone working in warehouse or a library, she added.

I seem to be in the way, I said.

I'm afraid I'm engaged, but I might be persuaded to change my mind, Klárika said.

Klárika was pretty. Enough to give meaning to a man's life.

So pull yourself together, I said to Father.

You see, your son says the same thing that I do. So please rest for an hour.

And I'll go downstairs for a cup of coffee, I said.

You, too, would do better having a proper meal, Klárika said.

Father laughed. She's got your number, son.

And yours too, Father. I'll be back in an hour.

(in the cake shop)

By the time I went outside, the first snow had turned into gray slush. It's all right if the snow comes early, it means that Christmas will be white. I went to the cake shop across the way and ordered a coffee. And then some scones. Father has started paying court, I thought. Klárika is making jokes, but she knows about the library, and she knows about the warehouse. And she's right, he needs to rest. Sára Rónai was also right, hope is important. And my mother was right, Christmas is Christmas. We must learn to be happy when it comes. And Kornél too is right. Basically, he's right about everything. As for that shit Kőszegi, at least he apologized. Then when I glanced out the cake shop window, I saw Lovas arrive. He's a decent guy, he saved my father's life, though he was probably the one who told my father your son doesn't give a shit about you. Of course, from where he was, the other room, he could imagine anything he wanted. But never mind. Father knows it's not true, and that's all that counts. Though Demjén could have said it as well, he was also his cell mate. Kőszegi didn't say it, he turned on Father when Father taxed him for being childless. I was very close to hitting him the day before. Luckily, I can keep calm, if I have to. Mother could keep calm as well, and actually, so can Father, even though he's lost his cool a couple of times in recent months. Which is understandable. I don't know what made me think I could search his room, especially after I'd called him to account once for searching mine. If he's got his heart set on organizing a world network, then let him organize one. He may be right, though he'll never turn Hungarians into good Jews. Hungarians are simply not suited for it. Their customs are different. That's all there is to it. Though the other way around may not be true. Kőszegi, for instance, makes a pretty good Hungarian. The problem with him is that he's a fanatic. Of course, when it comes to certain things, I'm a fanatic myself. Except, I would never kill. Father with his empty plates never killed anyone either. Not like Kőszegi with his Molotov cocktail. Of course you can hardly make revolution without killing people. That's the way the cookie crumbles. Killing is a necessity. The country doesn't need squeamish people. Bang, soldier. Bang. Like this. See? No need for Colonel Adler's crisis of conscience over it. He could have taught ethics at one of the better universities. An American university, for instance. And now, good luck to you in Budapest, Comrade Khruschev. Thank you, it's as good as done, Comrade Eisenhower. Still, I'm glad he stepped on that Kádár photo, even if he doesn't remember. When I go upstairs, I'll tell him. Klárika is right, he needs rest. The kidneys are not all that important. If he had a problem with his liver, that'd be a lot worse. And also, though he didn't take me seriously, I am going to finish high school. At twenty, it's still not too late. That's what night school is for. Some people graduate when they are thirty. Or forty. When they already have children. And I'm quitting my job at the printer's. It's not a solution, it won't solve anything. A one-night stand is not a relationship. Besides, I can't make ends meet from a part time job. There's the rent and the expenses, plus coffee and cigarettes. And there's nothing left for film and paper. And there's also the food. Even if he gets better, he'll be on disability. You can't work when you have cancer. He'll never recover enough to work. He wasn't this thin even when he got out of jail. I need a proper job, no two ways about it. I'm going to make a list of the bills and everything and go see that ID photographer I'd spotted from the cab once. I'll show him that this is how much I need, and for this amount I'll do all the work. He doesn't have to lift a finger. It'd be well worth his while. That's not even counting film and photographic paper, he still has plenty in his studio. And at least I'll be working with pictures and not the damned Political Committee and the classified ads. Must buy cradle. Gently used will do. With a coffin it would sound even more absurd. When I go upstairs, I'll definitely ask him who that Dr. Zenta was with his golden Schaffhausen watch in the photo. It's all right now, we can start talking about things. Lying in a hospital bed, suffering from cancer, it's time to talk about such things. I'm not a child anymore, and he can't act like he's going to live forever. It's high time he told me things. Like why we had to leave Mélyvár at all costs. And why he sold the house to a member of the Party Committee, of all people. Of course, it wouldn't have been a good idea to stay in the house where Mother died. We'd have ended up trying to keep out of each other's hair just as he and grandfather had done. Had we stayed in that house, I don't think he'd have been the one to teach me how to enlarge pictures. Or that he'd have sat down with Kornél for a chat. Or that I'd have taken anyone to the house. If he ever gets well enough for me to take him home, this Klárika would surely come and help now and then. She jokes around, but not like the other nurses. But it might be best if Sára Rónai doesn't visit him. I have no idea how she could have thought that I have as much right to be there as Father. Maybe I'd got it wrong, and she was Kőszegi's lover, not Father's. In which case, I'd be even more in the way. I'm almost certain that Father doesn't have anybody. The woman with whom he sat in the basement wine bar may have been his lover for a while, but I'm sure that didn't last long. I shouldn't have seen them. On the other hand, how was I to know? He must have met her around that time because, as a rule, people go to wine bars at the beginning of a relationship. Had I not ended up there, things would have taken a different turn, do doubt. I'd have felt uncomfortable, too, in his place. No, I won't have anything else. Or you know what? Bring me another cup of coffee. If my own child were to discover me like that barely a year after his mother's death, I probably would have also claimed that she was my cousin. If I had that woman's number, I'd call her now. I'm sure Father would be happy if she came to see him. And why doesn't Lovas come out already, when I'm sitting here so Father can rest. If they're still talking though, that means he's probably feeling better. In fact, I'm sure he's feeling better. A lot better than yesterday. It was horrible when I brought him in, but if he's doing better, maybe in two or three days I can take him home. They let all the patients who are not seriously ill go home for the weekend anyway. Anyone who has survived prison will survive cancer as well. Mother didn't die just like that. She decided when she would die. Just like Mária. But Father hasn't decided yet. Not by a longshot. You need to keep this in mind, otherwise you'll panic. And that's the last thing we need right now. When Lovas comes out, I'll go upstairs and ask the nurse to look after him at home. If he needs morphine, that can be administered at home just as easily. It eases the pain. The worst thing about cancer is the pain. But with morphine, you can tolerate it. I never want to see that woman again as long as I live. Kornél is right, I need a sane woman. Someone I could live with. And the countess, too, is right. If a woman won't give herself to you stock, lock, and barrel, turn on your heels and run for your life. But if a woman gives herself to you, make sure you appreciate her. Well, I've never met a woman like that, except for my mother. She gave herself lock, stock, and barrel. And she didn't play the martyr, not even when she had every reason to do so. If that's what makes a person oedipal, well, then I can only recommend it to others. And if need be, I'll sew it onto my coat, like my non-Jewish uncle did with the yellow star. Of course, they shot him in the back of the head for it. Reisz. József Reisz. That was the name of the photographer who takes ID pictures. I'm glad I remembered. He's here in one of the neighboring streets. I'll ask a cab driver where Szív Street becomes a one-way street from here. Father sat behind the driver, and I was to Father's right. Which means it's on the right. It's impossible that he won't hire me for a small amount if I offer to do all the work. Besides, we need next to nothing to live on. If I don't count the Leica, we've been living on next to nothing up to now as well. Come to think of it, it was really strange that both of us thought of St. Anthony at the same time. I thought of him because of photography, and Father, God only knows what made him think of him. If only someone could take a picture of us now, Mr. Doctor, sir.

(Kornél at the hospital)

Kornél was already at the top of the steps by the hospital entrance when I spotted him. He was just scraping the muddy snow off his shoes on the grating in front of the door. I called to him from cake shop door that I was there. He asked what happened. I said nothing, except I had to bring Father in.

When?

Yesterday. Or the day before. I don't know anymore.

What do you mean you don't know?

Just give me a minute, my head is in a whirl.

Why did you bring him in? How is he?

He's ok. But when I got home, he was howling in pain. I could hear him down on the street.

What are you doing sitting here?

Me? Oh. I just came in here to rest a while. Also, he's got a visitor, a former cellmate, and I don't want to be in the way.

Come on, let's go upstairs.

In a minute, but first, have some coffee.

I don't want any.

Then have a cream puff.

I don't want a cream puff either.

I had one yesterday. It was very good.

What the hell is wrong with you?

What do you mean, what the hell is wrong with me?

I don't know. You're talking like a child.

How am I supposed to talk? I'm his son. There's nothing wrong with me. If there's anything wrong, it's with Father, not me.

Fine. I'll have some coffee and you can fill me in.

Have mine. I don't want it. I just had to order something.

How long have you been sitting here?

Not long. Okay. I came home. My father was in a bad way. The doctor was with him. He called an ambulance and I came along. This happened the night before last. Then yesterday he was better, and now he's basically back to normal, and I think I can take him home tomorrow.

Kornél took the slip out of his pocket.

You wrote Péterfy, fourth floor, ward seven. My father will die today or tomorrow. Please come to the hospital.

I took the slip from him and read it.

Yes, that's what I wrote.

He drank the coffee and stood up. Come on, let's go upstairs, he said.

No, I said.

Fine. Then wait for me here, because I'm going upstairs, he said.

He was on the second-floor landing when I caught up with him. Lovas was gone. The nurse said he'd left about an hour and a half before. Father was looking at the ceiling. Lying on the bed by the window. Kornél barely recognized him.

Thank you for coming back, son.

I just slipped out for a coffee so you could rest, I said, and then I saw Lovas come to see you.

Never mind, son. I'm glad you're here now.

Kornél is with me.

Hello, Uncle András.

What a surprise.

I just came by to see how you're doing. I see you're alright.

Of course, I'm alright.

Father sat up and tried to drink his tea. I helped.

Look what my son gave me, he said.

An ashtray?

It's not an ashtray, it's a land mine.

All three of us laughed.

The Ruskies didn't dare tread on it.

You bet, Kornél said.

It's worth a lot more than medicine. In fact, I'm already flirting with a young lady here.

Good for you. Who is she?

For now, she's just the nurse.

Just make sure Klárika doesn't hear you.

You're right, son.

The man on the adjacent bed began whistling, but then stopped on his own. He sat up, drank some tea, then lay back down. It's all the same to me, he said.

He's a widower. No one's been to see him, father said quietly.

No children? Kornél asked.

He lives out of town. You have no idea how lucky I am with my son.

And he with you, Kornél said.

A drop of sweat rolled down Father's temple, then down his protruding cheekbone, then it made for the corner of his lip, and got stuck on the graying stubble.

You know where I've just been, Uncle András? The publisher's.

Well, well, Father said.

Well, well, I said.

You were right, Uncle András. I was a fool, and not for the first time either.

So you sold your soul to the devil? Father asked.

Yes, Kornél said. I signed the contract.

They placed the contract in front of you?

Yes. And they said the book would appear by next fall, or the spring after.

What happened exactly?

Tófalvi approached me a couple of days ago and asked if I've changed my mind. And I said yes, because you helped me. So if he invites me for another glass of beer. . .

You'd never say that, Father said to Kornél.

You're right. But I thought it.

So this time next year, we'll go on a drinking bout, Father said.

You bet, Kornél said.

And Klárika will be there, I said.

That goes without saying, son.

We fell silent. Somebody went to the bathroom, or just felt like going outside.

Have you got the camera with you, son?

No, I said.

It would've been nice, having a picture of the three of us sitting together like this. There's even a doctor on hand.

What do we need a doctor for? Kornél asked.

We could say to him, if only someone could take a picture of us now, Mr. Doctor, sir, Father said.

I don't get it, Kornél said.

Never mind. I'll fill you in some other time, I said.

This is what St. Anthony said when the four of us were on his bike, even my wife, Father offered.

I see, Kornél said.

I told you. I'll fill you in some other time, I said.

You were right to take it back to them, Father said.

Yes, I think so, Kornél said.

They might have laughed at an innocent plate, but you and my son are something they'll have to reckon with.

Who do you mean? Kornél asked.

I said I'd fill you in later, I said.

Do you know what I'm most proud of, Kornél?

What, Uncle András?

I knew that the camera would come next. It was terrible. Will a person never be rid of these paltry, false sentences, even on a hospital bed with an IV tube stuck in his arm?

That I gave my son that camera.

You have every right to be proud of that. Along with much else, Kornél said.

Klárika came in and asked us to leave and stop bothering my father.

They're not bothering me, my father said.

I know. But you need your rest, Professor.

In that case, get well, Kornél said.

And next year we're going to celebrate the publication of your book, Father said.

I'll take you up on that, Kornél said.

I'll be back, I said to Klárika.

But next time, come alone, she said.

Downstairs in the cake shop, I told Kornél that Father was doing much better than yesterday. Honest. He had months left. Kornél said that's great, but I shouldn't be alone for the night and suggested that I go back with him to Budafok. I said no thanks, I was going to stay in the hospital. Perhaps you're right, he said. I asked if he really returned the manuscript, or had made that up for father's sake? No, he returned it, and afterwards he went to the café where Évike had given him the slip. And without that conversation with Father, he'd have been a lot more scared the other day when Tófalvi asked him again to have a beer with him.

I'm getting an advance, so if you need money, just let me know.

What would I need money for?

For the doctors. What happened between you and Dalma?

I don't want to talk about it now.

Wouldn't it be better if you broke up with her some other time?

If I call a woman early in the morning and tell her that I had to take my father to the hospital and the only thing she can say is that it's not her fault, that cancer is what it is, it turns my stomach.

No wonder, Kornél said.

I'm so disgusted, I'm going to throw those damn pictures in the fire.

Don't do it.

It's none of her business. It's nobody's business, I said, looking steadily at Kornél.

That's true. Except, it was your father and not Dalma who put that Leica in your hand.

That's neither here nor there.

I know. Still, I wish you wouldn't do it.

(Kádár's picture)

The man at the hospital entrance didn't want to let me in. Visiting hours are over, he said.

But the doctor is expecting me. A lie, of course.

How am I supposed to know that? he asked. Anybody could say that.

I need to go in, I said.

I'm sorry, he said.

I knew that I had to remain calm. I remembered the hydrocephalic doorman when I went to see Dr. Zenta once. The way he talked over the phone. Yes, Comrade Chief Physician, I understand, Doctor.

Call him, I said.

Who?

The doctor.

Which one?

Anyone in the medical division. They can tell you that my father is here.

Go on home, son. You can come back tomorrow, after the doctors' rounds.

I had a fifty forint bill with me. I placed it on the counter in front of him. He pocketed it, and I walked right in.

In the spring of 1960, when Father was released and found us in the living room, me and Mother, he was utterly calm. He looked just like he did now, except without the stubble. But his face was just as skeletal, his two eyes sunk deep inside two black caverns. And of course, his head was shaved. No one would have recognized him then either, except for me, and Mother.

I told him that the film had come loose from the cassette.

Never mind, son, we'll remove it in the dark.

I couldn't bring myself to embrace him.

He took the Zorkij out of my hand and put it on the piano.

We stood there, next to each other, God only knows for how long.

Then he asked me to help him move Mother onto the bed.

He held her under her arms, and I held her by the feet. We didn't even have to exert ourselves. After her soul had departed, her body was as light as a butterfly's. It turned out that out of my mother's fifty-something kilos, at least fifty were her soul. It started to rain. The heavy raindrops knocked against the tin windowsill.

He embraced me only after we'd covered my mother with a white sheet.

Even her hands were like death's own.

Don't be afraid, son, you will be happy. I promise, he said.

The door to the ward was closed and the lights had been turned off. Some snow remained on the rooftops. When I sat down next to his bed, he woke up, though he may not have been sleeping.

I'd like to discuss something important with you.

Fine.

I have some money set aside in the back of the table drawer. When we moved to Pest, I couldn't afford it, but next spring I'd like to paint the apartment. I want everything to be in order. I know that you don't like people in your room, but your room should also be put in order.

Okay, I said.

The man in the other bed groaned and asked for the bedpan. I went and called the nurse. While she had him pee, I stayed outside. Earlier in the afternoon, when I was in the cake shop, I made a list of things I wanted to ask Father. Now I took it out and read it in the faint light of the corridor. Why did he really sell the house in Mélyvár? Who is Dr. Zenta and how did he manage to get me out of military service? Who was the woman in the basement wine bar? Why didn't Mother finish university? Why did he think it was better not to remarry? When we got on the train with our two suitcases back then, why did he ask me not to return to Mélyvár under any circumstances, as long as he was alive and the communists were still in power?

I crumpled it up and threw it out, then retrieved it from the garbage and put it back in my pocket. Meanwhile the nurse came out of the room with the bedpan and asked what I was looking for. I found it, I told her. It'd be best if you went home now, she said. I will. Soon.

So we're giving the apartment a paint job in the spring, I said when I sat down next to Father on the bed.

That's right, son. Also, I'll be as light as Mother was.

You're talking nonsense, I said. That's well down the road.

Only our souls are heavy, son. We've gone bad somewhere along the way. Life can't flow through us properly. Things get snagged in us.

That's not so bad, I said.

But you have your camera, and that's a great help. No matter what anybody says, don't put it down. If they beat you, or blackmail you, or leave you because of it, you mustn't stop taking pictures. Promise me.

I know. And I won't, I said.

And son, take me home. This place is worse than a prison.

I'll take you home first thing tomorrow morning, I said. But until then, I'll stay here with you.

You need some sleep, too. Go on home.

Okay. Once you're asleep, I'll go, I said.

You have nothing to fear. I'm fine. I'm much better than yesterday.

I think so, too.

I was a little afraid, but now I'm fine.

There's nothing to be afraid of, Father. Besides, in the morning we're going home.

He fell asleep, though he may have just closed his eyes. He was breathing through his mouth. A rattle issued from his throat, like mud rising from the depths, so I went outside to the landing to have a cigarette.

The night nurse was nice. Klárika had asked her to let me stay as long as possible, but I really should go home. I will. And I'm taking him with me. She just looked at me, but said nothing.

That damned slip was back in my pocket, next to my cigarettes. I could have made a much longer list, three times as long. But it was comforting to know that he would now never answer any of my questions, ever again. A profound calm descended on me the likes of which resembled nothing in my experience. Not the time I stopped myself from hitting Kőszegi, not when I hung up on Dalma Keresztes, nor when I filed down hammers. Those moments of calm were as weighty as a tombstone. But this calm had nothing incomprehensible in it, nothing unacceptable.

It started to snow again outside. I thought of how I'd forgotten to wax my shoes, and then that Father is absolutely right, the apartment needs a paint job. Maybe it was best not to ask questions that remained answered over the course of a lifetime. It had nothing to do with secrets, it was more profound than that. A secret is something that lies hidden for a long time. But something that cannot be known, that by its very nature cannot be grasped, is entirely different. God is not a secret, and neither is Father.

For instance, I will never, under any circumstances, tell anyone about the day and a half before Father came back from prison. Not because it's a secret, but because it can't be told. There are words for actual happenings. I could describe them, if I want. An event can be described with relative precision. Just like feelings. We have words to describe our feelings. Joy, fear, anger, indifference, gratitude, and so on. They can be understood by anyone. But there are things for which we will never have words and so cannot share with others, ever, because it's not possible. It's as simple as that. We have all seen a glass on a table, and we all know what it is like when a glass is on a table. On the other hand, no one has ever actually seen a glass on a table, because there is always a gap, an electron-size gap, just like the gap between two atoms of the glass. Without that gap, the world would collapse. Burn up. Explode. The secret of God is such a gap. And so is the secret of my Father. And me, too. Were I to ask him these questions now and were he to feel bound to answer them, I'd annihilate him. He wouldn't die, he'd be annihilated. Both of us would be. Like the world, were the atoms to touch. Isn't that right?

Yes, that's right, the nurse said.

There are certain things you can't ask a person. Not even on his deathbed.

When someone dies, they continue to exist, except in a different way. But if that person is annihilated, it's as if he'd never existed at all. Whatever is annihilated is robbed of its past.

Yes, I understand. You're right. Just don't go in there again.

Fine. I won't. I'll just stand by the door. What's that?

Morphine.

For the pain?

For the pain.

I have to go back in. I forgot to tell him something very important.

He won't hear you now.

He'll hear.

What do you want to tell him?

That he stepped on the picture of that bastard Kádár just before I brought him in. When I tied his shoes.

Fine, she said. Go on in, tell him.

(the hiding place)

The day after Father died, Lovas rang the doorbell. I was just doing the dishes. Actually, I'd been doing the dishes since dawn. I couldn't get myself to discard the curdled milk or the apple, even though the milk stank. I gave the kitchen a thorough scrubbing. The glasses, the cutlery. Everything. Three or four times over, the way we used to do it with Mother. Kornél had said I should sleep at his place, but I said no. In that case, he'd sleep over, he said.

No, you can't sleep in Father's room.

I'm not crazy, I have no intention of sleeping there.

You should go.

Fine. Have it your way. But if you change your mind, call a cab and come on out.

Maybe tomorrow. But not today.

I asked Lovas to sit down in the kitchen, but he went to Father's room and turned on the radio. When he came back, he didn't take off his coat. He wore a leather jacket, like the Secret Police. And a fur cap. A black sheepskin cap. Kossuth Radio was broadcasting music, so he tuned in to another station, because music makes it easier to make out a conversation.

You're on this list, he said.

This you clearly referred to the two of us. As if Father were still alive.

I don't have it, I said. Father took it.

He didn't take it, Lovas said. It's in the enlarger.

It can't be there. I use the enlarger. It's not there.

If your father said it's there, then it's there. Just go, look. It's important.

Fine. I'll look. But I know that he took it out. I told him to hide it in the enlarger, but he took it out. If it's that important, Kőszegi must have a copy.

I know. That's why it's important.

I don't understand.

300

Good. You mustn't get involved.

I have no intention of getting involved.

That's why you need to find it. Now.

I don't want to look for anything now.

If your father asked me to find it, I will find it. And if he said it's in the enlarger, then it's in the enlarger.

My father died! He's dead! Get it? The whole lot of you! And that means you, too. And Kőszegi, too!

Okay, calm down, he said. He finally sat down and lit a cigarette.

I'm sorry, I said.

Forget it, he said.

I promise to look for it, but you and the others need to leave me alone for now.

I can't do that, András. I can't because everything in this apartment is yours now. Everything. Including that list.

I see, I said.

That's good, he said. What did you tell Kőszegi in the hospital?

I said I'd fucking throw him out the window, like a piece of shit.

Good for you. But you shouldn't have said that.

How do you know about it? Did Father tell you?

Yes.

Which means he heard.

Of course he heard. It's hard not to hear a sentence like that.

Can you really imagine that Kőszegi. . . .

Yes, András. I can imagine it all too well, I'm afraid. And so could your father. Given half a chance, that man will wipe you off the map without a trace. And if he gets hold of this list, he might do it. You'll spend twice as much time in jail as your father without having placed a single spoon or fork next to those plates in '56.

Let's find it, I said.

Where's the enlarger?

In the kitchen. But it's not there. Take my word for it.

You take my word for it, András. If he said it's there, it's there.

We went to the kitchen, then I removed the dust cover and unscrewed the top of the lamphouse, but beyond the light bulb, there was nothing there.

Is this a drawer, he asked.

Yes. But it contains photographic paper, which is light sensitive.

Let's have a look.

I turned off the light, then switched on the red light. Altogether two boxes of thirty by forty centimeter paper fit in the baseboard drawer. One of the boxes hadn't been opened yet, so we opened it.

I don't understand, he said.

Well, if my father said it's here, then it's here. It must be here. I told him to put it here, because they'll never look for it in the enlarger.

But they will.

It took me ten minutes to find it in that damned tile stove.

Is that where he kept it?

Yes, I said. It sounded as if he were laughing at Father, as if he considered him naïve and foolish.

It was well hidden high up in the flue, I said.

Could you make some coffee?

Sure.

I switched on the light again, and as I turned back around, my eyes fell on the enlarger. All it took was for me to take in everything as one.

Wait, I got it! Hold it steady, I said.

What?

The baseboard, so I can dismantle it.

I loosened the lamphouse and pulled it off. It was in the angled column.

At last. Thank God, he said.

He took out a box of matches, intending to burn it.

Don't, I said.

It can't stay here.

It won't, I said.

But you can't take it to anyone else either, he said.

I'm not taking it anywhere, but I want to copy some addresses in my notebook.

He looked at me, then put the box of matches back in his pocket.

I'll wait, he said.

I went to get my notebook and pen. Meanwhile he set about making Turkish coffee. He was still wearing his coat and fur cap. The list was divided into countries. I copied out the Parisian addresses along with a few in Vienna.

Don't you try sneaking across the border, he said.

This fucking country should be so lucky, I said, and dug my nails into my palm to stop myself from crying.

He poured us two cups of coffee. That's when I remembered that he stole coffee grounds from the kitchen for my father when they were in jail.

Come have dinner with us tonight, he said.

Thanks, but some other time. It's better for me at home right now.

Come any time you feel like it. You remember where we live?

Yes, I remember, I said.

He burned the papers in the sink. The kitchen filled with smoke, so we went to Father's room. He looked at the curdled milk.

You should pour that out.

Yes, I know.

And you might as well make the bed.

Yes, I know.

He started fishing in the inside pocket of his leather jacket, found an envelope, and placed it on the table.

What's that, I asked.

A thousand forints.

Thank you. I don't need it, I said.

It was a loan from your father.

A thousand forints? I don't think so.

That's your problem. And as I said, you can come by any time you feel like it.

Thank you.

And there's no need to worry about Kőszegi anymore, he said.

(the funeral)

The funeral took place Saturday morning at eleven. Mother's grave couldn't be disturbed. It was still too new. It was against regulations. Four years ago, it didn't occur to either of us that we should buy a double grave. Fortunately, the first lot across the path was free, and so basically, they ended up next to each other, with just a gravel path that led from the Catholics to the Calvinists separating them.

Antal Lovas helped arrange the funeral, meaning the trip there and back. There were at least as many people as at Mária's funeral. I didn't expect so many people to attend. Some came from Pest, while others were locals from Mélyvár. Most of the mourners were unfamiliar to me. Lovas would have liked Tordai – the driver of the bus back in '56 – to bring the people down from Pest, even if it would have posed a certain risk. Lovas went to Mélyvár to speak to him about it, and learned that while he was in prison, Tordai lost the sight in both his eyes.

I asked the priest to say only as much as was absolutely necessary. He asked me why. I said because that way he wouldn't say anything my father would have objected to. Actually, I should have said that to Kőszegi, but I preferred not to say anything to him. He gave the funeral oration. It was actually a nice oration. It always came as a shock to me when I saw that there was hardly any relationship between what a person said and what they really thought. At funerals and award ceremonies, this was often painful and at times ludicrous. He gave his oration on behalf of Father's friends. Then Demjén recited a poem. That was fine, too.

Actually, it felt a bit like I wasn't even there, because except for Lovas, I had nothing to do with anyone. Except for Father, of course. Some of his old friends had come, and also some former colleagues and neighbors. They were all kind. But they were really

Mother's and Father's friends, not mine. They were sorry that Father had died so young. And my poor mother, too. Some of them asked if I was going to university. I said no, but I'd found employment with a photographer. That's good, too, it's a lucrative profession, they said.

Kornél and I had taken the early morning train. There was a light snow shower in the hills as we approached. I felt as if it were the first time I'd passed this way. I took a picture from the train window. I knew it would be blurred, but I didn't care. First we went to the station snack bar, then from there we headed for the cemetery. There wasn't much time for anything else. There's the Catholic, the Reformed, and the mixed cemeteries, though it's not actually mixed, because a wire fence divides it in two. The Jewish area is a good ways off. After the funeral, we took our leave of the mourners. Kornél asked if I was all right. I told him I was fine.

When the priest spoke I couldn't cry, but when Kőszegi launched into his schpiel, my tears came flowing, but not because of what he said. After all, I wasn't taking leave of Father in the name of his friends. As a matter of fact, I wasn't really taking leave of him at all. I was intent on looking at Mother's grave, overgrown with weeds. The snow had settled on the weeds. That's what made me cry. There was a moment when I thought I'd grab a shovel and drive everyone off, but I knew I couldn't do that. Besides, it was much better that they were there.

I was afraid that Dalma Keresztes would get wind of the funeral and show up, but she didn't. I'd have driven her away for sure. Sára Rónai was standing on Kőszegi's right. She'd wrapped her arm around his. Funny, how I'd forgotten to add her to the list of questions I had meant to ask Father.

Since there was plenty of time before the evening train, I showed Kornél around. On the way from the cemetery, we went to the café Mother and I had gone to after my baptism. Next we reached the main square, where that man had called my mother a fascist whore. Kornél asked if I knew anyone with whom we could spend the night. I said no. There might have been, had I spent more time talking with the mourners, but I had to get away. Kornél then said, let's go to a hotel. He had some money, easily enough to pay for a double room for one night.

I'd rather sleep on the side of a ditch in the snow than spend a single night in a hotel in this town.

Alright.

I showed him where Imolka had lived, and then we reached our old house. They'd chopped down the walnut tree, so now there was surely more light inside. Kornél said, let's go inside. We can't. There's no reason why we couldn't. Let's give it a try. He pressed the button by the new gate. It wasn't actually new. They'd just covered it with tin, so people couldn't see in. Then the creaking told me that someone had just opened the porch door.

A woman of around sixty came out. The wife of a member of the Party Committee. I knew her by sight.

Good afternoon. I'm András Szabad, I said.

Is that so?

I don't wish to bother you, but I'd like to show my friend—

What exactly do you mean?

I was born here, I said. The house was taken from us.

I know. So what?

Let's go, I said, turning to Kornél.

Okay, he said.

By then, the woman had bolted the gate.

(the white Christmas)

By Christmas Eve, everything was blanketed in snow. The countess had company and I didn't want to be in the way. I bought a Christmas tree at the Hunyadi Square market, then I went to the post office and sent Kornél a telegram. Can't go. Stop. Nothing wrong. Stop. We will meet tomorrow. Stop. Merry Christmas. Stop. I cleared some space in the corner and set up the tree in the same spot we'd put it when Father and I first came to Budapest. I lit the two candles and placed the camera under the tree. Mother had told me that a person who can't be happy is bitter, and that's dangerous.

There's always somebody.
Mother, Father, Hitler, Stalin, Imolka.
János Kádár.
Kornél.

I am happy, I said. I am András Szabad, I said. András Szabad, photographer. Je suis András Szabad. Ich bin András Szabad. I am András Szabad. Szabad, as in free.

As for the rest, we'll see.

PART TWO

(Peasant Katika)

Doggie. And also, Smart Doggie. This is what they called me. But I didn't mind. I got to be Doggie in fifth grade, when Katika Orosz started attending the girls' class at our school. She moved to Mélyvár from a small village and she couldn't find her way home. For minutes she stood between the two boxwoods in the park across from school, and she didn't know which way to start off for home. I showed her. I carried her school bag. The following day as well. Every day. I said to her that that's how it's done, and she believed me. I told Mother that I'd be late, because I have to see Katika Orosz home, and my mother said, all right, son. We always took a different path so I could show her the city. We couldn't go too far because she said if she wanders off, they'd beat her to a pulp. And I said that that's silly, because people should get to know the town where they live. And she said they'll also beat her to a pulp if she makes friends with boys. So I went with her only as far as the corner of Sáros Street, and from there she went home to the Milk Colony by herself. It was the housing estate of the dairy plant, but nobody called it that.

In turn, she told me all about Tarkövesd, first their house, the barn, the woodshed and the small corn field in the back of the garden. When Ida Galgóczi, the actress, was relocated and assigned their living room, people thought she'd go hoe the beets in the beautiful dress and shoes in which she came, but early next morning, she showed up in her bare feet, her head wrapped in a kerchief, and she hoed the beets and sang until a big automobile came for her and took her back to the theater in Budapest. She also told me about the streets, so that I know to this day who lived in which house in Tarkövesd, and also, if they kept pigs. They kept pigs as well, but then her father sold everything and they moved to the Milk Colony. Her mother worked at the dairy plant. She pasteurized the milk. On Tuesday, when school let out an hour earlier for us boys, I'd stay and wait for her. Then one time as I was waiting, a girl came up to me with her two girlfriends and asked me if I'd like to carry their school bags as well, and I said I'm faithful, and then the girl laughed in an ugly way and said, Peasant Katika's Doggie, and I couldn't think of anything better, so I said, bow-wow.

Then once, before we reached Sáros Street, we bumped into Katika's mother, though that's not how it was, because she'd been waiting for us in the bakery, looking out the window, and when we reached the bakery, she came outside and blocked our way, and Katika froze. There she stood next to me and she couldn't move. She couldn't even say hello to her mother. I said hello, but she just tore the school bag from my hand, then turned to Katika and said, is this what I taught you? Struck dumb, Katika shook her head. Then her mother asked me if my mother had taught me my manners, and I said she has, that's why I helped carry her daughter's schoolbag, and she said, then get yourself home, because if that's what we consider proper behavior, then she and her daughter will have none of it. Am I right, she asked Katika, and Katika shook her head once again, and then she asked Katika if she should tell her father that she goes around with boys, and then Katika broke into tears, please, mother, don't tell him, please, mother, forgive me, *you* punish me mother, please, at which point I asked what horrible thing exactly had Katika done.

And then something happened that I wouldn't have dreamt of in my worst nightmares. The woman gave me a long, steady look. There was neither anger, nor vengefulness, nor madness in her eyes. Actually, this emptiness was what frightened me most. Then, with a quick sweep of her arm, she slapped her daughter so hard that her nose started to bleed.

Do you want me to repeat it, she asked, turning to me.
No, I said.
In that case, don't you dare come near my daughter again, you hear? And now, get lost.

The next day, Katika Orosz passed me in the park without so much as a sideway glance, and she passed me the same way the second day and the third day and the fouth day after that. And then I drew her a map of Mélyvár so she could find her way home, and on the back I drew her a map of Tarkövesd with the two streams, the corn fields and the cows and the pigsties, and when she tried to pass me, I blocked her way and handed her the map, and then something happened that I wouldn't have dreamt of in my worst nightmares. There was neither anger, nor vengefulness, nor madness in her eyes. She looked at me with the same empty look as her mother. Then she tore the map into a thousand pieces and stuffed it in her mouth and began swallowing the pieces, all the while that she never took her empty eyes off of me. Then she walked away, without so much as a sideway glance.

(Éva)

One night in August 1968, I decided to go to City Park. I don't know why. I wasn't one to go out at night. Besides, I didn't much care for City Park. Even though the park is not what you'd call a labyrinth, if I leave the main paths, I invariably lose my way. I headed in the direction of the old Palace of Arts, though at the time it was more like a rundown exhibition hall than a palace, sometimes not even that. At the time, it was occupied by sculptors' studios.

A bunch of drunkards were kicking up a row along the tree lined path, so I almost turned around, but then I decided to cross to the other side. It was past midnight, and I thought I'd have the park to myself. The main staircase of the old Palace of Arts was surrounded by unfinished statues. They were as dark as any shadow. Some light filtered through a basement window, and a strange gurgling sound issued from within. I quickened my steps. Among the stone debris in the back, leaning against the wall, a couple were making love.

When the woman saw me, she brushed her hair out of her face. The light of the street lamp was reflected in her eye. Short of breath, the man, who stood with his back to me, was gasping for air. Spellbound, I sank down on a tree stump across from them. The woman looked straight at me over the man's shoulder, and I sat there as if I were the tree they'd cut down in that spot, the one that is not there any more. Then I took a picture. I knew that although I set the aperture, they'd be no more than shadows against the brick wall. But I didn't care. In order to capture the shadows at least, I kept the apperture open for half a minute, all the time that the woman looked into the Leica's view finder just as she'd looked in my eye a moment before. I'm not ashamed to admit it, I took two pictures. I'd have probably taken more, but I ran out of film. I wound the roll back up and removed the spool from of the camera. Then on a piece of notepaper I wrote, kindly send the rest of the pictures to this address, wound the sheet around the spool and left it on the tree stub. Then I headed home. I wanted to sleep so soundly that even if all of Budapest got blown sky high, I wouldn't hear. I was twenty-five at the time.

(the renovation)

When father died, I opened the door to our adjoining rooms, though actually, this was a couple of months later. That's when I made the bed as well. The milk I'd thrown out after the funeral. It smelled. But the dried-up apple I ate.

Sometime in spring, the mailman brought father a letter. I said my father is dead. He said that as long as there's a tenant living at this address, he's got to deliver the letter. And I said I'm not a tenant because this happens to be my home, and he better get lost. After I slammed the door on him, I started packing. Next day I bought some lime-wash and paint at the homewares shop. I thought I'd paint the apartment in one night. I finished in the fall. From time to time, Kornél lent a hand. I discarded the crumbling red sideboard from the kitchen, I constructed a workstation, and I painted the window black. Except for my bed, the lamp and the camera, I stripped my room bare, though later I had to move some things back in, because the rest of the apartment became so crowded, I could hardly move about. But in the end, there was a semblance of order. I then removed the door between our adjoining rooms. The desk now stands in a corner of my father's room. When I sit behind it, I can see the bed in my own.

Now that I had the apartment to myself, whenever I heard the sound of women's heels on the pavement below, I stopped doing whatever I was about. I put down my book, sometimes I even woke from a light slumber, and looked out the window. It became a habit with me. There are sounds that elicit instinctive responses. The crying of children, for one. Or thunder. For me, the clatter of women's heels was such a sound. It drew me to the window like a magnet, or like the way a dog sneaks under a bed, or the way we hush-hush a crying child. I don't know what I was expecting. Obviously, no one would ever look up to the fourth floor, and certainly, no one would ever ask if they could come upstairs.

At times, though, there was someone with me. It only happened once or twice, but still, it happened. Someone I'd been taking pictures of just moments before. Or not. Or else, she was just about to slip into her clothes. But this happened even less frequently. Still, it happened. Someone would be lying stretched out on the bed, smoking the occasional lover's cigarette. But when I heard the clatter of a woman's heels, and though I knew that I shouldn't be doing it, I got up, opened the window, and looked out. It didn't matter who it was down there, I kept looking until she turned the corner of Lövölde Square and was out of sight.

What happened? I wasn't any good?

Sure you were. I just needed some fresh air. If you're cold, I'll close it.

(the key)

It was four in the morning when I heard the clatter of her heels. I knew it was her. I also knew that from that moment on, I'd look out the window only if I heard her footsteps. And also, that I'd never mistake them. I opened the window. She looked up. She asked if she could come upstairs. I said, of course. I went downstairs, opened the front door and turned on the staircase lights. I just wanted to slip this in the mailbox, she said. Here. You need it, not me, she said, as she handed me the roll of film. I saw nothing of her except her eyes. Even without the light of the street lamp reflected in her eyes, they were the same as a couple of hours before, when she looked out at me from that goddamn embrace.

Thank you, I said.

Make me some coffee, she said.

Sure, I said.

We went to the kitchen. She lit the stove, took a pan out of the sink, and put the water on to boil. She moved about as if she were at home. Kornél would have never dared touch anything without asking first.

What happened, I asked.

Nothing. I just got tired of it.

Of what?

Never mind. How do you know I'm not a whore?

I brought the coffee and the sugar in from the pantry.

I just do, I said.

She wore a short, wrinkled summer dress. She must have been a couple of years older than I. Around thirty, more or less. Her hair was matted from sweat.

You live alone? she asked.

Yes, I said.

I'd like to take a shower.

The boiler isn't working. I'll warm up some water.

Don't bother. A cold shower will do.

I showed her the bathroom. I heard the creaking of the old tap, and then the drops of water hitting the cracked enamel. Meanwhile, I poured out the coffee so it would cool down a bit, and allow time for the grinds to settle at the bottom. Then I waited. Then I went after her. Her head bent, she was standing under the showerhead, looking into space. The cold water gave her goose bumps. I started counting the tiny birthmarks between her neck and groin. They made her body resemble a map of the starry skies.

I'm Éva Zárai, she said.

I don't have a clean towel, I said.

That's alright, she said. Yours will do.

She got out of the tub. I draped the towel on her back, and she dried herself.

How long can I stay?

I have to be at work by nine, I said.

I didn't ask when you need to be at work. I asked how long I can stay.

As long as you like, I said.

In that case, I'll wash my dress.

I'll wash it. You go, cover up with a blanket.

It was an American dress. I hung it up on the clothesline to dry, then took the coffee to my room. I found her on the bed with the blanket pulled up to her belly.

I like it here, she said. Your room is like a Chinese box.

What is a Chinese box like? I asked.

Whatever you place inside disappears as if it never existed. You open it and start searching, but only the weight of the box tells you that it has to be in there somewhere.

Why is my room like that?

If someone were to come in here now, they wouldn't see me.

I see you. I haven't seen anyone so clearly in a long time.

I know. That's why I feel my weight.

The pictures I had hung up to dry weeks ago were still on the wooden boards leaning against the wall. A young woman had come to Reisz for an ID photo, and I'd asked her up.

319

She's just like the woman in Bergman's *Through a Glass Darkly*, when she's standing in that empty attic in front of the door, she says, waiting for God to show up. Have you seen it?

Yes. You're just like her.

Me? I should hope not. Did you take those pictures?

Yes, I said.

That's all right, then, she said. Then after a brief pause, she asked, who is she?

I don't know. I only saw her once.

I see.

Then I asked who that man was. And she said, her husband. They're just getting a divorce.

And the two of you make love in the park?

Let's not talk about that now. I'm tired.

Fine. I'll sleep on the floor.

If I wanted you to sleep on the floor, I wouldn't be in your bed right now.

I lay down beside her, and she hugged me.

We're not going to make love, she said.

I know, I said.

That's good, then. Then, in that case, it's very, very good.

You have a piano, I see.

I can't play.

. . . I'll teach you.

Which means you do?

She laughed.

What's so funny? I asked.

Yes, I play, she said.

How well?

As well as you take pictures, she said. You realize, don't you, that this is one of the best pianos in the country? I'll have a look at it tomorrow.

Except, it needs tuning.

That's all right. I'll call a tuner.

Is it true that piano tuners can't play the piano?

I'm sure there must be some who do. But they don't need to. What they need is silence.

In which case, let's sleep, I said.

In the morning, I slipped into my clothes. I left my father's key on the bed. She'd kicked off the blanket. She was sleeping just like a child. She must have been dreaming, because she ran her fingers over the keys, like dogs when they start running in their sleep. I placed my arm with my watch on it in front of her and took a picture, so I'd know for ever and ever when it happened. Then I took a slip of paper and wrote that I'd be back around five. For years to come, I had no idea that someone had taken a similar picture around that time, except it's not Éva lying behind a Vostok wristwatch that is always fast, but a deserted street in Prague, soon to be overrun by Russian troops. Plus the Hungarian People's Army.

(József Reisz)

I'd had the same job for nearly five years, ever since I went to see József Reisz and told him how much money I needed, and that for this sum I'd see to all the work.

He just stood there, looking at me. He must have been about the same age as I am now. Fifty-five at most. He wore a gray cardigan and a shawl. He had an enormous nose. His studio was located in the back of the yard, to the right. At one time it must have been the laundry room or the super's apartment. The counter ran from wall to wall diagonally in front of the door, so you could barely open it. On the left there was just enough room for a chair and a coat hanger, plus a mirror. The camera, the backdrop, and the two lamps were behind the counter, and behind them the lab, the toilet, and the spiral staircase leading to Reisz's apartment upstairs. Until Reisz raised the hinged counter, the client couldn't step inside the studio.

What is your name? he asked.
András Szabad. And you don't even have to come to work, I said.
In that case, what am I supposed to do with my time?
I don't know. Anything. Anything you like.
This is what I like.
In that case, sorry to have bothered you, I said.
I was about to leave. A copper bell was suspended above the door, but it was missing the clapper. Instead of ringing, it made a thumping sound every time somebody opened or closed the door. It made that thumping sound now too.
Close the door, Reisz said, it's cold outside. Are you familiar with lab work?
I am, I said.
Who taught you?
My father.

Is your father a photographer?

No. He was a teacher. He died last night.

Last night.

Yes, I said.

He lit a cigarette, but didn't offer me one.

What did you do up till now? he asked.

I took pictures. I'm good at taking pictures. I also worked at a printer's as temporary help. I don't have a high school diploma.

Your mother?

She was a librarian. She died four years ago.

An alarm clock went off in the lab. Reisz headed for the back as if I weren't even there. He was either fixing or doing a stop bath, I don't know which. A couple of minutes later he came back out. I was still standing there. I was thinking that maybe I should tell him that I'll go to night school, if he wants.

From now on, you will be busy, he announced when he came back. You won't have time to assist me.

I'll find time, I said.

How could you? Besides, the holidays are coming.

Yes, I know.

There's no work here during the holidays.

I said nothing.

On the second, you will show up before we open. And bring a picture with you. I don't give a shit what's on it, a meadow, the mailman, or your lover. Just bring it.

Yes, sir.

I'll want to see how you develop film and how you enlarge a negative.

Yes, sir.

That's settled then. Consider yourself hired.

But you just said you want to see my work.

That's right. I want to know how much I have to fuck around, teaching you the ropes.

Thank you, I said.

And another thing. We open at nine and not at eight. I'm not running a slave colony. Promptly at nine.

Of course, I said.

He fished around in a drawer and brought out three hundred-forint bills.

Here. Your advance for January.

Thank you, but I don't need it, I said.

Take it.

I don't need it. Honest.

Okay, let's get one thing straight right now. No one in this place has ever told me or my father before me what to do. Understand?

Yes, sir. And I really am good at taking pictures.

That's the second time you've said that. Kindly get rid of this bad habit. It's not for you to decide.

I don't usually. Except, now I feel so. . . so. . . .

I feel the same way. So then, at nine o'clock sharp on the second of January. When I raise the shutter I want to see this overexposed moon face of yours outside the door.

(Gagarin's death)

By the time I met Éva, Gagarin was dead. He died a couple of months before in a plane crash. At least, that's what the papers said. Those who didn't believe it were reduced to guessing. A shaft caving in on him or him being shot accidentally during a hunt would have been a lot more credible, no doubt. This plane crash was a bit like Columbus drowning in a stream. Some people said that he died on the moon, except Moscow won't admit to the debacle of the moon landing. Others said that he'd never been in outer space to begin with, while still others insisted that he wasn't the first, because the Nazis had been up there before, except later the Jews denied it. There was even a version in which Hitler is living on a spaceship somewhere in outer space, waiting for the opportune moment for his return, and that's why his body was never found. I for one believed the plane crash. The fact that a government has every reason to lie, morning noon and night, doesn't mean that it is always lying. And of course, sometimes this can fool people.

Be that as it may, the night I went to City Park for a walk, Gagarin was already dead. For a long time I couldn't figure out what made me go there that night or, contrary to ingrained habit, what prompts someone in the middle of a sentence to put down a book, slip into a pair of shoes, and set off without any particular aim in mind. Today I think that there are things I have to understand, and there are things I don't have to. If a person believes neither in chance nor in God, then he has to accept that sometimes the reason lies suspended in a void, much like weighty steel balls in a vacuum. For some it is easier to accept this, for others it is easier to accept God's existence. I suspect that accepting God's existence is the easier option. No one has yet come up with a cause more compelling than God. It's not easy keeping these weighty steel balls suspended through a lifetime.

(fear)

After work I did some shopping, then from five waited for Éva. She'd left me a slip on the pillow. There was no perfume on it, and no lipstick. It just said that she didn't know when she'd be back. For a second, I didn't understand what she meant. Then in the evening, I heard the clatter of her heels on the pavement below. She didn't hear me open the window, so I had to shout to her. You're beautiful, I said. She laughed. She took what she'd bought for our dinner out of her string bag and put it on the table.

Have you got a fridge? she asked.

No, I said, but stopped short of adding that we'd buy one.

In that case, we'll have to eat everything tonight.

What did you bring?

Salmon and caviar.

That's good. I've never tasted salmon and caviar.

Then it's high time you did, she said as she unwrapped the bologna and the cheese. I heaved a sigh of relief.

I'm glad, I said. I'll open the champagne.

No lying allowed.

What do you mean?

Just as I said. You're not allowed to lie.

Fine, I said, then went to the pantry and came out with the champagne I'd bought earlier that afternoon.

The trouble is, I made dinner, I said. Homemade chicken *paprikás*. And there's no fridge for that either.

Will you kiss me? she said.

For a while, I said nothing. Then I said, I'm scared.

So am I, she said.

She took the champagne from me and headed for my room.

You bring the pot, she said.

I couldn't think of anything except me carrying Peasant Katika's school bag. Neither Adél Selyem, nor Imolka, nor Dalma Keresztes. Nothing. Just me carrying Katika's school bag all along the length of Liberty Road to the Milk Colony.

After I kissed all her birthmarks, one by one, she started to cry. I don't know what got into me, she said. Probably the same thing that got into me, I said. But at least, it was good. Very good. Then we watched the ceiling in silence. We drank and we smoked.

She took my hand.

I can't imagine why I'm afraid, she said, because I'm not afraid of your pictures. I'm not the least bit afraid of them.

Her voice carried no trace of reproach.

That's good, I said.

(the head cheese)

On January 2, 1964, at nine a.m. sharp, I stood waiting in front of Reisz's studio. And at nine-fifteen. And also at nine-thirty. An old woman from upstairs asked me what I wanted. I'm waiting for the photographer, I said. She said I should come back tomorrow. I said I'd wait. Then around ten I started for home. We ran into each other on the street. He was carrying a suitcase. He apologized. He'd spent the holidays out of town with relatives, and there was no train the night before because of the snow. I said no problem, I thought something like this had held him up. I didn't want to say that I'd lost all hope. He asked me to join him for breakfast.

Did you bring the picture? he asked.

Yes, I said.

The proper entrance to the apartment opened from the second-floor balcony. He told me to sit down in the living room while he lights the tile stove. The apartment was ice cold, so we kept our coats on. He switched on a lamp, but it was still pretty dark inside. A TV, a radio, a record player, books. Everything was new. The furniture, too, was bought after the war. There were a couple of family photos on the wall, but they were also new. They must have been ID pictures originally of which he'd made copies. The Hungarian royal seal could still be seen in the corner of one of them. Two shelves of the china cabinet were empty. The terrible cold in the apartment wasn't just due to winter. I worked for him for nearly fifteen years, but I never went to that apartment again.

Do you drink coffee? he asked.

Yes, I said.

We went to the kitchen and he made some. On the balcony outside, a child was playing on a scooter. He asked how come I went to him of all people. I said that I'd spotted his studio from a cab a while back, when my father and I were on our way home from the hospital. He opened the suitcase and unpacked the sausage and head cheese he'd brought from the countryside. They gave me this, he said. The pickle crunched as he bit

328

into it. I asked if he made only ID pictures. He said, yes. It's something people always need. The old woman I spoke to earlier appeared on the balcony and said to the child that this here is not a playground.

We drank our coffee in the living room.

He asked me to show him the picture I'd brought. I took out the Forte film manila envelope that contained five pictures of all sorts that I thought were good enough. They were pictures I'd taken earlier, but none of Dalma Keresztes, which were too big, though that wasn't the only reason I didn't bring them. He looked at them and said, alright. I waited for him to say something more, then I slipped them back in the envelope. He didn't ask about my father's funeral, nor anything else of a personal nature, like where I was born, or why I didn't finish high school. Also, his voice was different up in the apartment than downstairs in the studio. Up in the apartment, it carried a touch of reserve, whereas downstairs he sounded self-assured. I asked if he had a family. He said he's a widower. I asked when his wife died. And he said, a long time ago.

On the way home, I reflected that my own voice had also altered since my father's funeral, that it's less mature than it had been two months before.

Kornél said that it's only natural.

(the sundial)

Lots of people say that everything happens to you the first seven years of your life. But not everything had happened to me, not even up to when my father died. On the other hand, those twenty years are like the pointer of a sundial. It's stationary, but its elongated shadow is cast on the present. Which is just fine with me.

Once a Norwegian or a Swedish critic calculated that on the average only thirty-three per cent of the surface of my pictures show anything at all. He wrote decidedly positive things otherwise, only this one-third contained an implicit disapproval, as if I tended toward the dark, and can't help keep the world in balance. After I finished reading the review, I could just see the poor wretch sitting there armed with a ruler, a pair of compasses and his calculator, plus his obsessive fear that if something is not fifty-fifty, the world is out of joint, that if the days don't last six months and the nights don't last six months, the order of the world is imperiled, as if that's what it depended on, as if the gleam in the whites of a person's eyes couldn't emit more light than the amount of light emitted by eighteen months' worth of White Nights.

Kornél said not to worry. One-third is not so bad.

(just deserts)

I don't understand, she said, I haven't been so scared of anything since I was a young girl.

Well, that's what love is like, I said.

She kissed me.

What do you mean by young girl?

Eighteen.

You're lying.

I'm not lying. Seventeen. Alright, nearly sixteen.

What did you do till then?

Nothing special.

With these birthmarks? You're lying.

No.

And those eyes?

Alright. So I kissed a man when I was fifteen.

Where is he? I'll strangle him with my bare hands.

Too late. He's retired.

You were just fifteen and you went around kissing older men?

She got out of bed as if she hadn't heard, then opened the shutters. The sun was just coming up and its light drowned out the light of the reading lamp. Down on Lövölde Square, the first trolleys of the day clattered past.

Careful. The old woman across the way is an early riser, I said.

It wouldn't be the first time she sees a naked woman in your window, she said. Would it?

No. But I bet she doesn't remember.

Why not? Has it been that long?

I'd have liked to pretend I didn't hear, but I'm no good at pretending, so I said, yes it has.

Will you tell me why you watched us making love in the park?

I didn't. I left.

That's neither here nor there. What did you see? And how did you see me? As a prostitute? A whore? A woman who gets the hots when she looks in your eye while she's making love to another man?

If that's what I saw, would you have come here? I asked.

She said nothing. Then after a short pause she said, no. She closed the shutter halfway, lay down beside me, and took a drag on my cigarette.

I might have started out, she said, but I would've changed my mind. I know. Now I know.

How many times did you start out in the past?

Just once. Last year. We weren't in the midst of a divorce.

And how far did you get?

As far as the hotel's reception. He was an American guest conductor.

What made you change your mind?

The fact that my husband would have believed my lie. And that he wouldn't have slapped me.

I put out the cigarette and looked in her eye.

I'd have slapped you, I said.

She sat up without taking her eyes from mine, and drank from the bottle.

If I deserve it, you can slap me.

I wouldn't like to. So don't deserve it.

I saw her nipples harden.

I told you. If I deserve it, you can slap me.

And I said, I'd rather you didn't deserve it.

She stretched out on the bed and flung her arms to the side. Her stomach muscles tightened.

And if I asked, what else would you do to me besides that slap?

Her skin trembled like the hide of a horse, and I thought that these are birthmarks, not falling stars and not barn flies that'll fly away in a minute. They're birthmarks. One, two, three, four.

Out with it. What would you do to me?

I'd grab you by the hair and pull.

To make me scream?

Yes.

What else?

I'd fling you down on the floor and I'd call you a filthy whore.

I have no problem with that, as long as you don't call me a filthy slut.

That's why I said whore just now.

What else?

I'd grab your cunt so hard, your piss would start flowing, just so you'd know who you're dealing with.

What else?

I'd fuck you to kingdom come, even if you begged me not to.

We made love again back home, she said.

Who was he? I asked.

My husband, she said. Who else?

You're lying.

So what? I slept with him and I sucked his cock.

Shut up.

And I came. Like never before.

Shut up.

He fucked me so bad, I died.

I said, shut up.

When I came to, her eyes were still shut. She didn't move. She didn't even breathe. She lay in the middle of the room as if she'd just plummeted to earth from the sky, along with all her stars.

I grabbed the Leica and took a picture.

Have you got it, she asked quietly, without opening her eyes.

Yes, I said.

Then come back here, she said.

I lay down on the floor by her side.

You need a rug. I ache all over, she said.

We'll buy one, I said.

She kissed me.

Just don't sleep with them, she said.

From now on, I won't take pictures of anyone else.

If you do, I'll leave you. I don't want a man who swears off his soul.

I won't have to.

I wouldn't give up the piano either for your sake. Just as long as you don't sleep with them, because I'll know.

Alright, I said.

I didn't sleep with anyone else for seven years, and for a while, neither did she, though by that time, it made no difference. Or who knows.

(the ID picture)

On my first morning there, József Reisz said I should take an ID picture of him. I was stunned. I thought I'd help out in the darkroom, or maybe help set up the lights and the like. The camera was on a wooden stand. It was a folding bellows camera, and it bore a resemblance to the ones at the printer's, except those were much bigger. I said I'd give it a try. He sat down on the chair and waited. I fumbled with the two lamps. I was waiting for the bell over the door to give off that dull, thumping sound, hoping that someone would come, and then I could see how he does it. He got up and said, forget it. And I said, I'm sorry, I've never seen a camera like this. And he said he's not surprised, because it's a Linhof Technika.

He then explained how it works. Under the dark cloth, you set the focus on the focusing screen at full aperture using the loupe. Then you advance the film into the slot, cock the shutter, and pull the dark slide out of the film holder. You mustn't forget, or you'll end up making the exposure on the protective plate, and then you might as well close shop. You advance the film, cock the shutter, and take the next picture. Use your finger and not a cable release, because that's too slow. You can't feel it. That's for landscape photographers. Right hand, index finger. You barely touch it. When the client blinks your finger just barely reacts, as if in response to a light electric shock. You mustn't ask him not to blink, because he'll stare at the camera like a lizard. It's up to us to be on our guard. We're slower than his eyes. If we press the exposure after he's closed his eyes, they will be open by the time the shutter release clicks. And this way there's no blurred eyelid. We then advance the film right away, dark slide back in, film holder out, shutter open, so the camera will stand ready for the next client. You need to learn this sequence, so you can do it even if you're startled awake in the middle of the night, all the while that you're talking with the client. We concentrate on him, but we mustn't make a mistake. This isn't a Leica, you can't just snap away.

How does he know what kind of camera I have, I asked.

You showed me your pictures, didn't you? A Summicron 50.

How can you tell?

One of the photos is from a Zorki or FED, and the other four are Leicas. You made three out of the five exposures at f/2, one at f/5.6, and the Zorki at f/3.5.

Maybe, I said.

Not maybe, but undoubtedly, he said. Your watch is four minutes fast. It's precisely nine-fifty-six. Yesterday, it was just three minutes fast. You've got nine tiny mud spots on the bottom of your coat from a passing car. Yesterday it was clean. I know, and you don't. Whereas it's important for you, not me. It's an illness.

I've never heard of an illness like this.

Good for you. But don't feel sorry for me, it's something you can live with. Besides, what you do with your camera in your free time is none of my business. But when you're working for me, you must keep in mind that this camera has a soul.

A camera hasn't got a soul.

You must be a real shit in the pants if you parrot something you don't believe in yourself.

Fine. In that case, my camera's got a soul.

A shit in the pants, and touchy, too, I see.

Fine. In that case, the Leica's soul is different.

But at least you're reasonable, I see. It will come in handy in the future. So then, we measure the light, we use a number eight aperture and one-hundredth of a second. We don't use flat film, only roll film. Ideal format. Ten frames per roll. That's five clients. The pictures are ready the following day. If it's urgent, there's an extra charge. It's not because we're robbers, but because we have to develop the entire roll. And no enlargement, just contacts. The client gets one negative, the other remains here, with the client's name and address and telephone number, if there's one. But we archive according to the date, not the name. We're not the police.

And still, no one came. Business this time of year is slow. He sat back down. I turned on the two lamps and he told me to pay attention to the shadow cast by his nose. I said nothing. I didn't want to talk about his nose.

You do realize that you have just lost a regular customer?

336

Why is that, I asked.

Because if someone mentions his eyes or lips or ears or any part of him and you don't say anything, that customer will never come to the Reisz studio again. Nor will his relatives. And that's not good for business.

Fine. In that case, don't worry, Mr. Reisz, no official will even notice your nose.

Oh, dear, dear, Reisz said. Perhaps you should keep quiet after all.

When I covered my head with the dark cloth to adjust the focus, I was suddenly seized by a feeling as if I'd stepped out of this world, like when you're under water and you hear your own heartbeat inside your head. I saw the bleary, upside-down image of Reisz on the focusing screen, and I thought how he could tell time better than my watch. Then I remembered the car that had splattered me with slush earlier that morning. I hadn't noticed at the time. And I thought of my father, that during the last moment of his life, this was how he must have seen me, this bleary and indistinct. I started adjusting the focus, slowly advancing the lens on the rack.

Now you're in focus, Reisz said.

(the relative)

By the time I met Éva, the countess had moved out. I used to see her once, sometimes twice a week, until the spring of '67, I think. That's when a relative paid her a visit. He was middle-aged, from out of town. I hadn't seen him before.

When I visited the countess on Easter Sunday, I found this man sitting there. I almost said sitting in my place, because he was sitting in the armchair where I used to sit, under the Ripple-Rónai painting. He wore a suit and a tie. He also wore glasses. He looked like an engineer. The countess introduced us, but I excused myself. I said that I don't want to be in the way, I'll come back tomorrow for the traditional Easter sprinkling. That'll be fine, my dear, the countess said.

Cotton Tail and Bunny Tail brought me to your door today to wish you a very merry Easter holiday. This is the poem I recited for her every Easter for seven years. She tut-tutted me, saying that if I don't learn a proper poem, the folk traditions will die out. And I said that I have a feeling she's not familiar with folk tradition, because I'd just recited the least risqué poem of them all, and that she had to kiss me all the same. She had chocolate eggs wrapped in red tinfoil. She must have gotten them from Vienna, because they were not available in Hungary at the time. So much for tradition, I said.

I wanted to ask her who that man was, but then I thought that if she wanted to tell me, she'd tell me. I don't remember any more what we talked about. The usual things, I suppose. After my father died, we had an argument. She came over and found some dried up bologna on the kitchen table. My dear, she said, you can't afford to do this, and I said she's not my mother, and she apologized, she didn't mean it that way. I found a job, I'm working, I can stand on my own two feet, and I don't live among rotten bologna, it's just that I haven't had time to clear it away. And then she said that it's probably for the best if she were to leave now.

The next day I went and apologized. That's all right, my dear, she said. But if I weren't afraid of sounding like your mother, I'd suggest that you move out of this apartment, even though I'd miss having you around.

I'm not moving out, I said.

Yes, I know, she said. Why don't we talk about something else.

I unwrapped the chocolate egg and ate it. Then I washed it down with orange liqueur.

I have a serious problem with Karcsi, my dear.

Who is Karcsi? I asked.

A second cousin from the bourgeois branch of the family, she said.

What is your problem with him?

My problem is that unless I'm much mistaken, he's going to visit every week for months on end until he's confident that we're close.

Which means you haven't been.

No. Though the circumstances are partly to blame. He lives in Ózd.

That's not so far, I said.

In this country, nothing is far, my dear. Though come to think of it, my first cousin, who lives on Boráros Square, which is a lot closer, hasn't visited me either.

What does this Karcsi want?

That's the problem, she said. I don't know.

Sooner or later you'll find out, I said.

No doubt. Except, I usually know such things right away. I must be getting old.

Maybe Karcsi doesn't want anything. Why not give him the benefit of the doubt?

I don't have a problem with someone wanting something, my dear. My problem is what I just said. That I'm getting old. I'm not as quick on the uptake as I used to be. But after his third visit, I cried, Eureka!

You figured out what he's after?

I most certainly have.

A loan?

From me? From what? Karcsi is an engineer, my dear. He can count.

What then? An inheritance?

Worse than that.

What could be worse?

Switching apartments.

I don't follow, I said.

That's because you don't know that Karcsi has been offered a much better job here in Budapest than the job he has in Ózd.

I hope you're not thinking of moving to Ózd, I said, aghast.

Who would ever want to move to Ózd? Except, he's not living there because he wants to.

I said nothing. I knew that after a couple of visits she'd already made up her mind, even before Karcsi brought it up.

But don't you worry, my dear. We all look after our own interests, and that includes me. So don't worry. What argument could possibly make me move away from our shared toilets to a place like Ózd?

The decisive argument came in the shape of Karcsi's younger sister, who said she'd look after the countess. She was a teacher with two children, intelligent, kind. I met her a couple of times myself. And so it was decided after all that it would be better for the countess to move in with her in Ózd.

You said yourself that Ózd isn't all that far.

Yes, I know.

It was late summer, and I helped put her books in boxes. Meanwhile I thought that a couple of years ago, I'd have been a lot more upset, and also, that by now, at least, I can hold myself back from bursting into tears.

God damn it! God damn it!

Don't swear, my dear.

Sorry. I just bumped my hand.

Come, help me take this down.

I went over to the countess and helped her take down the Rippl-Rónai. She brushed the dust off with a rag.

I'll wrap it in newspaper, I said.

Don't bother. You can take it home just as it is.

I can't take this.

She stood so close to me, I could see myself in her eyes.

I've seen it long enough. So kindly pick it up and take it. Right now. This young girl has no place in the communist display case of heavy industry they call Ózd.

(seven conversations)

Who is this woman? Éva asked.

The love of my life, I said.

I can't say I blame you.

She went over to it and rising on tiptoes, gave it a closer look.

Original?

Of course.

Where on earth did you get a Rippl-Rónai? she asked.

I told you. From the love of my life. Countess Éva Szendrey. Except she's gotten on in years and left me. She lived in the back by the shared toilets.

Has she died?

I wouldn't be joking if she had. But last year she moved to Ózd.

Will you take me to see her?

Only if you deserve it.

She came over and hugged me.

You can do anything you want.

That's not good enough for me. I also want the anytime.

Alright.

Even ten years from now?

Even ten years from now. Just as long as it doesn't hurt.

What about the furniture? she asked.

Inherited, I said.

When?

Half at sixteen, the other half at twenty.

Which means you're not a child any more.

When I'm alone, I am.

Is that why you live alone?

She took a sip of the wine, then left her mouth open, and I watched the wine drip down between her stars to her belly button.

But I never said I'd wait ten years.

What's the first thing you remember, she asked when we came to.

Your cunt.

Don't be a pig.

What could be better?

I'm serious. What's the first think you remember?

A peacock. My mother tore it off me.

How old were you?

Two. It wanted to gauge out my eyes.

Two? And you remember?

I don't remember. I only remember it flying across the room from the tile stove to the crib. And the way it screeched. Though it may have been my mother.

You had a peacock?

It was a present from a German colonel who was quartered with us.

In Budapest?

No. In Mélyvár.

Did they hurt the family?

No. I think he fell in love with my mother.

Why do you say that?

Because he shot himself in the head. That was his farewell present. He was sitting in the chair that's standing by my desk now.

You sure you want to sit in that chair?

Absolutely. It's the only one with stable legs.

Once I went downstairs for bread and wine. I also called Reisz from the tobacconist to say I wasn't feeling well.

What are you most afraid of? she asked.

You leaving me, I said.

You needn't be afraid of that just now.

I'm not afraid of it. Not now, I said.

Though you shouldn't be so cock sure of yourself, either.

Well, I am.

I got up, walked over to my desk, opened a drawer, and looked for my old notebook. I read her the old black and white dream from '62 in which I went to the park late at night to take a picture of Gagarin, and a couple were making love under the swinging light of a street lamp. And then, without taking her eyes from me, the woman said something. She covered her belly with the blanket.

You scare me, she said.

Then go, I said.

Never.

She flung her hair in her face so I wouldn't see whether she was crying or laughing.

And what did that woman say?

What she said was meant for me only.

I bet she was lying.

Out of the question. I'd have slapped her across the face in my dream.

I told you. If I deserve it, you can slap me.

I'm exhausted. Let's wait ten minutes before you deserve it.

We hadn't left the apartment for three days by then. We ran out of cigarettes. I went downstairs. When I got back, she was standing in the bathroom in front of the mirror, repeating a single word over and over again. She was moving her lips, but no sound came out.

What did you say? I asked.

It's none of your business, she said.

I went up behind her and hugged her.

Come on, tell me.

I won't.

You're a coward. Tell me.

I looked in the mirror as she moved her lips without a sound. Then she suddenly turned around.

I am not a coward, she said.

Yes you are. A coward. And depraved, I said.

Okay. Time to go back inside, alright? To your pictures, okay? Let's go and look at your pictures. We can always decide later which of us is depraved.

I asked if she's sure she wants to see the pictures now. She said, of course. She lay on the bed belly down and looked at the pictures on the floor, the way others look out to sea.

These women are not depraved, she said.

Of course not. And neither am I, I said.

I'm not so sure.

I'm not going to wait for the verdict, I said.

Oh yes, you will, she laughed.

She asked how well I had known them, and I said, barely. Most of them I saw just twice, once when they went to Reisz to have their ID photo taken, and once here.

Did you sleep with them?

With one of them, yes.

And?

It lasted five days.

Why?

Because she had certain unshakable ideas about marriage.

Which one was it?

I didn't have a picture of her.

Okay. Show me the others, then.

Finally, I showed her some pictures of Dalma Keresztes.

You didn't meet her at Reisz, she said.

I said nothing.

What's happened to her?

I don't know. I haven't seen her since father died. Nor do I want to.

That's all right, then, she said.

We fell asleep, then made love again. Sometimes we chased the cigarette smoke from the room with a towel. We knew the time, but we lost track of the days. She leaned out the window and shouted to a man on the street, asking him what day it was. The man shouted back that it's Friday the thirteenth.

The last day she asked me to play the piano. I said that she should play instead, because a professional pianist needs to practice. She'll do that in a minute, but first me. Come off it, me of all people and for her of all people? She said that if I won't play, she's going to report me to the vice squad for harassment. I said fine, but first I need to throw some clothes on.

Harassment plus rape. Is that what you want?

I sat down by the piano, but my fingers wouldn't obey me. I couldn't even find the chords that came easily at other times, even if I woke up from a dream.

I can't, I said.

You'll be fine, she said.

Okay. I won't get dressed, but leave the room, or sit behind me on the bed.

I don't know what happened. I fumbled with the keys for a while, but then thunder and lighting, all hell broke loose. It wasn't music, mind you, because I can't play, just a couple of chords, and also, the repetitions and the rhythm. Or God knows. Black-white, black-white, nothing, black-white. Then she came over and lay belly down on the piano. Her face was so close to mine, I could hardly see it.

Go on, don't stop, she said.

She pressed her belly against the Bösendorfer.

Deeper.

Shut up.

Deeper! Please.

I'd lost all track of time. I was now just repeating the two lower octaves.

She reached between her legs.

Take your hand away!

More!

Take it away, I said!

I grabbed her by the hair and raised her head so I could see the delirious look in her eyes, while with my other hand I came down on those fucking keys so hard, I thought the strings would snap. I was past hearing anything, but I could see her scream.

And then I thought that Mother too had died atop that piano once.

(the mother)

As a rule, Éva came home late at night because she practiced in one of the rehearsal rooms of the Music Academy. I asked her why she won't get the Bösendorfer tuned. She said she needs to be alone. I could see her point. I couldn't have taken pictures either, knowing that someone was sitting in the other room.

Then one day I asked a woman if she'd sit for me. She must have been about my age. I said that if she'd like, I could make a proper portrait of her. She wasn't beautiful, and she had a sad look in her eyes, like a horse. Like El Greco's St. Bartholomew. She asked what she would have to do. I said, nothing, just sit still. Also, she should come in a dark dress with a high neck, so only her face would show. She seemed pleased. I gave her my address, we agreed on a time, and as soon as I got home, I set up the backdrop and the light. Then the bell rang, and when I opened the door, there she stood with her mother.

I had no choice, I had to ask them both in. The daughter felt ill at ease, but her mother didn't, not in the least. She came in, sat down, then said she doesn't want to be in the way. She had thick nails. She used polish. Also perfume. She wasn't like her daughter at all. I said she's not in the way, but could I please ask her to wait in the other room?
    Yes, of course, she said, that's only natural. Are you taking fashion photos?
    No, I said.
    Then what? Are you some sort of artist?
    I'm not an artist at all, I said.
    Still, there must be a reason why you want to take pictures of my daughter, she said.
    I thought I'd suffocate. I just take them, and maybe one day I'll get to exhibit them.
    Are you being paid for them?
    No.
    That's good, because it wouldn't be right, you being paid, but not my daughter.
    I assure you, I'm not getting paid, I said.

Have you taken pictures of lots of people for free?

Yes. Lots.

But I hope you're not taking unethical pictures. I hope you're not expecting my daughter to get undressed for you.

No. It never entered my mind. I take portrait photos.

That's all right then. In that case, why don't we get started? she said.

And then, out of the blue, a profound calmness took possession of me, the calmness of certitude that this woman has no right, not with respect to her twenty-two or twenty-three year old daughter, and not with respect to me. Meaning my work. And then I said to her that I'd like her to leave after all. She can come back in an hour.

The woman got up and said, fine. Aranka is very pretty, she'll make a good model. Then she turned to Aranka and said with a look of resignation and as sweetly as possible, I guess that's how it is, daughter, so I'm leaving now. Keep your wits about you.

And then something happened that surpassed my worst nightmares, like when her mother slapped Katika, and then asked me if I wanted her to slap her again. The girl, a gray mouse in stockings with a run in them, who'd been sitting on the bed next to her mother, and who hadn't opened her mouth, now turned on me like a fury. Who do I think I am, throwing her mother out? And what do I take her for? I ask her up after God knows how many other women, and God knows what I do to them, whereupon her mother said, it's all right, kitten, calm down. The young man has no evil intentions. As you see, I'm here. And she stroked her cheek. But Aranka did not calm down. She gasped for air as if she were being strangled with a rope, whereupon her mother told her how beautiful she was, and then she turned to me, isn't she beautiful, and then Aranka's tears began to flow, and she screamed right into my face, I'm not your play kitten, understand? She then sprang to her feet and stormed out, and then her mother shouted after her, you wanted to come here, kitten, I told you that this sort of thing is not for you. Then, feeling ill at ease, she apologized, she can't imagine what got into her daughter, she's usually not like this, she said, then she took off after her.

When Éva came home, I tried telling her what happened, but when she heard me say, am I some sort of artist, she abruptly began taking the clean clothes off the line. I asked what's eating her.

Nothing. I'm all ears. I can't get enough of stories with mothers in them, she said.

I don't know what's eating you. I really don't, I said.

Nothing. Go on.

There's nothing more to tell.

That's what comes of bringing such young women up here.

Is your problem with the mother or the young woman?

I don't have a problem. None at all. I just wish I knew why psychopaths cling to you like flies.

(the ex-husband)

I waited a long time hoping she'd bring it up, but then one evening I finally asked her about her husband. She said there's nothing to tell.

When will you get your divorce? I asked.

We're just trading our apartment for two smaller ones.

What does your husband do? I asked.

He's not my husband any more, she said.

Yes, of course. But still.

I already told you. He's János Radnóti.

But what does he do?

She looked at me as if I'd asked something truly idiotic.

He's a composer.

I see. And until you two find two separate apartments, you practice at his place?

I practice at the Academy. Besides, you needn't be jealous. He could be your father.

Not *mine*, he couldn't.

That's not what I meant. Besides, it's over. Actually, it was already over when we got married ten years ago.

Ten years ago you were just a young girl.

She crushed the burning cigarette she was holding in the palm of her hand, along with the hot ashes. I thought I'd never see her again.

I was not a young girl.

I'm sorry.

It's all right.

And I thought that as a matter of fact, she hadn't been a young girl, and also, that she's telling the truth. It really is over. Except, barely a month ago, I saw them making love. And then I thought that it wasn't him.

I'm not divorcing him so I'd have to talk about him.

Fine. I'll never ask you anything about him again. Still. Was that him in the park?

351

She didn't bat an eye, as if she hadn't heard. She got up, discarded the crushed cigarette, went to the bathroom, and turned on the tap. A couple of minutes later I followed her with a glass of wine. She thanked me.

So you're moving into your own apartment?

Yes.

I said nothing.

I can't live with anyone, she said. Just like you.

Well, you've been living with someone, I thought.

I'm taking my books and the piano. I don't have much else anyway. I'll have a place at last where I can practice whenever I want. That's what the apartment means to me.

Take the Bösendorfer, I said.

She said nothing.

You're the only one who can take it.

Come, join me in the tub.

I stripped bare and got in.

And what will you play for me?

Next day I looked at her ex-husband's picture on an LP cover. He could have been her father. Our features had nothing in common, which put my mind at ease. So she doesn't love me because of some fixation, because I'm like her father, or her older brother. Whatever. I didn't want to buy the LP because I was sure she wouldn't approve, but I listened to part of it in the shop. He'd written an orchestral piece inspired by Csont-váry's painting, *Mary's Well at Nazareth*. It was good, and I found that reassuring as well. The text on the back of the album said that he had studied in Pest, taught in Pécs for four years, then he started to work for the Opera. He's the recipient of the coveted Kossuth Prize. That, too, pleased me, because who would think of comparing us now? On the contrary. This meant that she doesn't care about such things. Then I made some calculations and decided that she must have been sixteen when they met. Or at most seventeen. So they got married after three or four years. Which meant that they had to keep their affair a secret for three or four years, which is not a good thing. Also, if I were in the middle of a divorce, I wouldn't like to talk about it either. But if she stayed with him for nearly fifteen years in spite of the age difference, that's a good sign. It should make me happy. What we dream about is important, but taking reality into account is at least as important. And the reality is that she embraces me in her sleep. In short, by the time I handed the LP back to the saleslady, I was calm as a cucumber.

In the evening she brought with her a couple of dresses, shoes, and some underwear.

I took my mother's clothes out of the wardrobe and packed them in two suitcases, then took the suitcases into the pantry and placed them on the top shelf, where I kept my father's clouds.

When she put her things away, I took a picture of her leaning into the empty wardrobe, with the empty hangers above her head.

I want it, she said, without looking back at me.

She pressed her trembling legs together and screamed, oh my God, oh my God!

Kornél said that it was high time I cleaned out that wardrobe, and I better not screw it up.

(the compass)

The three Gypsies were called Gábriel, Rafael, and Jonatán, I said.

Colonel Adler spared just the three of them? she asked.

No. They were newcomers. Brothers. But even the youngest was a year older than us, because despite the Party's recommendation, they couldn't attend the next grade. Besides, they didn't even show up for their makeup exams. They waited in Six B for the others to catch up. We knew that they'd be together in next year's sixth grade, and also, that they'd be five of them, because Zakariás and Eszaiás would be joining them. Lots of students envied next year's sixth graders, because five Gypsies would disrupt the class so much, teaching was out of the question.

They sold all sort of things during recess, from candy to ammunition. They refused to agree to an exchange. They wanted money, and a substantial amount of it. With them, a single Yugoslavian candy was worth the price of five rolls, all the while that they whined how they were losing on the deal. Nobody knew what they did with all that money, because the three of them wore the same outgrown pants in which they'd started sixth grade. This was more of a puzzle than how they got their hands on the stuff they were selling, because in those days, there were plenty of ways of getting your hands on smuggled goods. Whoever could afford it drank smuggled coffee for breakfast, and after the coffee, they smoked smuggled cigarettes, spread smuggled butter on their bread, and brushed their teeth with smuggled toothpaste.

Then once when Little Doggie, the best student in Six B, couldn't tell the East apart from the West and nearly threw up in front of the map of the world, the Gypsies screamed with laughter, because the day before, they'd sold him a compass on installment. It wasn't a run of the mill smuggled compass used by tourists, but a contraption the size of a big alarm clock. It was encased in a brass housing and it was equipped with a spirit level, and it had a ruby the size of the head of a match in the middle of the needle so it wouldn't wear away where it was attached to the spindle. It was a first rate precision instrument, and they didn't even show it around during recess, because they knew who was going to buy it. It could be passed off only on Little Doggie. They called him to the back of the schoolyard, showed him the compass, and added that bargaining was out. If he wants it, he'll give them his daily pocket money till the end of the year, including the days he's absent from school.

As for Little Doggie, the minute he laid eyes on the Askania Werke Berlin compass, he knew that it was worth even more than his father's salary. He also knew that the Gypsies didn't steal it from the storeroom of the sports shop. He saw that it's been tempered with at the three holes where the bolts had been. And then, with his usual equanimity, he said, he's going to bargain after all.

Gábriel, who couldn't believe his ears, offered to slap him, but Little Doggie said that there's been a misunderstanding, because he's going to give them his pocket money till the end of eighth grade, not just this year, except they must show him the place where they found it, because he wants the entire panel.

Gábriel and the others screamed with laughter and said, you'd shit in your pants there, Smart Doggie. Little Doggie handed back the compass and repeated, twenty fillérs a day till the end of eighth grade. Is it a deal? Including Sundays. He then turned around and headed for the stairs.

During the next class, there was no disciplining the Gypsies. They went wild. They called each other names. They realized that they'd been had, because the intact instrument panel was worth more than what their father brought home in a year. On the other hand, they knew that Smart Doggie was their only customer, and so they felt helpless, and it was this helplessness that infuriated them the most. Then, when they started tearing at each other's hair and shirts, the teacher slapped them. You either take a bath by tomorrow, or you go right back to the dirty shanty you came from. Do I make myself clear?

After school let out, they waited for Smart Doggie in the park near the school and said alright, twenty fillérs a day till the end of eighth grade. But if they catch you and you rat on us, we'll burn your house down, and you're going to be baked to a crisp along with your mother and father, understand? And he nodded that he understood, and in the afternoon, with the second twenty fillérs in the palm of his hand, he waited for the Gypsies in the deserted gardening center next to the backwater.

355

Half an hour later he was sure he'd been had and began searching every nook and cranny of the deserted greenhouses, but except for a bunch of broken glass, a cat's skull and some tin cans, he found nothing. There was no trace of anything that could be part of an instrument panel. He realized that they'd outwitted him, just as they had Laci Serbán the week before. Laci had paid for four ball bearings in advance, but was left with the one they'd already given him in school. He waited for the Gypsies in vain, and the next day, when he asked for his money back, they beat him up so bad, he had to go see the nurse because his nosebleed wouldn't stop, and he told the nurse that he slipped on the stairs, otherwise the Gypsies would set his house on fire, there was no doubt about that.

And so, Little Doggie realized that he'd never see the compass again, nor the twenty fillérs' advance he'd given the Gypsies in the park. And this is what enraged him the most, his helplessness against his own stupidity, that because of a precision compass, he ignored a simple, evident fact, namely, that Gábriel and the others always swindle everyone. Then all of a sudden, the Gypsies appeared out of nowhere, the two smaller ones from fifth grade and the two older ones who were eighteen. They'd come into the greenhouse so quietly, he hadn't heard them. They tread over the broken glass in their bare feet, because they wore shoes only to school, because it was compulsory. When Little Doggie saw them with their pants rolled up and their naked chests, his stomach was all in knots, and he handed them the cat's skull without being asked, as if it belonged to them, and he'd picked it up just now only to have a look. The oldest boy spit on the floor and said, okay, let's go, Smart Doggie, and they headed for the backwater.

When they reached the water, Gábriel said, well, how about it? You want to go in with your clothes on? He didn't understand why he should go into the water. And then it turned out it's because the fighter plane was down in the backwater, imbedded in the stagnant mud at the bottom. And then Little Doggie would have liked to say that he doesn't really want it, because he knew how to swim, but he was terrified of swimming underwater. He wouldn't submerge his head even in the bathtub. Except, it was clear that there was no turning back. A deal is a deal. Jonatán had already picked up a stone, and he threw it in the backwater to where the fighter plane was. In short, they'd already showed him the place.

There they stood, the Gypsies, watching him. The eldest, whose name he didn't even know, was twisting a willow reed between his lips, the way soldiers twist a Gillette blade. Then he lost patience and asked, what's up, butthead? You choke the chicken, but you can't swim?

And then Little Doggie began taking off his clothes, first his shirt, then his shoes and socks, but just then he saw that one of his socks had a hole in it, and he thought he'd die of shame. But the Gypsies couldn't give a shit about his sock with the hole in it. They were too busy laughing at him because he hung all his things, his pants and undershirt, everything, on a bush, so they shouldn't get dust over them.

The muddy water got stirred up under his feet. He couldn't see anything, because the sun shone in his eye from among the willows on the opposite shore. Gábriel told him which way to swim. Then when he reached the middle of the backwater, he drew a deep breath and touched his cheeks to the water, and then ducked his head below the surface, just so he shouldn't have to hear the Gypsies scream with laughter on the shore. He then drew another deep breath, and ducked underwater. It wasn't so terrible after all, and this was worse than the Gypsies' laughter, the realization that what had terrified him was actually so simple.

The water was shallow and he could feel the wing of the figher plane with his fingers almost immediately. Then he swam past the fuselage until he reached the cockpit. He'd counted up to twenty-five till now, and he knew that he could stay below till sixty, at least, because he'd counted the number of breaths a thousand times, to see how long he could stay if he ever dared swim underwater. At thirty he could feel the barrel of the machine gun, which told him he'd gone past, so he turned back around, but got stuck in the branch of a tree with seaweed on it. Actually, two branches. Two slimy tree branches. And then. . . . and then I opened my eyes, and in the grayish-green murk, I saw the pilot's face. Or what was left of it. And then I grabbed the two floating arms I'd mistaken for the branches of a tree and couldn't let go. Locked in a cramp, my hands wouldn't let go, all the time that I felt the bones through the pilot's jacket. Actually, I wasn't even scared, it's just that I forgot to go on counting. I couldn't think of anything else except my mother standing by the kitchen sink washing the dishes, then one by one handing them to me to dry, and I'm drying them, and then we're done with all the plates, but I never want it to end, ever, I want to stand next to her till the end of time, wiping those damned plates dry, except there aren't any more of them.

And then two hands grabbed me and the two older Gypsies pulled me ashore. They came down on the pit of my stomach with their fists to make me cough up the water, all the while screaming, fuck it, asshole, you're not going to die on us, you hear? Breath, Smart Doggie! Breathe! And then I came to and they took my clothes from the bushes and put them on me. My sock with the hole in it and my shirt. Two of them grabbed me under each arm and without another word, dragged me over the meadow to Vasút Street.

(the storytelling)

Tell me a story, she said when we came to. She lay on her back, listening, looking at the cracked ceiling of my sixth-district apartment as if it were the starry sky. It never occurred to me though that my words mattered. I just told her story after story. I told her everything from my great-grandfather Andás Szabad to Imolka, and from my father to Dalma Keresztes.

Now and then, she asked me to repeat a story. She liked my father, but she felt sorry for my grandfather. She took Imolka in stride. She said that for a teenager, any girl could be an Imolka. I said I know, but that doesn't change the fact that Imolka became *my* Imolka. And she said, of course. But my pictures aren't about Imolka.

Adél Selyem, on the other hand, she hated with a passion. Not just her red rag, but her slate eyes, as if her own weren't slate colored as well. She said she understands why that woman was the first, and it's not my fault. Oh, yes, it is, I thought. Some women are born martyrs. They choose the person who will hurt them with the greatest of care, then become his undoing. I said it wasn't her fault, I wouldn't have finished school anyway. She said she's not talking about that. Adél Selyem poisoned me with raw meat. Even a dog's dinner is cooked. Only a wild animal eats raw meat. And I thought, why is there so much hate in her toward someone with whom I'd spent only one afternoon eight years ago, and I said, she didn't poison me. What about Dalma Keresztes, she asked. I don't know, I said, and decided not to ask whether she'd lay belly down on the piano for anyone else.

Her favorite was the compass. Not the underwater part, but the greenhouses in the bright summer sun and me waiting for the Gypsies, and suddenly, there they are, walking barefoot over the glass shards, and the way the oldest twists the willow leaf round and round between his lips, and me hanging my clothes on the bush.

I love you, she said.
You better, I said.

A crack ran along the ceiling. I had my eyes pinned on it, and meanwhile I thought that for weeks afterwards, Little Doggie wet the bed in his sleep, and it stopped only when one night I finally told my mother about it. We sat leaning against the doorjambs facing each other, our knees pulled up. She was as white as the wall. If you don't want to go crazy, son, you must believe that the Little Doggie is you. Whatever happens to you in life, it's you. And as for that pilot, he was an unfortunate soldier who died along with millions of others. Do you understand, son? It's you, and everything is all right now.

(on solitude)

One day, when I got home from Reisz's studio, I found Éva standing in the kitchen holding a loaf of bread wrapped in a white tablecloth. She cradled it like a child.

Look what I made, she said.

It was still warm. We ate almost the whole thing on the bed in my room, just as it was.

It needs a bit more salt. The next one will be better, she said.

It's perfect, I said.

Really? she asked, her eyes sparkling. I'd never seen that sparkle in her eyes before, neither when we made love, nor after a concert. That's when I first thought that my mother hadn't been lonely, because she loved my father. That's when I first thought that the only thing that can keep us from feeling lonely is the beating of another person's heart in our own chest.

I was mistaken. I lived under this misapprehension for over thirty years. It didn't just take my father to keep my mother from feeling lonely. It took my father, as well as me.

(Éva's life)

Éva had lots of friends. Musicians, that goes without saying, but also journalists, paint-ers, butchers, hawkers, pilots, priests. She knew everyone. For a long time I thought that this is only natural when someone is, how should I put it, in the limelight. Then it turned out that that's not the case at all. She had just as many people around her when she hadn't sat down by the piano for some time. As for me, the same three or four people are around me today as when people who needed IDs or passport photos bought my pictures, and not museums.

I'm not talking about those who, for one reason or another, end up in one's address book or phone book, but those who are in fact part of your life, those who unexpect-edly ring your doorbell and come up for coffee, or ask you to go fishing with them. At first I thought that these people wanted something from her. But the woman from the Electrical Works who month after month came to collect her electricity bill and sat down with her for a quick chat and told her about her alcoholic husband, then rushed off, from one electric meter to the next, I don't remember her ever asking Éva for a free ticket to the Music Academy.

And needless to say, I also thought that it was due to her beauty. Or more like her erotic discharge, the power that makes the world go round at least as much as bread and water, the erotic centripital force that had once prompted even the agronomist's wife to look into Imolka's basement apartment through her big mirror. Except, unlike Imolka, Éva never neglected to close the two upper and lower buttons on her dress. She made no unspoken promises. On the other hand, I, just by asking them to stand in front of my camera in a darkened room, made more unspoken promises to people than she ever did with all her concerts, birthmarks, and dresses made in France.

Then one day I realized that Évike in the café, or the tobacconist across the way, know

362

a lot more about my life than I do about the life of the woman who, night after night, falls asleep on my lap.

Tell me a story, I said.

What do you want to hear?

Anything. Your Gypsies. Your peacock. Your compass.

I didn't have any Gypsies. I'd have told you if I had.

Then tell me about your grandmother, Éva Zára.

My mother isn't Éva. Much less my grandmother.

Yes, I know she's not Éva.

You also know that she lives in Sopron.

Fine. Then let's go to Sopron this Sunday.

Mother, dear, here's the love of my life, make your mutual introductions, then quickly make us two slices of buttered bread, because we have to catch the six p.m. express. I have a rehearsal in the morning.

So let's go some other time, I said.

Fine. But I have nothing to say about her, I swear. I have a normal mother and I had a normal father, who died of a normal heart attack, which crushed me in the ordinary way, just as one would expect. Now, on the other hand, I don't feel in the least crushed.

My mother was also normal.

I just meant to say that nothing turned our lives upside down. At least, not more so than is to be expected of ordinary lives. My father was not in prison, and my mother wasn't a librarian forced to sew on buttons in a clothing factory.

Well tell me about your Imolka then.

She laughed. She reached over me for her glass so I could see the starry sky on her belly.

What an idea. I never had an Imolka. But I gather, you wish I had.

I won't deny it. I wouldn't mind seeing you with an Imolka sometime.

She sat up, put down her glass, and lit a cigarette. The light of the small lamp was absorbed by her hair. As for her face, I couldn't see it at all.

And what has that got to do with love?

Nothing, I said. It was just a joke.

For a while, she said nothing.

Fine. If you get me drunk sometime and find me an Imolka to my liking, you can watch me with her.

Careful what you say. I already have the wine.

I don't wonder. And I'm sure you can find me an Imolka as well.

For a while, I said nothing.

You said you're not afraid of my pictures.

Why? Should I be? I just told you. Find me an Imolka.

I can't. Nor do I want to.

She took my hand and raised it to her lips, then blew the cigarette smoke through my fingers.

In that case, I'll find one myself. But you can only watch us in black and white.

Fine.

And just once.

Fine.

And only if you do me now.

I don't understand.

Screw me.

I don't understand.

Pump me.

I don't understand.

Fuck me till you break me.

Shut up.

(Nóra Kardos)

I didn't take a liking to Nóra Kardos, and I might as well admit it right at the beginning. There are few things in life that are decided in the blinking of an eye, but still, there are some. By the time we got to the café, she was already sitting at a table in the darkest corner of the establishment, drinking coffee with cognac. She was Éva's childhood friend. She worked at the Opera, in administration. Éva got her the job through her ex-husband, so Nóra could move to Pest. This is all I knew about her. And also, that I wouldn't like her, because nobody likes Nóra. I said that she shouldn't decide beforehand. She said she's not deciding beforehand, she just knows, but that's all right, no one will ever be more important to her than Nóra. And I said, what luck, the trams clattering past like that, so I can't hear what she's telling me. She hugged me and said, don't be silly, you're my life. Nóra is my coffin. I asked what she meant by that. And she said, fine, let's make it a leaden box in which a person keeps her life. And I said she better not keep me in a leaden box like that.

When we got there, Nóra was just telling her fortune with cards. Or playing solitaire. I really don't know. She quickly gathered up the cards and secured the pack with a rubber band, then put it in her handbag. She seized me up, then said to Éva, well, well. She looked like an adolescent boy. She wore pants and had a boy's haircut. There was nothing feminine about her. She asked what I do for a living. I said that I take pictures, and she said, anybody can do that. I waited for Éva to say something, but she didn't think it was important, and so I didn't say anything either, in the end. I'd have liked to, but my mind went blank. I couldn't think of a single thing to say. Éva laughed and said I shouldn't take everything so seriously. I said that I'm not. I'd have liked to leave that instant, but I didn't want to offend either of them. Still, she succeeded in making me try to formulate an answer, even weeks later, in case anyone should confront me with this "anybody can do that" again.

Nóra had just returned from Warsaw the day before. From time to time, she could go abroad with the Opera. She told us that during her last night there, she went to a circus tent with some strangers and swung naked on the trapeze. I knew perfectly well that there wasn't a grain of truth in what she said. But that's not what bothered me. What bothered me was the way Éva was listening to her, that she's looking at this woman the way my father had once looked at Kőszegi. That she believed whatever her friend says.

Before we met, I thought that she was Éva's Kornél. Now I saw my mistake. She was more like a shadow, a shadow that walks instead of you, a shadow that takes you in the direction she's headed. Give me three hundred forints, she said in parting. Of course, Éva said, took the money out of her wallet, and handed it to her. Nóra threw it in her bag without a word, not even a thank you.

On the way home, I asked Éva if she thought the naked swinging on the trapeeze was true. She said, of course. And also, it doesn't matter if certain things are true or not. I said that for me it does matter. It must matter to her, too, if what I say about my mother, my father, or anyone else, is true or not. She said that I'm not Nóra. I asked her what the difference was between Nóra and myself with respect to truth.
    She said nothing.
    Surely, you must know, I said.
    The difference is merely that your father didn't rape you, she said.
I said nothing, but the admiration in Éva's eye when she looked at that woman was now even harder for me to bear, and I said that the truth is the truth, whereupon she told me not to get my gander up, because of all the people she'd ever known, Nóra is the only one whose every word is true. Someone who has nothing to gain and nothing to lose doesn't lie. I thought that someone who has nothing to lose doesn't cast her fortune from cards, but I said only that I hope she wouldn't mind if I didn't like her friend, because I'd be hurt if she didn't like Kornél.
    Nóra is not my friend.
    What is she then?
    Is there bread at home?
    No. What is she then?

She kissed me on the forehead, handed me her burning cigarette, and went inside the shop to buy bread. I hated it when she didn't answer me, when she acted as if she hadn't heard what I'd said. I'd never met anyone else, ever, who was this good at it. Mother was the only one to whom I spoke in vain. But then, she was dead.

As I waited by the curb, I watched the cars drive past. An open snow-white Mercedes bearing a foreign licence plate drove along People's Republic Avenue. It was like a lie. I waited for it to disappear among the Skodas and Zhigulis. It had almost reached Heroes Square, but I could still see it.

So then, what is she to you, I persisted when she came out of the shop.

You want the heel? It's still warm.

I could have screamed. I wanted to grab her by the arm and shake her, fuck it, answer me when I'm talking to you! Instead, I tore off a piece of bread and halved it.

My witness, she said.

What sort of witness?

Admit it. This is better than what I made.

I liked yours better. What do you mean she's your witness?

I can't think of a better word, seeing how you didn't like *coffin*. My witness. The person who knows everything about me.

In that case, you're my witness.

She linked her arm in mine.

I'm not your witness, I'm the love of your life.

One doesn't rule out the other.

Oh, yes, it does.

In that case, Kornél is my witness.

No he isn't. You have no witnesses, just your photographs.

(the Shroud of Turin)

My first client was a man of about fifty years of age. He had a brush moustache and wore a sheepskin coat. Except for a short greeting, he didn't talk much. He hung the coat on the rack, sat down, and waited. I adjusted the lighting. A lousy silence followed. For want of anything better, I asked what the picture was for. He said, for a licence to carry arms. After that, neither of us spoke. I adjusted the focus, pushed the film holder of the ground glass into the spring back, placed my finger on the shutter release, and waited for him to blink. It felt like minutes had passed. He didn't blink. Well, what about it, he asked. I pressed the shutter release cable. Reisz called from the lab. Plate!

I pulled out the plate, I took the required two pictures, and wrote out the receipt. I was drenched in sweat. Soon as the man left, Reisz came out.
   Thank you, I said.
   You'll get the hang of it, he said.
   I'd have never thought that taking an ID photo was hell.
   You'll get the hang of it in no time.
   How did you know in there that I forgot to pull out the plate?
   From the sound. There was no twang, and the shutter clicked.
   You hear that from in there?
   Yes. And at such times, don't advance the film. Or if you've advanced it, take another picture of the client, so you'll end up with a pair. As it is, you've got an empty frame now.
   Fine. In the future, I'll do that, I said.
   And don't ask what the picture is for. It's none of our business. If the client wants to tell us, he'll tell us. If not, not.
   I just wanted to make conversation.
   In that case, ask him to lean his head forward a bit more, or something of the sort.
   Fine. He looked like a lizard. He didn't blink. Not once. He's some sort of hunter.
   He's not a hunter.

He said he needed it for a licence to carry arms.

He's not a hunter. He's a member of the Workers' Militia. Hunters never stop talking.

In a week or so, I got the hang of it. I liked doing it. Once I didn't have to attend to every move separately, looking at the focusing screen under the black cloth was a bit like looking at the iron shavings in the workshop, except now someone was looking back at me, if only for the time it took to take their picture.

I asked Reisz why he didn't want me to help with the lab work. He said it's because I already know that. What you need to learn, he said, is that taking photographs is not blasphemy. That you have no reason to be ashamed of yourself.

But it's blasphemy all the same, even if just a bit, I said.

You're wrong about that, he said. Who do you think is responsible for the first photograph ever taken?

Talbot, I said.

No way, he said.

Then Nieps.

You're off by a lifetime.

Then I don't know.

That's a shame, he said, because in that case, I'm afraid you're left with no other option than to be ashamed of your pictures all your life, because in that case, your pictures really are the greatest blasphemy in the world.

You hit the nail on the head. That's my sentiment exactly.

Alright, then, listen, and listen closely. Did the Lord paint?

Not that I know of.

Did he play music?

I don't know about that either.

Did he write?

Once. In the sand.

That doesn't count. Here today, gone tomorrow.

Still, it counts, don't you think?

Fine. You can let it count.

He also wrote on the stone tablets.

Maybe. Then again, maybe not. A man who has come from a distance can say anything he wants.

Still, the Holy Writ is the Holy Writ.

And so it is. And everyone twists it to his liking. But photography is no joke. That's why in the end, the Lord decided in favor of photography. That's why Jesus Christ is responsible for the first picture. A contact print. A life-size contact print of himself. If you want to be a photographer, don't ever forget it. It's the only thing that is personally from God. And within photography, portraiture. Human portraiture.

Which takes a lot of faith, I said.

Look. To be honest, I don't care about your faith or religion. I, for instance, if I belonged to a faith, I'd consider Christ, along with his shroud, a half-crazed prophet, if that, of whom there are at least a dozen running about out in the desert every Pesach. But if you want to work here in the Reisz Studio, don't let any rabbi, priest, or Party secretary, or any other wiseguy, tell you that photography is not from God, because if you fall for it, you can go wipe your ass with your pictures. Which is all for today.

Kornél said that Reisz is right, but the Holy Writ is from God, just the same.

(on photography)

When I think about it, in a certain sense, I'm the same amateur today who once knocked on Reisz's door. Can a photograph evoke in me what I felt when I pressed the shutter release button, this is the only thing that has ever interested me, and that's the truth. I look at a woman's face. Her ecstasy fills me with curiosity, yearning, fear, the wish to unite with her. I press the shutter release button. And then something happens. The ecstasy turns into tears, anger, hate, feelings that have nothing to do with what I felt just a moment before, when I took the picture. A photograph can even amplify what I felt the moment I took the picture. The photograph can't help it. It has no other choice. A photograph can't see into the future, and it can't see into the past, and this being the case, a photograph is merely the point where the future and the past connect. It is, if you will, the continuous present. Yes, perhaps I've managed to make myself clear to the extent, of course, that any discourse on photography can take us closer to its essence.

Come to think of it, I don't know why it should be more difficult for us to accept the void between photography and reality than it is to accept the fact that what we see up in the sky is no longer there. Surely, this must be because we're the ones on the photograph, our light and the light that we reflect. For all we know, perhaps it is, in fact, blasphemy when the light of a single moment of mine outlasts the moment itself, outlasting me. And so, in essence, there is no substantial difference between a photograph and the light of a star that reaches us millions of years after the star has vanished.

If I look at it this way, my photographer's attitude is hopelessly amateur. I took my pictures for the same reason that others take family snapshots. On the other hand, if some of my pictures have nonetheless been capable of guiding others to a moment that had never existed in their own lives, if that indeed is the case, then it's this amateur attitude they have to thank for it.

Of course, it may well be that this dynamic between the photograph and the viewer occurs not because of it, but in spite of it. However, if that's the case, I don't know the cause. I know only that the cause is not to be found in the factors considered by knowing critics. It is to be found neither in the light, nor the shade, neither in the composition, perspective, nor any applied technique, even if what these critics point out is no doubt valid, and even if these means and devices are undoubtedly essential. But nothing follows merely from them. Beyond a certain point, there is no difference between aesthetics and physics. Beyond a certain point, it makes not the slightest difference that one can be quantified, while the other can't. Our chances of understanding and describing the universe remain the same. It is impossible to approach the infinite any closer than we've done so far. Only a world from which we have banished the infinite can be described.

Throughout the years, I have discarded hundreds of my photographs, and I did so despite the fact that they would have fully satisfied the critics thanks to whom other of my photographs have appeared on several front pages or have made their way into museums and private collections. I discarded them because they didn't speak to me. Perhaps they would have spoken to others. Except, what has that got to do with me?

(kitsch)

In the homewares section of the department store in Mélyvár, the knick-knacks were displayed at the far end of the row of porcelains. Ballet dancers, rabbits, kittens with balls of yarn, chimney sweeps, *betyár* highwaymen smoking their pipes. There may have been other things as well. Father and I went there to buy a wash tub. The old tub we used to boil the wash got a hole in it. They were twenty-five or thirty-liter tubs, I can't remember, and they were made of galvanized tin. In the fall, we used these tubs to pick apples.

When my father was a teacher, everyone knew him, including the saleswoman in homewares. She helped chose a tub. Then she took it to the cashier so we wouldn't have to carry it with us, should we decide to have a look around. My father said that we should buy Mother a vase, not just the tub.

The knick-knacks came after the vases. I liked the chimney sweep very much. I asked Father if he's sure it's got to be a vase. He said that as far as he's concerned, he wouldn't like a vase, but he knows that Mother would like one, a narrow vase on the table for a single flower, because at home we only have vases suited for bouquets. I said that I think mother would like the chimney sweep as well. Father laughed. It was a sweet laugh. He said that he very much doubted it. I asked him why. He leaned on his cane and said, because it's kitsch.

I had no idea what kitsch was. All I knew was that I invariably heard it in connection with something I liked. The embroidered splash guard in Aunt Erzsike's house was kitsch, the Romanian glass fish atop their radio was kitsch, and the framed edelweiss above the glass fish was kitsch. I thought that whatever my mother liked, I like, too. I like kitsch, I told father. Fine. In that case, let's buy a vase for your mother, and let's buy this for you. I was very happy. We paid, then headed home. We carried the wash tub by its two handles, and inside it, wrapped in paper, the vase and the kitsch.

Then as we walked home along Dózsa György Road, Father explained that kitsch is the antithesis of art. It's the art of stupid people. All the sunsets and fawns drinking from pristine springs are lies. Not literally, of course. After all, sunsets exist, and so do fawns. They're lies only as art, because they convey the illusion of an eternal idyllic state, as if the bad were not every bit as much a part of life as the good, or the ugly as well as the beautiful. When he was just fourteen, Dürer made a drawing of his mother that few have been able to surpass, and not only because of his exceptional gift as a draughtsman, but because he dared to show his mother along with her ugliness. With the same immense gift for draughtsmanship, he could just as well have produced kitsch. He could have made a drawing that suggests that his mother is happy and beautiful, and what's more, so is every old woman. And no two ways about it, my son, that would have been kitsch, Father went on. It's their not lying that made Dürer and the others great. Michelangelo's David possesses strength, self-confidence, and tension, all at the same time. After all, he must defeat the Goliath. On the other hand, this chimney sweep smiles as if there were no greater joy to life than cleaning smoky chimneys. In short, kitsch is a lie. Forgetting life's darker side. Seeing the world as pink froth. That's kitsch.

I said to Father that in that case, I was very stupid just now for liking the chimney sweep so much. He said I wasn't stupid in the least, for I had no way of knowing what kitsch was. I'd be stupid only if I were to fill my home with such knick-knacks once I was a grown man, and leave them to my children. I said, possibly. But let's not show Mother the chimney sweep. He laughed and said that it's my kitsch, I can do with it whatever I like.

When I got home, I took the Michelangelo album off the shelf, took it to my room, and looked up David. I put the chimney sweep next to it. I thought I'd die of shame. My father was right. I didn't just believe it, I saw it. After dinner, I went to the raspberry bush in the back of the garden, grabbed a stone, and taking my time over it, crushed the knick-knack into tiny little pieces, ladder, grin, and all. Then I gathered up the pieces and wrapped them in wrapping paper. I cried like a baby. The kitsch is still there, buried in the ground.

Okay, let's go, Éva said.

Now?

Yes, now.

She got out of bed and began slipping into her clothes. She opened the shutters and the window. The sky was still gray outside.

Where are we going?

I want you to like kitsch again.

That won't be easy, I said.

Trust me, she said. You will.

You're not dragging me out of this bed for love or money.

She didn't say anything. She just pulled her dress down over her hips, then her panties, and with the same motion, flung them out the window.

Hurry up, she said, before somebody finds them.

She went to the bathroom and rummaged through the medicine box. She called to me, asking where I kept the the potassium permanganate. I said that it's not medicine but a chemical, so it's in the kitchen, in the lab cabinet. It's the brown bottle behind the fixer.

There it is, I said triumphantly when she came out through the front door downstairs.

Let others have a good day, too, she said, and pulled me away from where her panties lay.

The traffic on People's Republic Avenue was still very light. She linked her arm in mine and led me along so fast, I nearly had to break into a run. She hailed a passing cab.

I don't have enough money on me, I said.

But I do. To Elizabeth Bridge, she told the driver.

Are you sure? the driver asked.

Believe me, nobody knows better than I where I want to go, Éva said.

I believe you, lady, the cabbie said, except people generally prefer to jump off of Liberty Bridge.

Oh, we're planning quite a different sort of crime, Éva said and laughed.

I said nothing.

By the time we reached the bridge, the sun was rising. She paid the cabbie, and we got out. Since the new bridge was up, I hadn't been in the vicinity more than twice, if that. To the left, the Castle, to the right, Parliament, in the middle, shrieking seagulls. With Éva by my side, the city looked decidedly friendly.

This is not what I'd call kitsch, I said.

This? This is nothing. Come with me, she said.

We crossed the road at the Buda abutment, against traffic rules, I might add. She then stopped at the bottom of Gellért Hill, at the spot where the waterfall comes tumbling down into a basin. Her dress was soon soaked through from the mist.

In short, kitsch is a lie, you say.

Yes, I said.

Pink froth.

Yes, I said.

The lighter side of life. And you don't like it.

That's right. I don't like it, I said.

In that case, you provide the froth, and I'll provide the pink.

What?

Pour this box of Ultra in there, she said as she pulled the box of detergent out of her bag.

No.

Now!

I poured it in. She added all my potassium permanganate, and as if by magic, the light-purple foam began to grow in volume, then broke through the railing and flowed out onto the pavement, and there we were, standing in it. It had already reached the bottom of Éva's white dress.

Compared to this, your chimney sweep was a veritable Michelangelo, she said.

I know. Let's run, I said.

Are you crazy? You want to leave this?

I'm not crazy, I'm chicken.

So I see.

We climbed up to the statue of St. Gellért rising above the waterfall and watched the early morning drivers pass through what was left of the froth.

If you're afraid of it, she said, you'll die, even if your father was right.

I'm not afraid of it, I said. I just don't like it.

Come now. You bury it in the back of the garden, like an old dog, and you don't like it? You're suffocating. Afraid to breathe.

I'm not afraid. From now on, I'm not.

That's settled then, she said. You may now fuck me.

If they see us, that's three to five years.

She pulled her soaked dress up to her hips and lay belly down over the stone balustrade.

Someone's bound to come.

More than twenty years later, Kornél said that he never envied me for anything, ever, except for that dawn.

(the blind woman)

One day a woman came to Reisz to have her passport photo taken. She must have been around thirty-five. She was elegantly dressed. She had wavy blond hair that reached to her shoulder. She wore sunglasses. I was alone in the studio. Reisz had just gone out for lunch. There was a cafeteria on Baross Square. That's where we used to go for lunch.

Although only the counter was between us, the woman spoke very softly. She carried a snow-white umbrella. Its grip was shaped like a dragon. She hung it up on the counter. The dragon's eyes were made of some sort of red stone. The woman kept her hand on the carved grip, as if it were an animal. She was one of the most beautiful women I had ever seen.

When I told her how much the photo would cost, she paid right away. She took a wallet from her bag. It was full of neatly arranged one-hundred forint bills. I counted out the change and gave it to her. She folded the bills, then stuffed them inside another wallet, along with the coins. Only then did she ask when the photo would be ready. I said, whenever she'd like. She thanked me and said that in that case, she'd wait for it. I felt uncomfortable. I didn't want to tell her that if it's urgent, there's an extra charge, so I just said that it's not a good idea, because it'll take an hour at least. She asked if there's a free chair. I said, of course. She smiled and said, that'll be all right then, she doesn't mind waiting an hour if she's not in the way. I said I'm sorry, but this is the only way in, then I raised the counter and she walked in. She didn't even look at herself in the mirror. She asked what she's supposed to do. I said nothing. She should just sit down on this chair here. She nearly tripped over the foot of the light stand. I was about to warn her, but her foot stopped in mid-motion and she managed to step over it. She went to the chair, stopped just short of it, turned around and sat down. She moved like a marionette. I turned on the lights and watched her. She turned to the camera, or rather, toward me. Otherwise, she remained motionless. I pulled the black cloth over my head and adjusted the focus on the focusing screen. I don't know what I felt, what that something really was. Perhaps it resembled the feeling that sweeps over you when you look out to sea and your tears begin to flow.

I'd already inserted the film holder into the spring back and removed the dark slide when I remembered that you can't wear sunglasses when you have your passport photo taken. But they were so much a part of that woman that I'd forgotten all about it. I even adjusted the light so the dark glasses wouldn't reflect it.

Could you please take them off?

What for?

I said that with her sunglasses on, the police wouldn't accept the photo.

What a shame, she said. Then she took them off, and the blood froze in my veins.

Deep inside, her two empty eyesockets were covered with grayish skin.

Would you please take these? she said.

Of course, I said, and placed her sunglasses on the counter.

I'm sorry, she said.

I said nothing, pressed the shutter release button for her passport photo, then readjusted the lights.

What are you doing now? she asked.

Adjusting the light, I said.

She laughed. So that's why I didn't know, she said.

I couldn't get up the nerve to ask her to come to my place so I could take pictures of her.

I'll take another, I said.

Go right ahead. That's why I'm here.

There was a dark canvas backdrop we never used. Now I placed it behind her. But in the end, I couldn't keep myself from telling her that I wasn't thinking of a passport photo, but a proper photo.

Her lips barely just moved. The silence that settled over us was as profound as the silence of the grave.

No, she said.

In that case, I apologize, I said. We're done.

She remained seated.

Why do you want to take my picture?

I don't really know. Because I'm a photographer, I guess. I take ID pictures for a living, and I don't know why I want to take anything else.

But why me?

I said nothing.

What did you feel?

When you came in, or when you took your sunglasses off?

She said nothing.

I really am sorry, I said.

Give me your hand, she said.

I went up to her. She took my hand, as if she could see. The palm of my hand was drenched in sweat. She pressed it to her face.

That's alright, then, she said, and let go. Take those extra pictures.

I switched off one lamp, then placed the overlay on the other. Then I pulled down the blind, so the light shouldn't come in from outside. I wanted that single lamp to provide barely enough light, as if we were under the sea. I had nearly thirty minutes before Reisz was to come back.

Lower your head a bit, I said.

Like this?

Yes. And part your lips just a bit.

Should I wet them?

No.

How much of my eyes show?

They don't. They're in a shadow. Completely.

My hands?

It makes no difference. Whatever feels comfortable. They're not in the picture.

What a shame I'll never get to see it.

You know what it's like just the same, I said.

That's true, she said.

I shot two rolls of film. I'd have liked to go on and on, but I was expecting Reisz back. I put the film cartridges in my pocket. I didn't want him to know.

Thank you, I said.

She took my hand and pressed it to her face again. You're welcome, she said.

I raised the shutters and she replaced her sunglasses, then took her umbrella with the dragon's head.

I think I'll leave now after all, she said quietly.

Fine, I said. You can come pick up your passport picture tomorrow.

I won't be coming back, ever, so don't worry. I'll send someone in my place.

I developed the film at home. The baseboard was too small, so I turned the Agfa's projector away and enlarged the images on the wall to fifty by sixty. When Éva came home in the evening, the pictures were already drying on the boards. When she saw them, she stopped in the middle of the room, but said nothing.

Who is that woman? she finally asked.

I don't know. She came to Reisz's earlier today.

The way she looks at me, it makes me feel like I'm suffocating, she said.

She's not looking at you, I said. She's blind.

That woman is not blind.

Yes, she is.

You're lying.

Fine. I'll bring her ID picture home with me tomorrow.

She said nothing.

I told you. She has no eyes, just a shadow where her eyes should be.

It began to rain outside. Fall was upon us. Éva went to the window and watched the raindrops knock the dust off the tin windowsill.

Have you ever been happy? she asked.

I'm happy now, I said. I went up to her and kissed her eyes.

That's different. I mean before. Really happy.

Yes.

When?

When Mother and I did the dishes.

(the self-portrait)

Sit down there, Reisz said.

Why, I asked.

Just sit down.

I don't want to. I don't need an ID photo.

Don't you think I know that? Except, this camera has two sides, and generally, there's someone on either side of it.

I sat down. He adjusted the lights.

Don't look at me. Look into the lens.

I did so.

Raise your chin a bit.

I raised it.

Too much. Back.

I lowered it.

Sit up straight. Your shoulder is crooked.

I straightened up.

You're looking at the lens like a lizard.

I know.

Then stop it. Look natural. As if you were looking at me.

I'm trying.

If I were to press the shutter release now, it'd be a waste of film. I hope you know that.

I always stand on the other side of the camera. The people sitting here don't have to know how to adjust the lights or the focus.

Have it your way. Except, it's a waste of film. I just said.

I take very good ID pictures.

The district police won't reject them, if that's what you mean.

Why are you giving me shit? What did I do wrong?

Let me tell you a story. A woman used to come here, three, sometimes four times a year. She said it was for her passport. She lied, poor thing. That woman never went any-where, take my word for it. She didn't need those pictures. She was just crazy. I mean, she was one of those unhappy women who spread their ID photos out on the kitchen table to watch themselves grow old.

Okay. But what does that have to do with anything?

I'll tell you. That woman came here for fourteen years. She was fiftyish, and short. She held her shoulder awry. She wore a brown hat. She was a regular customer. I'm sure you'll remember her.

I thought I'd die of shame. I'm sorry, I said. Don't be mad at me.

I'm not mad at you. But fourteen years is fourteen years. In that time a child learns not only to walk, he finishes grade school as well.

I didn't mean to offend that woman.

That's neither here nor there. But that woman will never set foot in here again. Yes-terday, I ran into her on the tram. And do you know what she said? She said, Mr. Reisz, I had my reasons for visiting your studio and not someone else's.

I just asked her to sit up straight.

No doubt.

She came in asking who I was and what I was doing here, and asked if I was a relative? I said no. I'm working here. Then I asked her to please sit up straight. And she sprang to her feet fuming, shouting that no one has ever talked to her like that before, she's not a dog, nobody can bully her around. Then she stormed out.

If you say so, Reisz said.

What do you mean, if I say so? She's the one who spoke to me like a dog!

No doubt, Reisz said. But that's not the point. The point is, did you want to take that woman's picture or not?

Of course I did. And I'm very sorry she won't be coming back any more.

If she's not, she's not. She'll have her ID pictures taken someplace else. There's no rule saying she must turn to Reisz. As for you, if you want to take a picture of someone, even if it's just a simple ID picture, your place is not behind the camera. Your place is on that chair over there, from where you look straight into the lens.

Sure. I know, I said.

No, you don't.

384

Yes, I do.

You don't. You just think you do, because you've been lucky that no one has complained so far, because the ones you take home with you to take their picture follow you as if they were blindfolded. They're mesmerized, like charmed snakes at a fair. They're past caring what you do behind the camera.

They may be past caring, but I'm not.

A good thing. Otherwise, you'd be a great big fraud. But it doesn't follow that because you take good pictures of your mesmerized subjects, you know what it's like in front of the camera. You have to sit in front of it, and not just look in the mirror through your Leica, but sit in front of it. Naked. And let me tell you another thing. It's not the chair you need to sit on. You need to settle inside the person sitting on the chair and look into the lens with their eyes. And hear with their ears when you tell them to sit up straight.

It was late at night by the time I got up the nerve. I closed the shutters, so the old woman across the way wouldn't see me. Then using the mannequin, I adjusted the lights and the focus. I'd never used the delay-action release before. It was faster than I thought. After I used up half the film, I finally got up the nerve, threw off my clothes, and stood there as naked as the day I was born. Then I pulled my pants back on and slipped into my shirt.

In the last picture I took, I'm standing in my mother's Persian lamb coat.

(safety)

To make sure that Gagarin would be safe, they first sent a bunch of dogs into orbit. The first was Laika, the stray husky-spitz mix. The dog catchers caught her in Moscow. The space researchers trained her in Star City. This meant that they turned her inside a centrifuge faster and faster each day. At first they spun her too fast, and the poor thing couldn't even pee. Then they lowered the speed of the centrifuge. She was sent into orbit the year my father was put behind bars.

Actually, they just wanted to know if Laika would survive takeoff and weightlessness. Thus, instead of a return module, it sufficed to supply a poison capsule for her. She survived takeoff, this much we know. And also, that she didn't live to suffer the effects of the poisoned capsule. She was sitting inside an iron box, and by all odds, she saw nothing of which Gagarin later said, beautiful. It is so beautiful.

I don't know whether they've conducted experiments to find out what happens to corpses in outer space. Does the body start to decompose in a vacuum? Do we take along the vermin that gnaw the flesh off of our bones? Do corpses smell in outer space, or is there no place for them anywhere, except for the soil from which they spring? Be that as it may, Khruschev told Gagarin beforehand that he mustn't find God. "I don't see any sort of God here," this is what he had say over the radio. Which, come to think of it, is a rather peculiar way of conducting research. I wonder if Khruschev considered whether Gagarin would be able to follow his instructions should he find himself standing face to face with the Almighty. Of course, the odds of that happening were slight, and Khruschev was right in thinking that. But still. What if God can be seen from everywhere in the entire universe, with the exception of Earth? What if his light can't penetrate the Earth's atmosphere? The ozone knocks it back, like the ultraviolet lights. Even Khruschev couldn't have known this for sure. What can I say? That man was irresponsible.

Once Gagarin was in orbit, they didn't entrust him with mission control. Which was only logical. It would have been too risky. Just as there was no knowing in what way God's characteristics were different in outer space than on Earth, so there was no knowing how human characteristics and traits might be different up there. Besides, for lack of previous experience, Gagarin couldn't be trained to deal with too many eventualities. In this respect, the first man was indeed not unlike the last dog.

Gagarin's most important task was self-observation. To observe and take notes on what is happening to him. Which, let's admit it, is not an easy task, even under earthly conditions. He was supplied with a notebook and a pencil. Given the weightlessness, the pencil floated away, so we don't know what he might have noted down, only what interested him the most when he talked with Earth.

I'm doing fine. Can you tell me something about the flight?
I'm doing fine. I feel great. Is there anything you can tell me?
I'm doing fine. I'm feeling fine. Say something to me.
I'm doing fine. Perfect. Perfectly fine. Tell me something about the flight.
I'm doing fine. I feel great. But will you please transmit the flight data!

But they didn't tell him anything, because they got their calculations wrong, and for very nearly thirty out of the hundred and eight minutes, they didn't know which of the press releases they had composed earlier would be in place, and this despite the fact that unlike Laika, they furnished Gagarin with a parachute, so he could catapult out, should the space module begin to plummet.

In short, Gagarin was most preoccupied with what interested Laika and all the other great self-observers. Not weightlessness, not how beautiful it all is, not even whether God can be seen from up there, and if so, how that affects him, but whether after the self-observation, he'd make it back alive. In the end, he did.

(Persona)

One evening Nóra looked in on us. It was her first time at our place. Without even looking around, she lay down on the bed and lit a cigarette. She said, you should do something. You need a phone. I said that I can do only as much as anyone else. Wait. Éva asked if anyone wants something to drink. Nóra said we should hurry, there's an illegal film club out in Rákos, we have to be there by ten. They're showing *Persona*. I didn't feel like going to Rákos. I hadn't been to Rákos since Father stopped being a librarian there. I asked if she had planned to invite us to an illegal film club over the phone.

Give me an ashtray, or I'll get cigarette ashes all over your bed.

I took the ashtray over to her. Meanwhile, Éva started dressing. She put on a turtle neck just like the one Nóra wore.

You can see *Persona* in a proper movie theater, I said.

Except, they censored out the prick, Nóra said. But you, you can go see it at the movies if you want.

Dress warm, it's cold outside, Éva said.

They didn't censor it out.

Sure they did, Nóra said. Take my word for it. They censor out everything that's good.

I don't know about that. I've seen it.

I'm not surprised, Éva laughed. You've got prick on the brain.

I might say the same thing about you, I said.

Are you complaining? Nóra put in. It's the one thing I wouldn't complain about if I were you.

I wasn't complaining, I said. And for your information, it's in close-up and it stands up from right to left, and it's on the screen for half a second, if that. That's probably why the censors didn't notice.

Does he remember everything so well, Nóra asked Éva.

No. Just visuals, Éva said.

Poor man, Nóra said.

Éva handed me my coat.

Okay, come, because Éva and I haven't even seen the censored version. So hurry.

This apartment feels drab, Nóra said at the door.

There was a light drizzle outside. We took a cab. Nóra paid. She could write it off at the Opera as expenses. I sat up front. I was watching the driver, who was watching the two women through the rearview mirror instead of the road. Éva asked what the film is like.

You'll both like it, I said. As did I.

You've certainly made me curious, Nóra said.

The cultural center was pitch dark. We had to go in through the emergency exit in the back. The film club was managed by some people's educator, as they were called back then. I could have sworn that he was an informer. He was an acquaintance of Nóra's. The ten or fifteen people there practically disappeared in that huge hall. Only two lamps on the sides afforded some light, but at least, this way the red plaster star above the podium was barely visible. The padded seats were upholstered with red velvet, and there was a piano downstage to the left. I thought that Mother's Bösendorfer had stood just like this in a similar cultural center once, except back then, you couldn't run an illegal film club. We sat in the middle, where there was no one near us. Nóra sat furthest inside, next to her Éva, and I to her left. Before the film began, the people's educator asked everyone to refrain from smoking, because they'd smell the smoke the next day. Then he said, he knows that Bergman needs no introduction to those in the audience. This is the uncut version, everything's in it, including you know what. Everyone laughed. I've hated that conspiratorial laughter all my life along with *uncut* version instead of *uncensored* version. And also, people thinking the censor is an idiot, as if it weren't the censor allowing even these laughs. Then he went up to the projection booth and turned off the light.

When that penis had come and gone in half a second, Éva leaned over and whispered in my ear, is that all? I said, yes, that's all. You'll have to make do with it for tonight. I thought that in the scene with the camera, I'd tell her to pay close attention and see if she catches a really big blooper, because when Liv Ullmann sets the focus, she blocks out the viewfinder with her hand. You can't set the focus like that, because you can't see anything. The first time I saw the film, I couldn't understand. How could Bergman not have noticed? On the way home from the movies, it was the only thing that preoccupied me. Nothing else interested me except for this mistake. Then sometime during the night I remembered the broken piece of glass that the nurse sneaks in front of Liv Ullmann's naked foot, so she'd step on it. It was a pretty bad feeling. Luckily, except for me, no one knew about the satisfaction I felt all night over finding one measly little mistake in a Bergman film. It was terrible. Still, be that as it may, I thought I'd tell Éva to pay close attention when we got to that scene.

When the nurse started telling the mute Liv Ullmann how she made love to a woman who was a complete stranger to her and to an adolescent boy on the seaside, Éva took my hand. There wasn't even enough light in that fucking place so I could see clearly, to see if she also took Nóra's hand. When the nurse was saying that the boy pleasured the other woman with his hand, Nóra shifted position and put her feet up on the back of the seat in front of her, then put one hand on her lap, and with the other embraced Éva but so that her hand should touch my shoulder, as if my accident. Éva said, don't. Nóra said, what do you want then? Éva said, nothing. And I thought that if she thinks she can ask Nóra to be Imolka, she's nuts. Somebody called back and said, be quiet. Éva let go of my hand, bent over with convulsion and leaned her head on her two fists. She sat so still, you couldn't even hear her breathe. Nóra took a cigarette from a pack, knocked it against the pack, then put it back. I had to lean forward so I could see something of Éva's face. Her child's torn photograph was already under Liv Ullmann's hand when Éva finally straightened up and leaned back in her seat. She tapped her fingers on the back of the seat in front of her. Nóra removed her feet and sat up. After Alma told Liv Ullmann that she's mute because she hates her own child and would like to kill him, Éva said out loud, this is boring. I'm not going to watch this any more. In that case, let's go, Nóra said. She grabbed our coats from the seat next to hers and stood up. We meandered along the dark, labyrinth-like corridor before we finally found the emergency exit.

I'll hail a cab, Éva said, and left the two of us alone, very much on purpose. Nóra looked at me as if I were a serial killer.

If you've seen it and remember it in such detail, you might have told us not to bother.

For that I'd have to know something that apparently I don't, I said. Then I added, about the two of you.

What do you mean?

You know, I can't help thinking that that night in the park, it wasn't Éva with her husband, but you.

She lit a cigarette. Excuse me if I don't laugh.

I said nothing.

You're such an ass, she said.

I watched Éva as she stood by the deserted roadside in the drizzling rain, and I thought that never, ever would a cab come this way.

Take my advice, and instead of imagining all sorts of nonsense while you come on her belly so she won't get pregnant, take her home and get her pregnant.

Don't tell us what to do with our lives, Nóra. We'll have children when it damn well suits us.

(Kornél's wedding)

The other day, Kornél asked me why I hadn't written anything about the two of us since my father died. I said that that's not true, I've been writing.

He said nothing to that.

He comes to see me once a week, he usually brings some wine, and he sits in the easy chair where Éva used to sit. He usually stays two or three hours. We haven't played chess in nearly thirty years. I read him what I'd written in my notebook since our last meeting, much the way I used to show Éva my pictures at one time. Often she didn't even say anything, yet I knew that she approved, that something of what motivated me to press the shutter release came through. Kornél, on the other hand, offers a comment now and then, and says where there's not enough of something or where there's too much. Sometimes he reminds me of something. For instance, he reminded me of the mother who came with her daughter to my place to have her picture taken. But he now wanted to know about something specific, about why I'm not writing about the two of us. I said that what's important with regard to the two of us I've already written about. And he said, you know best.

Be that as it may, I'd have written about Klára Szentiváni and that one particular smile of hers even if Kornél had not called me to account.

His book came out after my father died. But his expectations were not fulfilled. It took nearly fifteen years before, standing in the middle of the Broch Gallery, I finally understood his disappointment. But back then, as I stood among the buckets full of whitewash in my father's room, his reluctance to accept what was happening with his poems irritated me. The reviews were low-key, but the high school students and the enthusiastic Hungarian teachers made up for it. Some of his books were read by hundreds of people. If you were a humanities student at university and wanted to impress a girl, reciting

Kornál Erdős alongside Ady, Attila József, and Radnóti put you at a distinct advantage. My father had seen it coming.

There are those who chastise themselves Jesus-like, and then there are those who flagellate themselves on a grand scale. Kornél was convinced that he's too weak for the one, and too much of a coward for the other. I believe that for a long time he didn't realize the power that lay in his cowardice and weakness, that at the point where every whip would be torn from its handle, that at the point where a concrete pillar is sustaining the truth, his refusal to blame himself created some sort of vague doubt, suspicion, and uncertainty. It made no difference whether someone was in love or was a Party functionary or a priest, a pillar teetered inside of him. He didn't walk on water. He walked in a swamp.

A couple of weeks after his first book came out, a woman looked him up. Actually, she was still more like a girl. Her name was Klára Szentiváni. She was twenty-four years old. She wrote poetry. I don't know what her poems were like, just that this was the reason they met. She never wrote poetry after that.

Kornél was scared. I was happy. He said he didn't want to ruin anyone's life. I said that he should start by not ruining his own with his fears. He dated Klára for about three months. Once they even came to Reisz's studio for ID pictures. I asked what they were for, and Kornél said, for passports. I asked where they were going, and Klára said, to heaven. They've already handed in their visa applications. It was nice. Back then there weren't any photo booths with curtains you could pull shut. This may well have been the first Hungarian ID picture showing two people kissing.

They held the wedding feast in the fall at the Trombitás restaurant. The leaves were falling, and they hadn't been swept up yet. When the air inside was gone, we went outside and danced among the leaves. Kornél had invited about fifteen or twenty guests, Klári about a hundred. I could say that it was a lovely wedding, but I can't make comparisons, because this was the only wedding I'd ever been to. Éva and I were never married. We never even discussed it, just that from the moment I put my father's key on the bed, she became my wife. I brought up marriage once, but by then it made no difference, because a couple of months later, she left. When I met Éva, Kornél had two children already, with a third on the way.

On their wedding day, I took a picture of them running after a tram, Kornél in a suit, Klári in her wedding dress. It was Kornél's idea, and I said fine, I'm game, but has he ever seen me take a funny picture? And he said, that's because I'd made up my mind not to beforehand. We screamed with laughter at this old saying of his. It didn't turn out well. I'm slow. I could never take a picture in a situation like this. In all the rush beforehand, his jacket got torn at the shoulder, there was no time to get it mended, so I lent him mine. That's what he danced in at the dinner.

It was obvious that sooner or later they'd get married, though it took me by surprise that it happened just barely three months after they'd met. Before that, we went to the café practically every night. Once I even went to a concert with them. When I finished whitewashing the walls, Klári helped clean the windows. She kept asking me about Kornél well into the night. She cried, because she felt that Kornél wasn't sure about the two of them. I said she should take it in stride, or she'll end up crying all her life, because except for his poems, Kornél will never be sure about anything. She said that that wasn't true, because he wasn't sure about a single line he'd written either. I said that she should believe me, he's sure, otherwise she would have never read a single line by him in print.

In the fall, when Sartre refused to accept the Nobel Prize, Kornél said that it makes no difference, he's a Nobel Prize recipient either way. At which Klári said he was mistaken, he was much more of a Nobel Prize recipient than anybody else, considering. Kornél said that he'd like to see a Hungarian Nobel Prize winner accepting the award one of these days. At which Klári said, God forbid. I asked her why. She said because, in that case, another Hungarian wouldn't receive the prize for a hundred years, which means Kornél wouldn't stand a chance. I glanced at Kornél squirming, ill at ease. That's a bad joke, darling, he said, and drank what was left of his coffee. I wasn't joking, Klári said. I pinned my eyes on the unsightly, flickering socialist-realist lamps that had replaced the Venetian chandeliers, and I said, there's nothing like love.

To this day I don't know why, but I learned about them getting married only at the last moment. I asked what's the rush. Kornél said that it's the honorable thing to do. There are things one must decide about, and he's decided for a lifetime. I couldn't think of anything else, so when Klári followed me to the terrace at the Trombitás, I asked if she was expecting. She laughed and said no.

In that case, why so soon?

It's not soon. Some things in life are clear-cut. Ady died, Babits died, so what other option do I have?

I said that I couldn't believe my ears, because those words should never be uttered, they shouldn't even be contemplated. And she said that I was wrong about a bunch of things, and I said that she's probably right, except this time I'm not wrong. If this was really what prompted her to hand in her visa application, then the passport is not for heaven, not even for hell, but to the most humdrum, the most commonplace of marriages. And she said that I was wrong about that, too, and from now on, her number one priority as a wife was to protect Kornél from my mistakes. And I asked if she sees any similarity between the woman who she was for three months and the woman she was now. She said that not only does she see it, its precisely because of questions like this that she's bound to protect Kornél and their marriage from me. And I said that she has no reason to protect their marriage, and as for Kornél, protecting him will be quite a challenge. And she said that I was wrong about that, too.

Kornél joined us. He was tipsy. Or maybe not. Maybe he was just happy. He put his arms around Klári and asked what we were talking about.

Nothing, I said.

That's not true, Klári said. We were just saying that it's either your friendship or our marriage.

Kornél looked at me and said, have you lost your mind?

Then Klári looked at me, and a smile for which I have no words flickered on her face, and she told Kornél, that's precisely what I just asked him myself.

I'd have liked to say something, but couldn't. I just stood there and watched the anger flare up in Kornél's eyes and that smile on Klári's face.

What exactly is your problem? Kornél asked.

Nothing, I said. There's been a misunderstanding.

Unless I'm much mistaken, his problem is that I compared you to Ady and Babits, Klári said.

You misconstrued my meaning, I said.

Well, it's pretty hard misconstruing something like that. And András, there's another thing that needs clarification. I'd never get myself knocked up just so the guy will marry me.

What the fuck's going on? Kornél asked.

I told you. Nothing. But since you ask, your wedding, that's what's going on.

Kornél flushed red as a lobster. He trembled all over. I'd never seen him like this. Klári put her arm through his and said, very quietly, calm down, darling, he's probably had too much to drink. Then she turned to me and said, in any case, it is painful to find out at your wedding that your husband's best friend considers you a slut.

I think I better leave, I said.

Yes, you better, Kornél said.

I remembered the time that man called my mother a fascist whore and my mother grabbing my arm, and I thought she was right, that whatever happens, whatever else Kornél or this woman might say, I mustn't open my mouth.

I watched as, arm in arm, they went back to their table. Kornél was wearing my jacket. I started to walk away and had already crossed the street to Moszkva Square, when Klári called after me.

Don't leave this with us, she said, and handed me my jacket.

I'll never understand what you're afraid of, I said. And I'll never believe that someone could sink so low and be so contemptible.

You're wrong, she said. Dead wrong. The only person who is afraid here is you, and this whole thing, it has nothing to do with how low a person can sink.

Fine. Then what has it got to do with?

Justified self-defense.

Against what?

Against you. Against the way you are. Against the way you live and think, and the pictures you take. Probably no one has told you so to your face, András, but you're poison. Maybe your pictures should receive pride of place at an exhibition, but they have no place in a family home.

(Gagarin's watch)

I stood uncertainly in front of the china cabinet for some time before I sprang into action. Then I imagined her coming into the studio: Mr. Reisz, I'm famished, if you won't let your assistant join me for lunch right now, I'll die of hunger. Then the empty orchestra bus parked by the gate and her wrapping herself around me, panting, we still have twenty minutes, I'll bribe the driver, and me saying, what lunch, you silly, I can't very well tell old Reisz that it couldn't wait until the next day.

And also, the way she's looking at that picture. This is no good, dear. Even if you enlarged it a dozen times, it's no good. I could say I like it, if you want, but by the same token, I could cheat on you.

And also, me standing by the window, waiting for her, but all in vain, it's been hours, and she's nowhere, and then she turns the corner at long last, and suddenly, like a flood, the mud beginning to surge behind her, reaching for the sky, and me shouting for her to run, but she can't hear, and then she shakes me awake.
Calm down, it's all right.
Don't you have dreams like this?
And she, laughing, never.

Before we went to Sopron at last on the twenty-fifth, I wanted to give her something no one had ever given her before, so I opened the china cabinet and took out the mahogany box with the stereoscopic viewer. I then took out the two photographs of my grandmother. Miraculously, the glass plates survived the war and the moving. I'd enlarged the picture with Éva and my arm with the watch that I took so I'd never forget when it happened the day before. Of course, it was not on glass, just film, and it lacked three-dimensionality, but I figured that even lacking three-dimensionality, the future would be just as clearly visible on it as the past had once been for my grandfather in this box.

I went to the Hunyadi market the day before and bought a Christmas tree. I'd have liked one that reached up to the ceiling, but the vendor just laughed. That's gone out of fashion, sir, he said. So I bought one just two meters tall. It was beautiful. Éva brought the decorations from her ex-husband's place.

After we did the shopping, she declared the kitchen off limits to me. From time to time she appeared, it's terrible, she hasn't even learned how to chop up an onion properly, all because of that damn piano. I offered to do it. She said I better not set foot in the kitchen, it's an unholy mess. She even burned the scones. And I said that in that case, she's not getting a present, because according to St. Mark, the Holy Family was especially particular about their scones. Then we decorated the tree together. Then she went to the bathroom to change, and from there she shouted, what has St. Mark got to say about dressing for the occasion? And I said, no unnecessary pieces of apparel. And she said, St. Mark was a great big dreamer.

What's this? I asked.
A piece of stone.
I took it out of the velvet box and looked at it. It was no bigger than a tiny pebble and as black as coal.
I'd have liked Gagarin's watch, but they wouldn't give it to me, she said.
What kind of stone is this? I asked.
God only knows. It fell from the sky. It's a star. It fell to earth about the time you were born, except in Siberia, and not here. But the dates coincide.
Where did you get it?
The museum.
You stole it?
I never stole anything in my life. I asked them for it.
Look me in the eye.
Alright. So one time I stole something. But that was ages ago. A friend stole this for me.

What's this? she asked when she started to unwrap the tissue paper.

Gagarin's watch, I said.

I don't believe you.

Well, then open it. I don't lie.

When she looked and saw herself lying on the bed behind my watch, she cried.

And what did you do with your grandmother?

Don't worry. She's in the china cabinet.

Kiss me.

The dinner will get cold.

According to St. Mark, you're not eating dinner tonight.

We were supposed to go to Sopron together the following morning, but when we came to, she said that she'd spoken with her mother. She slipped and needed a cast, so it was best if she went alone, but she'd be back the following day, because on the twenty-seventh she had a rehearsal. And I said, of course. Whatever is best for you.

Kornél said that when somebody had a star stolen from a museum for my sake, he can't understand why I wouldn't believe Éva when it came to a simple broken ankle.

(on music)

I've been attempting to write about this for days, but in vain. About Éva and music. I didn't like the way she played.

But first, I must confess that I'm no expert on music. This is important, because understanding something and loving something are intimately connected even if, like a chameleon, our understanding automatically adjusts itself to our feelings.

Of course, there are times when it can't adjust without the operation being detected, when the blood-red suddenly appears around our poor understanding as it tries to assert itself, when our understanding knows that the fault is not in it, it's just that it mustn't adapt to that particular color. And yet, it can happen to you at any time; it can happen that despite your common sense, your discrimination, your sense of justice and refined moral sense, you suddenly find out that your wife is a colossal whore. Let's face it, this breach can turn out to be the greatest tragedy for the individual, at times so great, it leads to suicide.

Of course, in our case, there was no such breach. I knew that she was a fine pianist, I just didn't like the way she played. And I told her so. I told her that I'm practically afraid of the way she plays. Though that wasn't quite true either. Had she played at her concerts the way she played when she began to rehearse, I'd have loved it. But that's not how she played. When she started to practice, you had the feeling that she was assaulting those keys with stones. But then after a while she began carting off all that stone, wheelbarrowing it God only knows where to, until that fucking Petrof was as immaculately sparkling smooth as if it hadn't been touched, as if, like a player piano, it played itself. Or as if Van Gogh decided to smear over his nervous lines with a brush generously covered with linseed oil until the wheat field turned into a photograph. Once I told her that for me, the difference between her rehearsals and her concerts was paramount to the difference between my photographs and the pictures of cell division taken in a lab, and she said she knows. And I asked, in that case, why is she afraid to play the way it's worth playing? And she said, believe me, this is how it should be done. This is how she needs to do it. And I said I didn't believe her. And she said, some people can afford to do it, others can't. What, I asked. She said nothing.

Then suddenly, she turned around and said, I, at least, go sit by that stupid piano when I need to, so shut up until you finally show your pictures in a gallery.

(Éva's apartment)

Éva moved into her new apartment a couple of weeks before the concert. Her ex-husband got it for her, more or less the way my father got his hands on our apartment in Szív Street at one time. What I mean is, her ex-husband surely had an easier time of it, because it makes a whole lot of difference if someone is a Kossuth Prize recipient or a political prisoner just released from jail. I asked if I could help her move. She said there's no need, she's all packed, and János will see to the movers. Actually, I was thinking of helping her unpack and settle, not stuff boxes at her ex-husband's place. But I decided not to pursue it further and just said, fine. Still, I went to Fő Street and found a pub from where I could see the entrance to the house from the window. I wanted to see her with her ex-husband. I thought it's only natural. I saw them just once, and then, too, they were making love. But then I decided against it. I realized that I had no excuse for doing so. Ferenc Vándor had an excuse to spy on Imolka from a woodshed, but what's my excuse? Also, I was afraid they'd see me. The apartment was a good distance away, and getting there from Szív Street was pretty difficult. I couldn't very well have said that I happened to be in the neighborhood.

When Éva came back after moving in, I asked what the apartment was like. She said that it's good for practice, but it seemed she wasn't about to say anything more. I finally got up the nerve and asked if she was going to show me sometime just the same. She laughed. Of course. Just that she didn't think I'd be interested. Of course I'm interested. We went the very next day. She fumbled around with the keys for some time. Second floor, the windows look out on the street and not the courtyard, forty square meters, a room and a half. Everything was packed together in the larger room, the mattress, the scores, books, and a couple of suitcases with her clothes. There was also an old wooden box. I don't know what it contained. And also, a desk. I asked if she'd like some more furniture. She said no, everything's fine just as it is. There was a postcard-size old photograph in a plaster frame hanging across from the desk. It wasn't hanging quite straight, as if the previous tenant had left it there. It showed a young woman walking a German sheperd in a park. I finally asked who it was. She said Nero, our dog. Then she added, with my mother. I didn't know you had a dog, I said. And she said, it's been ages. He snuck away and a car hit him.

I'd have liked to say something, for instance, that her mother is as beautiful as a statue, or something of the sort, but I couldn't very well, not after what happened to that poor dog. The Petrof just fit in the smaller room, and I thought that only the duvet was missing from the wall, that playing the piano in this tiny maid's room must feel like it felt for that Gypsy boy to play the violin in the pantry, and then I thought that if that boy had not stuck a knife in his mother, I'd have never sat in our own pantry, and then I wouldn't have had anything to write Adél Selyem on that sheet of notepaper, and then I'd have never ended up at that new housing estate. But at that point I got stuck. I couldn't find the next never that led from that new housing estate straight to Fő Street. And this put my mind at ease, the thought that the path here was entirely different. And then I thought that after the key opened the lock, it felt as if I weren't with the same woman with whom I'd left home earlier that day. It was like when I was upstairs in Reisz's apartment, where even the old man's voice sounded different from what it sounded like in the studio downstairs. Of course, I may not be the same either in this apartment. Also, I could never play this piano, much less spend a night here. A good thing we have a place to live. I'd brought a bottle of champagne with me, but then decided not to take it out of my bag.

So now you know, she said. Time to go.

(bumping into Dalma Keresztes)

I reached the Academy just in the nick of time. When I settled in my seat, the woman sitting in front of me said very quietly, without turning around, well, well, you acquired a taste for music?

I broke into a profuse sweat. The last time I heard this voice was through the tobacconist's telephone, and I was hoping I'd never hear it again.

I've always liked music, I said.

It's certainly not what you're known for, she said. Not in my book.

Nor you, I said. Or rather, just thought. I can't remember. Éva came out on stage and sat down at the piano. I had to applaud her.

I'd have liked to get up and leave, but clearly, I couldn't do that. I tried focusing on Éva, but all I could see was the silver and marcasite hairpin holding Dalma Keresztes's newly dyed hair in a knot. And also, the way the wrinkles ran down her neck. And I thought that given one or two more years, they'd reach her vertebrae, then wind round her neck, just like a rope around the neck of a man on a scaffold, and then she'd die. Finish herself off.

During intermission, I waited for her to leave before I stood up. She was talking to someone, while I headed for the snack bar at the far end of the foyer. I asked for a glass of wine.

People had already started to filter inside when she came over to me.

That woman's playing lacks spirit, she said.

I like it.

I'm surprised. That's not how I knew you.

You didn't know me.

Of course I did. I knew you and I loved you. But now I neither know you nor love you.

In that case, let's not talk, I said.

Don't be silly, she said. Now that chance brought us together? By the way, I'm terribly sorry about your father.

I'm going back in, I said.

It may rub you the wrong way, but I really am sorry. I still love him. Not like you.

Considering that you never met him?

Yes, considering.

I'm sorry, too. But I really must go inside now. They're starting.

I think I'll miss out on Madame Zárai's second act.

You do that. But for your information, Madame Zárai, as you call her, is my wife.

For a second the corners of her lips trembled, but she forced a laugh.

That's quite some joke, she said.

I didn't mean it as a joke.

Children?

Not yet. But we'll have some.

Just don't kick her in the stomach. It's not right.

I didn't kick you in the stomach.

You know something? It doesn't really matter.

It matters.

Sure. To you. And are you still taking pictures, or are you her page turner?

I can't read scores. My specialty is taking ID pictures.

In the good old days, it wasn't ID pictures you took of me. Remember?

I really must go in now.

It's the third time you've said that. Don't let anything hold you back, because should Madame at the piano spot the two empty seats, she might get ideas.

She's not the type.

She's that naïve?

She's not naïve. She simply has no cause for suspicion.

Oh, come off it. You couldn't have changed that much. Judging by the way she plays, you don't tear each other apart in bed.

I don't want to offend you, so don't offend me either.

I have not said anything offensive. I merely ascertained two facts. She plays like a cold fish, which doesn't prevent the critics from liking it. And as for you, you couldn't have changed all that much.

Meaning what?

You know perfectly well what I mean.

You haven't changed either, it seems.

Easy does it. After seven years, this sounds almost like a compliment.

I didn't mean it to sound like one.

You could have. I'm past the age when women are afraid of getting old. I hope what you just said about the ID pictures was meant as a joke.

It's no joke. I have to earn a living. But rest assured, I take other pictures as well.

In short, your wife doesn't have to support you. That speaks in her favor.

She's got a lot more going for her, I assure you.

No doubt. Were I to be utterly sincere, I might even entertain the possibility that the two of you tear each other apart after all. She's quite attractive.

Yes, you might put it that way. Attractive. Though if that's all there was, we wouldn't be talking like this now. You're quite attractive yourself.

Present tense? Careful. This is your second compliment of the evening.

You really haven't changed one bit. You have a way of misconstruing everything I say.

She looked around with a look of mock surprise, then secured the hairpin in her hair. The bracelets on her wrist slipped up her arm and her breasts tightened.

I don't see any misunderstanding here. What I see is that everyone has gone inside already, and unless my ears play me false, your wife is already at the piano, while we're still standing here. So where's the misunderstanding?

Rest assured, I'll be sitting inside in a minute myself.

No doubt. Did you take your father back to Mélyvár?

Yes, I took him back home.

Good for you. He was a true man of substance. You might have inherited a bit of courage from him.

I inherited other things.

Though possibly, you were just immature.

I was short on experience.

Maturity is not about experience, my dear, but what use you make of it. Even back then, you didn't have to go next door for experience.

For once you're right.

Do you know what your most mature moment was? Or your most manly, to put it that way?

What?

The first. When you had the courage to tell me that you bought swimming trunks for my sake. But from then on, ending with that shameful moment when you called me to account over the phone, it was all downhill.

For your information, before that shameful call, as you call it, my father howled with pain so loud, that by the time I finally made it home from your place, I could hear him down on the street. So don't think that your own most mature moment was when you locked me in.

She said nothing. She took her lipstick and a mirror out of her bag and rouged her lips. She put them back and drew out a cigarette. She lit it and handed it to me. She then took out another one and lit it for herself.

I'm sorry, she said.

I said nothing to that.

What else can I say? I apologize.

I can't accept your apology, I said.

You can't or you won't? What are you afraid of?

I'm not afraid.

Don't lie to me.

I said nothing. I watched the woman behind the counter of the snack bar wash the glasses. She doesn't even have to turn around, I thought, all she has to do is look up, and she'll see me in the mirror hanging above the shelves.

Don't worry, I'm not about to ruin your marriage.

I stubbed out the half-smoked cigarette. I'm not afraid. But please, go away now.

This is the Music Academy.

I know. But I refrained from going to the Lukács, so kindly refrain from coming to the Academy.

Fine, she said. She put out her cigarette, then smoothed her dress down over her hips. She had on a long, sleeveless dress, just like the one she wore at one time.

But I'm going to the ladies' room first, she said.

Fine. Don't let me keep you, I said.

She took two steps, then turned around, just as she'd done the first time on the terrace.

You can follow me, if you want.

That fucking mirror behind the counter was so misty, I couldn't see anything in it.

I don't want to, I said.

Oh yes, you do, she said.

After the concert, I went backstage to Éva's dressing room. I said that I have an upset stomach, so I'm not going out to dinner with them. She said all right, and she'd hurry home. At home, I took out the pictures of Dalma Keresztes, then I put them back again, because it occurred to me that burning pictures is just as senseless as burning books, and that when my mother cut Dr. Zenta off that picture with the dressmaker's shears, she was just as simpleminded as the savages who are terrified of having their pictures taken, as if a picture possessed some sort of power over them. Whereas it doesn't. It has no power whatsoever.

Then I changed my mind and took out the photo she'd wanted a copy of at one time. I went to the bathroom, turned on the tap, and watched the paper as it slowly soaked up the water in the tub, the blacks turning an even deeper shade of black, then the paper slowly rising with the water, and then I watched as it soaked up more water and settled at the bottom of the tub. I then retrieved it and put it on one of the boards to dry, but then I remembered that it wouldn't dry by the time Éva got home, so I tore it up and flushed it down the toilet. Then I thought that I could have hidden it behind the wardrobe, where there was just enough room to hide a drawing board.

I took my clothes off and slipped into the tub. I thought that I could have followed her, and Éva would have never been the wiser. And suddenly I felt such raging hatred for Éva the likes of which only my father might had felt for his guards.

Why didn't you come back after intermission, she asked.

I hadn't heard the key turn in the lock or her walking along the hall.

I told you. I had an upset stomach. That's why I didn't join you for dinner. Remember?

She didn't say anything to that, and I knew that she knew. I knew that she must have seen those pictures sometime and could recognize her anywhere, that it just took one look at the full house from behind the piano, and she'd know if that woman was there.

Also, I was talking to someone at the snack bar, I offered.

She began undressing.

Don't. It's cold, I said.

I know, she said.

She sat in the tub, then leaned her head back. Her hair floated, spread out, on the water. Her eyes were intent on the light flickering in the boiler.

Are you going to talk to her again, she asked.

No, I said.

She raised her head. The water came dripping from her hair. She didn't look in my eye. She looked past me. Somewhere behind me.

Did you fuck her, she asked.

No.

I believe you, she said and stood up. I need to get some sleep. I'm tired.

I'm coming with you, I said.

It's all right. Stay. Just add some hot water.

I didn't. Honestly, I said.

I know, she said, and wrapped herself in the towel. It's not your fault that I'm afraid of this woman more than any of the others.

You have no reason to be afraid, either of her, or anyone else.

We all have something to be afraid of, she said.

(the kris)

When I reached Miskolc station, I waited for my connection in the snack bar. The place was crowded with Gypsies, a large company of mourners, so I went and stood by the counter. They were heading to a funeral. The women were sitting on the floor by the wall. Some were breast feeding their children. One of the men joined me at the counter and asked what I was drinking.

I said wine. He asked the woman behind the counter for a bottle. She said that she only sells wine by the glass. The man spit on a hundred-forint bill and slammed it down on the counter. A glass, I said. The woman unscrewed the cork and placed the bottle and two glasses on the counter. She didn't return the change. The man poured, then looked me in the eye. His eyes were as dry as bone.

Let your mother and your father pass on, as long as your son doesn't die. Not your son, he said. He gulped down the wine as if it were water. Your son never, he said.

I'm sorry, I said.

Don't feel sorry for me. Feel sorry for the Lord God, because I'm going up there today to see him. These Gypsies don't know, but I'm going up there this very day and I'm going to ask him, where is my son?

Don't go to see him, I said.

So you don't know what it means, having a son, he said, and left me without further ado.

The trip to Ózd would have taken less time by bus, but I don't like buses. On a train, you can lean out the window. Then in Ózd, I had to walk well over half an hour from the station. I hadn't done much traveling. Only now did I realize how much more the streets in Pest had to offer, that you could see anything there. Trabants, Wartburgs, Skodas, Zhigulis. In Pest, even the mannequins in the shop windows have a soul. In Pest, there's no end of cinemas, cafés, and post offices. And trams. The countess had drawn a map on the postcard, so I'd know the way. At least, she didn't move into a prefab apartment house, but a house with a garden. Her niece lived in another part of the house. She brought us cake and coffee. A kind woman. Her two children were playing catch out in the yard.

The countess asked where I'd put up that girl with the parasol. I said, between the two windows. She said that that's the darkest wall. I said, not anymore. She laughed.

It was a much bigger apartment than the one in Szív Street. She used only one room. The other stood empty. She said she didn't need it. I asked how she felt here. She said fine. She can see the huge chimneys in the distance. A a whole forest of them. A forest of brick. I took a picture through the curtain. I'd have liked to take a picture of her in the empty room, but was afraid to ask. Instead, I took a picture of the empty room without her.

She continued to receive chocolates and biscuits from her Western relatives just as before, the small table stood in the same place, just as before, and the *Life and Science* magazines stood stacked up, just as before. She asked about Szív Street. I told her that Korbán, the superintendent, had died. A truck backing up pressed him against the wall. It was early morning. They were delivering the coal.
    Poor man. He was pretty unfortunate himself, she said
    Not necessarily. For some people, being a superintendent is a piece of luck, I said.
    No, my dear. All informers are unfortunate.

I asked her if she'd like to come to Pest with me sometime, and we'd go to a museum or the movies.
    Don't give me the run around, my dear.
    I can't think of anyone I'd rather run around with.
    Just the same, find yourself someone else. No one's going to shout up to you on the fourth floor and ask if she can come up.
    Well, that's what I'm waiting for.
    I'd take exception to that, my dear.
    And meanwhile I wondered, did that Gypsy say what he said because he was bitter,

or was he in earnest, and he really is going up to the Lord today to ask him why he killed his son.

People in this part of the world are not familiar with the *kris*, or if they are, it's only from crossword puzzles. It's a knife with a wavy blade that's used somewhere in Southeast Asia. The first time I visited the countess, she was preoccupied with this dagger from Java. Actually, seeing how she'd be spending her last years in the City of Iron, she thought that she might as well read up on iron and metallurgy. That's when she came upon an article in an issue of *Life and Science* about the *kris*.

Just imagine, my dear, she said. With these savages, as my dear departed mother would say, everything still possesses a soul. I have no idea how they do it.

Do what?

Take the *kris*, for instance. They've been melting the iron for it in an open-hearth furnace for a long time now, and now they've been fashioning it with an electric grinder, but to them, it still possesses a soul. It can balance on its tip, at night it slips out of it sheath and flies around in the air, it signals earthquakes and volcanic eruptions ahead of time, and it takes offense if its owner doesn't smear it every month with the oil of a flower with an unpronounceable name.

My camera also possesses a soul, I said. Ever since Reisz called me a coward, it never occured to me that my Leica might lack a soul.

You're trying to turn this into a joke, my dear. But I'm serious. Besides, I don't think that your future bride would want to be wedded to your Leica.

Well, she'll have to. Okay. I won't joke about it anymore. But are you saying that when they tie the knot, the Javanese kiss their *kris* as well as their brides? Sorry about that!

You said you wouldn't joke about it.

But I'm in the best of spirits. Could I move into that empty room?

Forget it, my dear. You'd have to age forty years in one night for that.

Who knows. Maybe I can manage it. But what about that funny knife?

Don't manage it, my dear. As for the knife, if a man can't be present at his own wedding, the *kris* can stand in for him when they tie the knot. It doesn't just symbolize its

413

owner, you see. As far as the Javanese are concerned, his soul is inside it. The marriage will be every bit as valid as if it were sanctified at the corner rectory.

Perhaps even more valid, I offered with a bright smile, because I'm not at all sure that our local priest believes in transubstantiation.

As far as that goes, neither do I, my dear. Except, for us this is a piece of luck, because it saves us from having to worry about reconciling the rational with the irrational. As far as we're concerned, these two are mutually exclusive. We have to work hard for our God. Can you imagine the poor Pope, the nightmares he must have because of Darwin? Don't think it's easier for him than it is for you or me. I wish I knew why.

It's called Enlightenment.

Oh, please, my dear, don't bring Enlightenment into this. You know, as long as they forged these *krises* from meteorites, well, what can I say? But those people are no longer savages, my dear. What's more, they weren't savages even in my mother's time. Those people were building cities the size of Rome when we weren't even speculating yet about conquering the Carpathian Basin. Furthermore, the soul is still there in their grasses and their trees, possibly even in their bicycles. And they don't see a problem with it, some irreconcilable contradiction, while, when it comes right down to it, our priests feel as much ill at ease with the Eucharist as you feel with regard to your camera. We have lost our way, my dear.

When?

When we thought that this depends on Enlightenment or the open-hearth furnace.

Well then, what does it depend on?

If only I knew. Do excuse me, she said, then she stood up and went to the bathroom. I ate a piece of cake and waited. When she returned, her eyes were red from crying.

The trouble, my dear, is not that I have grown old. The trouble is that now that I'm old, I have lost faith. I can't see the soul in the grasses or the trees anymore.

Oh, please, I said, for lack of anything else.

Alright, I can still see it in you. What a shame you're not my grandson.

(Pasiphae)

One night I took the world atlas off the shelf. I like looking through it. Éva asked where I'd like to go. I said anywhere, with the exception of Sopron, of course, because Sopron doesn't exist. She didn't seem to hear. Then with a sudden motion of the hand, she opened the atlas at random, and without looking, she pinned her finger to a spot. It was the Pacific Ocean. Let's not, I said, I'm not a good swimmer. We laughed. The second time around turned out to be a bit more promising. She nearly lighted on the shores of Sumatra.

Okay. Now let's see where *you* would like to swim.

No need to guess, she said, and turned the page to Greece.

Why Greece? I asked.

Because from Prometheus to Oedipus, the Greeks came up with everything.

I asked what her favorite story was. She said, Theseus and Ariadne. She asked if I was familiar with it. I said, sure, and raised both hands to my forehead, as if I had horns, and I said that if that's her favorite, she better start running, and fast. She laughed and said, you should have it so good, you're no Minotaur. For that, Pasiphae would have to be my mother. I said I don't know any Pasiphae. I got stuck at Ariadne. Ariadne is not bad, she said, she's the daughter of the woman I just mentioned, except, she wasn't conceived by a bull. And poor thing, when she got pregnant, Theseus threw her out of his ship.

I'd like to slap that Theseus.

You'd better not fight, Ariadne was probably no better, considering how thoughtless she was, getting herself pregnant. The apple and the tree.

What did her mother do wrong?

You seem a bit ignorant, just a bit.

If the only reason you want to go to Greece is to prove it, don't bother, I can be ignorant right here.

I can see that. Well, there's the Trojan wooden horse and the Cretan wooden cow. They're basic, so you should commit them to memory.

Fine. I'll do that. But would you kindly tell me what her mother did?

What did she do, what did she do? She got herself knocked up, that's what she did. She got the hots for a white bull so bad that she had Daedalus, the master craftsman, fashion a hollow cow of wood, she slipped inside and offered up her cooch, and the fornication was a success.

Please don't say cooch, it has a proper name.

Okay, her cunt. I just didn't want to make it too graphic, or I might get into a state, and then I won't be able to finish the story. But wait, the best is yet to come.

I doubt you'll do much better than interspecies fornication. Would you please show me how Parsipi, or whatever her name was, did it?

Would you please pay attention? You really should at the very least know that the Minotaur was fathered by the bull that Ariadne seduced.

That doesn't surprise me, I said.

Fine. In that case, I'll tell you about an even greater miracle, namely, that Minos had the labyrith built by the very same Daedalus who fabricated the wooden cow. But that's not the strangest part of the story, the strangest part is that everyone gets bogged down with Theseus and Ariadne, because it's such a beautiful tale, but nobody cares what became of Pasiphae.

I bet she got what was coming to her from Minos.

You're straying off track, my dear. From then on, poor Pasiphae lived in that labyrinth with her freak son. And don't you forget it when you're all agog over Ariadne and her ball of thread. Ariadne and Theseus are not the key figures of the story, but the mother.

I said that if this whole thing was true, I want nothing to do with any of the key figures. I'd rather stick with Theseus and Ariadne. What's more, I'd like to fuck the latter, and I do mean fuck, and not just smear her with my sperm, and if she should get pregnant, we wouldn't set sail anywhere, I'd stay with her on Crete, and take pictures of her suckling her little nymph, though I realize that this just shows how ignorant I am, because nymphs are not small.

I thought I'd said something to please her, but she got up and put her robe on and said that in that case, I should find myself an Ariadne. Then she headed for the kitchen, and I heard her open the fridge and pour a glass of milk.

I joined her and said, I already have an Ariadne.

I'd rather be alone now, if you don't mind.

I have no idea what I've done to upset you, but I promise to take you to Crete sometime and prove to you that I'm right.

You'll have to go on your own.

I'd like to go with you.

The glass of milk exploded against the wall like a hand granade and she screamed, go back to your labyrinth, asshole!

Kornél said that I'd been known to fly into a rage myself.

(clever management)

For a while I thought that if she wouldn't take me to Sopron, I wouldn't take her to Ózd. Then I thought how stupid that was. It's just defiance, and defiance has been the ruin of countless lives. One morning I asked if she'd like to come with me to visit the countess. She glanced at the Rippl-Rónai and said, fine, but only if she's really old. She wanted to know how I'd introduce her to the countess. My love, my lover, my model, possibly my pianist, because, as we know, aristocrats generally like music. I told her I'd like to introduce her as Éva Zárai, an umbrella term that contains all of the above. She then stood in front of the bathroom mirror for twenty minutes.

I made a mistake, though. I didn't tell the countess that I'd be bringing Éva along. She made no reproaches, and she was kind to Éva, but the situation was awkward. Halfway from the station it began to rain, and we got soaked to the skin. Also, the countess's niece had gone to Miskolc, so the countess had to watch the two children. They couldn't very well be sent outside to play in the rain.

When I introduced her, Éva said that she's Zárai with an *i* and not a *y*. Whereupon the countess said, it makes no difference, dear. Besides, I know. The love of our lives gave me your Schubert recording. I thought Éva would be pleased, but she got flustered. And I was surprised by this *i* instead of a *y*, that she'd want to let the countess know that she's no aristocrat. She never gave the least hint until then that such things bothered her. Nor did she later. It's just that she didn't know what to do with the countess's aristocratic *y*.

The countess offered us American cookies and homemade cherry liqueur. Then she said to Éva that when we get old, our imagination diminishes. It hadn't been a year since she told me that no one would ever look up to the fourth floor and ask if they could come up, and just look now! Éva said with an amusing little smile, well, well, she'd have never have thought that I would go into such detail about my love life. Whereupon the countess said that she and I have no secrets.

Basically, all that happened was that she took to Éva right away, and talked to her the way she talked to me. She had no idea that before we left, Éva had stood in front of the mirror longer than when she had an appearance at the Music Academy. The children also took a liking to her and kept at her to go to the other room and play Clever Management with them. The countess told them to be patient, but her admonishment fell on deaf ears. Éva finally said that she'd join them. At least, that way we could chat undisturbed.

It seems an angel has flown into your home, my dear. Just make sure she doesn't fly away, the countess said.

She can't. I've closed the window, I said.

You should know better than that, my dear. An angel doesn't stay put because of a closed window, but because she has a reason to stay put.

She can never have a better reason than that she loves me.

Of course, my dear, of course. That's what I'm talking about, the countess continued. This reason calls for clever management, otherwise you lose, like I did today when I played with the children. I didn't learn to play parlor games in time, so now I ended up losing more apartments and furnishings than when my belongings were nationalized.

Do you think that the Americans are really going to the moon? I asked, wanting to change the subject.

They have no other choice, the countess said. They have to.

All the way home on the train, Éva talked about nothing else but what a sweet old woman the countess is and what a shame that the poor thing had to live in Ózd, and how she'd like to visit her if only she had stayed in our house, and how nice that she doesn't play the aristocrat, and how lucky for me that I've found such a lovely surrogate grandmother, she must've been a great help to me at one time. I knew perfectly well that she meant every word she said, but I also knew that if I were to ask her again if she'd like to come to Ózd with me, she'd always have a rehearsal.

(the moon landing)

In July of '69, Éva said we should watch the moon landing at a friend's home. There'd be lots of people there. I said it's not New Year's Eve. She took offense. I was stupid. Or to be honest, I was a coward. I was afraid to tell her that I'd rather watch the landing in Ózd with the countess, and not with her friends. I'd only visited her once the entire year.

She sat down by the piano and kept repeating the same sound made by the key that's missing the elephant bone. She kept striking it for minutes on end. I think she even forgot I was there. Then out of the blue she said, my mother in the dark.
What about your mother in the dark? I asked.
Nothing. I was talking to myself, not you.
Well, tell me.
She said nothing.
You really ought to tell me.
Sometimes I feel like I'm suffocating here, she said, and headed for the bathroom.
I followed her and apologized. I said she's right, of course, she's right, let's go.
But what would *you* like? she asked.
I just told you. Let's go.
Fortunately, she hated fights, so we generally climbed out of such precarious ditches.
I'd like to go, she said. I don't intend to sit home when someone is going to the moon.
I see your point, I said.

Outside, July had settled in among the houses. Even after sunset, the air was still. We took the subway to the last stop, crossed the Chain Bridge by foot, then walked up to Úri Street near the Castle. I never liked Buda Castle. From a distance, from Pest, yes, but to walk along its streets was another matter, to stroll along its promenades, its small square, Fishermen's Bastion, I never liked that. I didn't like the area around the Castle either, the Chain Bridge, the tunnel, the Vérmező sprawled out just below the Castle.

I didn't like any of it. Every time I happened to be in the vicinity, I felt cheated, as if I were in an amusement park or an outdoor village museum. Of course, this sense of being cheated is still preferable to what I feel in a prefab housing estate.

As we silently walked up the hill, the shadow of our afternoon fight trailed alongside us on the gray stone wall. I wondered if the American astronauts would meet Laika. Then I thought, will Neil Armstrong's camera be lost in that state of weightlessness, like Gagarin's pencil. After all, as far as weightlessness is concerned, it makes no difference whether it's a camera or a pencil.

Éva asked what I was thinking. I said I was thinking about the countess. She said that in that case, why didn't I go to Ózd instead. I said nothing. Also, I didn't know the acquaintance whose house we were going to. The truth is, neither did Éva. At least, not very well. Only that she's some sort of journalist or newspaper editor and Nóra's friend.

When Adél Selyem opened the door to us with a baby in her arms, I began to sink. Or rather, my lungs, my stomach, all my interior organs began to rise like when a person falls into a goddam pit, faster and faster into the dark. Actually, it's not such a bad feeling. It came to an abrupt end when she held out her hand and said, Adél Bauer. Then she added, and this is Eszter. András Szabad, I said. She and Éva also made their introductions. Éva kissed the baby.

Adél made such a point of not knowing me that I had no choice but to play along. There I stood, at the bottom of that goddamn pit, with neither sky nor ceiling visible. Nothing. I had no idea how I'd find my way back to the surface. Meanwhile, Neil Armstrong's space module was approaching the moon and the landing strip.

And I thought, it's probably better like this. It would have never occurred to me to pretend that I don't know her, but that's what she needs, it seems. And possibly, Éva, too. Eight years take their toll on a woman, especially if she becomes a mother in the process. But there, in the door, with her child in her arms, Adél Bauer seemed to float as weightlessly as Adél Selyem had done when I handed her the sheet of note paper with the single sentence telling her that I can stay in a meter-and-a-half pantry for half an hour of my own free will.

I thought that if she's so afraid of Dalma Keresztes, it's a whole lot better for Éva if she doesn't know that this is the woman whose red rag I had once told her about. It was a big apartment with lots of guests. Bauer must have been a collector of some sort, because sabers, halberds, and carbines hung all along the walls, and a full suit of armor stood by the coat rack in the hall. I thought it was awful.

The living room had a gilt sofa and chairs, china cabinets, and a small marble table that held the television set. The picture was grainy. On the other marble table, there was a record player playing dance music. There were also enough chairs to fill the auditorium of a small theater, but now, only a couple of people were inside. Because of Eszter, the rest of the guests were smoking out on the terrace. We went outside to join them.

Bauer was fiftyish and short. He wore blue jeans and an unbuttoned yellow shirt. His arms and chest were hairy. I knew I'd seen him before. Then it dawned on me. Comrade Selyem dancing with Gagarin's wife.

Their terrace was huge, with fan palms and a panorama of Budapest by night. Everything, save for the Danube. Adél told Éva that the buffet was in the other room, we should go serve ourselves. She didn't say anything to me, though. Nóra was the only person I knew. She was forcing a smile, putting up with two elderly men sweet-talking her. Éva found a couple of acquaintances, but I tried to get away before she could introduce me to them. People were busy discussing whether going to the moon made sense.

Someone said that Moscow should just lean back, relax and wait, because the American economy is not robust enough to finance the Apollo Program without draining its resources.

Everyone was standing with the exception of Bauer, who took a sip of his cognac and without even looking at the man said, Imre, don't play the provocateur.

A shocked silence ensued. Bauer waited, took another sip of his cognac, then added with a grin, if you go on like this, I'll have to conclude that you're working for the Americans.

The tension dissipated, and people laughed.

Eszter began to cry. Bauer waved to her, but Adél didn't see him. Then he said, well, what about it? Bring me my daughter. Adél brought her out and placed her on his lap. Bauer pointed to the sky. Lookie there, angel. A great big, ugly American man is going up there today. He's going up there and he's going to gobble up the moon, like this. Humm, he said, and quickly put Eszter's hand in his mouth, as if to swallow it. The child stopped crying. Bauer handed her back to her mother. Take her inside. She'll catch cold, he said.

And I thought that this Bauer has definitely nothing in common with the Bauer who at the age of seventeen wrapped himself in a blanket soaked in gasoline and, with the red, white, and green flag in his hand as a sign of protest against Communist oppression, set himself on fire in the Museum Garden in January.

After Adél went inside I waited a bit, then I told Éva that I'd bring us some wine. I stopped by the door of the child's room and watched Adél play with her daughter on a blanket spread out on the floor.

You have a beautiful daughter, I said.

Startled, she turned around.

Not here!

All I said was that she's beautiful.

Not here. I beg you, she repeated, distraught.

Fine. It's probably for the best, I said. But your child is beautiful all the same. Then I headed for the other room to get the wine.

When the broadcast started, we went inside. There weren't enough chairs, so I told Éva to sit on my lap, but she didn't want to. This had never happened before. I went and stood in the corner. Adél Selyem sat next to Bauer in a snuff-colored armchair. Eszter started to cry again, so Adél put the edge of a diaper in her mouth.

She's teething, Bauer said to the fiftyish woman sitting next to him.

Poor child, the woman said.

All through the broadcast, I couldn't take my eyes off of the child chewing on that diaper. Of the moon landing, I saw nothing.

As it turned out, this was in fact just the landing, and Armstrong would go and step out on the moon only sometime during the early morning hours. Bauer asked the guests to move the chairs against the wall. He then turned off the TV and upped the volume of the record player.

Some of the guests said goodbye, and that they'd watch the rest at home, while others went back out to the terrace to discuss what they'd seen. What I saw I couldn't very well have discussed with anyone.

Adél Selyem put the child to bed. I asked Éva what she'd like to do. Dance, what else, she said. But first, she and Nóra went to the other room for some cognac. She asked me if I'd like some. I said, sure. But then they didn't come back. They sat down somewhere to chat. For want of anything better to do, I sat down in the snuff-colored armchair and watched Comrade Bauer dance with Adél Selyem as I thought of Éva repeatedly hitting that piano key on the Bösendorfer earlier in the day, and then her saying, my mother in the dark. It sounded like a curse. And then I thought that she probably said it because of me, that she really can't breathe by my side, then I thought of Adél Selyem pretending not to know her former lover, and that she gets more air in this goddamn museum of military history than Éva gets when I can't come up with anything better to do than see a Bergman film for the third time, or go for a walk, or go to a basement pub. I also thought that if I wracked my brain for a year, I still wouldn't come up, ever, with throwing detergent in a waterfall. And that I have doubts when someone says that she swung naked on a trapeze in a circus in Warsaw – but why shouldn't she have done so? After all, I got on that borrowed bicycle myself and instead of filing hammers, rode to the greenhouse. Berecz didn't even slap me. I also reflected that I didn't fall into this goddamn pit when Adél Selyem opened the door earlier in the evening, but way before that. Before Laika was sent off to outer space. Or Gagarin. And also, that somebody's sitting there, God knows how many thousands of kilometers above me in a space capsule, smiling, and waiting for the door to open so he can emerge and step outside. He must be afraid. How could he not be. But he will take that step, while for nearly ten years now, I've kept my pictures in the drawer of a desk. Then I thought that the last picture I took was of that blind woman and I haven't asked anyone up since then because I knew that Éva was afraid. She doesn't mean to be afraid, but she's more afraid than I am. She didn't believe me when I said that the woman was blind. I brought home the ID photo from Reisz so she'd see that she's really blind. She didn't ask, she didn't so much as mention it, but I knew that she wouldn't believe me otherwise. And what about me? I believed her when she said that her mother broke her ankle. But where did it get us? Where did it get us, me believing that she sometimes practices until midnight, or that when she goes to Vienna or Berlin, she sleeps in a single bed, or that for one reason or another, we can't go together somewhere, and should the prospect of us spending three days together should come up, she suddenly needs to go to Sopron to get rid of moths for her mother, and then she comes home a nervous wreck, because she had a fight with the conductor on the train. I wonder. My mother put lavender in the wardrobe, and the moth problem was solved. If we have a child, I wonder who will get rid of the moths for her mother. Probably, we will. The three of us. We'll take a whole bunch of lavender. Or formalin. Or whatnot. Mothballs. I wonder if she'd take her child to her mother at all. On the other hand, I didn't like it either when Dalma Keresztes insisted on taking me to Mélyvár. Also, she went to see my father, though that was different, of course. I doubt that we'd have had children. The problem was that the child would have been more like her grandchild. But that wasn't the problem. The problem was that I didn't really love her. To be perfectly honest, except for Éva, I never loved anyone. That was the problem with Adél Bauer too. It's so easy, learning somebody's new name. Bauer. It's enough for her to have said it just once, and I learned it for a lifetime, especially with her holding a little Bauer in her arms when she opened the door. An ugly man is going up there and he's going to gobble up the moon. Humm. That's not the way I'd introduce my child to the moon, that's for sure. The moon, I could see it sometimes between the lilac bushes growing in front of my window. I didn't even check if they cut them down, or just the walnut. Not that it makes any difference. Come All Souls' Day, I'm going to ask Éva to go with me. I'd been back just three times in six years. Actually twice, because the third time, I turned back at the station. That grave will never be finished properly. If only it hadn't rained. Why don't they have All Souls' when the weather is nice? Then the second time, it rained so hard, I missed the night train back,. No way will I spend another night at that station. Luckily, my ID says I was born there, or the policeman would have taken me to the police station. But he was ok. I bet he knew my father. Everybody knew him. If Éva comes with me, I'll write someone and ask if we could spend the night with them. Not that she'd come. She'd have to go to her own father's grave in Sopron, I'm sure of that. I wonder if she'd have introduced me to her father. Maybe not even him. In any case, if my mother were alive and I were a pianist, she'd attend all my concerts, even if she had to come to Budapest all the way from Mélyvár. It's sure as god's sandals. Most, if not all, anyway. Just like my father, who'd come to my exhibitions. Of course, I'd have to have an exhibition first. Also, my father would have to be resurrected first. Which makes it problematic, of course. The truth is, that blind woman's picture is my best. The trouble is not that Éva's afraid of them, but that I can't exhibit just one photo by itself. Though there might be a few others good enough to be included in a show. Just wait it out. Kornél, too, waited years before he compiled his first volume of poems, and even then, he asked for it back to prevent them from turning him into an informer. On the other hand, he didn't wait ten years. And also, with a poem it's different. A poem is inside you, from the first line to the last. Kornél can write a poem whenever the fancy takes him. But I couldn't have taken that picture, ever, if that woman hadn't come to the studio and hadn't removed her glasses. To give him his due, he's smart. He's satisfied with a piece of paper and a pencil. I don't care how great the weightlessness, Neil Armstrong's camera will never float like Gagarin's pencil. Let's put it this way. The two won't stand comparison. What will stand comparison is that they already have three children. Perhaps Klári was right when she said that my pictures have no place in a family home. Which doesn't mean that three years had to pass before I could visit them. Kornél was a great big shit of a coward. On the other hand, if he ever dared call Éva a stupid bitch, he couldn't set foot in my house for thirty years, not even if he was right. That's the way the cookie crumbles, I fear. I was no doubt right in the short run, but Klári was right in the long run. After all, they're sitting at home now in front of the TV, watching the moon landing, instead of watching the twelve month old Eszter Bauer chew on a diaper stuffed in her mouth. He's made a life-long decision, and his poems are none the worse for it. Éva wouldn't play either better or worse, would she? And my

426

pictures wouldn't be better or worse, would they? Also, why am I so afraid of finding out that she might not be going to her mother's to kill moths. She's right. We all have someone we're afraid of. Though why it should be Dalma Keresztes is beyond me. In her place, I'd be more afraid of Adél Selyem, and not because she was poison. Raw meat round my prick. At fifteen, you were already kissing. I was still looking at Egon Schiele's drawings when you'd been fucking your composer for two years by then. To the right Schiele, to the left those frescoes from Pompeii, and in the middle yours truly. Do you know why I'd be afraid of Adél Selyem if I were you? Do you? Because she's not scared of a thing, except maybe of her subhuman husband. Because even with a child in her arms, she dares to float. She opens the door and she floats. It's not a matter of physical makeup. It's a matter of daring. Never in this life will she have breasts or an ass like yours. Never in this life will she have the starry skies on her belly. But she made a decision, just as Kornél had made a decision. And also, Klári. And my mother. Everybody. Bauer may be subhuman, but with all his sabers and carbines, he could never keep Adél Selyem there if Adél hadn't decided to stay. If from time to time she didn't go kill moths, just when I can't think of anything else, except Bergman. Besides, I never said that we should all see *Winter Light* at least once a month. Which makes floating pretty difficult, I admit. Only a person who is not terrified that she actually might like something else can float with a child in her arms. The truth is that all of us want everything. I want everything, too, just as Gagarin would have surely liked to be a deep sea diver as an extra added plus. But he had to decide. The Mariana Trench or the starry sky. Don't come to me suggesting that I'm the one who hasn't decided, while you're the one threatening to leave if I only take pictures of you. Don't try to suggest that it's me who hasn't decided, when in six months I spent just ten minutes in the apartment that your ex-husband got for you. Don't try to suggest that I haven't decided, when I can't even be sure your mother is still alive. On the other hand, what is it you don't know? What? From my half-crazed great-grandmother to this whore's red rag, what haven't I told you?

You find her attractive? Éva asked. She came and sat on the arm of the chair and handed me the cognac.

Who?

Mother Devotion, that's who.

Don't be silly, I said.

This Mother Devotion had more derision in it than I'd detected in her voice toward anyone in the nearly twelve months that we'd been together.

Well, you're certainly intent on her.

It's not her I'm intent on, but the way she's dancing with her husband.

Interesting, she said.

What?

That when you're watching them like that it doesn't occur to you that you might ask me to dance. You haven't even noticed that I've been dancing here with Nóra for ten minutes to catch your eye.

Nóra? So that's why I didn't notice. I'd notice her only if she were swinging naked on a trapeze.

Don't get your hopes up.

For your information, I'd rather see you with her than with Mother Devotion. At least, she's boyish.

She's not boyish.

Well, I wouldn't call her mannish myself.

At least we agree on that. She laughed.

You're getting bold. Must be the cognac.

Come, I said. I gulped down what was left of the cognac, then dragged her along to the other room. I poured some more, then drank that as well. She laughed.

You need this much alcohol to dance with me?

I have no intention of dancing. Bedroom, library, baby's room. Don't they have a marble bathroom somewhere?

They do.

Kitchen, pantry, toilet. Ah, this is it. Get inside.

Comrade Bauer wouldn't like it, she said, but she was already unbuttoning her dress.

Fuck Comrade Bauer, I said.

What if Mother Devotion won't like it?

Her too. How come they have three locks on their bathroom door? They're crazy.

They probably had them installed because of you, so you won't crash in on Mother Courage.

If you don't stop this Mother Courage business, I'm taking you right back to the dance floor.

Fine. I'll stop. Come to think of it, she dances pretty well, considering she's a mother. Love me?

Of course I love you, András Szabad.

In that case, you'll be dancing pretty well yourself, because you're about to become a mother.

She pushed me away. Everything in that fucking bathroom froze. The toothpastes, the perfumes, the robes, the towels, they all froze as if the Good Lord had scattered them from that space capsule into the black, empty void.

I'm sorry, I said.

Just don't say that again, she said.

Alright, I said.

Never again, you hear? Don't you dare forget, ever again, to ask me if I want it, too.

Alright, I said. I won't.

By the time the moon dust stirred under his feet and like a novice god just learning to walk on water, Neil Armstrong took his first step on the Sea of Tranquility, I was already looking at the wall from Colonel Adler's armchair. And also Éva, turned to the wall, sleeping. Because of the reading lamp placed on the floor, her shadow reared up over her. There they were, the two of them, she and that hulking shadow, and it occurred to me that if I were to lie down between them now, one of them would disappear. I grabbed the Leica and took a picture. I hadn't taken a picture of anyone for six years. For six years, it never occurred to me that what I was feeling just then is what people call gratitude.

(father's grave)

One day, Lovas came to see me. I'd last seen him when my Father died. After the funeral, I visited them once or twice, but then I didn't look him up any more. I felt awful eating the fried chicken they gave me out of respect for my father. I explained to them why I wasn't moving back to Mélyvár, although I could have bought a house with a garden for the price of my Budapest apartment. My father and my mother are buried there, they argued. Besides, photographers are needed everywhere.

He stood in the door wearing the same leather coat he always wore. I was home alone. He caught me by surprise. That was the only reason I kept my hand on the door handle without moving. He asked if he could come in. I said, I'm sorry. Of course.

He walked around the apartment as if I weren't even there, taking a mental inventory of everything that had changed. Then he sat down in my place, which used to be my father's. I felt like a fistful of shit, as if my father had sent him to check up on me. And I thought that if either he or my mother were to come back from the dead, I couldn't live with them anymore, that I'm no longer the man who had buried them. I have learned to live with their deaths, so they mustn't come sneaking back into my life, ever again. Then I told Lovas that I had to rearrange certain things. He nodded.

From where he was sitting he could see the drawing board in my room. I hadn't removed the pictures yet, the ones I'd taken at the Music Academy. Éva asked permission for us to go into the concert hall at night, and I took pictures of her on the empty stage. You're still taking pictures, I see, Lovas said. And I said, yes.

I asked if I could make him some coffee, and he said he doesn't drink coffee at this time of day. I asked what brought him here, and he said, he hoped he wasn't intruding.

I heard the key turn in the lock, then the door being opened. I was even glad that this silence would be broken. Then Éva shouted, wake up, András Szabad, your lover is here! Not a muscle twitched on Lovas's face.

My wife, I said.

I didn't know you were married.

We haven't had the wedding yet, I said.

Then I asked Éva to come in and I introduced them. My wife. My father's former cell-mate. When I said wife, Éva said, you should have it so good, András Szabad. Lovas kissed her hand. Éva asked why he was not taking off his coat. Lovas said he'd only come for a short visit to discuss something with me. Éva said he should take it off anyway. Meanwhile, she'd make some sandwiches. She took the leather coat out to the hall, then brought wine from the refrigerator, along with three glasses.

Thank you very much, Lovas said, but you really shouldn't bother. I'm not hungry.

I'll make some anyway, Éva said, and we'll see if you can resist. Won't you pour, my dear?

Of course, I said. We clicked glasses and Éva went to the kitchen to make the sandwiches.

Your girlfriend is very nice, Lovas said.

Yes, she is, I said.

As far as I can tell from here, that's her in those pictures.

Yes, that's her.

Of course, that's none of my business, he said.

I felt so on edge, I began shaking all over.

She's a pianist, I said. She often plays Bach on stage. And suddenly I remembered my father telling the Gypsies that his son was an art photographer. That's why he keeps a manequin in his room.

Love each other, Lovas said. That's what counts. Your father would have approved of her.

And she'd have approved of my father, I said.

He drank some wine, then rolled his cigarette between his fingers to soften it.

Since we're on the subject, I've come because of him. But it's confidential.

431

What concerns me concerns my wife, I said, to let it sink in that I'd have none of this girlfriend business.

As you wish, he said. You disappeared. I thought you'd keep in touch with us.

I'm busy, I said.

I wanted to ask what he meant by us, his wife, or the whole bad lot who came to see my father during his last months. Instead, I asked about Kőszegi.

I don't know much. Last I heard, he got married.

I bet he married that librarian, I said.

He said nothing. Then he said, yes, and I thought that there's one person, anyway, who benefited from my father's death, then I thought about how much duality there is in a person's life, that God himself wouldn't have believed that my father and Kőszegi could fit into the same woman's life. On the other hand, it's probably just as much of a mystery what I'm doing in Éva's life after János Radnóti. And of course, what Adél Selyem, or anyone else, for that matter, was doing in my life before Éva.

I've come because I went to Mélyvár last week, he said.

Yes, I said.

I took a look at your house, too, though only from the outside, of course.

It's not our house anymore, I said.

Éva brought in a plate with the crescent rolls cut into rounds, butter, salt, some sausages, and paprika cream. She asked if she was interrupting anything.

Of course not, I said.

Just that family matters don't necessarily concern me, she said.

I was about to say that I don't have a family any more, but then decided against it.

Lovas took a sandwich and said, very nice.

Éva smiled her acknowledgement, then said, you see, I managed to tempt you after all, and Lovas said, yes, you did. Then he added that had service been like this in prison, they'd have fared much better. He said it the way the agronomer had said to Imolka that for two gilded roses like that, I'd gladly trek home even from Kamchatka, just don't tell my wife. And I thought how he'd never forgive me for discarding that rotting red sideboard, while he'd let Éva get away with anything without a second thought, even those five photos, and this wouldn't be any different, even if I were the one to force those sandwiches on him. I'll never know what it depends on. Some people have been dealt a certificate of absolution without an expiration date. Éva is like that, and so is Kornél, and it doesn't matter if she flings a glass against the wall that explodes like a hand grenade, and it doesn't matter if, out of cowardice, he avoids me for months after the wedding, I end up sweeping up the splinters, and I end up waiting yet another month. And not just me, but anybody. Except for this certificate of absolution, I've never envied anyone for anything. My mother had a certificate like that. But she didn't use it.

Éva said something I didn't hear.

Lovas laughed.

I asked if he had any other news from Mélyvár.

Lovas clearly felt ill at ease. He hadn't counted on Éva. He answered me, but he turned to her as he did so.

Not much, he said. From where he sat, he could in one glance take in Éva and the pictures behind her in the other room.

Have you been to Mélyvár? he asked.

Not yet, Éva said.

You don't have time to travel, I guess. The two of you must have lots of concerns, Lovas said.

Yes, I said, though I couldn't think of a single concern just then.

In short, I visited your father's grave.

Yes, I said.

I came to see you to ask your permission, Lovas said. A couple of your father's cellmates and I agreed to have your father's grave properly seen to, to make it worthy of him.

I think I must have said something like I'll see to it myself.

Éva put down her glass, stood up, came over to me, sat down on the arm of the easychair, and threw her arm around me. From then on, I didn't care about anything, and while I listened to their conversation as if it were a radio play, or as if the sounds came from the neighbor's apartment, or God knows where, I kept my eyes pinned on the pictures in the other room. The picture where she just stands in the middle of the stage was the best. Always, there's one picture better than all the rest. The very first. There are few exceptions. And yet, you use up an entire roll of film. Or ten.

433

It's all right, Lovas said.

Éva then said that we're very grateful, and naturally, we'd reimburse them, but it would definitely be a tremendous help if my father's cellmates were to see to it, because I'd never manage to arrange the headstone myself. She said this as if I weren't even there. Then Lovas said, he was glad that I have such a wonderful woman as my wife, and then Éva saw him to the door, and I thought that the time has come for me to lie down between my wonderful wife and her shadow, except the next morning I'd no doubt wake up, only with the shadow.

When she came back, she just said, you're terrible.

(the two men)

When Reisz had to go to the hospital with his stomach ulcers for a month, I took over. He asked if I could manage. I said sure. Once I asked Éva to sit for me after I'd closed up. I had nothing specific in mind. It's just that except for that blind woman, I'd never taken a proper picture of anyone at the studio. Also, the Linhof is entirely different from the Leica. You can't go around pressing the exposure button all over the place. What can I say, Reisz was right about that. She sat down and asked what she should do. I said, nothing, then spent about ten minutes adjusting the lights.

I'm not blind, she said.
Of course, you're not. I pretended I didn't know what she meant.
You can take as many pictures of me as you like, but I am who I am.
Of course, you are, I said. You and the Lord, both.
When you see me, it's me you see, so it's no use fiddling with the light.
Oh, yes, it is.
No, it isn't. Whatever you do, I can't light up your imagination any more than this. I put the camera aside and pulled down the shutter curtain. It was now pitch dark inside. And I said, let's see.

I had no need of lamplight to see the starry sky on her belly. I knew perfectly well that it's been decided for a lifetime. It wasn't even me who decided, but something far more powerful than me. And I knew, too, that these stars will be long dead when I will still see their light. I held her so tight that her heart fluttered in my hand.

Suddenly she shrieked, fuck me more, fuck me more!

(at Imolka's place)

When Mrs. Ferenc Vándor, née Imola Kocsis placed that cardboard with i was bad around her neck and hanged herself, for a couple of weeks the basement apartment was left empty. I climbed through the same back window from where I'd formerly taken my pictures. The city council had left it slightly open so the place could be aired out before the new tenant moved in. I'd taken along a flashlight with alkaline batteries, not that there was anything there I wanted, though the truth is, I wouldn't have dared filch anything anyway. I sat down at the table, across from the window. I sat there for about an hour. That's how long the batteries held out. I wouldn't have dared sit in that pitch dark place. I then took the lamp and placed it on the floor shade down, so some light should filter out onto the plank floor. A cat scurried past outside. Someone went to the woodshed, gathered up a basketfull of kindling, then walked away. A mouse scratched around in the sideboard. From time to time, a drop of water fell from the kitchen tap. I knew perfectly well that the person outside had seen me.

(Winter Light)

I told the woman not to be afraid. She should just sit straight and look into the lens. It'll be all right. It'll take a hundredth of a second. She won't even notice. She should hold her hands as if she were begging. Alright, she said, she's not afraid, she trusts me. She was around forty, with black hair. The veins shimmered through her light skin. I asked her to raise her hands just a bit, to just about her navel. I don't know what'll happen either. We'll see. When I ask, she should imagine that she's ill. Her heart. She's so ill, her heart will break. Now. Blinding flames shot out of her palms. I pressed the shutter release. The azure flames shot up to her breasts. It was beautiful. They lit up her whole body. Except, that hundredth of a second had long passed, and the light was still blazing in her hand. And by now she saw it too, not just me. The Linhof's shutter wasn't working. It opened, but wouldn't close. Should I stay as I am, the woman asked. Close your hands! Tight! Desperately, I kept pressing the shutter release cable, but it was no use, the shutter didn't respond. It's beautiful, the woman said as she watched her flaming palms. Press them together! You hear? Can I have it, the woman asked, and I said no, it's mine, but she didn't hear or else didn't care. She didn't even put her clothes on before she headed for the gate across the dark yard.

The notebook remained on my desk. I don't know whether I'd forgotten it or left it there on purpose. I may have left it there on purpose, though I always put it away and lock the drawer. I locked it even when I lived alone. Ever since my father said that he was just looking for my birth certificate. When I got back from Reisz, I found Éva at home.

I asked if she'd like to go anywhere. She asked where I wanted to go. I couldn't think of anything, so we ended up seeing Bergman's *Winter Light* again. Then we took a walk in City Park. I said that I'd ask Reisz if I could sometimes work in the studio after we close shop. Éva asked why I wanted to work there, and I said, because of the Linhof. The Leica is like a notebook. The pictures I take with it, they're basically my life. But

437

there are things I can capture much more precisely with the Linhof, though precisely is not the right word. Just differently. That picture of the blind woman isn't so improbable because of the eye sockets left in the dark, but because one sees something that's only visible in one's dreams. Also, flat film is like a mirror in which we see things in black and white.

We were just passing the spot where I first saw her. She sat down on the tree stump where I sat when I watched her with her ex-husband.

Who do you want to take pictures of, she asked.

You.

Two dogs fell at each other at the end of the path. They were biting each other. Their owners could hardly separate them.

There's a cellist, Éva said. I'll ask her to come. Take pictures of her.

I want to take pictures of you.

In that case, you'll have to take pictures of the two of us. Her skin is like glass.

I said nothing, and we continued walking in silence.

When we reached the Institute for the Blind, she asked if I think that Jonas Persson in *Winter Light* really shot himself in the head because he was afraid of the Chinese. Can you imagine a fisherman reading a newspaper article in a remote Swedish village about the Chinese teaching their children to hate and developing an atom bomb, and this fills him with so much dread that he commits suicide?

Yes, I can well imagine it, I said. Anxiety is like a dog. It goes around smelling and digging until it finds a bone. The bone hasn't got any meat on it, and it can't satisfy his hunger, and he may not even be able to chew it. But if anyone tries to take it away, it'll snarl. It could kill for it. Yet it wasn't the bare, chalky, dried-up old bone that made him go searching. I don't think my great-grandmother ate a single bite of the horsemeat she gathered up. It's just that she found the cause for her anxiety in the danger of famine, and Jonas Persson in the Chinese.

Still, it wasn't the Chinese who killed Persson, but the pastor.

Oh, come on, I said.

He went to see the pastor hoping he could help him.

438

He didn't go. His wife took him. He had no intention of going to see the pastor.

Never mind. The point is, he went. And he committed suicide only after Tomas Ericsson dumped his own anxieties on him.

A pastor suffering a crisis of faith is in no condition to help. How could he?

He could have at least refrained from complaining to the poor fisherman. That's not what his office was about. If he's lost faith, he should pack up and go and become a locksmith or a truck driver. But he shouldn't destroy others with his own doubts.

I suddenly felt very nervous.

Look. I don't know the real reason for Persson's anxiety, and neither do you, I bet. But let's agree that it wasn't the Chinese and it wasn't that poor unfortunate pastor's emptiness of heart. Let's not chastise the pastor because at one time his father had humiliated Persson, or because his mother didn't feed him.

Or that he no longer wants to sleep with his wife, Éva said.

I said nothing.

What exactly are we talking about? I then asked.

Bergman. At least, I started talking about Bergman. But what you're talking about only you know.

Still, of the two of us, I'm the one talking about him, don't you think?

Great. In that case, we're both talking about the same thing. In short, you insist that the pastor is not responsible for Persson's death.

He's responsible, but no more than the journalist who wrote that article is responsible, or the Chinese, who will no doubt have atom bombs, or his wife, who kept at him to talk to the pastor about his fears.

Well, that's not how I see it, Éva said. Somebody asks for his help, and he spouts drivel about his cold.

He wasn't talking about his cold, but his doubts. Who knows? It might have helped someone else.

His doubts? I don't think so.

A pastor is not a physician. And just because you can't help someone doesn't mean you're responsible for their death. If someone goes up on the roof and you can't grab his arm in time, it doesn't follow that he climbed up there because of you or plunged to his death because of you.

439

You scare me.

Will you tell me why?

I don't know. I just find it strange that you should be defending that pastor so vehemently. You come with all sorts of things, mother, father, bone, dog, when, though he's a pastor, he treats that teacher like a dog. The nonbeliever Marta has more love in her heart than he does. That woman loved him. She insisted on being with him. She humiliated herself for him.

We were talking about the fisherman, not the teacher.

The way you manage to separate these things, I find it a bit strange.

What I find strange is me leaving my notebook out on the table and. . .

Really? What sort of notebook did you leave out?

Don't pretend you don't know. The one in which I record my dreams.

You didn't just *leave* it out. You left it out on purpose.

Unlike you, I tell you about my dreams.

I have nothing to tell, my dear. I don't dream about men with skin like glass. Nor women, either. I don't even dream about you. Or the two of us, you're the one who sees into the future, not me.

I saw the future just once, but even that wasn't about someone saying I'm insensitive because I'm not convinced that a pastor who has lost his faith is to be blamed for the death of a fisherman who is hounded by depression.

That's not why I think you're insensitive, and you know it.

Then why?

Next time, think twice before you dream.

Fine. I'll try.

And if despite all your trying you can't succeed, then at least, lock it up. Don't leave it out on the desk for me.

Fine. From now on I will lock everything up, I promise.

Good.

Still, it's a shame that of all my dreams, this particular dream means so much to you.

What means so much to me?

That someone's skin is like glass.

Don't be ridiculous.

Please let's not talk about it anymore, I said when we got back to the old Palace of Arts in the park. This is where I first saw you, so let's stop it here.

This is not where you first saw me. You first saw me in a dream, and that's where you'll see me for the last time as well.

(flat film)

When I asked Reisz if I could use the studio, he said I could have asked him earlier.

I'm slow, I said.

You're lucky you have so much time on your hands, he said. And here I was thinking you'd been given sixty, seventy years at best, like me.

In which case, I'm not even halfway there, I said. The best is yet to come.

You know what? I'll save you five years by pointing out to you that the Linhof is really a flat film camera.

I know. You mentioned that six years ago.

Well, well, what memory. Just make sure your exceptional memory doesn't do you a disservice.

It won't.

You know best. So then, bring a box of flat film with you tomorrow and I'll teach you the art of photography.

Will you?

Of course. I was a camp photographer in the army. I even had an exhibition in the physician's room.

For a while, I didn't say anything. Will you tell me about it sometime?

What? There's nothing to tell.

I can wait.

Don't wait. Go take pictures of your lover.

She's not my lover, she's my wife.

Ridiculous. She'll be your wife if and when you get married.

The following day I bought a box of flat film, and after we closed shop, Reisz showed me how to insert it into the cassette and the camera, how to develop it, and so on. And I said that I'd like to take the first picture of him, like the time when he taught me how to take ID pictures.

Just watch the shadow of my nose, he said.

Just make sure your exceptional memory won't backfire, I said.

It won't, he said. You had nine mud spots on your coat.

Eight.

Nine.

Then and there I would have never thought that this man, who took me in, a complete stranger, after my father died, would one day disinherit me like a father, for good and without reprieve, because of a single sentence uttered by a half-crazed, complete stranger.

(the mansard)

There's so much humbug, there's so much lying going on when artists talk about their work. It doesn't matter, writers, painters, photographers, nonsense comes pouring out of them, especially when they think it might work to their advantage. When I could have done the same, I made sure, very sure, not to make this mistake myself. Not to lie, ever. Not ever say anything like I'd never had a chance to exhibit my photographs in Hungary. Let's face it. I hadn't even tried. So I can't possibly know. If, for instance, someone asked me how I spent the fifteen years from the time my father gave me the Zorki until I signed a contract with the Broch Gallery, I had no qualms about saying that I was working at a printer's and then I took ID pictures. I even liked doing it. I didn't think it was below me. Besides, what I know about technique I mostly learned from József Reisz. Nothing has given me as much satisfaction as reading this in various interviews and short biographies. Nothing reveals the full truth as well a couple of incontrovertible truths.

Éva had a friend. His name was Kálmán Varga. He was a painter. We visited him now and then in his rented studio in Zugló. I liked going there. It even occurred to me that I would ask to borrow it for an afternoon so I could take pictures of Éva there. He generally invited five or six people. There was everything – sandwiches, domestic wine, the smell of linseed in the air. At such times he'd show us his latest works. He was an outrageously talented painter, even in the eyes of those who'd had their share of canvas and paint themselves. But the moment Martonyi set foot in the room, Varga got going and he couldn't stop talking about painting, holding forth on inner reality and the possibilities inherent in materials. I'd heard it three or four times before, from beginning to end, so when he launched into it this time, I said, Kálmán, when you stand in front of the canvas, are you really intent on your inner reality?

He looked blankly at me. I don't know what you mean, he said.

Okay. Let me put this another way. When you're in bed with Anna, are you engaged in analyzing the nature of your innate drive to propagate the species, or do the two of you fuck like rabbits?

What they do is hardly any of your business, dear, Éva said.

I think we're talking about the same thing, except in two different ways, Varga said.

I don't know. If you ask me, Anna would freeze up for a lifetime if you were to reflect on what you're doing, instead of doing it. So we're not really talking about the same thing.

Anna, who sat across from me, looked at me with the gratitude of a dog when it's finally given its dinner.

What exactly is your problem? Varga asked.

My problem is that you're lying, I said. Month after month you sit here with your friends, and you're a very decent person, but the minute Martonyi walks through the door, the lies come pouring out of you. Lucky for you that you never, ever really delved into anything. Not really. Lucky for you that as long as you don't see a critic on the horizon, you just paint, or fuck Anna, all this colossal nonsense doesn't occur to you.

I take it that what I write is colossal nonsense, Martonyi said.

You take it wrong, I said. You can go discover the possibilities inherent in a painter's material all you want, but standing in front of a bare canvas, Kálmán will do nothing of the kind, ever. It would never occur to him to occupy himself with such bullshit.

In short, you're some sort of instinctual being who won't let creative consciousness get in the way. You discard it, Martonyi said.

Thank you, Varga said.

Take it easy, Éva said.

I'm not discarding anything, I said to Martonyi. I'm just saying that you know all there is to know about escape velocity and weightlessness, but you've never been in space. Nor will you. The only difference between you and a physicist is that without him, no one would reach outer space, while without you, Kálmán can paint just fine.

Now it's my turn to thank you, Martonyi said.

Don't mention it. Of the two of you, it's you who'd starve to death without the other. And yet, he's the one who starts in on all this theoretical bullshit whenever you show up.

You're lucky, András. Except for taking ID pictures, you don't do anything, and so you don't have to lick the ass of a Party secretary, or the Pope. Nobody. Such purity is no doubt edifying. Still, I don't envy you, Varga said.

The wine decanter was right in front of me. I watched it gradually disappear, then everything else disappeared along with it. The glasses, the ashtray, the table. Kálmán Varga, Martonyi, and the others. Fortunately, Éva grabbed my hand, and I could see clearly again.

You're both right, I said. I apologize.

Don't mention it, Varga said.

I'm sorry. I don't usually do this.

We know. Forget it.

Alright, let's go. It's late, Éva said.

Yes, of course, I said.

I'm sorry, Éva said to Anna when she saw us out.

Forget it, Anna said. They're all alike.

I thought I'd never get away from that mansard studio. When we were out on the street, Éva abruptly blocked my way. She was as cold as ice.

I'm fed up, she said.

I understand, I said.

I don't want you to understand. I want you to gather up your pictures and show them to people. It's high time you mounted an exhibition in a cultural center, if nowhere else. I hope you realize that what you're doing is crazy.

I don't want an exhibition.

What are you afraid of?

I'm not afraid of anything.

Well, you should be. I meant it when I said just now that I'm fed up.

I understood the first time.

She walked away as I watched the light of the cars flicker across her dress. I followed five or six steps behind her. When she reached the corner, she stopped, but did not turn around, waiting for me to catch up with her.

I can't look up to a coward, she said.

I grabbed her arm and shouted that of the two of us, she's the coward. The person who doesn't dare play the fucking piano the way she'd like, that's what I call a coward. I take pictures of what I want, and not what I dare. So don't concern yourself with my pictures, I said. I have no need of a guardian.

The passersby stopped, and an elderly man asked if he should call the police. Éva said, don't bother.

She threw her arms around me, and I sobbed on her shoulder like a disconsolate child.

(under the window)

In 1973, Éva gave me a camera for my thirtieth birthday. I'd have liked to feel happy, but I just couldn't. About six weeks earlier, she went to see her mother in Sopron. She said it would be for two days. Then she called me at Reisz's, something's come up, she can't make it back until the following day. Then she called to say that her rehearsals have been canceled and she's staying an extra day. She ended up staying almost a week. On the night of the fifth day, I went to Fő Street. The light was on. I thought I'd lose my mind.

I didn't know what to do. I stood outside for half an hour. Then I went upstairs and knocked. She didn't open the door. I'd have liked to break it down, but I was afraid the neighbors would call the police. So I went downstairs again and stood around for another two hours. She turned off the light, but nobody came outside. The sun was coming up and traffic began to flow, so I went home.

The next day, when she came back, instead of saying hello, Éva turned on me. She said I better not try that again. I better not spy on her, because she gave me no cause. I said that if the light is on in her apartment at night when she's supposed to be in Sopron, I consider that adequate cause, not to mention the fact that she goes for two days but ends up staying a week, all the while knowing full well that I'm standing under her window the whole night. So now, it's me who's going to do the screaming and not her, and she better not try this ridiculous the-best-defense-is-offense business. She said she has no reason to defend herself, because Nóra regularly uses the apartment, and I know it.

No I don't, I said, you forgot to tell me. Besides, I can't imagine what reason Nóra would have for not opening the door.

The same reason you'd have for not opening it if you were fucking someone, she said.

And I said that as things stand, I'll soon be free to open the door to one and sundry, especially seeing how Nóra can come and go in the apartment where I was allowed up only twice.

She said that what she does with her apartment is none of my damned business.

Suddenly, I felt as calm as a millpond, and I asked her never to say this none of my damned business again, if she knows what's good for her.

Why? You're going to hit me?

I'm not going to hit you. I'm going to slam you down on the floor like shit.

I watched her throw her clothes out of my mother's wardrobe, then I watched her stuff them in her small carry-on suitcase. Less than half her stuff fit inside. The rest she left in the middle of the room.

You can go burn them, she said.

The key, I said.

She slammed it down on the floor.

You're scum, she said.

Get out of here, I said.

She grabbed her bag, then when she reached the door, she called back.

It was Nóra, you asshole.

I caught up with her on the corner of People's Republic Avenue. She said I should take my hands off her. If I didn't trust her, why should she come back with me? And I said that screaming your head off is not the way to make a person trust you. If things were the other way around, she'd have equally good reason to be suspicious. Imagine me going to Mélyvár, I said, but the lights are on in my place. And you come knocking and begging and beating on the door, but nobody comes to open it. What would you do? What would you think? What would you feel? And with that, I rest my case.

She looked at me, her eyes calm and level, and I thought that she finally understood me.

You know something? Back then, I believed without the least reservation that that's when you saw Mrs. Bauer, born Adél Selyem, for the first time in your life.

I felt as if they had pulled the pavement of People's Republic Avenue from under me.

She didn't recognize me. She didn't want to recognize me.

All the same, you could have told me why you dragged me into her bathroom.

It wasn't because of her.

449

Maybe. Still, I don't remember ever bringing it up against you in the past four years.
I said nothing.
And now I'd like to take a walk, she said. Alone.
Fine, I said, and took her bag from her.
I went home and hung her clothes back in mother's wardrobe all the while that I was keenly aware how contemptible it was of her to put that shit moon landing on the same footing as last night, even if it really was Nóra at her place. I felt more cheated and more miserable than if I'd walked in on an orgy in that apartment. It scared me. I felt that she could do with me anything she liked.

(the thirtieth)

In short, for my thirtieth birthday, Éva gave me a camera. She said we must hurry. I asked her where. She said, it's a secret. Once she said she's going to arrange an exhibition for me without me suspecting. I had asked her not to do it. I wouldn't like it. She can take my word for it. Now I remembered it, and it scared me. Really scared me. I quickly checked the drawers. My pictures were in their portfolios. I felt relieved. She said I should put on something that I won't mind soiling. I said that that's all I have.

We got out of the cab on Elizabeth Bridge just as we'd done at one time when she brought me here to make me appreciate kitsch, except back then it was sunup, and now it was sundown. Or late afternoon. Basically, it makes no difference. An elderly man was waiting for us at the Pest abutment of the bridge. He was around sixty, with a beard. His name was János Szentesi, and he was the bridge guard. At the pylon he opened the iron door. He said I should go up front, Éva in the middle, and he'd climb up behind us, because it's safer that way. Some of the lights were not working. He gave each of us one of those lamps that go on your head, the kind that miners use. I started climbing the damp iron ladder up into what seemed like nowhere.

On one of the landings, Éva kissed me. She said, you'll never guess. I said that I couldn't guess last year's Nadar album either, the one she brought me from Paris. Except, back then I didn't have to guess who's burning the midnight oil in the Fő Street apartment either. When we reached halfway up the pylon, my lamp went out. The bridge guard wanted me to take his. I told him I could see. Meanwhile, my mind was occupied by what I'd been thinking every night for the past six weeks, namely, that I should have kicked in the door. Every man worth his salt would have done so. He'd kick it in, with the frame included for good measure, and slap the person who deserves it. That's how it's been done for the past five millennia, regardless of what part of the world we're talking about. More people have killed from jealousy than hunger. And let nobody tell me that it's not right, that it's not proper. Fuck what's proper, and fuck the moon landing. A man standing for hours, like an ass, on the sidewalk, staring at a window, what's proper about that? Is that what we call normal? What's normal about a man being hauled over hot coals because he forgets to introduce someone to you? Or a man whose chest feels like it's in a vice from some dresses being dragged out of the gardrobe, what's normal about that, with his heart, too, in a vice, as if he were standing by a freshly dug grave? It's none of my business, you say? Fine. Whose business is it then? Your mother's? Anybody's except mine? You're intent on overseeing my dreams, but I mustn't ask where the fuck you've been for a whole week? I haven't taken pictures of anyone but you for years, lest your delicate soul comes unstrung, but I have no business asking who you're fucking? Instead of standing around, I should have kicked in that door, along with the frame.

When we reached the top, she said, happy birthday.

Up inside the cross-bridge there's a hole in the steel floor. It's a water runoff, or God knows. But it's been there ever since the bridge was rebuilt. It looks out on the road below. It's just big enough to allow the traffic to be reflected upside down on the steel roofing opposite. The rows of cars, the buses. The entire Elizabeth Bridge is a camera obscura.

It's yours, just so you'll get a camera from me, too, she said. And by this time next year, you'll have an exhibition, I promise.

You'll have to wait a lot longer than that, I said.

She kissed me.

János Szentesi, the bridge guard, drew a small bottle of peach brandy from the pocket of his coat and passed it around. He said, happy birthday.

I thought of what Kornél had said when my father gave me the Leica, that I should thank him and be happy. There I stood, in an iron box up in the sky, looking through a hole at a city that I can't relate to, like Imolka had looked at Ferenc Vándor up on the crane before she hanged herself. It took all my resolve to hug Éva and say, thank you. At least, to say thank you.

(silence)

When we got home, Éva also gave me ten rolls of Kodak film. She got it from abroad. She said I should save them for a special occasion, for example, if I'm going to take a picture of her together with an Imolka. I said I'd rather not wait until they're past their due date. She pretended she didn't hear. She asked if I knew what pictures I'd like to take. Of course, I said. But poor Imolka, she won't like it. I never cared about two women showing off in front of a camera. If she doesn't want the film to be wasted, she'll have to forget Imolka. Do away with her. It's her own face that interests me. Her anger, her jealousy, her cruelty. Her madness.

What if she tries to do away with me, she asked.

I wouldn't recommend it, I said.

Someone rang the doorbell. I thought that Kornél had come, and I felt relieved, because his presence would put an end to this uneasy conversation. Since we had that fight about my dream in City Park, I avoided the subject like the plague.

I went to open the door. The young cellist with the glass-like skin was standing there with a chocolate cake in her hand. I'd never seen her so close up, but I'd known even back then that Éva was talking about her. I think that a lot of people attended concerts exclusively because of her. I was so badly shaken, so angry, it took all my self-control not to slam the door in her face. I knew perfectly well that in exchange for this cake, I was now expected to forget that I had stood under that Fő Street window all night.

The girl handed me the cake and said, happy birthday. Her name was Lilla. She must have been at least twenty-five, but now, with her hair gathered up in a ponytail, she looked more like a high school girl. Éva hurried to the door and they hugged each other. Lilla said, you're so beautiful. Then she asked me if I like the camera Éva gave me. I said, yes. She said, she'd like to see the view from up there, on the bridge. It must be vertiginous, and she loves feeling giddy.

We went inside. Lilla took a bottle of cognac from her bag and said, this is also for you, and Éva said, no, it's for us. But he has to set the focus first.

When I went to get the three glasses, Éva followed me to the kitchen. She hugged me and said, I promised, did I not, that I'd find you an Imolka.

I asked what she'd told the poor girl.

And she said, all things bright and beautiful.

I said that as for me, I promised that I'd see them in black and white only.

I don't recall asking you anything of the sort.

Well, I do, I said. Then I added that even if she hadn't asked, that's what I'd do.

She kissed me and said, have it your way, it's your birthday. You do whatever you wish. As long as they're good pictures.

And I thought that I very much doubt that she's interested in my pictures right now. Except for boasting throughout a lifetime of years that she gave me the Elizabeth Bridge and Lilla Hámori, she doesn't care about anything.

I'll do my best, I said.

By the time we went inside, Lilla was standing in front of the picture that Éva had hung above the piano some years back.

Well, well, this guy really is crazy, she said to Éva as if I weren't there. Except, her comment was clearly meant for me. But I was in no mood to have Éva cry and slam the door on me because of something I might say.

Only when I take pictures, I said.

Don't be so modest, Éva said, because I have stories to tell.

I asked her to bring plates and a knife for the cake. When she was out of the room, I said to Lilla, just don't aim for vertigo now. And don't be so beautiful.

As you wish, she said. I can wait.

What did you say? Éva asked from the hall.

I just said that the two of you are far too cheerful. Why don't you paint dark circles under your eyes?

After the cake I poured them some cognac, and some water for me. Then I closed the shutters, put on a Gregorian chant, and began assembling the lamps.

454

Éva and I slept on pillows on the floor. Lilla slept on the bed. Éva woke early. I heard her leave the room, brush her teeth, then slip into her clothes. I pretended that I was still sleeping. Lilla did the same, though possibly, she woke up only when Éva left to get us something for breakfast. In about half a minute after she left, some of the plaster came crashing down in the kitchen where the ceiling was wet.

I went to the kitchen and swept up. I put on the coffee and waited. Lilla had still not gotten out of bed, though when the big chunk of wet plaster came crashing down, her eyes were open. I saw it from the mirror. I poured some coffee for her and took it inside. She was naked. She never even attempted to pull the blanket over her. I had slept in my clothes; I didn't even take off my shoes. I handed her the coffee. She placed the mug on her belly. I sat at the foot of the bed. As she pinned her eyes on me, took a sip, then placed the mug on her navel. I thought I'd suffocate. I said that the pictures turned out fine.

I agree, she said.
She folded the pillow behind her back and sat up.
What do you think the two of us are doing in this room now?
I have no idea, I said.
I'll tell you. If a woman is afraid, she tries to steer things along a certain path. Even things that can't be steered. Which is impossible, of course.
What?
Oh, come on, she said.
She rested her foot in my lap.
Éva has no reason to be afraid. I've never cheated on her, I said. And she knows it better than anyone.
Well, I don't think she knows, Lilla said. She knows only that you're too much of a coward to fuck anyone except her, even if she gives you permission, but she doesn't know that you haven't cheated on her.
Can't you imagine any other reason besides cowardice?
I don't go in for imagining things. I say what I see.
I took her foot, kissed it, then placed it back on the bed. I sat down on the floor. I didn't want to have to stand up abruptly from beside this girl when Éva showed up.

We ate breakfast sitting on the floor. Lilla just put on a light robe. Early in the morning, the sun shines in, and a wide ray slowly swept over the room. I watched Éva step over this shaft of light, sit down by Lilla's side and lean her head on her shoulder. Then she regarded me at length. I felt as if I were in front of a judge and jury. She didn't speak. I said that while she went to the store, part of the ceiling fell down in the kitchen. She said, yes, she saw. Lilla pulled the robe tighter around her. Éva said, don't, the sun will reach you in a minute. And I said, sorry, I've used up all the film.

The light shifted from Lilla to Éva, then onto the china cabinet. It penetrated right through thirty years' worth of knick-knacks, then shifted. What was left of the cake stood on the left side of the table next to the three glasses, the empty bottle of cognac, and the soda. The three small dessert plates were packed with cigarette butts. On the right side stood the used-up film cartridges neatly arranged in pairs as if I were an engineer or what have you. At other times I wouldn't have taken this many pictures in an entire year, and I knew they were good. Except, right now, it didn't matter. Lilla asked if she could have some more coffee. I said, of course. I was about to stand up, but Éva beat me to it. I knew that she'd be watching us from the kitchen door. She brought me some coffee as well. She placed the coffees in front of us, then sat back down, and we smoked another cigarette without speaking. Then she opened the window and said, you know what? In that case, let's go to the movies. I was about to ask what she meant by in that case, but decided against it.

While Lilla was in the bathroom dressing, Éva said how strange that actually, you can play anything perfectly well even on a mute musical instrument that didn't have strings. I asked what made her think of that now. She said she didn't know, she just did. And not only can you play it, she went on, but if someone understands music, they can even hear you play. I said it was a pity that I didn't understand music. She said she wasn't thinking of me. But, for instance, if Lilla were to play a prelude on a cello without strings, she'd know what Lilla was playing, and also, how well. Which got me pretty upset, and I said, we can't very well try it now, can we?

I've already tried it, and believe me, it's true, she said.

Still, I doubt that you'd have lain belly down on this piano if it didn't have strings.

456

She gave a laugh, stroked my cheek, and kissed me.

You're right, she said.

When we got to nearby Lövölde Square, we checked the movie schedules posted on an advertising pillar. They were showing *The Silence* that morning at the Kinizsi. Éva said she'd like to see it, even though she knew how I hated that film. We all have a Bergman we love to hate. Hers was *Persona*, mine was *The Silence*. Lilla asked what it's about, and was it exciting? Éva said it's about two women and an innocent young boy. A trolley pulled up by the church and Lilla said she'd rather go home after all, she was tired. In parting she hugged me and kissed me on the cheek, and said she can't wait to see the pictures. Meanwhile, she pressed my shoulder with her hand.

Éva and I walked on foot to the Boulevard. When we reached the self-service cafeteria on the corner of Mayakovski Street, Éva suddenly stopped and turned to me. She said that she wouldn't want me to use the excuse of the pictures to be with Lilla, and I said she could rest assured, I wasn't going to be alone with her, nor would I be with the two of them together. She started to cry and said, I'm sorry, I don't know what's got into me. And I said, the same thing that would get into anyone who tries to steer something that can't be steered. She asked what I'm talking about, she had no intention of steering anything in any direction whatsoever. And I said, never mind. I was about to ask her if she understood now what it feels like standing in front of a window the whole night. But instead, I asked what would have happened, had I taken her offer seriously the previous night and fucked Lilla. And she said, it might have been better than my lousy pretense.

We practically had the movie house to ourselves. When the old lady who checked our tickets and showed us our seats finally left, Éva said, let's move to the last row. I hated that film with a vengeance and tried to sleep with my eyes open. I thought I'd develop the negatives that afternoon. There was a certain frame, and I knew perfectly well that it was the best picture I'd ever taken. I didn't do anything special. I used the same dark background throughout. Éva put her arms around Lilla, but not as if she were another woman, but more like her younger sister or her daughter, the way Klára Meyer hugged Iván Hollós's daughter in the pantry when the soldiers moved the sideboard aside and kicked down the door. I thought that Lilla would show up at Reisz's within two days. But then realized that fortunately she didn't know where I worked. I could find her at the Academy, but she couldn't find me. During the scene in which Anna watched a couple making love in a private box, Éva slowly slipped her hand under her skirt. I grabbed her wrist and pulled her hand away. She didn't so much as look at me. After we left the cinema, I asked her if she'd like to make love with two men at the same time. Whatever would make you ask such a disgusting question? she said. I didn't realize it's any more disgusting than what you call my pretense, I said. But since she asked, I thought of it because she's pretended more than once for my benefit that she's making love with two men. Is that so? She remember nothing of the sort. Well, unless my memory plays me false, I said, that's how I met her, she was making love with one man while looking another steadily in the eye. She said nothing. At home, I pulled the films out of the cartridges one by one. She asked what I was doing. I said that at least that way I wouldn't have an excuse to see Lilla Hámori again. She said that she's taking the night train home to Sopron. I said, fine.

When she came back from Sopron, we actually spent several months in peace.

(the meteorite)

In February of 1974, a black iron meteorite five meters in diameter and twelve meters in height crashed into the earth smack in the middle of Kerepesi Cemetery. The snow that covered the graves melted. The tram tracks stretching along Kerepesi Road melted, and new tracks had to be laid down between Keleti Station and Teleki Square. The rubber factory's fence in the back collapsed, and for a long time afterwards, the dogs wandered into the cemetery through it, and from time to time, the horses also wandered in from the nearby racetrack.

Some people said that the meteorite resembled a cathedral, others said it was more like an observatory, and still others, that it reminded them of the Anthem. People came to like it, and whoever could manage, secured themselves a nearby gravesite. No government dared remove it. Today, it is surrounded by a rail, and tourists consider it one of the top attractions in Budapest. They think it's like the remnants of the Berlin Wall, or the empty space where the Bastille had once stood in Paris. But it's not.

It soon turned out that the meteorite attracts stray dogs like a magnet. Sometimes as many as ten or fifteen mangy dogs scratch themselves in its shade. Researchers have not found the reason to this day. Initially, the Street Department tried to deploy dog catchers, but then gave up. Those emaciated strays sit there like an unruly bunch of numbers strewn about at random under the shadow of a sundial.

I don't know why I'm writing this. None of it is true. If it were, even less would have remained of Budapest than of Dresden or Nagasaki.

Kornél said I should leave it in. He thinks it's important.

(the obituary notice)

One evening just before closing time, I wanted to do some shopping. Éva was with her mother and wouldn't be back until the following night, and there was no food in the house. The string bags and shopping bags were on a hanger on the inside of the pantry door. I don't like string bags. The bread gets stuck in them. Sometimes I can barely extricate the loaf because the thin nylon strings cut into the crust. There was a black shopping bag with a white screen print of the bridge at Mostar. Éva brought it back when she gave a concert somewhere in Yugoslavia. I took it to the store with me.

I even remember what I bought. Half a loaf of bread, fifteen dekagrams of cheese, a bottle of yogurt, mustard – because I'd run out – and a knackwurst. Then, when I paid at the cashier and was about to put everything in the bag, I found a wrinkled envelope at the bottom. András Szabad, Budapest, 6th District, 8 Szív Street. There were also some old receipts. I put the envelope in my pocket. Then I packed what I'd bought for dinner and came out of the shop, thinking I'd look at the envelope back home. But when I got to Mayakovski Street, I took it out, even though it was already pretty dark outside. I stopped in front of the window of the bridal gown rental place, where some light came filtering out the display window. I opened the envelope with the help of a key. It contained a printed text. Only the countess's name and the date of her funeral were written by hand.

When I got home, I put down the bag, unpacked, cooked the knackwurst, and sat down to eat. I ate all the bread, too, and the whole jar of mustard. Then I drank the yogurt. Then I looked around in search of something else to eat. I found some cheese and a can of liver paté in the pantry. Then I threw up. After cleaning the bathroom floor and the tub, I lay down and waited. I heard the sound of women's heels on the street, opened the window, and looked out. A light snow had begun to fall. I couldn't see the woman, just her umbrella as she turned the corner to Lövölde Square.

When traffic had died down, I went to Kerepesi Cemetery. There's a spot by the Jewish graves, in the back where you can climb through. I found the grave without difficulty. The wreaths were still on it. Her relatives probably didn't know how much to give the gravediggers, because the marble slab was split in two lengthwise. God damn it, I said. God damn it! And she said, pull yourself together, my dear.

The following night, when Éva came home, she repeated the same three sentences that had become habitual with her at such times. Her poor mother doesn't get proper medication for her high blood pressure, she's got to see to everything herself, it'd be so much easier in Vienna. Also, she's exhausted after her trip. Me, I was as sick and tired of these three sentences, along with their variants, as rain is of dogshit.

You forgot to show me this, I said.

She glanced at the obituary notice and turned as cold as ice.

I'm very sorry, she said.

So am I.

Then, as if nothing had happened, she asked if there's anything to eat.

I said there was, but I threw it up.

I'm not going to spend the rest of my life listening to you say that I forgot to give you the obituary notice.

You can rest assured, you won't.

Besides, it wasn't in an envelope with a black border. If they'd placed it in a proper obituary envelope, I would have noticed. I'm not that dumb.

That's true.

There must be something that you forgot at some point as well.

That's true.

If I shopped more often, I'd have found it in time.

That's true.

You can't resurrect the dead by going to their funeral.

That's true.

Your father's grave was looked after by others. You don't even go. Ever since I've known you, you've only gone once.

That's true.

She started yelling at me, that I better not try giving her a bad conscience.

I wouldn't think of it, I said.

And she said, I couldn't, even if I tried, because there's no reason she should feel bad. Of the two of us, it's my soul that's like a cesspool, not hers.

No, mine isn't.

Well, everything bounces right off your thick skin. You slander me, lie right and left. You poke and probe. You spy on me. And like an idiot, I put up with it. Yes. Here I am, shuttling back and forth between my half-crazed mother and my crazy lover, like an idiot, when God only knows what you're up to. I wouldn't be surprised if you hid that letter in the bag yourself, because of your graveside phobia, and now you have a bad conscience and you're taking it out on me.

Your clear conscience makes me sick to my stomach.

Is that so? I make you sick to your stomach?

She began taking her clothes out of the wardrobe, meticulously folding them, and placing them one on top of the other. Then she gathered up her shoes.

Stop it, I said.

That is precisely what I'm doing.

She placed Father's key on the table without it making the least sound. Don't even think about coming after me, she said quietly.

You have nothing to worry about there, I said.

She held the suitcase with her clothes in one hand and the bags with her shoes in the other.

Don't forget the bathroom, I said. She went to the bathroom and gathered up her lipsticks, nail polishes, and her toothbrush.

If you find anything else, just throw it out.

Fine, I said. I'll do just that.

And another thing, she called back from the door. If you ever dare exhibit just one single picture of me. . .

You have nothing to fear on that score, I said.

But you do, she said.

Fine, I said. Now get out.

I opened the window and took a blurred picture of her dragging her belongings through the slush as she headed for People's Republic Avenue.

(the pub)

After the countess died, I began frequenting the pub on Fő Street from where I could see the front door to Éva's place. I'd go there after I finished work at Reisz's studio and would leave only when they closed up. The bartender was a huge guy. I took an instant dislike to him. He treated people like trash. Here you are, Józsi, drink up. An elderly woman who smelled of powder was also one of the regulars. Her name was Vera. She was not an alcoholic. At least, I never saw her drunk. She drank just one mug of beer the entire night. She occupied a corner table by the toilet. She probably had nothing to do at home, and it's better to be with people, no matter what they're like. I'm lucky. I have my camera and my makeshift darkroom at home. If I had only books, or a radio, I'd have gone crazy by myself sitting at home all night. At least, that was the case just then. When Vera finished her beer, she took out a handkerchief and wiped the lipstick off the rim. Sometimes she didn't succeed and then, after he gathered up the glasses on a tray, the bartender held up the mug to one of the customers at the counter, like some incontrovertible evidence. See? This is what you people are like, leaving me to do the dirty work. You're lucky, Józsi, that you don't use lipstick, and everyone had a good laugh at Vera's expense.

He didn't dare use his banter with me, he reserved it for the locals. The fourth or fifth time I went there, he asked if I'd moved into the neighborhood. I said no. I'm a journalist. I even placed my camera on the table. Oh, he said, and from then on, he left me in peace. He didn't want to jeopardize his job. Come to think of it, it's strange, but back then, when almost nothing could be published, a journalist had more power than today. In places like this pub, at any rate.

Once I saw her come out the main entrace with Nóra. They headed in opposite directions. And once with an elderly man. I didn't recognize him at first, but by the time they got in the car, I realized that it was her ex-husband. It put my mind at ease. Then she was gone for a week. She must have gone to Sopron, I thought, to see her mother. Then, when the light was on again at her place, she had company. I was sure they'd come to see her, because two of them were carrying instrument cases. One was a violin case. I don't know about the other. Lilla Hámori was not among them. I'd have recognized her. That's when I remembered that it was her birthday. I quickly finished my beer and headed home. Luckily, my pictures are in order. My mother had been a librarian. I found the proof of the first picture of her I'd taken in City Park. I had no reason to enlarge it properly, but she knew perfectly well who those two indistinct shadows were on the brick wall. I wrote Happy Birthday on the reverse side, and went back in the middle of the night and threw it in her mailbox. The window was dark by then, but I could hear dance music. And I thought, why not, it's her birthday. And also that years ago, when I put that picture on my father's desk one night, the next morning I found a slip in front of my door: Thank you, Son.

Kornél told me to stop it, it was a blind alley, I'd never have a normal life like this. I chose not to see him for a couple of months after that.

(at the Opera)

I thought that if she finds that picture, she'll come to the pub the following night. She knew that I was a regular there. Her not knowing was out of the question. I thought that she'd come in with her things, I'd knock back what was left of my beer, and then we'd head home. But for a week afterwards, there was no light in the apartment.

I decided to go to the Opera to see Nóra. She asked what I wanted. I said that she knows perfectly well. I want to talk to Éva. She said to wait for her in the snack bar. I waited half an hour and drank two coffees. She sat down and said, listen, András, I'm not going to play the intermediary between you two. You're a big boy, solve it on your own. And I said that I didn't want her to play the intermediary. I just want to know if she's with anyone.

Why do you want to know?

Because it matters to me.

If it didn't matter to you when you met her, then why should it matter to you now?

That was different. They were in the middle of a divorce.

Is that so? Oh, the things one finds out on a lovely morning like this.

What do you mean by things?

My dear, they were already in the middle of a divorce when you were still in elementary school, and they will continue to be in the middle of a divorce until János bites the dust.

I felt like a man struck by lightning. What do you mean, they will continue to be in the middle of a divorce?

She said nothing for a moment. Calm down. He's not her lover.

In that case, what do you mean by saying they will continue to be in the middle of a divorce?

There are women whose husbands are divorcing them over a lifetime. After six years, I'd have thought you realized that Éva is a woman like that.

Well, I did not realize it.

So I see.

Were you the one in her apartment that time?

When?

Don't play innocent. Were you or were you not?

She said nothing for a while, then she said, yes, I was.

And what did I do?

What do you mean by this what did I do?

What did I do? How did you know that someone was there? Did I ring the doorbell, or what?

She laughed so her belly heaved. Are you for real? András, you're an idiot.

I'm not an idiot, so kindly answer me. Did I ring the bell, or did I knock?

The way she looked at me, I burst into tears.

Calm down. You knocked, and it was me in the apartment. Not that it makes any difference who was there. Women whose husbands will never divorce them don't keep lovers by the dozen. She's slept with only three men her entire life, if you must know. And that includes you.

I only know about János.

I'd be surprised if that were not the case. So take it in stride.

I said nothing.

What should I do? I asked.

Go to her and admit that you'd left the obituary notice in the string bag, or make up something. Tell her it was your fault and apologize. Then wait.

Except, that's not true, and you know it.

You asked what you should do.

I know. But it's still not true.

Okay, what do you want? The truth, or Éva?

Okay. I'll apologize.

She put out her cigarette and stood up. Also, after six years, you might try getting to know her better.

I know her pretty well, I said.

467

Just make sure she'll never find out, should you decide to go up to her apartment alone one day, as if on a whim, one might say.

I'd never do that, I said.

Okay, get going, because I'm busy. You're not a bad guy, just a bit dense in the upper quarters.

(the diary)

When Éva moved back, I took the soap one night and made an impression of her key. Then when she went home to see her mother, I headed for Fő Street. I still had the flashlight that I used years before to climb into Imolka's dank basement apartment. I had it with me because I didn't want to turn on the light. I was terrified, lest someone sees me. It was past midnight. I heard someone slam a door, and I didn't dare move for minutes. I was drenched in sweat. Then I realized that I needn't worry, because sometimes Nóra used the apartment, and so did others. I'm the only person who is not free to come and go there. I switched on the light.

I looked through the chest first. There was a throw pillow on top, so you could sit on it. It was a simple tool chest. I inherited a similar one from my grandfather. Ever since they don't fit in a drawer, I've been keeping my notebooks with my dreams in it. Once I asked what she kept in hers, and she said, nothing, just stuff. There were a couple of old dresses, a pair of shoes with worn-down heels, and scores with all sorts of notes in the margins. Also, the receipt from a dinner at a restaurant in Sopron, a lock made in China, a bunch of dried flowers, and some black beads from a torn necklace in an envelope. Just what I'd expected. A board game. A book of ten picture postcards bound together and perforated, so you can tear them out. It was published in Rome. The postcards showed the blueprints of famous labyrinths with the proper paths indicated in pencil. The first had been torn off. She probably sent it to someone. Or else, she got it like that. Also, a leash. I'd seen the picture on the wall where her mother is walking a German shepherd. It was probably the same leash. Had she not said so, I'd have never guessed that the woman was her mother. She was more like a stone statue.

I expected to find old letters and family photos, but there weren't any. By the record player on the floor, a bunch of records. János's records were stacked up separately next to the others. Which is only natural, considering that for ten years she was his wife. The reviews in two folders, some of which I'd seen before. I looked at a couple. In one, the reviewer praises her for playing Bach like Bach and not letting her personal feelings get in the way. I don't know how he came up with such nonsense. He must've been Bach's page turner. Apparently, something is personal only if it intrudes on the performance, while something repressed is impersonal. I looked at the books lying in piles. Three of Kornél's books were on top, and that made me happy. Balzac, Kosztolányi, Ady, Stendhal, Antal Szerb, Dostoevsky, etcetera. The same as anywhere else. Philosophy, a couple of psychology books in German and English. Sigmund Freud and Carl Gustav Jung. I didn't know she could read German. I thought she could only talk on a basic level. The spine of one of the books was missing. I thought it was a notebook. I picked it up, but it was Nietzsche's *Zarathustra*. Translated by Dr. Ödön Wildner, nineteen-hundred and eight, *"For my wife and my little ones, in memory of one of the chapters in Zarathustra. Ö.W."* Father gave me the same edition once. He'd stolen it from the library. In Éva's copy, the "Ö.W." was crossed out with a pen, and below it, in pen, it said, "János Zárai." That's her father. I knew that. Except, it seemed strange that he left the words "my little ones" in the original dedication. But then I thought that those were the translator's words, and he didn't want to cross them out. I found nothing else among the books, nor was there much else in the apartment, with the exception of the piano, of course.

I was about to leave when I remembered that I hadn't checked the desk. The drawer was locked, but these locks generally take the same key. My mailbox key fit.

Divorce papers. So divorce is a possibility, after all. Some official documents, a couple of picture postcards from abroad, sent by János. I looked at the first, but didn't read the rest. This made me feel better. A small album of photographs. At last! Pictures! But they were just pictures taken at various concerts and recording sessions. I found the five A4-size spiral notebooks to the left, in the back. Just like with everything else, I made a mental note of where they lay, so I could put them back the same way. The one on top slightly awry, and they don't touch the side of the drawer.

I knew perfectly well how low minded I was acting, but then, that's what I came for. She read my dreams, too, when I forgot them on the table. She started writing her diary when she moved to Pest. At least, that's when she started these. She wrote in a small, elegant hand, like my mother. I quickly thumbed through the first notebook. After all, her marriage is none of my business. Just like the postcards from János. The fond expessions they used for each other are none of my business either. My Sweet Fawn. To me, she's not my fawn, she's Éva. My sweetheart, my love, my whore, my wife. But not my fawn. As I said, I gave the first couple of notebooks only a cursory glance. She wrote in a breathless style, she filled up every line, every page, there was no articulation. The previous entry came to an end, the date in the middle of the line, followed by the next entry, like a river that overflowed its banks. Detailed descriptions of rehearsals. Travel. Exhibitions. Movies. What the film was like. Some quotes copied from books. Four lines of verse from Kornél, written in one line. Most of the entries, about her visits back home. I'm going home tonight. Same old story. I couldn't arrange mother's disability retirement, that damned doctor wants loads of money. I was home for two days. As if they held my head underwater. I gave Ádám a thousand forints. Mother said I should have the rights to the apartment, János should move out, and good riddance. We had a terrible fight. Ádám has been ignoring me since Easter. He comes in to see Mother as if I weren't even there. I tried to recall what happened three years ago at Easter, but couldn't think of anything. It took me some time to realize who the hell this Ádám was, but then I realized from one of the entries that he's some sort of relative who sometimes takes care of her mother and shops for her. As if her mother were a cripple. Though once she'd broken her ankle, that I remembered. At home, Ádám got started again about how there's no money for Mother's medicine, and also, he doesn't have time to shop for her every day, I should pay someone to do it. I told him that I can't give any more money, I send half my pay the fifth of each month, the money I got for the Chopin, that, too, I spent on the bathroom, all of it. Nóra said we should pour Ultra cleansing powder in the waterfall. I'm going to try it. And here I was, thinking that it was her idea. I have an apartment now, forty square meters, just right. I called Mother and told her to calm down, but she got started again about how János was just using me, and how he threw me out on the street with nothing to call my own except the panties I had on, just as she said he would. I put the receiver down. After today's concert, Lendvai came in to congratulate me. I was so happy. Something may come of the Beethoven concert. I skipped several pages, I didn't want to stay until the early morning, when the tenants would start leaving home. Today, Nóra took me along and introduced me to the bridge guard, except we didn't have time to go up. Incredible. The entire Elizabeth Bridge is a camera obscura. Well, well, I wouldn't have thought that Nóra came up with this idea as well. Of course, it doesn't matter whose idea it was, I got to see it thanks to Éva, and no one will take it away from me now. I turned back the pages and found the week when she was supposed to be visiting her mother, but found just one sentence. I'm suffocating, one of these days I'm going to blow this house sky high, I swear. Except, this didn't tell me how much time she spent at home. I found nothing whatsoever that could have been important to me. Nothing whatsoever. Except, of course, for the fact that she and her mother don't love each other all that much after all. At least, the tension between them is substantial, you could cut it with a knife. Which is not surprising, if indeed she sees to everything at home, from the bathroom to the disability retirement, and also sends the better half of her income to her. It's actually a good thing that we don't go to Sopron together. I put the notebooks back just as I'd found them. When I tried to lock the drawer, I panicked, because the mailbox key opened it with ease, but wouldn't close it. But then I managed. I turned off the light, closed the door, and left. I had almost reached the end of the street, when suddenly, a feeling of emptiness, of something lacking, swept over me with such force, I thought I'd drown in it. I turned right around and hurried back to that damned apartment, and beginning with August of sixty-eight, I read everything, letter by letter. I didn't find a single word, not one fucking word to indicate that I exist.

(humiliation)

When I got home, I searched through the drawers of my desk until I found an empty notebook. I decided I'd start a diary. I'd fill an entire notebook before she got back from Sopron. I'd fill it with anything. Whatever comes to mind. But not a single word about her. And I'm going to leave it out on the table. Not forget it, but leave it out on purpose, so she'll read it. And then I thought that I couldn't even fill half a notebook. If I didn't write about her, I wouldn't have much to write about. What happens at Reisz's wouldn't fill a single page per day. I see Kornél once a week, which is worth a whole week of Reisz, but that's still not enough. The rest is Éva.

You keep a diary, don't you? I asked Kornél.

Yes, he said.

What kind? The usual, or literary?

A simple recording of events.

Do you write about me as well? I asked.

Of course. Why?

Nothing. I just asked.

Fine. Except, I don't understand, he said.

You will, I said. Just bear with me. In short, you write a simple diary and you mention me as well. Our conversations, as well as what happens to us. Of course, not much happens. But, for instance, I show you my pictures, and then they get into your diary?

That's right. Of course, I don't record our conversations word for word. But I do record the subject of our conversation.

And you don't restrict yourself to just the good or just the bad things?

No. I write about both. Though more about the bad things, I guess.

So if something bad happens between the two of us, you write about that as well?

Of course. But look here, Kornél cut in. If it's my diary you're interested in, I'll show it to you. It doesn't contain any secrets.

473

I'm not interested in your diary, I said. But is there anything you don't write about?

Anything or anyone? he asked.

Anyone, I said.

He said nothing. I don't have a lover. Klára and I get along fine.

I know you don't have a lover. That's not what I meant. Just that is there anyone you won't write about purpose? I asked. Not a word?

No.

But can you imagine yourself doing it? For instance, you decide that from now on you won't write about me. Not a word. Regardless of what happens, if we had a falling out, or you wish me in hell, or it could be something very good, but you decide not to write about it?

Say something very good.

I can't think of anything now. But that's not the point, I said.

Well, for me, it's more and more the point, Kornél said. So go on, say something very good.

I told you. I can't think of anything just now. So then. Can you imagine not writing a single word about me? Not for years?

That's out of the question. To do that, I'd have to concentrate harder than anyone's capable of, Kornél said. At least, any normal person.

What do you mean by normal person? I asked.

I don't know. The same as you. Because, in that case, writing a diary would be about what I don't write about, and not about what happened.

So then, if you were to decide that from now on you're not going to write about me, that wouldn't be normal? *You* wouldn't be normal?

No, I guess not.

And what kind of illness would you have? Depression? Schizophrenia? Paranoia?

I don't know. I know nothing about psychology, and it doesn't particulary interest me. On the other hand, I'm very much interested in finding out at last what it is that you want to know.

Just bear with me. It's a game.

I don't see any game here. You know what I see? That you're about to burst into tears.

You're wrong. But never mind. It was a stupid game anyway. How is your novel getting along?

Let's not talk about my novel. But to answer your question, it's not.

How much of it is left?

Don't skirt the issue, András, and tell me what this bitterness over diaries is all about.

What bitterness? I said.

Éva keeps a diary, doesn't she?

Éva? I don't know. How could I. If she does, she certainly doesn't keep it here.

Why? Have you looked for it here?

I haven't looked for it anywhere! I don't understand this sudden interest of yours in Éva's diary, I burst out.

Kornél didn't say anything for a while.

All the same, this bears a striking resemblance to the time your father shouted at you and said that he never searched your drawer, he said.

I thought the shame and humiliation would get stuck in my throat and choke me. I made a key, I said.

You what?

I used a file. A nail file. Who cares. The point is, I had good reason for doing so, believe me.

He said nothing.

She's been writing a diary ever since we're together. Actually, since way before. There's not a word in them about me. In six years, she hasn't written a damn word, not one damned word, to the effect that she knows a person by the name of András Szabad, who lives in Szív Street.

He said nothing. Then after a while, he spoke.

I think you two should split up, he said.

We're never going to split up.

Well, you should.

Should I leave her just because she doesn't write about me in her diary?

No. You should leave her because you go to her apartment to read her diary.

I said nothing.

Because you are now doing things for which you'll spit at yourself in the mirror, things you're too ashamed of to tell me about. And because she's driving you nuts.

It's not having her around that would drive me nuts.

You have no way of knowing that.

Oh, yes, I have.

I need to go, Kornél said. I'll be late for kindergarten. But I'll come see you tomorrow, if you'd like.

(the mirror)

For weeks, I fell asleep listening to her breathe, the air filling her lungs. The nothing. One morning when she was about to leave for Sopron, I stopped her at the door. I said, I hope you know that I have no one else except for you. She said, yes, I know. I said that I'd given her everything she wanted, and it would be the same in the future as well.

She said nothing.

I asked why she's going home again, when she went last week.

My mother is ill, that's why.

What's wrong with her?

I just told you. She's ill.

She wore a dress with a French lily pattern. She said that she bought it the other day. Black lilies on a white ground. It would have looked better the other way around. She also had with her the same small red suitcase she always used when she went to Sopron.

I asked if she had someone.

She said, no. I'd know about it.

I'm not so sure, I said.

Yes, I would, she said. She'd go crazy, having to lie.

Just then, the mirror came crashing down in the bathroom. It fell with such force that the fragments came flying into the hall.

She didn't bat at eye. I have to go, she said. I'll miss my train.

Go ahead, I said, I'll sweep up.

Just be careful you don't step on the broken glass, she said.

(Karcsi)

The next day, a woman came to Reisz's studio. I knew I'd seen her before, except I didn't know where. She must have been about my age. She was rather pretty, if a bit common, though I'd be hard put to say what that means. The word, as we know, means that she's a dime a dozen. And also, that she's ordinary. That anyone can give her the eye. That she's all out there, that she displays her entire storehouse of drives and impulses on her face and by the way she dresses. First I thought that I must've seen her on the tram and then, for some reason, that perhaps it was at a concert. I hoped it was the latter. At least, that's something I could ask about. And so, I asked if she used to go to the Music Academy.

Why do you ask? Are you a professional musician or something?

Not really. I just thought I might have seen you there, I ventured.

Hardly, she said. Besides, she doesn't live here, she just came to visit her aunt for a month, that's why she needs a picture for her pass, so she can get around town.

I asked where she's from.

Mélyvár.

So am I, I said

Really? What a coincidence.

So that's why you seemed familiar.

Now that you mention it, so do you. Which school did you attend?

The vocational training school, I said.

Well, then it's not from there, she said. But by then I knew. By then I saw the park as if it were yesterday, the boxwoods, the white gravel on the straight path to the war memorial. There stood that poor Soviet soldier, poised to attack, his bayonet pointing at the elementary school. Once Gábriel and the others flung my coat on the tip. I couldn't reach it and had to ask the janitor for the broom, but I couldn't reach it even then. I ended up throwing the broom repeatedly, like a lance, while the Gypsies guffawed at the sight. But that was before Peasant Katika visited our school. Later I waited for her day after day, and meanwhile I watched the boys baiting this girl and her two friends. Everybody baited them or, at least, those who dared, especially this woman, who was now sitting across from me, her hair blond from a bottle, in a khaki dress that stopped short above the knee, whose top and bottom buttons she forgot to close. I watched her face become indistinct through the ground glass as I pulled back the lens on purpose, until her face became one big blur. Then I adjusted the focus. Wet your lips a bit, I said from under the black cloth, and grinning, she licked her lips all around, and she had no idea that her lips had said Doggie to me for the first time in my life.

Another client was already waiting his turn. She gave me her name in parting. Her fingernails were painted, as well as her toenails. I said that if she comes to pick up the picture just before we close, we could go somewhere for coffee. She said, fine. The other client, fortyish, turned his head after Kata Bárdos and didn't take his eyes off her until she disappeared through the door. Which unsettled me.

When Reisz came out of the lab for the negatives, he said that he listened to Éva's Chopin recording again the day before, and I should convey his congratulations to her. It stood the test of time. I knew he was lying. I doubted that he'd listened to her Chopin more than once, if that, since the recording came out two years ago. Also, he listened to nothing but Bach. So why would he come with such blatant nonsense? I haven't cheated on Éva till now, nor will I in the future.

At night I looked at Éva and counted the breaths she took. She'd been quite put out when she came back from Sopron. I asked what happened. She said, nothing. If I'd made notches, like prisoners, to indicate these conversations, the walls of both rooms would be covered with them.

Then I thought that I'd take this Kata up to the top of Elizabeth Bridge, let her lead the way, because it's safer that way. At the printer's Karcsi once said that you can't make it with girls, not with a camera the size of a wardrobe. Well, Karcsi, this camera here happens to be bigger than the one at Reisz's, but I'm going to make it with her anyway, the likes of which you'd never imagine, not in a lifetime. What's more, it's not borrowed, it's my own. It was a present from my wife. Also, there'll be three of us, because the bridge guard has to be on the scene. What about that, Karcsi? You think she'll discard her panties for my camera like the virgins and wives do for yours? Because this Kata is neither a virgin nor a wife, that's for sure. Most probably, she had already lost her virginity when I was still Peasant Katika's Doggie. Katika and Kata. Not bad, Karcsi. I'll put that in my diary. And I'll be sure to add my wife, so she won't take offense. Get her gander up. Or grow suspicious. And while we're at it, we'll make a list, from Peasant Katika to Éva Zárai. One, two, buckle my shoe. I bet you have a list yourself, Karcsi. It's nothing to be ashamed of. On the other hand, it's a bit of a challenge, keeping your priorities straight. If, for instance, I take Kata Bárdos up inside the pylon and fuck her so hard that the Elizabeth Bridge collapses and they'll have to build a new one, she still can't be on the same list as Peasant Katika, who looked me steadily in the eye while she swallowed the map of Tarkövesd. That's the trouble with lists, Karcsi. The considerations they go by are either too wide or too narrow. That woman with the lemon who drew a red circle around me with her lipstick, I can't very well put her on the same list as the one who stuffed a red rag in her mouth. On the other hand, with other considerations in mind, they belong on the same list. On the other hand, Dalma Keresztes and Sára Rónai don't belong on the same list. For one thing, Sára Rónai was my father's girlfriend. And Köszegi's as well. What have you got to say to that, Karcsi? From another angle, though, they're the same. However, it's even more complicated than that, because if I include the Éva Zárai whose lungs are filled with nothing with every breath she takes, if I include her, I will need another list for the Éva Zárai who screamed so loud atop this piano, that I couldn't hear it any more. And yet, seen from another angle, if another consideration comes into play, they're very much the same. For one thing, neither of them wrote a single word in her diary about me. Now do you see the problem with lists, Karcsi? Do you? Of course, I could take Kata Bárdos up the pylon regardless. Except, I couldn't arrange it. Only Éva or Nóra can arrange such things. Did you know that the pylon of a bridge is a military target? Did you, Karcsi? That Elizabeth bridges are military targets even when they're not being blown up? It'd be wiser to take Kata, Katácska out to the park, to the old Palace of Arts. For one thing, it's much closer to Reisz's place. I might ask Éva along. Provided she's not busy buying a dress adorned with French lilies. She'll sit down on the tree stump and watch. I once watched her fuck her ex-husband,

480

now she'll watch her ex-husband fuck Kata. Generally, it's as simple as that. And don't you come telling me, Karcsi, that with someone from Mélyvár it's too banal, because, for your information, Karcsi, this is too banal with anyone at any time. This is what my mother taught me. She said, Son, never listen to Karcsi. Never. And how right she was. Had I listened to you, I'd be taking pictures with a shitty Rolleiflex, and not with the Elizabeth Bridge. Though who knows? You might be better off, Karcsi. You're more mobile. With this hole-camera that's higher than Pest, I keep seeing the same thing. Of course, I pretty much see the same thing with a proper camera. And also, the same way. That's what they call style. Did you know, Karcsi, that this 'same way' is the same thing as style? Because, for instance, when I take a picture for an ID, let's admit it, that's a pile of shit. No backdrop, no lighting. No face. But if I were to fill up the Palace of Arts with all the ID photos I've ever taken, and I could, believe me, that'd be style! And we're right back at the Palace of Arts! If only I knew why I can't imagine to the end me pressing Kata Báros against the wall and doing a number on her. Why do you think that is, Karcsi? I bet you know. Stuff like this you know a lot better than me.

(Kata Bárdos)

The following day, Kata Bárdos came to pick up her pictures half an hour before closing time. Instead of her slightly wrinkled khaki dress, she was now in white. The kind of white that blinds you. Up until then, I'd seen white like this only when I looked into the spotlight. Or when I filed hammers. She asked if we're going for coffee. I said, yes. Reisz said that the workday wasn't over. I said I'd make up for it later.

We headed for the park. I never felt so light in all my life. Not light as in nothing, just light. I asked a flap-eared black dog if he thinks I can bark like a dog, more or less, or am I talking total nonsense when I bark. Kata Bárdos laughed. And I said that a dog like that would suit her. Black and white. She said she knows, except they're so much trouble. Piddle and poop, and cooking stinky meat every day. And I said, that's true. When we reached the old Palace of Arts, I decided to go someplace else. I said I know a pub on Hermina Road. She asked if I was the son of the teacher who was put in jail. I said, of course. But he's out, isn't he? He's been out for ages. In fact, he's dead. Oh, she's so sorry to hear that.

I asked if she remembers little Doggie. What Doggie? The one who tried to get into Peasant Katika's good graces. No. She only remembers Peasant Katika. Why? What's with Doggie? Nothing. I just asked. What about Katika? Does she know anything about her? Sure. Everybody does. She went to work at the dairy plant where her mother worked, then on a sudden impulse, drowned herself in a tank of milk. It happens, I said. Well, she doesn't get such things. You gotta be soft in the head. She had a really nice boyfriend, then she went off the deep end, poor thing. It's been ten years, and he's still telling everybody that it wasn't his fault. In that case, I'm sure it wasn't, I said, and stood up with our two empty glasses. Bring me something hard as well, she said. It'll be worth it, she said, a bit of wind in my sails. Then, just like in the studio the day before, she grinned and licked her lips all around. Fine, I said. In that case, I'll have one too.

It was as stifling hot in that pub as it must be in hell, and that probably also tipped the scales. While the woman at the bar poured us two more spritzers, I drew a map of Tarkövesd on the wet tin countertop. Meanwhile, I threw back one of the spritzers and asked for another. Kata Bárdos was sitting with her back to me. Because of the sweat, her white rayon dress clung to her like a second skin. I threw back the hard liqueur I'd ordered for her as well. And I thought that once I'm back at the table, I'll be barking like a dog. Nonstop.

I waited while she applied her lipstick in her small pocket mirror, then I waited while she lit another cigarette. The woman at the bar asked if I'd be wanting anything else, or what? I picked up the two glasses and went back to our table.

Listen, Kata, I have a wife.

That's all right, Doggie. I figured as much.

(the child)

If only something had happened. An abortion. An occasional lover. Anything. Some canker in the heart. But there was nothing. We weren't unhappy. Nor completely happy either, for that matter. But who is happy? If we can't live without the other, it makes no difference if we're happy or not, no? There's no light in which we don't cast a shadow, no? Even in steady dispersed light, the shadow is there under our feet, no? At the bottom of every life, there throbs a curse of some sort. Who has been happy here, lock, stock, and barrel? Not my mother, not my father. No one. It's simply the way it is. Why can't someone understand this and accept it? What the fuck is someone expecting of America? What's there? What's so damn important about America to make us leave the other person for it? I'll tell you. Nothing. Except for those ten thousand kilometers, nothing. That's all it's got going for it, those ten thousand kilometers. The same thing that compels people, when they've grown tired of it, to take a dog a good distance into the woods. So it'll never find its way back home.

The night before, she said they're showing *The Silence* at the Kinizsi and she wants to see it. I told her to go by herself. She knew perfectly well I'd say that. Seeing that film twice was more than enough for me. Especially the second time. The way that woman laughs until she cries. And the way that man looks at her. That pitying, contemptuous look, you see it for two seconds, if that, but I don't want to see it again. I don't care that I, of all people, should have a more nuanced opinion of that damned film. I hate that boy, the way he washes his mother's back. The way he looks at the rising sun from the train. The way he keeps wiping his eyes. An innocent little shit who in twenty years will fling his arms apart and say it's not his fault.

(Éva leaves)

I'm leaving tomorrow, she said.

A concert appearance? I asked.

No.

You're going to see your mother?

No.

The silence in that fucking kitchen was so dense, you could cut it with a knife.

Well, then, where are you going?

She said nothing. Then after a while, she broke her silence.

To America, she said.

I knew exactly what she meant, but I asked nevertheless.

Alone? Tomorrow?

Yes. I just got my visa.

You live here with me and I don't know you're applying for a visa?

I am not living with you. I live alone. And so do you.

That's because you said you can't live with anyone.

That was seven years ago.

Well, then, why didn't you say something in the next six years? Or five? How was I to know that what you once said was no longer valid?

Don't fight. I don't want to fight. What for?

A fly was circling above the table, then it landed on the soft-boiled egg.

You're not leaving, I said.

I'm all packed. I'm leaving. And I'm not coming back.

You got someone in America?

She said nothing.

No.

That's not true.

I just told you, no.

485

You're not leaving. I'm going to report you. Have you taken off the plane.

She got up and went to get the salt. On her way back, she stroked my forehead.

You'd never report me. Nor anyone else.

Meanwhile I thought that there were just as many flies when my mother died.

When did you decide?

I don't know. Probably when I was a child.

Forget it. If you spared me the details for seven years, this is no time to start. Here, by my side, in our bed. When did you decide?

I didn't decide in our bed.

Well, then? I asked.

She said nothing.

I can't live together with your pictures.

My pictures? My pictures of you?

Of me. And the others.

I never slept with any of them, and you know that.

That's not the point.

Yes, it is.

No, it isn't. That's not why I'm leaving.

You once said you'll leave me only if I stop taking pictures.

Let's not quibble over who said what at one time. It's history.

I wouldn't mind if we did. I'd say the same thing now that I said in the past.

I know. Maybe that's the problem.

That what I said seven years ago still stands today? Is that your problem?

Yes, perhaps. That nothing has changed, except that in the meantime I've grown old.

You're not old. And besides, what should have changed? What? I said we should get married. You didn't want to move in with me, you didn't want to marry me, you didn't want children. And now you're leaving me because you miss what you pointedly didn't want?

That's not why I'm leaving.

In that case, what didn't I give you? I think I have a right to know.

There's nothing for you to know. You gave me everything you possibly could, and I gave you everything I possibly could. So don't call me to account.

I shouldn't call you to account for leaving me?

She said nothing.

Who are you going to?

I told you. Nobody.

That's not true.

That conductor.

The one whom you didn't go see in his hotel room?

Yes. Him.

Because you couldn't have lied to your husband? But it's all right, lying to me?

Please stop. I'm not going to him. He just sent me the invitation I needed to apply for my visa.

I'll kill you. I have nothing to lose. And I'll kill him, too.

Don't kill me. I must go.

You must? You must leave me? You call that 'must'?

It's not you I'm leaving.

Well, then, who?

Everyone. My mother. The piano. Everything.

The piano.

Yes.

You said you would never give up the piano for anyone's sake.

I've changed my mind.

You'll be left with nothing. You'll go crazy.

I won't go crazy.

So what are you planning to do in America?

I think I was already crying when I asked.

I don't know, she said in earnest. Obviously, I won't clean houses.

Obviously.

Don't be mean.

Why didn't you write about me, ever?

She looked me steadily in the eye. Did you go up to the apartment?

Yes.

How can you be so contemptible? Not that it matters.

It does. Why didn't you write a damn word about me, ever?

Because a life can't accommodate two realities.

I'm the reality. I'm at least as real as your mother. Or the piano.

Yes. By now, you are.

But you don't want it anymore?

She said nothing.

You wouldn't leave a dog here.

I don't have a dog.

How can you be so contemptible?

I'm not contemptible.

I wish you'd die.

I know.

(the letter)

When she left, she took my pictures with her. Mostly the negatives, though also some enlargements. Not everything, just the ones she selected out. I didn't notice for weeks. She left most of the pictures of her behind. Probably so I'd have something to remember her by.

She asked me to see her to the airport. She said that her plane was leaving in the evening, she was transferring in Paris, but I should go to work now, she'd like to be alone while she's packing, she's already gathered up her things in the other apartment, she'll call a cab and bring them over in the afternoon.

Reisz asked what happened. I said, nothing. He said, go home. I knew that Éva wouldn't like it. I went to the park and sat on a bench. Then I walked to the Circus. I thought that we should have come here once. And also the Zoo, and the Amusement Park. That nothing bad could happen to a person if they visit the Amusement Park. And when she comes back in the evening, I'll tell her that we'll visit the Amusement Park one day.

A child of about seven or eight years of age was learning to fly by the tree stump where I had sat at one time. He climbed up, spread his arms, and jumped. Then he started all over again. His mother called to him once to be careful and not get his pants dirty. I thought that this child must have been born around the time that I watched Éva in the embrace of a stranger from this same tree stump. And also, that if she were to leave in earnest, I'd know. And that if she fell in love with someone, that wouldn't last more than a couple or months. Possibly, a year or two. But for a lifetime, we love only one person. If she were not coming back, I'd know that, too. I'd have known the first time I lay eyes on her. This calmed me.

I went home only when I was supposed to finish at Reisz's. At Lövölde Square I asked a cab driver to come to 8 Szív Street in half an hour. By the time I walked through the door, she must have been flying over Vienna. My father's key lay on the table, and next to it a slip of paper: I loved you very much.

(the strings)

The first couple of hours were okay. I thought of calling Kornél, but then decided against it. What for? I did the dishes. I opened the wardrobe. Only a couple of hangers were empty. The coats were still there, and under them, the shoes. I took a picture of everything. They were very good pictures, the shoes under the coats, as if they were standing flat up against the wall in the hall, and yet, not. I looked inside the mahogany box with the stereoscope viewer, to see her lying doubled up behind my wrist watch, like at the start of a race, when the referee starts the stop watch, when someone starts to dream. I saw only the milky whiteness. She'd removed the two pictures from it. I started to cry, but I knew that it was only natural. I thought of breaking the viewer. Then I thought I'd put my grandmother's picture back in it. But it was not mine anymore. It's been hers for the past seven years, even if she couldn't take it with her. I have no right to break it.

I sat on the bed and took stock of everything. My mother's mirror is no longer just mine, the small writing desk, the table, my father's cane. The piano is no longer just mine, though she hardly played on it. And she didn't teach me to play, though she said she would. Or read scores. I kept all my promises. Each and every one of them. I didn't hit her. I didn't beat her. I didn't drink. I didn't cheat on her. During the past seven years, I yelled at her three times. Or four. Whatever. Others yell at each other on a daily basis. I hear what goes on here, in our building, and not just with the Gypsies, but all the tenants. They're all shouting and screaming. But me, just four times in seven years. Also, I didn't lie. And I didn't keep anything back from her, except for that one time, when Adél Selyem opened the door for us, because that's what the situation called for. But if she had asked, I'd have told her. I didn't make a habit of lying.

I took one of her dresses out of the wardrobe. Not just any dress, but the American dress that I washed when she asked how long she could stay. Be that as it may, I took that dress out of the wardrobe and placed it on the bed next to me. Then I thought, I'm being ridiculous. It's something kids do with the handkerchiefs of poor Imolkas who end up hanging themselves. I was thinking that we'd never been to Mélyvár, not once, just as I hadn't been to Sopron, and that in seven years, I hadn't been in her apartment anywhere near seven times. To the left the books, to the right the suitcases with her clothes, in the middle that damned mattress, as if she didn't own anything. Like squatters.

It was too late to call Kornél. I stood up, went to the pantry, and grabbed the pliers. I opened the top of the Bösendorfer, and one by one, removed the strings. In some places the keys gave way, others I had to cut. I rolled them up, wrapped them in newspaper, and placed the whole bunch in the wardrobe, among her dresses. Now try to play, András Szabad.

(the conversation with Nóra)

I got the Sopron address from Nóra.

I hope you know what you're doing, she said when she handed me the slip. I understand you, except you should really learn that we *can* live without the other.

I wouldn't like to learn that, I said.

We were sitting in the same café where Éva introduced us seven years ago. I asked if she had any idea where Éva was. I've gotten nothing from her, no call, no letter.

Ask her brother. I'm sure he knows, she said. He knows everything.

I could feel that fucking café sinking under my feet, along with its plastic flowers, along with Nóra, along with everything. Just like when I found my mother in our living room.

What brother are you talking about?

Oh, this is going to be interesting, she said and exhaled her cigarette.

What brother, I asked again.

What brother, what brother. Her brother. Their mother's firstborn, the psychological cripple. There's a psychological cripple in every family. Haven't you heard?

No. Our family didn't have any.

If you say so.

I say so. Does her brother live here in Pest?

No. Of course not. He lives in the yellow house.

What yellow house?

The yellow house where your loving mother waits for you day after day, and dies of grief if you don't go home to do her bidding at least once a month. My friend has led you down the wrong path, I see. Hasn't she mentioned Ádám to you?

She hasn't led me down the wrong path, but she's never mentioned him. There must be something you don't talk about either.

She gave me a steady look.

You mean my father? I'll tell anyone for the asking.

That's not what I meant.

Sure you did. Believe me. A father fucking you a couple of times is preferable to a mother keeping you in chains at the age of sixteen. Like Éva.

They keep all sixteen-year-old girls in chains.

In dog chains? Fixed to your neck with a padlock every night while your brother holds you down so your mother can check if you're still a virgin? I hardly think so.

I said nothing. I don't believe you, I said at length.

That's your problem, she said.

She loves her mother.

Did I say she doesn't love her? They're the only people she loves even more than you.

I look at the street through the nylon curtains, all the people heading somewhere.

Who else knows about it?

She said nothing.

Who?

The person because of whom she became a chained dog. Her ex-husband.

I went to the men's room and threw up. The cleaning lady was wiping a mirror by the door with toilet paper. Someone had written on it with lipstick: I love you just the same.

Are you all right, Nóra asked when I sat down again.

I'm fine.

I ordered this for you, she said, and pushed a glass of cognac over to me.

I don't want it.

Go ahead, drink it.

I gulped it down.

She told me that her father died of a heart attack. Is that true?

Yes. Except, it makes no difference. They never exchanged more than ten sentences between them all her life. Her husband was her first father.

I wasn't her father.

I know that. János brought her up, and by your side, she could have been a mother at last. And now someone else is going to get her pregnant. Or else, bury her. That's the way it is. Though I bet it's the latter. In my opinion, you were the only one who could have gotten her pregnant.

She didn't want a child, I said.

And you believed her? You know, sometimes it's very comfortable, believing someone. There was a piece of lint on her turtleneck. I couldn't take my eyes off it. I was thinking that it should be removed.

Why do you think I don't have children? she asked.

I don't know.

Sure you do.

Because of your father?

Don't make me laugh. What's a poor, half-drunk prick compared to a mother who scrubs everything sparkling clean, then irons it to perfection, and all the time pretends she doesn't see her husband's spunk on her daughter's sheets. Anything to keep the family peace intact.

I said nothing.

And believe me, my mother was a saint just the same. So don't tell me that Éva had nothing to fear. If a woman whose husband loves her, who gets whatever she desires, who is served up the Music Academy on a silver platter along with a hundred and twenty square meter apartment in Buda nevertheless decides to have an abortion, she has good reason, you can be sure of that.

She never told me this either.

What was she supposed to say? Look, my dear, motherhood terrifies me so much, that I preferred an abortion? That I even left my husband? I doubt that this is the usual subject of conversation between two people when they fuck.

Our lives were not about fucking.

But if there's nothing between two rounds, then that's exactly what it's about. I live the same way. I should know.

You may live that way, but we don't.

You're right. The two of you don't live any which way anymore.

I said nothing.

I've never met a woman as cold as you, I said.

She knocked her cigarette against the table, then lit it.

You fucked my one and only friend for seven years, András, and she left. My problem is not that you don't even know her name, you shit, but that she's gone. Don't expect me to love you.

495

I said nothing.

But never mind. You can put your mind at ease. She didn't leave because of you. You're the only person who could have kept her here. She really loved you.

If she loved me, why didn't she tell me anything?

Because by János's side, she learned that it leads to no good if a man knows everything about her.

Still, there's a lot of room between everything and nothing.

Maybe for you. But not for her. She's stuck with the nothing.

Still, she could have told me that she has a brother.

It seems that she thought it best if her family didn't pass judgment on your lives.

The worst possible judgment would have been better than this.

Are you sure? Her marriage collapsed under the weight of their judgment after just a week, and after that, she and János were in the middle of a divorce for the next ten years.

She was no longer a child when I met her.

Meaning?

She was a grown woman. They couldn't interfere any more.

Listen, András. Your own mother's been dead for more than twenty years, and she still interferes whenever the fancy takes her.

(the dog chain)

One of the best-known pictures I have ever taken shows an old woman sitting by the kitchen table. Her son is standing by her side. He's in his pajamas and is holding a fork. His hair has turned gray, and his face is covered with stubble. He is probably feeding his mother. Both are looking straight into the view finder.

Some people say that the two characters are posing. That I made it up and took the picture in the studio, like so many of my other pictures. Some people say that's out of the question, because they're looking into the camera as if they'd been caught sinning. Some people say that they're simply mad. There's no question about the old woman, but by all odds, so is the man. He's holding the fork in his right hand at chest level, and the light of a lamp is reflected off of it. Behind them, nothing but the bare wall. Above them, on the wall, the clock says eight minutes to twelve. Many people think it's nearly midnight. Because of the pajamas and the lights, the assumption is no doubt valid.

My train pulled into Sopron at eleven forty in the morning.

I wasn't familiar with the city. I gave the taxi driver the address. He stopped in front of a yellow, single-storey house. The acacias had nearly covered the four windows. I told the driver to wait. The garden gate was open. In the back of the narrow, stone-paved garden stood a dog house. It was empty, and its roof had caved in. A wire was stretched out between the back of the dog house and the left firewall. There was a dog chain hanging from it. When the dog was alive, it must have rutted on the five or six meters of space between the two walls.

I didn't want to ring the bell. I wanted to see them just as they were at that moment. I'd decided this earlier on the train. The porch door was locked. One of the glass panes to the right was broken, the shards were still attached to the frame. I hesitated at the top of the steps. I was afraid. But then I reached inside between the broken pieces of glass and felt for the lock. I had no idea what I'd say.

The piano on which Éva must have learned to play stood on the porch, and on top of it, a rolled up rug. On top of the keyboard, some winter apples. I took a picture. The house exuded the smell of mothballs. When I walked into the kitchen, the man was feeding the old woman. I said, I'm going to kill you.

The old woman looked blankly at me. The man raised the fork. I said, don't move, or both of you are as good as dead.

    There's no money in the house, the old woman said.

    Calm down, Mother, he's not after the money, the man said.

    What does he want then? the old woman said.

    He's the photographer. The knight in shining armor.

The bitter, desperate helplessness I felt nearly suffocated me. Then I said, you will never die. Never. I swear. Then I took the picture, turned around, and left. Out on the porch I could still hear the mother shouting, get out of here, and her brother, laughing his head off. Once I was back in the cab, my tears began to flow.

(the negatives)

After Éva left, I freaked out. Actually, I freaked out on the train back from Sopron. A man came into the compartment. He felt like talking. He asked where I was from, what I do for a living, stuff like that. The sort of things people generally ask on a train. He was around sixty. He wore a moustache and had two suitcases with him. The pocket of his plaid shirt was full of ballpoint pens. I thought that it would be better for me, too, if I spoke with someone, so I launched into it. I told him that I've just been to my wife's mother's house and that it was the first time I'd ever seen her. Then I told him everything, from the brother she kept a secret from me for seven years, down to the dog chain. As I was telling him that Éva had left the country, the man excused himself and said he had to go to the toilet, and I didn't see him again until we pulled into Keleti Station and he came to collect his suitcases.

After that, I said all sorts of things to all sorts of people. About Mélyvár, my mother and Éva. I told no lies, I stuck to the truth. That's probably why neither Kornél nor Reisz caught on to my state of mind. After all, if I mentioned anything to them, it seemed very much in place. For instance, that in '56, my father could have left the country, if he hadn't been an abject coward. He held up the Russian tanks with soup plates instead, preferring to spend three years in jail. But when I told the cashier at the Keleti Station cafeteria the same thing, she said that if I knew what's good for me, I should button my lips, and I agreed, but that's how it was all the same.

Then on Boráros Square I told the waitress about Adler, though without going into detail, namely, that at one time, a German colonel had shot himself through the mouth in our house, and I think it was actually because of my mother, because that's what love is like, and that I can get on pretty well by myself without my mother and my father, but without Éva, it was a lot more difficult, she told me to calm down, it would pass, and I told her it would never pass. She laughed. Well, that was my problem, she told me. She

499

would never shoot herself through the mouth for anybody's sake.

At the Hunyadi Square market, one of the vendors asked what happened to the beautiful woman she always saw me with. And I said, she's in America, and I removed the strings from her piano, and as soon as I find out where she lives, I'm going to send the whole lot to her, so her heart will break, just like my mother's.

I don't know what came over me. It lasted as long as I had nothing to hold on to. Then one afternoon about three weeks later, I decided to cover the piano with her pictures. That's when I realized that she'd taken the negatives, and from that moment on, I knew that even if she doesn't write, even if she doesn't send so much as a postcard, even if she's with that conductor or anyone else just now, she had not left me, nor would she, ever.

And then I found my peace of mind.

(the letter)

During the Cold War, the United States Gold Reserve at Fort Knox, Kentucky, next to the army base, was guarding a crate with the label: *Radioactive UFO*. They'd been guarding it for twenty-seven years. The soldiers guarding it held it in as much awe as any guards would hold extra-terrestrials, the Ark of the Covenant, or the Holy Grail, though I doubt that the American army was in possession of the Ark of the Covenant. Or the Holy Grail. Even they couldn't have been that lucky. Though who knows. But this particular crate existed, and I had this radioactive UFO to thank for, among other things, being called into room three-hundred-something-or-other of the Ministry of the Interior in the fall of '75.

I hadn't heard from Éva for six months when the mailman brought me a letter from America. I was afraid to open it. I'd been waiting for that stupid piece of mail from Éva for so long, that when I held it in my hand, I stood like a post. The mailman asked if I got bad news. I said, no. I signed the receipt and tipped him. Then I closed the door. I took the letter to my room and first placed it on the table, then on the bed. I thought that in seven years, the crack on the ceiling had grown twice as big as when I had told her everything, from Imolka to my father.

Then I got up and went to the piano. I played a couple of chords, but there was no sound. I forgot that I'd removed the strings. I closed the lid, grabbed the Leica, and left the apartment. To the right the Castle, to the left Parliament, behind me a passing tram, under me the bridge, reverberating with its load.

I had waited for that letter as if that damned envelope from across the seas contained my whole life. I walked toward Fő Street. The lights were on. Someone must have moved in. Then I came back to Pest over the Elizabeth Bridge. I don't know what I was expecting from that letter. After all, I knew that Éva would never return. She couldn't have, even if she'd wanted to. Not in those days. It was past midnight by the time I got home. I sat down by the desk, picked up the letter opener, and opened it. It was an official letter, written in English. I couldn't make out a single word. Not that I cared.

I got into the shower. For some reason, the boiler wasn't working. Then I found the dictionary from which I'd learned a few words with my mother, and by morning I understood that this was an official letter from the Broch Gallery in New York to the Hungarian authorities saying that they would arrange for my accommodations, pay my travel expenses, and would like to invite me to attend my exhibition. At the time, I thought I'd stay for good.

(the Holy Crown)

They wouldn't let me go for the opening. I don't think that they had any particular reason. I think it was just routine. Most probably, my application got stuck at the lowest levels of the passport hierarchy – at such a low level, just like me, they couldn't have known yet about the radioactive UFO at Fort Knox.

The truth is, it took nearly three years until Jimmy Carter, the new American president, put an end to the bumpy negotiations, and decided that it was time to open the crate. I bet that the men at the army base must have been pretty disappointed when it turned out that the Holy Crown of Hungary was neither radioactive, nor could it fly. Though, come to think of it, this must have been a disappointment for quite a number of Hungarians as well.

In short, it took nearly three years from the time I received that letter of invitation for János Kádár to admit that it'd be judicious for him to make certain gestures toward the Hungarian emigrants and the expectations of the White House. He also admitted that he had no business being near the Holy Crown when the US returned it to us. For one thing, he's not the king, just the General Secretary of the Party which, if nothing else, he admitted in the end after all. And for another, if four hundred people, more or less, are considered a crowd, then considering the executions following '56, he is, simply put, a mass murderer. Which he never admitted. But he knew it.

In short, he admitted that it would be wiser for him to be called away on urgent business and not be in the House of Parliament when the crown was delivered. By all odds, he accepted this condition because he never suspected that ten years later pretty, young girls would be doing a survey among the population, asking which should be the new Hungarian coat-of-arms, the Kossuth, or the one with the crown. As I said, in '75, when the lowest echelons of the passport office rejected my passport application, neither János

Kádár nor I would have thought that on January 6, 1978, when the Holy Crown would be brought back home from Fort Knox, he wouldn't be in the House of Parliament, but I would.

Actually, all that happened was this. Aaron Broch, one of the few people who formed the artistic taste of New York's upper classes, happened to say in front of a couple of journalists that he thought it peculiar that Kádár had set his sights on the Holy Crown, but wouldn't let the best Hungarian artists out of the country to attend their own exhibition openings.

This sentence was not Éva's idea, nor the conductor's, but Aaron Broch's, who grew up in a world where he learned that in certain situations it was more prudent not to appeal to the truth, value, or freedom, but to personal or political interests. In face of any one truth, there's always another. My truth is here with me, his is with him, and neither of us is interested in the other's.

Keep this in mind, dear Éva, no one is ever interested in your truth. Truth is not negotiable. Give me a piece of bread because I'm right, there's no such thing. So let's see what we have that Kádár's been after for years. But it's also important that it shouldn't be on center stage in Hungary at the moment. It should have no news value there, so you won't have to launch into explanations back home should the subject come up here. The other thing you must learn here, dear Éva, is that there's something that even the atomic bomb can't destroy. And that is defiance. The cancer at the heart of pride. In short, we must appeal to self-interest and self-esteem, while keeping defiance at bay. And it's all right to spring a surprise on the other party, if we spring something on them they wouldn't have dreamt of in a thousand years, because there's no reason they should have. After all, what we want and what we say have nothing in common.

What in your opinion is the last thing that your photographer friend has nothing to do with? All right. It's time we had a look at what's inside that crate in Kentucky.

(the passport)

They showed up at Reisz's studio. Actually, this is what worried me the most. That they came straight to Reisz instead of Szív Street, as if it made a difference, as if it weren't absolutely evident that they knew where I'd be at ten o'clock in the morning. The man was reserved, but not threatening. Official. He must have been the same age as me. He waited patiently for me to finish in the lab. He apologized to Reisz for the inconvenience. He said that we just needed to clarify a misunderstanding at the passport office.

In the car on the way to the Interior Ministry, all I could think of was that I had no way of proving that Éva had taken my pictures without my knowledge. And also, that if my father could survive the three years, then so could I, though that's not strictly correct. That's what I was thinking, but there was no trace of the visceral fear that I had felt fifteen years before, when I spotted that car in front of our house. This was a feeling more akin to what a person feels with respect to the Almighty, and which has nothing in common with the abject fear you feel when they take you for interrogation or to the scaffold.

In room three-hundred whatever, Comrade Varjas was already waiting to receive me. His voice, his clothes, his shirt, unbuttoned at the collar, the cheap coffee cup and the slightly awry calendar hanging on the wall, the cheap aluminum handle on the door, and the picture of two adolescent boys under the glass table top, were all meant to indicate that Comrade Varjas is just like you or me, that this whole thing was as little to his liking as it is to mine, that we eat the same Hungarian bread kneaded from the same Hungarian wheat, and that after working hours, we teach our children to be fair and square the same way, except now it's working hours.

We shook hands. He asked if I'd like some coffee. Then he said that it was a shame that my papers got lost somewhere and my letter of invitation had just been retrieved from a lower department. But this is an important exhibition, was it not, in an important place, was it not? One that the Hungarian People's Republic should also be proud of, was it not so? In short, the passport office is dutybound to correct this unfortunate mishap.

I knew exactly what they wanted. They now wanted from me what Kornél feared without real cause they'd wanted from him years before.
    And what if I don't come back, I asked.
    We'll take the risk. But I don't think you'll stay in America, he said.
    Why not?
    It's just a hunch. Why would you? Why would it be better for you in America?
    My wife is there.
    He laughed. Are you referring to your former companion?
His laughter held no trace of cynicism, but rather, the cheapest sort of pity, the pity that one man feels for another who is caught talking nonsense. It took all my self-control to stop me from grabbing him by the neck and pressing his head to the glass table top until he agreed to tell me everything he knew about Éva.
    You need to sign here, he said.
    I said nothing.
    And what do you want from me in return? What are the concomitants, if I sign?
    His manner, when he spoke, was as artless as if we'd been discussing the weather.
    We are not planning to enlist you as an agent, if that's what you mean.
    What's the guarantee?
    There's no guarantee for such things, he said as he offered me the pen.
I took the passport and signed the receipt.
    Au revoir, he said. Until we meet again.
I detected no trace of a threat in his voice.

I told Reisz that I'd be going away in a week.
    Where to?
    America.
    He screamed with laughter.
    What's so funny? I asked.

506

And he said, what luck that I compiled a list.

A list of what?

A list of how much paper and chemicals and film you stole in the past ten years. And now it's time you paid me back.

Some other time, I said. Right now I need to buy a proper suit.

(the game)

I didn't mention it before because I didn't think it was important, but somebody's playing games with me. It started about a week ago, more or less, at the time I went to the stationer's and bought this new notebook. It may even have been a bit before. I don't remember any more.

I'm the only tenant left here on the fourth floor. The apartment opposite has been empty for years. Her daughter put the old woman in an institution, but they can't see eye to eye about the future of the studio. One of the daughters said I should buy it, and for a while I considered it, I thought I could use it to store stuff, but in the end, the other daughter vetoed the idea. Which is just as well. It would have made sense only while Éva and I were living together.

In short, except for me, no one comes up to the fourth floor over the main staircase. Then about a week ago, someone placed an apple on the windowsill at one of the landings. As I was coming upstairs, the light fell directly on it through the cathedral glass, so I picked it up and brought it home and put it on the table. I don't know why. The next day, there was another apple on the windowsill. I left that one there.

Kornél denied having put it there.

(the departure)

The day before my departure, I went to the Otthon department store and bought an iron. I ironed my shirts. I thought that I was no longer who I used to be, that I'd gone bad inside, that even when Father died, there was no doubt some purity in me, but it has since disappeared without a trace.

When I finished packing, I went to the pantry and took down the box containing Father's photographs. I hadn't looked at his clouds since he died. I spread them out on the floor in my room. I placed them side by side until they filled up all the space. Then I placed my suitcase in the middle. I climbed on top of the Bösendorfer and took a picture. And then I thought that he never got to see clouds from above. I slept with my clothes on, so I wouldn't miss my plane in the morning.

I dreamt that I'm leaning on my elbows by the window, looking at the square below. The square is in a small town down south. In Spain, or possibly Italy. Across the way there's a cinema, and on the corner, a narrow street. Someone's standing on the street, but only his shadow is visible on the cobble stones. Then there's a long, white wall. The sun is shining on it. A man is standing, chained to the wall. He has a sack pulled over his head. In front of him stand soldiers in white uniforms. The soldiers fire, the man collapses, his head jerks forward, only the chain attached to his wrists is steadying him. I stub out a cigarette on the tin windowsill, and I'm about to close the window because I have to leave, but the man straightens up. I light another cigarette and lean on the windowsill once again, even though I should be leaving, because there's already a line in front of the movie house. They're showing the film someone compiled from my photographs. Afterwards, there's going to be a public conversation. I'm afraid. I'm not an accomplished speaker. I try to put my mind at ease by repeating what a prostitute once said, that it doesn't matter what I say. What matters is that I have a nice voice. The usher opens the door. I must be off. I shout to the firing squad downstairs to get it over with already. The officer looks up at me, as if to ask, what business is it of mine. The man in chains begins to pull and tug. He tries to shake the sack off his head. Meanwhile, he's screaming, Son!

(America)

My first time there, I saw no more of America than I'd seen of the moon landing. I was so excited to see Éva that I couldn't sleep a wink on the plane. I wasn't even interested in that crazy dream. I'd forgotten to take pictures of the clouds, whereas that's why I'd taken that picture of my father's photographs. I had planned to take a picture of the clouds on the next frame, then enlarge the both of them, uncut, on the same piece of paper.

I flew Malév to Frankfurt, but from there on in, I didn't understand a word the stewardess said. The compact dictionary that I bought before the trip I'd stuffed in my suitcase. I'd have liked to ask for water, but couldn't think of what it's called in English. I communicated my wish to the stewardess with gestures. She was kind and brought me a glass of wine. I decided that I'd rather not ask for anything else. I went to the toilet and drank from the tap. I knew it would be all right. I'd drank from the tap even on a train. From time to time I took out Éva's last letter from my wallet, then put it back. It said, I loved you very much.

When I saw her waiting for me with her husband by her side, I very nearly burst into tears. She said hello, hugged me, and kissed me on the cheek as if I were a long lost friend. Then she introduced me to her husband. He was about the same age as her first husband. He even looked a lot like him. We shook hands, and he asked about the trip. Éva translated it for me. I said thank you, it was fine. He said I shouldn't feel constrained, Éva and I could talk in Hungarian, it's all right.

In the cab, Éva said they live in Brooklyn, but that's too far from the gallery, so they made reservations for me in Manhattan. I said thank you, I understand. Then she handed me an envelope. I asked what it was. She said, a thousand dollars. I mustn't be without cash. I asked what I was supposed to do with so much money. She said that Broch had sold some of my pictures and this is the advance, we'll settle the rest tomorrow in the gallery, but now I should rest. I asked if she loved me. She didn't even hear. She said that Edward is very sick, he gets infusions every day, that's why I can't stay with them, but I'll be visiting them, that goes without saying. A lot can be packed into two weeks. I was looking out the window. We were passing over a bridge. It was ten times the size of Elizabeth Bridge, and I thought I'd kill myself. Éva said, believe me, it's difficult for me as well.

When we got to the hotel, she saw me to my room. Her husband waited downstairs in the cab. I asked why she invited me here.

Because your pictures belong here.

And me?

Come. I'll show you how the faucets work in the bathroom.

What are you doing here?

I told you. I'm looking after Edward. He's very ill.

Is that why you came here?

Yes. Here's my number. If you need anything, just call from the room. Broch is footing the bill. I must leave now. I don't want to keep Edward waiting too long. And don't hate him, because I have him to thank for you being here.

You do, or I do?

We both do.

Don't worry, I don't hate him. I didn't hate your former husband either.

I very nearly said that except for her, I'd never hated anyone, but checked myself.

That's good. But now, get some sleep. I'll pick you up in the morning.

Fine. But I'm not staying for two weeks.

Oh, yes you are.

She turned to leave, but stopped short by the door. Then without turning back she said, Ádám said you've been to Sopron.

I said nothing.

Not that it matters now, she said.

To me, everything matters, I said.

I know, she said.

I wrapped her in my arms and didn't want to let go of her, ever.

Let go of me, she said. The cab is waiting. I'll see you in the morning.

(canned soup)

It was still light outside, and I couldn't sleep. I sat by the window and smoked a couple of cigarettes. I studied the fire escapes and the water tanks on the rooftops opposite. As the sun set, the shadows of the fire escapes stretched longer and longer along the brick walls. In one of the windows, a woman was watering flowers. Seven stories down, a man was preaching about Jesus through a loudspeaker. With the help of the few dozen works in English that I knew, I tried to make out what he was saying, but the traffic noise drowned him out. I thought that in just a couple of months, I'd be thirty-three. Like Jesus. And then, that from this window I'd have never heard Éva's shoes knocking against the sidewalk. And that she'd have never looked up from this street. And that this street hasn't even got a name, just a number.

By the time it got dark, I'd smoked my last cigarette. Also, I was pretty hungry. I hadn't eaten since the plane. I thought of calling room service, but I'd have had to speak to them in English. I took everything out of my pocket, my passport, the money, my key from home, the zú, and hid them under the pillow, along with the Leica. But then I took them out and decided to hide them in the laundry basket in the bathroom. I took only fifty dollars and some matches with me. I looked out the window again. A light snow was beginning to fall. I took the stairs because I didn't have any change to give to the elevator boy. I thought how for years Kornél and I had been to the New York Café, but we never tried to imagine this city, not once. It never occurred to us that it really existed. Before I left, he said that it would probably be much like Pest was after Mélyvár. I'm not so sure. At least in Pest there's the Lenin Boulevard and there's the People's Republic Avenue and there's Szív Street. A cleaning woman passed me. She told me to use the elevator. I pretended I didn't understand.

I took a mental inventory. This was my first time abroad. What's more, on another continent. This was my first time in an airplane. The first time I'd seen the ocean, even if only from the sky. The first time staying in a hotel. The first time I didn't have a clue what people were saying around me. The first time I had so much money, at home I could live off of it for a year. My first exhibition. The list lasted to the third or fourth floor. After that nothing remained, except for Éva at the airport standing by her husband's side, looking at me. Ádám said you've been to Sopron. As if I were the most despicable man on the planet. As if I were the one to keep half my life from her. As if I were pressing a thousand dollars in her hand, here, be happy. As if I'd kept her on a dog chain.

I figured that if I kept to the block where the hotel was located, I wouldn't lose my way, and I'd find a tobacco shop and a grocery store without having to cross the street. I looked at the shop windows. Plenty of things for sale. The man preaching about Jesus left when it began to snow. Even though Kornél and I had spent an entire night pouring over a map of Manhattan, I had no idea where I was. An obese black woman was selling umbrellas in a doorway. Some people bought them. I hesitated, but the snow wasn't that heavy. Also, I didn't want to pay with a fifty-dollar bill. Not on the street.

I couldn't find a tobacco shop, but after a while I found a shop where they sold groceries. They didn't have bread, cold cuts, and the like, so I ended up buying canned soup. I figured I'd run it under the bathroom tap and warm it up. They had cigarettes by the cashier. I asked for Marlboros, because I was familiar with them. Then suddenly I felt so tired as if I hadn't slept for months. Or more like since Éva left. The man at the checkout counter said I should step aside, I'm holding up the line.

I put the canned soup in my coat pocket, then lit up in front of the shop. That's when I remembered that in all the rush, I'd left my father's photographs on the floor of my room, and when I get home at last, I'll have to start by gathering up his clouds and putting them back in the pantry. I decided that since I've gone partways, I might as well finish going around the block. Turning around is bad luck. It was snowing heavily by then, but so what? Then as I turned the corner, I came face to face with myself. I couldn't believe my eyes. I thought it must be due to fatigue. There I stood on an advertising pillar, large as life, wearing my mother's Persian lamb coat. And then my tears began to flow.

(breakfast)

In the morning, I told Éva that I've decided to stay, I don't mind if she's married. She stroked my cheek and said, but first, let's go downstairs and have some breakfast, then we'll go to the gallery. Broch is expecting us at noon. In the restaurant downstairs, gilded angels hung from the ceiling. Hundreds of them. From time to time, an angel would descend about a meter or so on an invisible string, then was pulled back up again, and then another angel would descend. I found it irritating. But then, it was almost time for Christmas. Éva asked if I'd had dinner. I said, yes. I was about to ask if this was really the most important thing on her mind right now, if I had dinner, and how the faucet works, but I checked myself and asked why she hadn't told me over the phone that she's married and would be meeting me with her husband, and that I couldn't stay with them.

I told you. You can't stay with us because Edward is ill.

Is that why you wouldn't marry me? So you wouldn't have to arrange our divorce long distance?

How can you be so contemptible?

Me?

I took her letter out of my wallet and put it on the table.

She said nothing.

How do you think I felt? How do you think I've been living since then?

I know how you've been living. I told you. It's not easy for me either.

You don't know anything. I didn't love you, I still love you.

She said nothing.

Do you love this man?

Yes.

Then what am I doing here?

She took my hand.

Edward is homosexual, dear.

I didn't ask if you sleep with him. I asked if you love him.

(the cab)

You couldn't see as much of the sky from up there as from a carriage path. Éva said not to take the subway but go everywhere by cab so I wouldn't lose my way. I said that I wasn't going anywhere without her. In the cab, I asked her why she gave up the piano.

Because I'm a good pianist, but not a good musician.

That's ridiculous.

She said nothing.

Your pictures belong here.

I removed the strings from your piano. I wanted to bring them with me, but they didn't fit in the suitcase.

That's your piano, not mine.

There's nothing left that's mine. Only the pictures were mine. You could have at least asked before you took them.

Had I asked, you wouldn't be here now.

You bet I wouldn't. I saw that fucking poster last night. Is that how things happen here? Your husband said, go ahead, do it, and I become street display?

No, that's not how things happen here. Your pictures are good, and someone realized. Someone people trust.

I don't believe you.

No one would be interested in your work just because of Edward if your pictures were not as good as they are. In fact, outstanding. There are more very gifted people here than there are half-gifted people back home. All I ask is that you listen to me. But first and foremost, listen to Broch.

I usually listen to myself first and foremost.

Fine. Listen to yourself back home. But not here.

And I felt my chest tighten, just as I did every time she sprang a sentence like this on me.

Fine. In that case, I'm going home.
Yes, I know.

(Broch)

I saw nothing from the street except the name Broch on the black glass front and the picture of me standing in my mother's Persian lamb coat on the door. The women passing the gallery wore much nicer coats.

There were no lamps inside. On the other hand, the suspended ceiling provided the gallery space with evenly dispersed sunlight. They did it with mirrors. I'd never seen anything like it. And of course, I'd never seen my pictures together like this either, displayed on snow white walls. On the other hand, most of them were not strictly mine. They were enlargements made by the gallery. I could have never made enlargements this big either at home, or at Reisz's.

How do you like it? a man behind us asked. Éva introduced us to each other.
Then I said, they're pretty good, but right away felt ashamed of myself.
In that case, he said, we're already agreed on what counts.

Broch had a limp, just like my father, except not from a dislocated hip, but from the Normandy landing. The handle of his cane was in the shape of Hitler's head.
What's this? I asked.
Éva didn't want to translate it. Broch laughed.
You Hungarians love to be shocked before you take a proper look at what you see. This is a cane. I use it to lean on. It's made of the same medical platinum as the clasps in my leg. He pulled out Hitler's face, from his eyes to his mouth, like a drawer, and held it out for me.
Have some. It's granulated sugar. My bloodsugar tends to go down. It was designed by a pragmatic friend.
Salvador Dalí, Éva added when she translated this for me.
That's good. In that case, that's very good, I said.

Éva declined to translate this as well.

And then I remembered that it was Éva and not Broch who said Salvador Dalí, that it was more important to her than I'd have thought. And that by all odds, she saw me the way she always wanted to see me only when I was displayed on an advertising pillar in New York City.

An old woman decked in diamonds came in, walked around, retraced her steps, and stopped in front of the picture of Johanna Vészi, the copy of which I tore to pieces years ago and gave to that girl from the Catholic high school.

I told Éva they should take it down. She said, that's not the way things are done here.

Broch leaned closer to Éva and said, interesting, old women seem to take a special liking to that picture.

I'd never felt so dispossessed and helpless in my life. Here I was, having to say a quiet thank you for everything that I'd like to howl about, the hotel, the thousand dollars handed to me in an envelope, the cane with Hitler's head, and Johanna Vészi. When Broch went to his office to summon his driver, Éva asked, do you know who bought your blind woman?

I don't give shit.

You're as defiant as a child.

(lunch)

In all of New York, it wasn't at the gallery but at a cheap Chinese eatery that I could feel like a full human being again. Broch said he hopes he's not disappointing me, but this is the kind of place he likes. He used to come here as a child. I said that I like it, too. He asked if I like Chinese food. And I said, I have no idea, but I'll eat just about anything, except, I wasn't hungry yet, but he should go ahead and eat. Éva didn't translate this.

He asked if I'm really satisfied with the exhibition. I said, no. Then I asked Éva in English to translate what I just said. Éva looked at me as if I'd slapped her in the face. I told her not to look at me like that. Broch asked what objections I have. I said that my pictures are all I have. I exist through them, whether they're good or bad, and the picture I took of my father may not be my best work, but it should have been included in my first exhibition.
   He said nothing.

Then I told him that the picture that the old woman liked so much I'd torn to shreds once because they asked me to, and the fact that that woman will probably never find out that she ended up on the wall of a New York gallery fifteen years later is no excuse for her photo being included in the exhibition.

Also, I know perfectly well that pictures and words are very different, I went on, but they still share certain things in common. When I speak, the meaning comes from me arranging the words in a certain order. It may well be that this exhibition is better than if I'd curated it, except for me it's as if someone had cut my sentences into pieces, then rearranged them to their liking and not mine. Every single photograph is mine, that's not my point of contention. I also admit that each one must speak for itself on its own. But now they're together, and that being the case, it would have been better had the picture of the blind woman, for instance, been hung next to the picture of my father.

Still, couldn't someone be of a different opinion? Broch asked.

Naturally, I said. Except, they must convince me.

Are you free tomorrow?

Yes.

Fine. In that case, I'll have your father enlarged, and we'll see how you'd arrange your works yourself. The photograph of the blind woman, though, I can't take down, because I've sold it.

It doesn't matter, I said. But thank you for my father.

It does matter, Broch said. It was bought by MoMA.

I didn't know who this Moma was.

He said he'd like me to hear him out. It's awkward, he said, that we can communicate only with Éva's help, but in any case, we should both be grateful to her, because without Éva, we wouldn't have met. But from now on, he went on, that's neither here nor there. If we are to work together, your private lives don't concern me. Also, you should understand that I am not a merchant. For me, profit is a means to an end. Culture. I've never sold junk, not even from the best names, and if someone is good, I won't sell their work to just anyone. You could say that my mission in life is not to whip up shit to look like chocolate mousse. I sold four of your pictures for an amount that is within the bounds of decency for a very good but as yet unknown photographer. In any case, for a year or two, you won't have financial problems back home. If we're to work together, I have a couple of conditions, though. I will to determine the number of prints. You will not exhibit your works anywhere without my consent. The gallery is entitled to fifty percent of all sales, even if the pictures are not sold directly by us. This shall be in effect until we terminate our contract, but all of your work until then shall be represented by the gallery. While you are in New York, we will edit a book to be financed by future sales. Only a couple of art journals interest me. You can publish your pictures where you like, but all future books shall be negotiated between myself and the publisher. Except for Hungary, of course. What happens in Hungary is, unfortunately, of no consequence.

And though it may seem the obvious thing to do, I have no intention of turning you into a victim of communism. That could be of interest for a year or two, but I'm not selling a photograph to a museum for the short run. If you agree to these conditions, he said, we can sign the contract tomorrow.

Naturally, I agree, I said. But what if I can't get the pictures out of Hungary?

Leave that to me, he said. The pictures as well as you will leave in the most legal way imaginable.

So I shouldn't stay here?

That's none of my business. But it doesn't seem to me that you're in any danger back home. And as far as your work is concerned, I see no reason for you to stay. For the time being, you can live off what comes in better there than here.

(the last day)

When we got out of the car and took our leave of Broch, Éva hugged me and said, I'm proud of you. I said, thank you for bringing my pictures to New York. He's a good man even if he does have an idiotic cane, and even if he never sells more than these four pictures. To the left Times Square, to the right West 43rd Street. In the middle, I wrap her in my coat and say, I don't want you to leave me ever again.

She kissed me. No. Then she breathed into my mouth, do me. We went up to my room. I was as scared as the first time. I couldn't think of anything else except her standing under the shower in the bathtub with the cracked enamel and looking into space, and me counting her birthmarks.
    Ninety-two, I said.
    What?
    That's how many birthmarks you have.
    How do you know?
    I counted them on one of the pictures after you left.

She said she had to leave so she could be back by the time the doctor got there to see her husband. I told her that I'd rather not go to their place. She said she understood, that it may be better for everyone involved. I said I understood. Though Edward didn't pose a threat, not really, I didn't want to go to their place just the same.
    I didn't leave the room until the following morning. I waited for her to come. I enjoyed sitting by the window and watching the street below. Also, I didn't want to spend my money. When she showed up, we made love. Then we went to the gallery. We put up Father's picture. Then she wanted to show me the Statue of Liberty, but I said I'd have a look some other time, let's go back to the hotel instead. She helped select the pictures for the book, and there was an interview, and she helped translate. She warned me not to say anything that could get me into trouble back home. Once we went with

Brock to the rooftop terrace of a skyscraper for some sort of reception. There were a lot of painters, writers, and musicians, mostly those for whom people stood in long lines one-hundred stories down. Without Éva's help, I couldn't talk to anyone. Also, I felt pretty awful in my suit, made by the Red October Clothing Factory back home. One of the painters with gray hair stopped in front of us for a moment and said, you've got a good face, and that fur coat is fucking perfect. Be sure to take more self-portraits. I said, fine. Éva asked if I knew who that was. I said, sure, I never could stand him, and he did nothing now to change my mind. Then I asked if we could leave.

This is what it's like, you need to learn.

You can teach me, but if we don't go back to the hotel to fuck this instant, I'll go up to that prick and slap him.

Oh, please don't. In that case, let's abscond.

In short, this is how our days were spent for an entire week. I thought that the decision had been made and I could stay there, that we'd rent a room in one of those houses with the fire escapes, and I wouldn't even care if she went home to her Edward every afternoon. I'd take a hundred self-portraits every day, if necessary, just as long as she comes home at night. I'm fine during the day, but the nights, they're like a quagmire. It's not natural for a man to fall asleep all by himself, if, instead of the beating of someone's heart, he hears the drip-drip of the faucet.

What's this? I asked.

Don't open it, she said.

When can I open it?

Back home, at Christmas.

Nothing happened. I didn't even blink an eye, I think.

At least, tell me.

You'll see.

I want to see now. I opened it. It was a watch.

Neil Armstrong went to the moon with a watch just like this one.

Thank you.

I'll give you a present only if you lie down by my side.

We must hurry, we have a very important lunch appointment.

There's plenty of time. I removed her dress. I thought of how, during the moon landing, she pushed me away in Adél Bauer's bathroom.

This is all I can give you, I said.

She wrapped herself around me like creeping vine. When she came, I felt her heart beating in my chest.

I held her down.

Be careful.

I really love you, I said.

What are you doing? Don't come inside me. I held her arms down.

Let go!

Never, you coward.

Let go, I said!

I pressed her down on that damn hotel bed, you'd think I was crucifying her.

If you're afraid, kill it, I said.

She spit in my eye.

That's the last time I saw her.

(Aczél)

After Reisz retired, I took over the shop. I kept it open so I wouldn't have to give it back to the Council, but I no longer used it to take ID pictures. My book was already out by then, and I'd had my first exhibition at home, too. I'd also been to Rome and spent a month in West Berlin. I even learned some English.

Once, over the phone, I asked Broch about Éva, but he said he has nothing to do with my private life, and he prefers it that way. The second time I went to New York, I learned that she and her husband had moved to the West Coast. After my opening, I stayed just three more days, even though this time around Broch said I should move there. And I said, what for?

At Reisz's, I dismantled the counter. I bought some lamps and bought a forty-by-fifty wood-frame enlarger for the Linhof. It was almost as big as the one at the printer's had been. I wanted it so that nothing of the lights and shades should be lost in the process of enlargement, so that the pictures would be like black and white mirrors.

I wasn't very well known at home, but that suited me just fine. Or rather, I was known just enough so that it didn't interfere with my life. But I never worked for magazines, I never took pictures for advertising campaigns, I didn't participate in group exhibitions, and so I didn't deprive anyone of their livelihood. Once they asked me to join the Association. I asked if it was mandatory. What an idea, dear András. I said, thank you, but in that case, I'd rather not. There must be those for whom this is important, and I envy them for it just a bit, because an association gives you a sense of belonging. It means you're not alone. But I wouldn't attend the meetings, I wouldn't serve on a jury to judge other people's work, I have no desire to take advantage of the free holidays, and so it wouldn't make sense for me to join. I'm satisfied with the occasional exhibitions of my work.

As you wish, dear András. But you're welcome here any time.

When I came out of the office, I immediately recognized the man sitting at one of the tables in the outer office. I had meant to ask him once, this was when only the pylon of the blown-up Elizabeth Bridge was still standing, what it took for me to become an assistant. He didn't recognize me. I am absolutely sure of that. What I mean is, he recognized me, except he didn't know that I was the man to whom he once said that if I felt the overpowering urge to hang a five-hundred dollar camera around my neck, I might as well learn proper exposure. He wore a gray sweater. He stood up when he said hello. My stomach tightened just like back then, when I wasn't even Reisz's assistant. I couldn't sleep all night. I took stock of all the possibilities, starting with going up to him and thanking him for egging me on to learn, and ending with offering him a much better job at my studio than his present job as a clerk. By the time the sun came up, I was no longer occupied with my former bitterness, but the shame at the amount of defiance, hurt, and infantile pettiness that had lain dormant in me for nearly twenty years, all because of a single sentence that a former scapegrace had said to another former scapegrace, and that it's just such bad sentences against which there's no remedy, not the passing of two decades, not the Andráses, nor a review in *The Times*, and that under the circumstances, the best I can do is to be careful and give no indication of the pettiness and bitter defiance I feel, and though I have managed not to hurt anyone with similar quips, the willingness is there inside me, just as it is inside practically us all. I finally took a sleeping pill, and never went near the Association again.

Most of us knew each other by sight, and also, there were some people who hated me at first sight every bit as much as I hated them, but then, that's how it is. Still, most of them left me in peace. And no wonder. From Biharkeresztes with its Scythian relics near the Romanian border, to Hegyeshalom with its borderguards, right by the border to Austria, I wasn't in anybody's way.

I stayed here because that's the price I paid for my freedom, and I could do so without having to take any more ID pictures. Needless to say, my freedom meant more than this, I know that. It's one thing to live deprived of something, and quite another to reject it. Had I stayed in America, before I realized what had hit me, I'd have been forced to take advantage of all the opportunities that presented themselves. I'd have had to participate. Strange as it may seem, possibly even displeasing to some, but the fact is that I was able to preserve the freedom I'd gained abroad by coming back home behind the Iron Curtain.

There was just one price I had to pay, namely, that at times they held me up in triumph, like a bloody rag, at others, like a white flag. Fortunately, I didn't have to participate in either endeavor too often. Once I met Aczél. It would have been difficult to tell if he was ordering me to see him or inviting me to see him. Comrade Deputy Minister Aczél would very much like to meet you in person. He's expecting you in his office tomorrow at two-forty-five p.m. That resembled an invitation, though dubiously so. When I put down the phone, I lit a cigarette, then called Kornél to ask him what he thinks the culture czar wants from me. He said he had no idea. Probably the same thing he wants from everyone else. I asked if he'd ever met him. He said he'd have told me about it. I was about to say that I wouldn't bet on it. He said that all told, it's better if he wants to see me than if he was bent on ignoring me. I said the latter would please me more, and if he wanted, he could go instead of me. He said nothing. I'm fed up with these silences. We'll meet afterwards, I said. Sure thing, he said. Then he added that he's only free in the evening, after the children are in bed. He called me back five minutes later and said that I shouldn't do anything that I might regret. I said, of course not. But then added, thank you. I hated it when he behaved like my father. It was as bad as his offended silences.

When I went in to see Aczél, the first couple of minutes were awkward. Or official, rather. I'm so pleased, I'm so pleased, coffee, a drink, etcetera. Then, in an effort to lighten the mood, Aczél said, you know, I'm a bit afraid of you.

I asked him why.

Because I don't understand you. And what a person doesn't understand, he is naturally afraid of.

What it is that you don't understand?

Other people in similar exceptional situations would take advantage of it, don't you think? Or take certain liberties. Depends on how you look at it.

I asked who he had in mind. He said he couldn't offer too many names.

You have every reason to be afraid of them. They're writers, and it takes just one sentence to topple tyranny. Unlike a photograph taken in a studio.

He gave a wry smile, wagged his finger at me and said, watch it, that was a sentence.

I told him I didn't mean it as a joke. I really believe what I said, and I'd understand his worrying a lot more if I were not taking my pictures within four walls. I'm aware of my exceptional situation as well as my abilities, and I'm not a master of words. At least, not enough to make it worth my while to bother with them.

Why didn't you stay in America? he asked. You'd have been better off, all told.

I don't know, I said. My uncle didn't leave in '44, my father didn't leave in '56. Surely, that, too, weighed in the balance. What can I say? I just stayed, that's all. And unless I feel I must, I don't really want to leave, even though I'd manage much better with my pictures in the West than a writer with his mother tongue to contend with.

Good, Aczél said. Then you don't feel any such thing. Why should you? As for words, you're quite right, the devil dwells in words, ours as well as yours. Everyone's. However, as luck would have it, words can't be photographed.

For a brief instant I considered saying something to Comrade Minister Aczél for which Father got slapped so hard, he saw stars. Then I saw no reason why I shouldn't.

One can't take a picture of God either, yet that's what I'm endeavoring to do, I reflected.

That's great. I'll keep my fingers crossed, he said and laughed.

It took me years to realize how sly he was, making me feel that I came out of his room the same man I had been when I entered it, whereas obviously, I didn't come out the same man. No two ways about it, he was a good politician.

(Reisz)

Two years after Éva left, I met a woman. Her name doesn't matter. We made love just once. She was the first woman with whom I hoped to have a lasting relationship. I liked her a lot.

Which is not true. It was Lilla Hámori. I waited for her in front of the Music Academy one night only because she had something to do with Éva. I might even say that I took a bit of Éva from her. Also, ever since that night of my birthday gone wrong, I knew she wouldn't say no. I walked back and forth in front of the Academy until the concert was over. Then when she came out and saw me on the street, she came over. It's been ages, she said.

She came to the studio that very night. I didn't want us to go to Szív Street. I didn't want her to see Éva's coats on their hangers and her shoes under the coats. I didn't want her to sit down at the Bösendorfer and ask what happened to the sound. She asked how I was. I said, fine. What a shame poor Éva gave up the piano, but then, America isn't kind to everyone. Do you have any knews of Éva? No, I said. Then she asked if the pictures I'd taken were actually ruined by a bad developer, or if poor Éva made that up. I said that they were ruined because of a bad developer. Well, she could've sworn that Éva had a hand in ruining them. A lot of women find themselves in a threesome, but few really enjoy it. I said that Éva wasn't jealous. Oh, come off it, she said. Then she asked me why I didn't move to New York, I'd have it made. I was about to say, why should I, without Éva, but instead I said, who knows, I just might.

When we got to Reisz's, she asked if I had anyone. I said, no. She asked if she could use the phone. I said, of course. I wanted to go out, but she waved to me to stay, it's all right. She said just three sentences. Don't wait up for me tonight, dear. Just because. Because I can't make it tonight. I asked if someone was waiting for her. She said, not as

530

much as she'd waited for me after I took those pictures. But she's not blaming me. She knows that I was with Éva back then. And I said, that was a long time ago. I opened a bottle of wine and said, I'm still sorry about those negatives. They were probably the best pictures of my life. When we clicked glasses, she looked in my eyes as she'd done from the door of the trolley at one time. She's sorry, too. But now she's here, and I don't have to hold back either, I can take any pictures I like. I said I'd like to take a picture of her hands. She laughed and asked what she should do with her hands. And I said it makes no difference, it'll be the way I see them anyway. I put a Gregorian chant on the record player and went to the dark room to insert the flat film in the case. Meanwhile I thought that probably no one, not Lilla, not Éva, probably not even Kornél would believe that in seven years my most serious cheating was when Éva went to the store in the morning and this woman put her feet on my lap. Except, she was probably right. Just because we haven't got the guts to cheat on someone doesn't make us the models of fidelity. My grandfather, too, was right. Just because we commit a contemptible act doesn't mean that we'll be contemptible for the rest of our lives. It's high time I came up with a similar truth myself, I reflected. Just because we're tra-la-la, doesn't mean we're tra-la-la. I inserted film in the cassette. When I went outside, I said that I'd like to take a picture of her feet as well. I thought so, she said, and held out her feet for me to remove her shoes.

I adjusted the lights and took the two pictures, then we made love. It was terrible. It wasn't her fault. It's just that without love, we can't plunge back into the whirlwind of our former lives, we plunge into emptiness. The closer a stranger's body is to us, the more acutely we feel that this draughty, uncomfortable solitude is our life now. Though possibly, it's just me feeling this way. In short, I slept with Lilla Hámori once. I'll never know how she could have enjoyed it.

The following evening, she showed up at the studio. I wasn't expecting her. She wanted us to make love.

It won't work, I said.

Why not, she asked.

Because I have to leave soon, I said.

She started unbuttoning her dress. Meanwhile she said, Fine, she said as she started unbuttoning her dress. You'll leave soon.

Don't be mad at me for last night, I said as I buttoned her up again.

I'll be mad at you only if you don't fuck the daylights out of me again, she said.

Don't be mad, I said, but I love someone else. I want her, but I'd be looking for another woman in her, and I'm sure she wouldn't like that either.

She looked at me as if I'd spit her in the eye. And not just me, but Éva, too.

You might have said so yesterday, she said.

I had no way of knowing yesterday. I haven't been with anyone in two years, I said.

Don't make me laugh, she smirked. You've been taking pictures of all those whores, but you haven't been with anyone in two years? Who are you trying to kid?

And suddenly, I had no idea how this woman ended up here, or what happened to me, why didn't I see it coming, or if I did, then why her, of all people, because the truth is that I saw it coming, I saw it all very clearly even when I took pictures of her and Éva. That's why I felt the pressure of her hand on my shoulder for days afterwards, and that's why the wet plaster came tumbling down.

I'm sorry, I said, but you were the first woman in my life since Éva left, and it seems you'll also be the last for a long time to come.

You're pathetic, she said.

And I said, possibly. But if you really think that I fuck whores here every night, I added, what makes you think you're the exception?

What did you say? You bring me here to fuck me, then you call me a whore?

It wasn't me. It was you.

Who do you think you are? What makes you think you can do anything with anybody you like?

I don't think anything of the sort, I said. And will you please leave now.

You're some sort of gods, the two of you? First your whore seduces me, then you?

She toppled over the Linhof, I told her to get out, and she fell on me.

Go call your mother a whore, you piece of shit!

I held down her hand. She screamed. Just then, Reisz came home. When he heard the scream, he opened the door to ask what happened.

Nothing, I said.

Let go of her, he said. Stop it.

And I said, keep out of this.

Don't call me a whore, you piece of shit, Lilla continued, or I kill you.

And that goes for you, too, Reisz said. Stop it. Think of the other tenants.

And then Lilla Hámori said, who is that shit Jew?

I let go of her arm. She grabbed her bag and stormed out. Reisz stood by the door. She pushed him aside in front of the door of his own studio. His hands began to shake. Not tremble, but shake, as if he had Parkinson's. He gave me a look as if. . . As if. . . I don't know. I think it wasn't even me he was looking at.

I'm sorry, I said.

I barely heard his answer.

For God's sake, it's not my fault, I said.

Get out, he said.

Didn't you see? She's crazy.

Get out.

Fuck it! Fuck her, fuck you, and fuck Auschwitz, too! I screamed.

Get out of here, Reisz said one last time. Get the hell out of here.

(the free elections)

On July 6, 1989, János Kádár died. Some people count the change in regime as having started with the actual fall of the Iron Curtain, some from the declaration of the People's Republic, some from the start of certain negotiations or the setting up of one or another of the new parties, and some from the first free elections. I belong to the last category. Kádár died on the day that the Supreme Court rehabilitated Imre Nagy. Some people say he called a priest. Not that it matters. The priest's job is to answer the summons and listen, then grant absolution to anyone who wants it. Even János Kádár. Besides, none of us know beforehand what we'll do before we die. My mother didn't know that instead of doing the dishes, she would sit down at the piano. My father didn't know that his major concern would be to have the apartment painted. Until his dying day, he never cared about tidying the apartment. Kádár must have been the same way with the priest. It suddenly occurred to him. It's as simple as that.

I joined the demonstrations. At one of the torchlight marches, a woman even kissed me. She said she'd be right back, she'd just find her friends. Then she disappeared in the crowd and I never saw her again. But that's all right. I think I must have felt the same euphoria as just about everyone else at the time. I know because a couple of times I caught myself not thinking of Éva, sometimes for days.

Sometimes someone would look me up and ask me to sign something, or protest, or join. I signed the first couple of protests, but I never went as far as joining anything. Day by day, I found the argument that it's my duty less and less convincing. Some said I should join because of my father, others said, because of my uncle's family, whom they killed, still others, because for decades, they said, these people forced us to have dozens of ID pictures taken of us. Well, I must be the exception, because they didn't force me to do anything. Someone even looked me up from Mélyvár. He said that it's my bounden duty to sign, because I was born there. It soon turned out that anyone who doesn't honor his bounden duty in this country is a traitor. Either a traitor or a silent accomplice. Or lives in an ivory tower.

When I came back from Japan after a six month stay, I suffered from double vision for days. The minute I got off the plane in Pest, the picture slid apart, like in the Leica's viewfinder before the focus is adjusted. It lasted for minutes, stopped, then started again. It was scary. I thought I'd go blind. That's when I met Dr. Péter Várnai. Afterwards, we talked a lot. I even had dinner at his place a couple of times. He was a very good eye doctor, and the founder of a major party. What's more, he never was, nor did he turn, into a scoundrel. Except, once he came to see me and asked me to join.

Can you seriously imagine my name on a list of candidates, Péter?

Dear András, I most certainly can.

I'm sorry, but the answer is no.

Must I be satisfied with that, or will you honor me with an explanation?

I have just one explanation, I said. Your aims are impeccable. But if I were to see your means to those aims from up close, I'd have double vision again, I'm sure of that. There must be quite a few with which I could never identify, just as there must be a part of my work with which you could never identify. It's these two parts that make up the whole.

I don't understand you, he said. You know perfectly well how much I admire your work. And not just your work. That's why I'm here.

I took my album of Japanese photographs off the shelf and placed it on the table. What do you think this picture represents? I asked.

A woman. The face of an Asian woman, he said.

A Japanese woman. And what do you think this woman is doing?

Oh, András, it's one of your best-known pictures.

That's why I'm showing it to you. What is this woman doing?

I hope you're not accusing me of being shocked by a bit of eroticism.

I'm not accusing you of anything, Péter. I'm just asking you what she's doing.

How should I know? Only her face is visible.

Come on, Péter, out with it.

She's having sex. Is that what you want to hear?

Yes.

This is ridiculous. I don't know what you want to hear, but you're mixing up two very different things.

God forbid. So let's continue, if you don't mind. How do you think this picture was taken?

I have no idea. I know very little about photography.

You don't have to. Can we agree that she's not pretending?

If she is, she'd doing a very good job, he said and laughed. Of course she's not pretending. Still, I have no idea what you're getting at.

I'll help you. If I adjust the aperture, the time, the focus, the light, then who do you think she's fucking?

He said nothing.

The fact that you're there doesn't turn it into pornography.

Definitely not. Especially not a portrait.

Well then, tell me, he said. I told you. I don't know what you're getting at.

Péter, this woman is dead.

He looked at me as if I'd lost my mind.

She's a bride whose groom knifed her in a hotel in Kyoto. Look through it at your leisure. No one in this album is sad, no one is sleeping, no one is watching TV, no one is fucking, no one is stroking their dog. They're all dead and their glance is exactly as their neighbors, the hotel's cleaning staff, or the police found them.

He said nothing.

Well, think of your means to your end the way you think of this picture. Beyond a point, you find my freedom too much, and I find your means to your end too much.

It's time I left, Péter said. I'm sorry. He walked out of the room, but stopped short in the hall.

I didn't mean to hurt your feelings, András, but as far as I'm concerned, this is profanation, and you know I'm a doctor. Because these pictures have nothing to do with artistic freedom.

That could well be, I said. Except, I started taking pictures by committing profanation. First, my mother's. Believe me, I have no more nor less to do with freedom than, let's say, your defamation campaigns. Which is why I don't try to pass off the questionable criteria of my questionable freedom on anyone else.

That's politics, András.

And *this*, this is how it is, I said.

(my life)

I need to make something quite clear. Besides Mélyvár and this sixth district apartment, I've lived in West Berlin, Hamburg, Paris, Barcelona, Velletri, on the outskirts of Rome, as well as Crete. Also Shanghai, Kyoto, and Central Java. And in New York, too, for a while. Though I spent less time there than anywhere else. By living I mean that I've spent months, sometimes even years in these places. I had my own home, meaning a rental, my own acquaintances, a couple of brief, bitter affairs, and duties. Some of these acquaintances turned into friendships. I liked my homes, I satisfied my duties, and the bitterness of my affairs was due solely to the fact that I wanted someone else. Also, besides the places I just mentioned, I spent a day or two practically everywhere where they weren't shooting, and even some places where they might as well have done so. I need to clarify this because I leafed through my notebooks, and what I've just said doesn't necessarily follow from what I've written so far – this despite the fact that I know that my works, my books, my exhibition catalogues, plane tickets, and hotel bills would lead others to conclude that my life is a lot more exciting than in fact it is.

By the way, there's no contradiction here, just that now as I write these lines, my visible life is stripped away from me the way a casting mould is shattered into pieces once it is removed. One would think it's the other way around, that my mother, my father, Éva, Reisz, Imolka and Kornél are the moulds, and once we remove them with a hammer, we'll find the essence because, after all, the essence is what can be seen from ten to six at the Neue Nationalgalerie. Well, hardly. At least, as far as I'm concerned, it's the other way around, and my pictures interest me only to the extent to which they help me trace my steps back to the core from which they have originated.

I'm not saying that during the six months I spent in Kyoto, nothing happened inside of me. I'm not saying that the countless food stands in Shanghai or the heavy downpours in Java did not permeate my life through and through. I'm just saying that almost nothing was decided there, that, for example, a whole lot more was decided in the bathroom of an apartment in Úri Street as Neil Armstrong landed on the moon. Éva was right. I pulled her inside the bathroom because of Adél Selyem. Except, that's not the sort of thing you can say to another person.

(Camera Lucida)

Two years ago, I found Lilla Hámori standing next to me in front of a book shop. Neither of us had planned it. I was soon to give a speech at an award ceremony in Zürich, and I was preoccupied with that. I don't like speaking in public, but they said that this time, I had to. Photography as simplified death. This was going to be the subject of my presentation. I couldn't find Barthes's *Camera Lucida* on my shelves, so I went to the bookshop near November Seventh Square. Pardon. It's now the Octogon. And when Lilla Hámori saw me, she came over to me. She was so close, her shoulder nearly touched my arm.

I hadn't seen her in at least ten years. I caught sight of her in the shop window. She had on a sleeveless yellow summer dress. I will never forget it. There I was, my mind occupied with a damned speech, all the time that I was fixated on what she was wearing, and deciding that the past ten years had hardly left a mark on her, and yet, although I had no intention of starting up a conversation, I stayed put. She said hello. I said hello. She said she'd seen her hands at my exhibition at the Ernst Museum. I said that except for her and me, nobody knows who the hands belong to. She said, that's true. Then she said, it's terrible, the way poor Éva had to die. I had no idea what she was talking about.
     What Éva?
     Éva, who else?
     I just stood there, looking at her confusedly.
     Haven't you heard?
     No.
     She doesn't know the details herself, she said, except that Éva died in an accident in Sopron when she came home for her mother's funeral last spring. Then she said she's sorry that I had to hear it from her, and like this, on the street.
     That's all right, I said. It's not your fault.

(with Mother at night)

It was noon. I felt only an overwhelming weariness. I went home, closed the shutters, and fell asleep. Then I got up and drank some water, then peed. Then I fell asleep again. I think I must have slept for two and a half days. I woke up in the middle of night. What was left of my coffee from the day before was still in the mug. I drank it and ate a slice of bread. Then I remembered how she stood in the door with the bread wrapped in a kitchen towel. I threw up. Then I started collecting her things. I filled three big plastic bags with coats, shoes, underwear, and dresses that had been waiting for her for seventeen years.

In the meantime, my mother showed up and asked what I was doing. I said that Éva died, and I was gathering up her things, and she shouldn't leave, I'll be done in a minute, I have just these couple of shoes left. And it would be better for me if I didn't have to be alone now.

But Son, now that she's gone, you *are* alone.

Yes, Mother, I know.

I was thinking that up till then, they were all mistaken. Kornél was mistaken, the parson was mistaken, my lovers were mistaken. They were wrong. All of them. They were incapable of understanding that thirty years after the war, deserters who'd been hiding were still appearing from the depths of the forests, that prisoners of war were still returning from Siberia, that at the age of seventy, those who hadn't seen each other for half their lives now stand before the altar, that as long as we are alive, anything is possible.

You had no news of Father for three years, yet you wrote those letters and put them on his table, I said.

I know, she said. But now, please call Kornél.

Fine, I said. I'll call him.

Klári picked up the phone. She said it's midnight, and I said, I know. She asked what happened. I said, Éva died. She asked where I was. I said I was at home. And she said, don't move, wait for Kornél. And I said, alright.

(Éva's death)

Two years ago in the spring, Éva came home. Which is all I know. János Radnóti told me. Kornél said I should look him up. She didn't come to Pest, because her brother said he'd pick her up at the airport in Vienna and take her straight to Sopron to bury their mother. Which is all I know.

And also, that Ádám was a psycho. A schizophrenic, or some such thing. Which is all I know.

And that he thought he was a mathematician and wrote all sorts of nonsense about parallels. Which is all I know.

And that after their father died, he took charge of his sister, who was seven years his junior. He started to teach her to play the piano, because music and mathematics are the same, and a man's soul can be cleansed only by these two. Meanwhile, he kept Éva in check by telling her that she'd killed their father. He died because he couldn't bear the shame that his daughter was a whore who started masturbating when she was just six. Which is all I know.

He'd warned their mother that Éva snuck out the window at night, and he got hold of the padlock and the key, too, then he detailed all the things he could do to his chained-down sister, except he won't, because he loves her. Which is all I know.

Then after Éva got married, her brother lived in one room with his mother. The rest of the yellow house stood empty, because his mother had a heart condition of which she complained every single day, until she was eighty-something. Because her son knows what love is, she had said, while her daughter left her, like a piece of rag. And for what? For a nobody who seduced her, and he calls himself a teacher. Ádám couldn't follow her

543

to America to bring her back because he couldn't get a passport, because the vice squad had once initiated an investigation against him because he'd been accused of being a homosexual. Except, he got off because they had no proof. Which is all I know.

All I know is that Éva left János Radnóti for the first time when he wanted to report her brother and mother for abuse, the second time the day they got married, the third time when she got pregnant, the fourth time when she saw me in the park, and the fifth time when she went to America. Except for Ádám and myself, that's when she left everyone else behind. Even Nóra. Which is all I know.

Their mother died two years ago. Ádám went to pick Éva up at the airport in Vienna. Just before they reached the city on the way back, he ran into a tree at full speed. Which is all I know.

But before he went to pick up Éva, he left a note on the kitchen table, saying they should hold the funeral for the three of them at the same time. Which is all I know.

In the end, Edward took Éva's ashes back to America. Which is all I know.

And that instead of taking that damn photo, I should have killed them. Wiped them off the face of the earth. Burned down the house with them inside. The both of them. Let them burn in that madhouse, restrained by dog chains. Let their souls be purified. Let cancer eat out their hearts. Let them rot in hell. Let them rot.

Sorry.

(the travel agent)

A couple of days later, I went to a travel agent on the Boulevard. I asked if they had any trips to Crete. I knew perfectly well that there was nothing there, no trace of the labyrinth or the Minotaur, but I felt I had to go there.

How much do you want to spend? the young travel agent asked.

I said it makes no difference.

But I need to know, because they have lots of trips, I can't go listing them all.

Then try to sort them according to some other consideration, I suggested.

She gave me one of those uncomprehending looks, so I asked if they happened to have a map.

They don't have a map, only a prospectus, she said. But she could show me a video of the accommodations.

I opted for the video. She took me back to one of the rooms, had me sit down in front of a TV, and asked which tape she should insert, the one with the hotels, or the one with the apartments.

The one with the apartments, I said.

Apartments are cheaper, she said, but not all of them have air conditioning.

That's all right, I said. If they survived for five thousand years without air conditiong, I think I can survive a week or two months.

She's sorry, but they offer only one and two week tours, she said.

In that case, I'll take four two-week tours, which should solve the problem, I said. At that moment I was thinking that just the other day, I'd have turned on my heels long before I asked for the map, or at the air conditioning part I'd have put this young girl in her place in no uncertain terms, so that afterwards I'd have felt even worse than her. I'm not saying that I wasn't irritated, or at least, not enough for me to do something that would make me ashamed of my actions. The girl inserted the cassette in the VCR, and I asked her for the remote control. Then I set it on fast forward, so neither of us should have to suffer from each other's company more than was absolutely necessary.

The video reminded me of something on local cable television. After the main title with the beautiful sunset, a woman wearing a green pants suit showed us the medium category apartments located along the shores of the Aegian Sea. She showed us each building first from the outside, then from the kitchen and bedroom, after which she turned to the recreational amenities. Meanwhile, in most of the short scenes you could see the cameraman's shadow with the VHS camera on his shoulder. Judging by that shadow, he must have been bored stiff. I'd almost have liked to forget the whole damn thing, but I stopped the fast forward out of courtesy when the staff arrived at the Evangelia apartment complex. I rewound the tape, wondering if I saw right, but I did. There it was, on a sign between two poplars: Evangelia. The Bringer of Good News.

Where is that, I asked the girl, and she said, probably near Heraklion, but she'll check in the catalogue.

And I said, that's the trip I want, and if possible, I'd like to leave tomorrow.

That's not possible. Our charters leave only on Wednesdays, she said with a trace of satisfaction in her voice.

In that case, get me a regular ticket for tomorrow, I said, then I paid for two months' accommodations in advance, along with the extra charge for single occupancy.

(the customs check)

All through the customs check, I couldn't help thinking that it might have been wiser for me to go to America. At least, I could see Edward. Then I thought that it wouldn't make any sense. The customs agent asked what was in my bag, at which I said, somewhat irritated, that they're personal belongings. He asked me to open it. I hadn't been expecting that. No one has ever been interested in my carry-on bag. They scanned it. That was all.

They're very personal, I said, all the while knowing that when you enter a country, that's not taken into account, and that if I grew even more irritated, that'll only make things worse. And so I fished the key out of my pocket and opened the carry on.

What're these, the customs agent asked, whereas he could see what they were.

Negatives, I said. I almost added, of my wife, but then I thought that I have no reason to enter into an exchange of a personal nature with a complete stranger.

The man took out a roll at random and turning to the window, gave it a closer look. As far as I could tell from the other side of the counter, they were the pictures from Ózd, when Éva got drenched in the rain. He rolled it up and put it back in the black cassette, then he took out another roll. The pictures must have been taken in the dressing room after a concert, but based on the negative, I couldn't tell when. The man felt pretty awkward when he saw the naked breasts. The veins bulged on the back of his hand, and from the way he swallowed, and how often, I could tell that he began salivating. He realized it himself, and in order to hide his discomfort, he tried to look over the roll as thoroughly as he'd done previously, then he rolled it up just like he'd rolled up the previous batch.

I told you. They're very personal, I offered, and in an attempt to alleviate the awkward situation, I pretended to feel awkward myself, whereas only the hand luggage that was still open worried me. I expected to be questioned further. I looked behind me, because if there's a long line, they generally keep it short. But there was no one waiting. Then

547

I remembered that because I didn't want to push and shove, I was the last one off the plane.

What do you do, the customs agent asked.

After a brief pause, I said that I'm a photographer. Then I thought that if he demands proof, I won't be able to supply it, that these more than a hundred rolls of film about Éva are not proof, in which case, there's nothing left to do, I'll slip him some money. I hate it, but in the south that's how it's done, even more so than back home. Maybe I should have started with that in the first place. Fifty or a hundred dollars is a lot of money anywhere, I thought, but instead of asking me more questions, the man closed the carry on, and with the most blatant disdain imaginable, he looked me up and down as he handed me the key.

Have a nice stay, he said.

(Heraklion)

I stood at the empty carousel, waiting for the suitcase with my clothes to come round again from behind the rubber curtain. There were plastic flowers all over the place and making a lot of noise, a child of about eight years of age was busy pushing the trolleys that were left behind into their place. Leaning against a doorpost, a young soldier was chewing a match. All in all, the Nikos Kazantzakis airport is not much different from a narrow-gauge railway station on the Great Plain, I thought, and for some reason, that calmed me down. After a while, the rubber curtain opened, and my suitcase appeared. I tore the Budapest–Heraklion tag off the handle, but I couldn't find a trash can anywhere, so I sunk the tag in my pocket, then found a cab to take me to the Evangelia.

It was a pretty bleak place. A small bedroom, a small kitchenette, a shower, but I didn't need it to be a home. I settled in. The following day I went into town and bought photographic paper, trays, chemicals, and a used enlarger. At least, for the two months I spent selecting through the pictures, I didn't feel anything. That's the good aspect of photography. It's just film and paper. Low grade paper. Work. Black, gray, white.

(Theseus and Ariadne)

There's a long stone wall in Heraklion. The waves come crashing over it, and the spray disperses the light. To be sure, it's a rare phenomenon. It's like when my mother and I shook out the wet sheets in our yard in Mélyvár. In the early evening, when the air has cooled down a bit, two old people in wheelchairs sit out on the shore. A man and a woman. I never saw them from up close. They don't do anything. They don't wheel their chairs up and down, they don't chat, they don't play cards. They sit, their eyes intent on the sea. Or who knows. They sit there till sunset, then wheel themselves in the direction of the market.

I watched them every evening from the terrace of the café by the shore. The truth is, I went there because of them. On my last day there, I finally decided to ask the waiter if he knows why they're crippled. He gave me a look of surprise, like the people down south do, when what is evident to them isn't evident to the rest of humanity.

Of course I know, he said. Everybody knows they're Theseus and Ariadne.

Why, I asked.

Because they're crazy, poor things, he said. They're waiting for the boat. But at one time they were acrobats with a world-class act. They performed everywhere in the country. They even performed abroad. The act consisted of Theseus jumping off the trapeze without a safety net. He did a salto mortale, and Ariadne threw the rope after him. Theseus caught it in mid-air, and he was saved. As I said, there was no safety net. Nothing. Just the sawdust in the ring. Then once in Thessaloniki, the rope got entangled on Ariadne's leg and she couldn't throw it, and she leaped down after Theseus to catch him, because Ariadne was secured around the waist. And she managed to catch him, and they were very nearly safe, but Ariadne's safety belt could only support one individual, and so they became cripples. That's the circus standard. Just one individual.

I paid, then went back to the Evangelia. I had to pack. I wondered if there was a moment in our lives when I would have dared to leap off the trapeze, when I could have been a hundred per cent sure that Éva would hurl herself after me. I think she probably would have, every time. She just made sure that I shouldn't trust her that much. And so I probably took pains myself to make sure that she shouldn't be sure about me either. Or the other way around. God himself wouldn't know by now. There is no more potent poison than fear. I thought of what she said to Kornél when her Chopin recording came out and the three of us went to the New York Café for dinner. A person afraid to give life doesn't deserve life.

The night before I left, I took a picture from the terrace of the café. Down, on the narrow path under the wall, a young girl was rolling a wooden hoop. It was getting dark, the shadows were long. High above her, the breaker was deserted except for the two old people in wheelchairs, Theseus and Ariadne. It's the last picture I took. And if it's kitsch, then so be it.

(the exhibition)

Nobody understood why I wanted to exhibit my pictures in a tumble-down old building in City Park. I couldn't very well say it's because this is where I first saw Éva in the dark shadow of the building twenty-two years ago. Something like that won't hold water. Except for me, nobody cares. Why should they? Also, the interior of the building is not suitable, they said. The nearby Palace of Arts was being renovated, and the offices were temporarily moved here. I told them that the offices didn't bother me. I wanted to stage the exhibition for just one day, and they should turn the exhibition space into a dark-room. The director said it's crazy, the museum can't possibly finance it, and so on. I said I'd take care of the finances. He hummed and hawed, it can't be done, he said. Besides, he's looking out for my best interests, it would be unworthy of my achievements, that I can't see it, because I'm in no condition to do so. I asked him if I should organize the exhibition here, where it belongs, or would he rather I take this material abroad, like my first pictures during the Kádár years.

I'm sorry, but I don't know what got into you. What does this have to do with Kádár? This idea of yours is sentimental, infantile, and amateur, and that's the truth.

You're right, but I don't give a shit. I stood up and left without saying goodbye. He caught up with me in the hallway and said, fine. Do what you want.

In the end, I needed a week to black out the windows, paint the space black, have a curtain put up at the entrance, and assemble two kinds of lighting. I realized that it would be much simpler to have the paper delivered by the factory and I'd see to the enlargement myself. Two assistants helped do the enlargements on the papers stretched out on the walls.

Kornél opened the exhibition. In his opening remarks he said that anyone who can't let go goes mad or becomes a photographer, and if he becomes a photographer, he'd rather let go of his own life than his camera. Or his pictures. Capa, Diane Arbus, Mapplethorpe. Yet now someone is letting go of his pictures, probably so he won't go mad, and we are standing in a darkroom now so that we may see what he sees before the white lights are turned on, and he can witness what he's letting go of disappear.

What he had to say rubbed me the wrong way, to say the least. I had asked him to open the exhibition because I thought that he would be able to describe what this whole thing is about. It's about the fact that Éva died. And also, that there's no state more pure than mourning, and that after my mother died, I could still put my hopes in Éva, but now that Éva is gone, what can I possibly pin my hopes on? Others might have things to cling to, but I couldn't care less about the things they believe in. I'm no longer particularly interested either in God or the Fatherland. I will never see except through a glass darkly, and the Fatherland only interested me as long as János Kádár was alive. The present situation, the Hungarians calling Jews names and the Jews calling Hungarians names and the former Party functionaries turned billionaires laughing up their sleeves, this is worse than what my father prophesied. I'm no longer interested in the power of sexuality, nor the power of death. As I see it now, what's the use, why belabor the subject yet again and delve into the possibilities inherent in materials yet again, just because I'm still alive? Death will never be more clearly visible to anyone than to the individual standing in front of a dead person they love. As for the chatter of the living among themselves about death, it bores me every bit as much as my own pictures, because what's the point? Except for the fact that they have satisfied my ambition, they did nothing for me. I experienced nothing of what people call personal development. Whenever I hear it mentioned, I break out in a cold sweat. In any case, I experienced nothing of the sort from the time my mother died to the time Éva died. I feel now, and I can say this with full confidence, exactly what I felt when I was sixteen. I have exactly the same amount of canned food and pasta at home as a family with five children would need in a month. Except, I don't have children, and from now on, I obviously won't, though it's the one thing that would give meaning to life. Kőszegi may have had a firmer grip on the various ideologies than my father, except, as we know, ideologies are easily replaced. Abandoned, dropped. Like pictures on a wall. But as far as my father was concerned, I could not be replaced. That's what these pictures are about. About Éva's cowardice. And needless to say, my own. That except for the glowing reviews she received for her

Chopin recording, she left no trace when she died. Only the two of us together could have left a trace that would have mattered. Life. Except, I can't express this properly. That's why I asked Kornél. Instead, he talked all sorts of rubbish about letting go and going crazy. I have not gone crazy. I know exactly what I am doing. I'm not letting go of something, I'm finishing something. Except, just as I was too much of a coward to show my pictures at an exhibition, for the same fifteen years I was also too much of a coward not to exhibit them.

Next, Kornél asked those present to imagine that gravity ceases for a couple of seconds, which is plenty of time for the seas and the rivers to reach the sky, for the sands in the desert to blend with the slop in the sky, for the moon to break free from its course, and we float like we wanted to when listening to Gagarin's account of his experiences. For just a couple of seconds, nothing has weight, but those couple of seconds suffice for us to want, once again, all the weight, all the burden that had been our lot. Well, this exhibition is something like that. Thank you for coming, he concluded.

Laughter. Of course they had come, what an idea!
    This insider laughter irritated me even more than Kornél's speech. I asked Zoltán to turn on the light. *Mehr licht*, someone quipped, at which point I very nearly said, fuck you, buddy. I was sorry that I hadn't seen to everything myself. And then Zoltán cut the darkroom red and upped the spots trailed on the pictures to a thousand and five.

Actually, this is when I first saw the pictures myself. They left me cold. What should have happened, happened only chemically and, of course, optically. Except, deep inside, neither chemistry nor optics count for much, and no one lives forever just because someone takes a picture of them. On the other hand, no one stops existing if we destroy their photographs. However, that's neither here nor there. At least the pictures she didn't take with her because she didn't want to see them in her miserable, real life are gone without a trace. The two realities could not exist side by side, and in the white light, the images that had not been processed began to fade. For some reason, the picture I took of her on the empty stage of the Music Academy held out the longest. But then that, too, disappeared.

The room was crowded and the TV people grumbled that they couldn't film properly. The museum assistant ran all over the place so he could document the opening on video. A woman journalist asked if the exhibition was really over, or would there be a repeat the next day. I said, no. I was fed up and regretted having come up with the idea in the first place. I wanted to go outside for a cigarette.

And then something happened that surpassed by worst nighmares. Barabási, one of the men responsible for the change in regime and a new investor who had started to buy my pictures before it occurred to anyone else, took my arm and confidentially asked, the negatives are gone, you swear? Whereupon I asked, if they existed, what, in his opinion, would be the point of this exhibition?

And is it really true that you don't have a single negative left of Éva? That you burned them all? he asked.

It's true, I said. Though I still have the first.

In that case, let's say that I'm buying the whole batch. We'll settle the rest some other time, he said, extending a hand.

You don't understand. These pictures no longer exist, so they're not for sale, I told him.

I understand, he said. Still, I'll give you ten million for the whole thing.

I told you. Look around. The pictures are gone.

Consider, András. No one's ever paid you this much for photo papers that have gone bad. Not even in America, he persevered.

Whereupon Guttmann turned around, and gleefully said, make it eleven million.

You're frauds. Both of you, I said, and turning on my heels, I left them high and dry, because I'd never slapped anyone in my life, and I wanted to keep it that way. It was like a nightmare. This is not what I wanted, not in the least, except I'd miscalculated something, like so many times before. Eleven-five-hundred, Barabási called after me, but by then, I didn't care. By then, Éva wasn't with me to hold my hand.

(Mother dies)

The day my mother died, the following happened.

When she got back from work, she started to clean the house. When she got to my father's room, she stopped. She asked me to clean it.

It doesn't need cleaning, I said.

It's really the least I could do.

Maybe, but you won't like the results.

This is not what I expected of you.

I took the dust rag, the broom, and the dustpan and went in. I pulled up the blinds. The light outside was gone. Three years' worth of letters lay on my father's desk. My mother wrote him once, sometimes twice a month, then placed them on his desk.

She wrote on typing paper with pearly letters. *My dear. . . .*

I opened the window. I swept up and wiped off the dust. Then I sat down at the desk and started to read the one on top. They weren't really letters. They were more like diaries or accounts than letters. They were about what happened to us. Our lives. Everything.

I didn't have the patience to read them all. The neighbors. The garden. My marks. What books I'd read. The foreman at the clothing factory started playing up to her. They contained nothing I didn't already know. She cried when she told me about the foreman She'd have told Father, too, if he were home. Of course, were he home, she wouldn't have had anything to tell, because she wouldn't have been working in a clothing factory.

I went and told mother I was done. She was sitting in the kitchen. She wasn't doing anything.

You should clean up properly, we can't wait for your father like this.

Fine.

I went back. I grabbed the letters, crumpled them up and threw them in the wastepaper basket. Only after I'd gone out to the yard and set fire to them did she come and ask what I was doing.

I said nothing. She saw perfectly well from the kitchen window what I was doing.

She then went back inside.

She laid out our dinner, and we ate.

What'll happen next? I asked.

I don't know, but something always happens.

It's like Father had been dead for three years, and now he's being resurrected.

She said nothing.

Should I do the dishes?

I'll do them. In the end, she didn't.

I went to my room and got into bed. Then I got out of bed and took out the Schiele album. A bookmark was on the page with the woman lying on her belly. It got me upset.

I heard her packing in Father's room. I don't know what she could have been packing; there was nothing there to pack.

I thought that it would have been better if my father had died, because then at least we'd know what's up, because that's permanent, it doesn't change. I turned the page to the other woman, then shut the book. I turned off the light and imagined Imolka.

Just as Dorvai pressed her against the table, mother went to the living room and began to play Grieg's Concerto in A minor. This was the only piece she played. And only when she was by herself.

Then she closed the lid and said, oh my God.

I thought she was crying.

I could hardly wait for Dorvai to grab Imolka's hair and fuck her until she started screaming, oh my god, oh I can't take it any more, do me! But I couldn't hear her voice. I heard nothing but the silence issuing from the living room.

In the morning, Mother was supposed to come in and was supposed to say, rise and shine, Son, rise and shine.

And I was supposed to say, I will, mother, I will.

(the game)

That apple is there again today. I don't know who it is or what they want, but it's unnerving. If I take it, the next day there's another in its place. If I leave it, they put another one next to it. If I put another one next to it myself, they take the one I'd left. When I went out for bread today, I took a bite of one, just for the heck of it. I don't particularly like apples, but I did it anyway. I buy apples only because they last. By the time I came back from the store, I'd forgotten all about it. But tonight I see that they left mine as it was, with my bite out of it, but chewed a ring around the other. It's not the Gypsy children from the back stairs, that's for sure. If anybody wants something from me, let them knock and say so.

(my sister)

Last year, when my exhibition opened in London, a woman came up to me. She must've been a couple of years younger than I. She looked like a vulture.

Your pictures scare me, she said in Hungarian.

That wasn't my intention, I said.

She was unpleasant. Or more like there was something unsettling about her. I thought that she must be a member, or possibly the head, of the local Hungarian community, and next thing I know, she'll be asking me why the communists are still free to come and go on the streets of Budapest. Or something of the sort. For the last three years, they ask me this almost everywhere I go, and I don't have the answer. Once I told someone that allowing these people to come and go on the streets of the city is still a lot less outrageous than the alternative, but he wasn't satisfied. On the other hand, the way the communists put up their posters before the free elections, still believing that they had something to offer, was just as outrageous. But never mind. This woman with the vulture's face just stood there, and I didn't know what to do with her.

Well, they scare me, she said again. Especially when I think that you're practically my brother.

Really, I said, forcing a laugh.

I'm Klára Zenta, she said, and offered me her hand. I think your mother was my father's first wife.

I just looked. I looked right through her, as I tried to make sure the glass I was holding wouldn't shake in my hand.

I thought you knew, she said.

I didn't, I said. Which was true. It was also true that even during his last day, I meant to ask my father about that Dr. Zenta, who had me exempted from the army.

In any case, it's strange.

Yes, it is, I said.

In which case you probably never knew that we had a half-sister, she said.

There I stood with the wine glass in my hand. I looked around. Fifty of my pictures were hanging on the wall. I was fifty. I thought that I'd seen and experienced just about everything. I hadn't touched my camera in a year, and I thought that now I had only these exhibitions to look forward to.

Let's go outside, I said.

We sat down on the steps of the museum. It was a stuffy early evening. A dog was barking on the other side of the square. An ambulance shrieked past, then stopped in front of the cathedral. I asked what she was doing here. She said that she's working at the embassy. She even wrote me once.

I'm sorry, I said, I don't remember.

I'm not surprised, she said, I just write the letters, but somebody else signs them.

She told me that Johanna Zenta lived just one day, though not even that, and that she's buried at the Kerepesi Cemetery, though she doesn't know where. Probably in the back, with the children. Also, her father was my uncle's best friend, that's how he and my mother met, and also that my mother couldn't have been even twenty and had to be dragged to the funeral by force, and also that when they got the divorce, she broke off all communication with her ex-husband.

How do you know all this? I asked.

We talked to each other, she said.

So did we, I said, unable to hide my irritation.

She laughed. It's easy for you, she said, even if your pictures *are* gloomy and depressing.

Why? I asked.

Because at least your father wasn't with the secret police, she said.

I'm sorry, I said. I was about to ask how come he was with the secret police. I thought he was a doctor. But I didn't, because she'd have realized that I'd met him once after all.

Would you like to have lunch with me tomorrow?

My plane is leaving tonight.

In that case, bon voyage.

(the holding officer)

I asked a friend, a historian, to find something on Dr. János Zenta – to the extent, of course, that one can find anything on anyone around here. János Zenta graduated as a doctor, then got his Ph.D. in neurology. He practiced hypnosis, but later gave it up on Party orders. He joined the Communist Party after the Arrow Cross killed his friend, Iván Hollós. As a medical expert, he helped set up the ÁVO, Hungary's State Security Agency, but then he left. He did not join the ÁVH, the State Protection Agency. He practiced as a neurologist. Then he worked in the Ministry of the Interior again. He was a holding officer, one of the best, thanks to his knowledge of manipulation. Then he became a training officer. He wrote the handbook on how a holding officer should treat an informer. He was twice married. Klára Zenta was born of his second marriage. He shot himself because of some corruption business. If my calculation is correct, he was the colonel whose name had to be kept a secret, the one who got my mother's piano back for her.

Kornél asked why I didn't want to meet that woman again. After all, we have the same roots.

We do not, I said.

(the award)

In mid-October, a woman from the prime minister's office called. They would like to give me an award, and will I accept it? Meaning, will I accept it in person, or appoint someone. I said that of course, I'd go myself. She said they're very happy. The ceremony will take place on the 23rd of October. That's when I realized that it was already October.

On the twenty-third, I went. To the right the Castle, to the left Parliament. And I reflected that when I took my very first picture of the bridge with the Zorki, I would have never thought that I'd ever set foot inside the Parliament building. Not that I had any such ambitions. Of course, back then, Kádár was in the middle.

Those who were there to receive their awards, including myself, knew each other only by sight, or not even that. It's pretty awkward going to a place like that unaccompanied. I looked around for the waitress with the champagne glasses. Not that I wanted champagne, except, it helps to pass the time. There was no waitress.

Várnai had been a member of the democratic opposition when I'd come back from Japan and suffered from an onset of double vision. He placed an awkward hand on my shoulder and said, I'm sorry, and walked off. I thought he meant it as a joke, for the protocol. Then I thought that perhaps he was sorry that it's not his party giving me the award. But that wouldn't have been any better. Or maybe that he's a doctor and knows about the test results. I remembered that the day before the phone kept ringing all morning, but I didn't pick it up. I was sure that they were calling me about the test results, and I didn't want to know. I finally yanked out the plug. I was about to go after Várnai to ask what he'd been told, but then remembered that he can't know, he's an ophthalmologist. Which put me at ease.

The ceremony began: the President, a couple of ministers, and so on. The presentation box contained a large cross and a small one that you can pin on your lapel without it weighing your collar down. The master of ceremonies said that the cross was presented to me for my tireless efforts in popularizing Hungarian art and culture abroad. First I thought that this is already the second cross awarded to me not for my work, but for my accomplishments abroad. And that nothing has changed. And then, that it's only natural, it's precisely things like this that can't change in just a couple of years. And then that if I accepted the first one, what excuse did I have for rejecting the second? And that this box would just fit in the lower drawer of the china cabinet. And that I wonder what motivates people to display their awards behind a glass pane. Or what motivates us to look down on and laugh at those for whom such a china cabinet is important. And then that I could be laughed at just as much, because for the past ten years I've been using a Leica manufactured to my specifications, and not the camera my father had given me. After we all shook hands and I turned around, I saw that it was one man, one woman, one man, one woman. I froze. The master of ceremonies discreetly motioned to me to go back to my place, it's all right.

Right after the presentation, I gave a TV interview for the midday news. It was conducted by a young, enthusiastic reporter. After listing my foreign awards, he asked if a Hungarian award means anything to me. I said, of course. He asked, what. I said, a lot. Could I please be more specific? Look. I was born here. I took most of my pictures here. I am one of the few individuals who didn't become well known elsewhere because they'd left Hungary. It is only natural to wonder, though, how Hungary can handle this. An award is a bit like a camera. There's someone standing on both sides of it. The one who sees, and the one being seen. Except, in this case, the roles are reversed, and if a bona fide picture is to be taken in this reversed situation, they should at least clean the windows of Parliament.

What do you mean by that? the reporter asked.

I meant it literally, I said. It wouldn't hurt if we could see through them. For the time being, it seems that my Western awards are clearly visible from inside these walls. Except, they were clearly visible to György Aczél as well. And so I'd like my next cross to be awarded to me solely on the basis of my work. And I'd also like it if I were not the only photographer here, because several others are equally worthy.

Yes, you're right, the reporter said. And the solidarity with your colleagues is commendable.

Whereupon I said that this is not solidarity, just common sense. The red star atop the dome of Parliament acted as a potent centripetal force. But if they continue to award the cross only to people who have been recognized abroad, even those who, under Kádár, felt it their patriotic duty to stay will end up leaving, because they'll have nothing left to wait for.

Then came the bombshell. He said that I'm right, of course, and he's sorry to bring up such a sensitive subject, and needless to say, I don't have to answer, but he'd like to know my reaction to what has just come to light about my father, and he was sorry for this embarrassing coincidence, especially because just two years earlier, my father had received a posthumous award for his actions during the revolution of '56.

I don't understand the question, I said, because I really didn't.

Your father was an informer, the reporter said. He's on the list that was made public just the day before yesterday.

What list, I wanted to ask, but I couldn't. I just stood there, watching this young man watching me with the obligatory public service smile on his face, and in his hand, the public service microphone.

Have you any idea what they used to blackmail him? he asked.

I was still dumbstruck.

As I said, don't feel that you have to answer, he said.

There was nothing to blackmail him with, I said.

Are you saying that he volunteered? the reporter asked.

I thought of the three of us sitting in my father's room, Father, Dr. Zenta, my mother's first husband, and myself, the two of them in the two armchairs, and me on the stool I'd brought in from the kitchen. The wine and two glasses were on the table. Also matches, cigarettes, and an ashtray. And me asking, so what's it to be? Should I go hang myself?

He didn't, I said. I told him to sign.

Excuse me?

I asked him to do it, and let's leave it at that.

Turn it off, Józsi, do you hear? Turn it off! The sound, too, the reporter uged. Then he turned to me.

Do you know what you're saying? he asked.

I do.

(at Kornél's home)

I called Kornél from the Kossuth Square metro station across from Parliament. He said he tried calling me all morning the previous day. He wants me to go see them.

They'd moved to Óbuda two years ago. I'd visited them two or three times. It's a nice spot, except you have to cross the new housing estate. I forgot to validate my ticket on the bus and got fined. The woman was nice, actually. She told me that if I pay on the spot, there's a reduced fine. The money was in the pocket of my jacket, and I couldn't have taken it out without also taking out the box with my award. I told her to write a ticket instead. She said that we can half it, but I'd have had to scrape the money out of my pocket even so, so she ended up giving me a ticket.

Though I could afford to do so, to this day I can't get myself to take a cab to Óbuda.

I liked their house in Budafok more, but it's been gone for about twenty years now. The new owners demolished half of it, then rebuilt it properly. No loose stairs and no squeaking gate, I bet. This is also a nice house, except I can't relate to it. Though possibly I should just go sit in the garden and watch an ant for thirty minutes. I have time. It's the fear holding me back. I don't want to be confronted with the fact that whether seen from my own point of view or the point of view of an almighty god, I haven't gotten much further than when I was eighteen.

By the time Kornél sold Budafok and two apartments in Pest and bought the house they now lived in, two of their three sons had already moved out, and the third kept his things at home only out of regard for his parents' feelings. Be that as it may, I felt a sense of satisfaction that I'd taken photographs of the three boys suited for display in a family home.

Kornél showed me the newspaper and I ran my eyes down the list. It only contained those who took part in the events of '56. It must have been compiled by someone with an eye out for the next elections, I thought. Lovas was also on the list, but Kőszegi was not. On the other hand, that doesn't mean anything.

What should I do? I asked.

Kornél said he had no idea. Sometimes he's scared himself. What if something comes to light about his own father?

Rest assured, I said. There's nothing about your father that could come to light.

Just two days ago, I'd have said the same thing about yours, Kornél said.

We were sitting in his room. In the window of the house opposite, a woman was watering her flowers. It reminded me of the old woman behind the nylon curtain of whom I'd taken a bunch of pictures. I thought that if I were still taking pictures, I'd grab hold of my Leica now, just as I had back then.

Do you know who was his holding officer? My mother's first husband.

Where did you get that?

I didn't get it anywhere. I know. He recruited my father when they went to see him.

Please don't start that again.

Start what again?

You know perfectly well. The self-flagellation.

Just don't start in on me, alright?

You have no way of knowing, Kornél went on. This list is probably a lie.

Yes, the list may be a lie. Except, I lived with him. I should know.

I told you, András. Don't start that again!

Klári brought us some coffee and asked if my test results were back yet. I said, maybe tomorrow. She said, not that it matters, I couldn't go to a hospital here, they're slaughterhouses, all of them. Kornél said, don't exaggerate, dear. And Klári said, that's what she's known for, but just the same, she wouldn't go to a hospital here, she knew somebody in Stockholm. I'm afraid it makes no difference, I told her. She looked silently at me, then said, it may make no difference to *you*. Then she left.

As it turned out, she was right.

I knew I was scared, but I'd have never thought I'd be this scared, probably because I'd seen my father. Or more to the point, because I'd heard him scream in pain down on the street. I have no idea who he informed on, or what he said about whom, nor will I ever know. On the other hand, I know the way he stood every morning in front of the mirror, and I remember the time I discovered them in that pub on Thököly Road, the way he yelled at me under the street lamp, that I better not question his decency. And of course, there was the time when I said to him that he'd had his stint in prison for nothing, so he might as well sign. As if a man could pay the penalty for the future ahead of time. Who would have thought back in '61, at the age of seventeen, that in thirty-three years' time, we can turn gray from a single sentence we once uttered.

(the newspapers)

The news editor decided not to cut out that sentence. I don't have a TV. I learned about it when some people called me that night. Some said how sorry they were, others heaped dirt on me, anonymously, I should add, while still others asked how I dared soil my father's name like that.

In the morning, I went down to the newspaper stand on Lövölde Square. I asked the vendor which were the most important dailies. He just stared. I said that I don't generally read the papers, that's why I'm asking. He continued staring, then he said that there are several, it depends what I'm interested in. He clearly felt awkward, confused. I said that in that case, he should give me one of each. He gathered them up. That's when I realized why he'd been looking at me like that. Despite all my exhibitions, books and crosses, never before has a picture of me been spread all over the front pages.

"András Szabad admits he was an agent." "Government awards Order of Merit to agent's son." "Son takes his father's sins upon himself." "Nude-photographer's conscience makes him tell all." "Photographer forced father to work for secret police so he'd be a success abroad." That's the sort of stuff they said. The rest I don't remember.

I thought that when all is said and done, a picture is more clearcut than words. Less equivocal. A man is standing on the Boulevard, a cane is hanging from his arm, he's placing soup plates on the ground. Were I to conclude that he's a beggar or a street artist, I'd still be closer to the truth than any sentence. For instance: I told him to sign.

When I got home, I thought I'd pull the plug out to stop the phone from ringing. But then I thought better of it. Anything, I thought, would be preferable to silence. Then I ate something. Lovas called first. He said I must demand they print a correction notice because this list is slander, he never informed on anyone. I said that I believe him, but

I can't ask for a correction notice in his name. He said that this is not what he expected to hear from me, especially after what he'd done for my father, and why won't I give my name to clear his. I said that only he could clear his own name. He said that my father would be disappointed in me for being such a coward. I said that I think he's wrong, my father wouldn't be disappointed. Then a couple of journalists called, and I told each of them the same thing, namely, that what I had to say about this whole thing I'd said on television the day before. Yes, I understand. You think I was irresponsible. Yes, I understand that public opinion has a right to know, though strictly speaking, at most the public has a right to know, dear lady, but not opinion. Yes, I realize that this will stir things up in the West as well. No, I'm not afraid of it. Rest assured, sir, in Berlin of all places, because of this sentence of all things, they're not about to take my pictures off the museum walls. Yes, I know, dear Péter, I know you sympathize, but I have nothing more to say, not even to you. Then they called from the hospital that my test results are in. Positive, I bet. It's alright, you can tell me over the phone. I don't care that it's not that simple, and I don't care what infected the culture. Yes, I know what positive means. No, dear Gábor, I don't want to mount an exhibition. Yes, I understand. You think that this is the ideal time, but my answer is no, and not because I'm afraid, but because I didn't want one in the past either. What has changed, you ask? Nothing. Yes, dear Sári, you're right and you're very kind, but at the moment, I'm not interested in who else was an informer.

Then the phone didn't ring for five minutes, and in the silence I wouldn't have even minded had Lovas called me again. It was Kornél. He said not to look in the papers.

I've already looked, I said. Hand the phone to Klári.

Why?

Because I want to talk to her, not you.

What do you want to talk to her about?

Kornél, will you please hand the phone to your wife.

While I waited, I could just see him hesitating, afraid that something might disturb the long restored peace between us.

Didn't you hear me, jerk? I said, give me your wife!

I'm his wife, jerk. What's up? Klári asked.

Nothing. They said it's positive, but they want to run one more test.
Ridiculous.

I agree. If death were inside me, I'd feel it. I've been practicing for thirty years.

Practice something else, Klári said. Meanwhile, buy yourself a ticket for Stockholm for this coming weekend.

(the dog)

Years ago, Éva showed me a picture. It was of a painting by Goya. I hadn't seen it before. It shows a dog, though actually, just his head, and even that is barely visible, lost in a strange sort of sky, huge, weighing down on him. A strange sand dune or a surging wave of mud is rising in front of him. That's what he's looking at. You get the feeling that he's about to drown, as if he had just minutes left. It reminded me of the dog that had been to outer space on the advice of circus trainers and came back alive, which meant they could send the next one. Seen from the usual distance, one would think that the dog is in distress. Only if we lean very close do we realize that he's actually surprised, that simply put, he's at a loss. As I see it, this painting is one of the most accurate representations of the human condition.

Last night, I found a picture postcard in my mailbox. It had this painting by Goya on it. There was no stamp. She must have dropped it in. It was signed: "To my Dog Father, Anna Zárai, Hotel Gellért, Room 127, Budapest."

I'm more afraid now than when I thought of hanging my pictures on a white wall. Or during the last three months, until I learned that the lump in my throat was benign.

She'd given her my mother's name.

(the white Christmas)

It snowed today. In the early morning, I decided to look through the old pictures of Éva, hoping I'd find one in which she looks into the eye of the camera like a mother. I forgot that I had destroyed them all for the sake of a stupid exhibition. On the other hand, I had no way of knowing that they're family photos. Then I thought I'd send her my last picture with Theseus and Ariadne in their wheelchair and the little girl with the hoop. And then I thought that I'm not going to give my daughter my last picture when I'm seeing her for the first time. I finally made up my mind and picked up the Leica. I took a picture of the apples lined up on my desk. I had no time to waste, because around nine a.m. in winter, the sun shines on my desk for just a couple of minutes. It turned out no better than my first pictures had been, but that makes no difference now, I decided. I made a postcard-size enlargement, and wrote on the back that I'd make dinner for us tonight.

I went to the Hunyadi Square market and bought the tree. Then I called Kornél to tell him I wouldn't be going. He asked what happened, and I said, nothing, I'll come over tomorrow and tell you all about it, and Merry Christmas to you and Klári. I cleared some space in the corner and stood the tree up in the same spot Éva and I used to place it every Christmas for seven years. I set the table, lit three candles, then placed the postcard with Goya's dog under the tree.

I have almost no one left. I have no father and no mother, neither János Kádár, nor Éva, and yet everything is practically the same. Knit one, purl one, knit one. Last year they reinterred Horthy, blew up the bridge at Mostar, and fighter planes flew over Sarajevo every night. This spring, the socialists won the elections hand in hand with those who defeated them four years before. I found this strange, but that's politics, I guess. I'll be fifty-five when someone will defeat them in turn, and not even sixty by the time my grandchild will learn to walk. And by the time he or she will learn to read and write, I will still have no idea why my mother died on that particular night, or why I take pictures, or if my father harmed anyone besides himself, or if I'd been a good Hungarian, or whether there's a God.

I'm so happy she sent me that stupid dog.
I'm so happy.
Which is as much as anyone can hope for.